I0690500

Constantine

E.L. STEVENS

NOTE FROM THE AUTHOR

I WOULD ADVISE AGAINST READING THIS BOOK AS A STANDALONE. CONSTANTINE IS A TRUE PART II, AND DOES NOT DO AN EXTENSIVE RECAP OF THE EVENTS THAT OCCUR IN GEORGIA, BRITAIN'S STORY PART I.

For my friends,
the best hype girlies anyone could ask for.
You know who you are.

And for the readers who gave Georgia a chance,
may this book bring you peace.

CONTENTS

THEN

ONE

BRITAIN
  18 years old

You've got two choices, Britain; you can stand under that pavilion with all those strangers and mingle. Ugh. *Or, you can stand alone, in the sun, and bake to death.* I'm having a hard time deciding which is worse.

It's 105 degrees today, making it, quite possibly, the worst day for a picnic. Worse even still, is that *I'm here.* Well, technically, I'm in the bathroom, splashing cold water on my rosy red cheeks and chest in an attempt to cool down after helping my mom get this whole thing set up. But also, I can probably squander away ten minutes without anyone noticing my absence. Not that Georgia would even realize I'm missing either way. She doesn't pay much attention to me.

My jaw practically hung open with disbelief when she told me I *had* to come to her company's picnic. Never, in my 18 years, has she invited me to one of these, let alone *mandated* my attendance at an MS Group company function. Aubrey and I had plans today, none of which included me sweating my ass off at some dusty lake in the hills, setting up picnic tables, and filling ketchup bottles for the last hour.

It's not that I don't like being social per se...well *sometimes*. It's not that I even dislike *those* people specifically. It's just that I don't know anyone here besides my mom. Everybody else here is tight. They're one big, happy family — one that I'm *not* a part of. And even though Georgia has worked at the MS Group since I've been alive, I've only ever met her boss, Connie, on three separate occasions. Everyone else is a mystery to me. Well, mostly. I know about them, but I don't *know* them. And they don't know me.

Georgia will occasionally let slip comments about people from the office, and while it's certainly not for my benefit when she does talk about work, she gets...lighter. Her mouth extends into a smile, and her color rises. Like when she told me how Liam fumbled his first big pitch, calling Mr. Prattle *Mr. Pittle* for the entire meeting.

She came home practically bursting with laughter. But then, it's like she remembered who she was talking to and she dimmed herself back down. I wanted to ask more, hear more, even see her smile more, but she just walked back to her bedroom and shut the door. Her anecdotes aren't invitations. They never lead to something more, no matter how many times I've hoped they would.

I also tend to soak up whatever information she shares with me, like the attention and love-deprived sponge that I am. It doesn't help that I'm also cursed with a wicked memory. So even though I've never met Connie's kids, I could tell you all their names, from oldest to youngest, and their approximate ages based on details Georgia's dropped throughout the years about birthday gifts or their grades in school.

I've always been that weirdo, though. The one who remembers other people, but never the one remembered. *Yup, that's me.*

I still cringe when I think about my computer science teacher asking me mid-year what country I was from. He thought *I* was the new foreign exchange student. Not me, Britain, who was in his class the previous year and again that year. But that's pretty typical crap for me. I mean, when your own father pretends you don't exist, and your mom barely acknowledges your existence, you get used to it. Sometimes, it even works to my advantage, and I can fade into the background. For some reason, I get the feeling fading won't be an option today.

I don't really know why — it's just a gut instinct. I mean, it makes sense, though. I'm the outlier, the odd one out. They'll look at me and know. Or, more likely they'll look at me and think, *she doesn't belong.* They wouldn't be wrong. I don't belong, not here, *maybe not anywhere.*

I drag my vision up to the cloudy mirror mounted on the cinder block wall in this glorified outhouse California State Parks has deemed a bathroom, and thankfully, my cheeks are starting to look less beet red now. Just more sunkissed, and I no longer feel the sweat rolling like a river down my spine. Unfortunately, the evidence of my heat exhaustion is still visible. Thanks to the sweat beading along my hairline, the baby hairs framing my face look light brown instead of their typical golden hue. *Christ, it's hot.*

I've just got to last — I look down at my phone perched

on the sink ledge — *two hours and 53 minutes*. I whimper quietly, dreadfully, letting my shoulders droop and fall.

Looking back at my reflection, I thank the heavens I at least had the forethought to put on a sundress before I was forced into spending my day at this outdoor oven. I shimmy and twirl my hips slightly, willing the fabric to stop sticking to my damp skin, and send out a prayer of thanks that my little black dress with dainty white flowers is hiding my sweat spots surprisingly well. I guess miracles *do* happen every day.

You can do this, I think to myself in an attempt to combat the overwhelming social anxiety coursing through me.

Grabbing my phone and inhaling deeply, I place my hand on the cool, metal door handle before letting loose an exaggerated exhale. I push hard on the heavy door but am immediately stopped from opening it fully by a wall...of man. Well, I don't so much as stop it, as his forehead stops it.

"Owww, FUCK!" The man-wall drops his phone and brings his hands immediately to his forehead, applying pressure where there will surely be a huge, swollen knot any minute.

"*Shit!* Shit, I'm so sorry! I had no idea someone was standing right outside the door!" The metal door swings back towards me, the impact causing me to falter. *Yeah, that's a heavy fucking door.*

"Fucking hell," the man groans, clenching his eyes shut while pressing the palm of his hand against his forehead.

Way to fade into the background, Britain. I look around briefly to see if anyone has noticed, but not many people have arrived yet and Georgia is nowhere in sight, thank God.

"Just wait here, just a second. I'll be right back!" I take off, running over to the picnic pavilion, grabbing my purse, a bottle of water, and a half bag of ice that wouldn't fit into one of the coolers. When I get back, the man is still standing where I left him, palm to his forehead, groaning.

I snatch his phone off the ground where he's dropped it and lead him into the bathroom, taking extra care to guide him, safely, out of the door's path. I drop the bag of ice in the sink, perching his phone and the bottle of water on the ledge while letting my purse land somewhere on the grimy floor. I'm too concerned about the head trauma I've just perpetrated to care, though.

Emptying a portion of ice into the sink, I use what's remaining to make an ice pack. Winding the excess plastic tight, I move the man's hand, gently, from his forehead and replace it with the bag of ice. His eyes stay clenched, but at least he's no longer groaning.

"Again, I'm so, so sorry; I didn't know you were right outside the door." *I'm absolutely killing it at first impressions.*

The man takes a deep breath. "It's not your fault. I didn't know anyone was in here and my stupid, fucking phone distracted me." I let loose a little breath of relief. Hopefully, this means he won't blame me for the concussion he might have — or the hospital bills that might be coming his way.

The man starts to sink back, looking for something to lean against, but his hands are just groping blindly behind him, so I step forward to guide him. My one hand is still holding the bag of ice to his head, while my other presses his left hip back and to the left until his hands find home and he rests against the sink's edge. When I let go of his hip, I feel a tingle. My body responds before my mind can, causing my cheeks to heat rapidly. That touch felt...*intimate...not platonic. Huh.*

I'm in a bathroom. Alone. With a man I don't know. *Cool.*

I give him a once over, up and down. *A very attractive man I don't know.* He's got thick, sandy-colored hair and is dressed handsomely, leaning against the sink like a damn J. Crew model. *Handsomely? Who am I?* I should hand the bag of ice over, make a final apology, and leave. I should get him two ibuprofen from my bag, tell him there's a bottle of water on the sink, and walk out that door. I should definitely do that, but...the longer I stay *in here*, the less time I have to spend *out there*. So, I keep holding the bag, and surprisingly, he doesn't move to take over.

"Would you like some ibuprofen?" I ask him quietly. At the sound of my voice, he starts to ease his eyes open...and *fuck*. They're the most beautiful blue eyes I've ever seen. *Jesus.* It's not even like the color is particularly bold. It's just that they're his eyes, on his face. And he's striking. His strong, sharp jaw, perfectly straight nose, and dirty blond hair accentuate his tan, creating a perfectly balanced harmony with those gorgeous blue eyes.

I could have stood here for hours in quiet companionship as long as he kept his eyes closed, but damnit, with his gaze fixated on me, I'm getting hot again. The small bathroom starts to feel stifling, and as if on cue, I feel a drop of sweat bead and roll down my spine, getting trapped in my panties. I can't help but fidget under the weight of his focus, which he hasn't broken since opening his eyes. To be fair, I haven't either.

"I have some ibuprofen in my purse if you'd like some," I offer again quietly, "for the swelling." He's still staring at me, and I don't understand why. We've definitely gone past the point of polite eye contact, with no talking.

"*Crap*," I whisper mostly to myself as a wave of panic

takes hold. "Do I need to call an ambulance? Do you know where you are? Do you know who you are?" *How bad did I hit this guy?* He just laughs a low, calming laugh. The sound puts me at ease while simultaneously exciting me.

"I know where I am, I know who I am...What I don't know is who *you* are." He cocks his head slightly, questioning.

"Oh, um, I was just helping set up the picnic." I give him a half smile. I don't know why I didn't answer his question. Well, I guess he didn't really ask me a question, though, did he? He made a statement. A true one at that; I don't know him, and he doesn't know me.

"Huh," is his only response, but the questioning look lingers. I finally break eye contact when his Blackberry begins vibrating on the edge of the sink. It's behind him, so I instinctively reach for it to pass it to him, and while I shouldn't, I do. His phone is still open to the chat he was reading when I hit him with the door...and I read the message. *More like a novel by the looks of it,* but I only have a moment to glance at the first couple of lines before I hand it over to him. Immediately, I wish I hadn't.

I hold the phone out for him to take, but he doesn't. He just keeps looking at me, completely ignoring the phone in my hand. When it vibrates again, I push the phone towards him, and when our hands touch slightly this time, I feel that hint of intimacy again. There's this heat between us, and it's growing.

What is happening right now? Am I imagining this? Stuff like this doesn't happen to Britain Palomino, and after reading *that* text, I should absolutely not be feeling the kind of warmth that I am right now. The kind that makes you rub your sticky thighs together and squirm with anticipation.

Ugh. *Why? Why won't he take it?* Probably because he knows *"Nancy"* is leaving him — for someone else. He makes no move to take the phone, though, leaving us stuck in this strange standoff. Me holding ice to his head, holding his phone out for him to take. Him staring at me, bracing his hard and muscular body against the sink. My fingers are still slightly touching his hand when I have the realization that I'm being weird. *What the fuck is wrong with me?*

I clear my throat and look away, setting the phone back down behind him.

"I should probably get going..." I begin to lower my hand from his forehead when he grabs my wrist to stop me. It's not hard — quite the opposite, actually. He does it with so much tenderness I can't help the burning in my pelvis.

"Please," he pauses, dropping his gaze to the ground, "can you just stay a little longer?" I reply wordlessly, with a simple nod and move my slightly trembling hand back to his forehead. He releases my wrist, and I feel his thumb slowly graze my underarm as he does, but maybe I'm imagining the intent behind it. I guess it's just been a while since anyone has touched me. *Huh*, it's been over a year since I've been touched. At least not intentionally or, warmly...or intimately. *That's fucking depressing.*

"Do you believe that everything happens for a reason?" His question breaks through my mental fixations about *the touch*, startling me.

"Wh-what?" I awkwardly stutter back.

"Do you believe in fate?" He asks again. I'm struggling to comprehend why handsome Mr. Blue Eyes is asking me this. I flounder for a moment, blinking awkwardly.

"Do you want my honest answer?" *Stupid question,*

Britain, you idiot. Would anyone *want* you to lie to them? I die in embarrassment slightly.

Thankfully, he doesn't seem to notice and just replies solemnly, "Always." His striking blue eyes pierce me with their intense focus and I muster the courage to tell him what I really think.

"Well, no," I sigh. "I think believing in fate means believing in fairy tales and happily ever afters, and I don't believe in those. So no, I don't think things happen for a reason. Things just...happen. Good things, bad things, things that don't make us feel anything at all. Constantly and for no reason at all. At least that's the conclusion I've come to so far." I shrug my shoulders and his face transforms, his mouth turning up into a smile. *Damn*, his smile is contagious. It makes me smile. And for what seems like no reason at all, I'm smiling with this man. In a shitty bathroom, at a dusty lake, on a day that feels like hell reincarnated on Earth.

"Do you? Believe in fate?" I ask.

He hesitates before laughing out his reply, "Nope." His voice comes out a low, rumbling chuckle. The sound vibrates and shakes me to my core, but there's something about his response that niggles the back of my mind, and I don't laugh with him. Something about his response feels wrong, and my smile fades.

I move away from him, removing the bag that's mostly water now from his forehead, and when he averts his eyes, I know that's my cue to leave. I've spent a lot of years honing my ability to read social cues because I'm awkward enough as it is. Something about this moment feels definitive, and I know it; our time is up.

I drop the bag in the sink and bend over to get the

ibuprofen out of my purse. I fumble for what feels like minutes until I find it, hidden under my swimsuit and cover-up. Popping the cap, I slip two red tablets into my hand.

I don't attempt to hand them to him, avoiding another uncomfortable standoff. Instead, I drop them on the sink next to the water bottle. Even though I can feel him watching me, I do my best to avoid eye contact as I pick up my purse, straighten my dress, and head towards the door.

"Well, again, I'm very sorry about the door...and the head thing." I look down at his phone and almost say, *and I'm very sorry about your girlfriend, or maybe even your wife*, but I don't. I stop myself.

Instead, I say, "And it was very nice to meet you." I give him a soft smile and turn to leave, instantly regretting my choice of words because did I meet him? I didn't. I have no idea who *he* is.

As I walk towards the picnic pavilion, a feeling of regret engulfs me. It's so intense I come to a complete stop halfway to the picnic area. I pause for a moment, letting some weird, internal debate wage well below my conscious mind. This feeling is like an invisible tether, tugging at me to go back. Back to *him*. But I immediately shake it off, mentally berating myself for being foolish.

I may not know much about life yet, but I do know that men like Mr. Blue Eyes aren't interested in girls like me.

TWO

BRITAIN

"There you are!" I've only heard Georgia use that high pitched voice maybe five times in my life. It surprises me. She sounds...delighted.

"Yeah, sorry. Just needed to use the restroom." I sidle up to her in the pavilion that's now teeming with people. The picnic went from 0 to 60 while I was helping Mr. Blue Eyes. The sight instantly activates my all-too-familiar anxious dread of socializing.

"Come on, there's some people I'd like you to meet." Georgia slides her arm into mine, and I look down at the seemingly foreign attachment. Georgia doesn't seem to think twice about it, though, just winding us through groups of people who are all chatting and laughing together.

"Do you really work with all these people?" I ask as we weave and bob through the crowd.

"Well, yes, and no. About half of them work at the office

full-time, the other half works on-site, but I still have to work with all of them." I just nod along to her answer. I honestly don't know what my mom does for a living. I'm pretty sure she's a secretary, but a high-level one. The only thing I know for certain is that she works for Connie, the co-owner of the MS Group.

We reach the far end of the pavilion, closest to where the makeshift bar is, and when we get to where we're going, the group of people part for us like the Red Sea. Like Georgia belongs.

Connie is instantly recognizable with his thick black hair set against his tan skin. He's wearing a white polo with khaki shorts, a watch that probably costs more than my car, and boat shoes. I don't know much about wealthy people, but if I were to imagine a rich, middle-aged man, this would be pretty damn close to what I'd picture. The moment he sees us, Georgia and me, his entire demeanor and attention shifts, falling on us. He straightens, and his face turns up into the brightest smile. *We should find out who his dentist is.*

Constantine is a good man. On the few occasions I've met him, I've always remembered how kind he was. He always asked me questions about school and what sports I was playing, or what books I was reading. My dad was never in the picture as a child, and Georgia didn't date, so my only interactions with grown men in my adolescence were, ironically, the dentist and Connie.

Georgia leads me straight to him, a smile on her face. I can't figure out why, honestly, because she rarely smiles. It's then that I realize I'm seeing a different version of Georgia today. *Work Georgia*, not "mom Georgia" or "home Georgia," this is a woman I don't know.

"Britain! My god, you've grown so much since the last time I saw you!" Constantine beams at me. He moves to set down his beer, then opens his arms wide for me to step into a hug. I'm trying so hard not to be awkward so I move in closer and return his embrace. I wasn't really expecting a hug as a greeting. I'd expected maybe a handshake, at most — perhaps even just a polite smile.

While his hug is warm and kind, I do think it lasts a moment longer than it should. You'd think I was a long-lost relative, not his secretary's daughter. *Weird.* When he finally relaxes his embrace, he holds me away from him, refusing to relinquish me completely, and I blush.

"Hi, Mr. Scala. It's so nice to see you again."

"Darling, please call me Connie," he says gently. I smile at him and nod my head. He slowly drops his arms, picking his beer back up. And I take that as my cue to fade to black. I check behind me before I can take a step away, but I don't get the chance.

"Georgia told me you're staying local for school, going to State?" *Oh*, okay, he wants to talk...to me.

"Oh, um, yes. I'll be staying in town." I smile, trying my absolute best to be the polite human Georgia raised me to be.

"Georgia also mentioned you got into Stanford, but you're not going." My cheeks heat uncontrollably; I hate talking about myself.

"I did, but I think I'd rather stay here. No use spending all that money when I haven't even decided what I want to do yet." I laugh nervously, "Also, I sort of like it here." I shrug my shoulders, but it's the truth. I know most people are itching to ditch this place, but I've never really had that same drive. I like the valley surrounded by majestic mountains with hidden lakes and the ocean just a stone's throw over the coastal range. I like the rolling hills and driving by the ranches with my country music turned up to ten. I don't even know why I bothered to apply to any colleges *besides* State other than my counselor advised me that I should.

"You know, my son, Matt, just graduated from Stanford?"

"Oh, I didn't know that. That's awesome." *Lie.* I did know that, but I don't want to seem like the weirdo who knows everything about these people even though I've never met them.

"He really loved it there. You should talk to him about it. You know, it's not too late to change your mind." Connie gives me a wink and a smile.

"Oh, I'm sure he's busy, and I'd hate to bother him-" Connie cuts me off.

"He's not busy at all. In fact, he's right..." Connie looks around the group of people Georgia and I just entered, which has now splintered into several smaller groups, *"here."* Connie rests his hand on the back of a tall man's shoulder, and when he turns in Connie's direction...*holy crap*. He's fucking gorgeous.

Tall, dark, and gorgeous turns and joins our small group that I'm just now realizing is just Connie and me. That's it, that's the group. Well, now *Matt*, too.

"Matt, I'd like you to meet someone," Connie says to him.

Before Connie can continue, Matt speaks up, "You must be Britain." He smiles when he's done. And oh my *god. He* knows who *I* am? It's like his movements are in slow motion when he reaches a hand up to push a piece of black hair up and off his forehead making me salivate.

"Hi, yes, I'm Britain." I extend my hand to shake his, and

when our hands meet, it feels electric. Not in that corny romantic way though. It feels unnatural, new...different. It feels like something that wasn't supposed to happen did. Now I know I'm blushing again. *Stupid pale skin always failing me.*

"Matt," he replies in his deep voice. "It's a pleasure to finally meet you. Honestly, I've heard so much about you, I feel like I practically know you!" He laughs. *What in the actual fuck?* This drop dead gorgeous man knows about me? I laugh nervously in response, I mean what am I supposed to say to that?

Connie pats Matt on the back in a loving gesture, and for a second, I feel jealous. Not because Connie is touching Matt but because Matt gets to have Connie as a dad. It's irrational, but I wonder what it would have been like to grow up with a father like him.

"Matt, I thought maybe you could talk to Britain about-"

Matt cuts him off, "Stanford?" He chuckles, "I know, Dad, you only brought it up three times on the way over." *Ahh.* So that's how Matt knows who I am. Connie gets a sheepish look on his face before letting out a low laugh. I also could've sworn he blushed for a moment, too.

"Well, it's important!" Connie defends himself. "I'll let you kids talk for a little bit." He shoots me another wink before patting Matt on the arm, then turns to join another group, leaving me...with Matt. I could just curl in a ball and die right now. It's so fucking embarrassing that he's basically *pity talking* to me because his dad made him. Matt turns to me, giving me that luminous smile. *I bet it's so easy for him to talk to people.*

"It's okay; you don't have to talk to me about Stanford.

15

We can just pretend to talk for a minute and then you can go." I give him the out he's probably dying for.

"Absolutely not! Let's talk about it," he says, seemingly taken aback by my dismissal. *Oh.*

"Umm, okay?" I let out another nervous laugh for what feels like the fiftieth time. He looks over my head, and around me then gently takes my arm, guiding me away from the crowded bar area.

It's a lot quieter on this side of the pavilion so he immediately jumps back into the conversation. "So, what are you planning to study?" I laugh at his question.

"That's the million-dollar question, isn't it?" I sigh, "Well, I honestly don't know. I'm sort of hoping I'll find out when I get there. I'll take a course, and there'll be this spark, and I'll know then, this is what I want to do." I shrug my shoulders.

"And why can't you do that at Stanford?"

"It's just...it's a really expensive school for general ed when I don't have a set path. I mean, my mom told me not to worry about the cost, that she would take care of it, but I do worry. You know?" He probably doesn't know, though. He's been brought up in a world of wealth. I don't know why I just told him that. It's not polite to talk about money, but I just felt like if I told him the truth, he might drop this whole subject.

"I think, if Georgia said she would take care of it, you should let Georgia take care of it. If that's the only thing holding you back, you shouldn't let it." Of course, he would say that. It's easy to tell someone else to let their parents go into debt for six figures for college when it was never even a question for you.

I'm thinking how best to respond when a skinny guy with spiky blonde hair walks up to us.

"Hey, bro! Been looking for you!" Spiky-haired guy butts right into our conversation. He's even wedged himself between Matt and me like I don't exist. *Typical.*

"Hey, Jake," Matt says as he side-steps around Jake to stand next to me. "I'd like you to meet Britain. Britain, this is Jake."

"Hi there, nice to meet you." I don't extend my hand, though. This guy seems like a douche.

"Sup'?" Jake responds to me, but I don't reply. He's not actually asking me what's up. Jake doesn't wait for a response either, redirecting his attention to Matt. "Ready to take the boat out? I've got a good group together." It's so awkward when people talk about their plans in front of you, especially when those plans *don't* include you.

Without waiting for Matt's reply, I just politely excuse myself. "Matt, it was very nice to meet and talk to you. Jake, nice to meet you as well." I give a tight-lipped but courteous smile, then dip my head in farewell and head in the opposite direction without looking back once. I immediately start walking with purpose except...I have no direction.

I could go stand next to Georgia for the next couple of hours, but that sounds torturous *and* especially lame. *God, I hate coming to things like this.* I mean I absolutely loathe stuff like this. It brings all my feelings of inadequacy to the surface. I feel like I'll never really belong or am worthy, and these intrusive thoughts cause me to spiral. I get this outsider mentality, and then I latch on to those thoughts, and it hurts physically. There's a pain in my chest, and tears start to line my eyes. *God, I'm pathetic. I've got to get out of here.*

There's a small dirt path winding beside the lake connecting different pavilions and beach areas, so that's where I direct myself. No one will notice I'm missing. I'll wander around and hopefully kill another hour. At least that's what I'm hoping for, but I only get about 50 feet from the picnic pavilion when someone calls out to me.

"Britain, wait!" I turn to see Matt walking quickly up the path behind me. I wait for him to catch up, confused about why he's here.

"Where are you headed?" He asks once he's reached me. I almost look around to see if he's talking to someone other than me, but I refrain.

"Just going for a walk down to that beach area." I point to a spot about a quarter of a mile away.

"Can I join you?" This time I actually do look behind me, to make sure I'm not being delusional.

"Listen, if this is about the Stanford thing, I really don't think you could say or do anything to change my mind. It's just life. I'm fine going to State, really."

"If I don't bring up Stanford again, *then* can I join you?" *What? Why? Don't look a gift horse in the mouth, Britain.*

"Umm, sure...why not?" I can't fathom what would make this man want to walk around a lake with me on a scorching hot day when he could be drinking under a shaded pavilion or wakeboarding on his boat with friends. *But*, I will accept the distraction he'll provide.

"Cool," is his only response. So I turn towards the path and start walking again, this time with Matt at my side, yet neither one of us talks. I look out at the lake surrounded by golden foothills sparsely dotted with dry brush and low oak trees. Occasionally, I zone out, following the path of speed boats as they zoom through the wake before eventually growing smaller and disappearing over the horizon. It's... amiable, at best.

It doesn't take much for me to notice that Robles Lake is *not* like Spearhead Lake, my favorite place in the world. Robles Lake isn't up in the mountains surrounded by pine trees; it's down in the hills, which means 1. It's hot, and 2. There's hardly any shade and a lot of dirt. The trees here don't get tall, either. Oppressed by a brutal valley sun beating down on their backs, they have no choice but to bend to the sun's will. I inhale deeply trying to appreciate the natural beauty, but nothing but the smell of dirt fills my lungs.

By the time we get to the beach area, we still haven't spoken and the heat is starting to feel unbearable, so I slip off my sandals, leaving them on the sandy beach, and head straight for the water. I'm not planning to go all the way in, but cool water lapping against my shins sounds amazing right now. Not bothering to check what Matt does, I just do my own thing, desperate for the cooling relief above all else.

When I step into the water, the dry sand turns to cool mud beneath my toes, and I sigh. *It feels so good.* I take several more steps into the lake until I'm knee-deep, the cool water seemingly my only relief on what is turning into a miserable afternoon.

"Britain, don't move," Matt says in a stern, low voice. I don't move, but the urge to turn around and look at him is strong. "There's a water snake by your right foot." He's nearly whispering it like the volume of his voice is somehow impactful.

"Oooookay," I reply quietly, "what should I do?"

"I'm going to get closer to you, and you're going to slowly walk back towards me. If it starts to move, hopefully, I'll be close enough to pull you away." I don't like snakes. I like the thought of water snakes even less, but I'm not sure this is necessary. It's not like water moccasins are native to this area. I think if I just take a couple steps in the opposite direction it'll be fine.

So I slowly take a step back and to the left, but my movement causes the snake to move. Well that's what I'm assuming happens because before I know it, Matt has pulled me back into him, which would have been fine, except the quick movement startled me. Instead of a graceful drift into his waiting arms, I flail, he yells, and we both fall. Into the water. Off the drop-off. In the opposite direction of the shore.

When I come up from the water, I see *it*. A gnarled tree root has floated to the surface in our wake. A root that looks a lot like a snake. I don't even attempt to hold the laughter in.

From behind me, Matt says in a quiet voice, "It looked like a snake." His statement only fuels the ridiculousness and makes me laugh harder, until eventually, he starts laughing, too.

Once we've swum close enough to the shore that I can walk, I turn back to look at him, and *Christ on a cracker*. His wet t-shirt should be fucking illegal the way it hugs every muscle in his toned torso. I try to cover my blatant stare with a smile at him, which he returns, and that's when I feel it. There's a spark burning low in my abdomen. *I want him.*

Stop it, Britain. I have absolutely no business wanting *him*. He's Matthias Scala, and I'm me. I turn away from him, embarrassed by my cringey thoughts, and attempt to squeeze water from my dress, but it's useless. When we get back to the pavilion, I'll just have to change into my swimsuit and cover-up.

"I'm really sorry about that, Britain," Matthias says as he walks towards me, shaking out his hair as he does, making my pelvis burn and yearn. *I guess that's what it looks like to hit the genetics lottery. Awesome.*

"Honestly," I clear my throat to regain some composure, "it's fine. It's so freaking hot, it felt good to just get all the way in anyways." I shoot him a soft smile because it's really not a big deal. I mean, how much worse could this day get anyway? He stares at me for a moment before responding.

"Can I take you out sometime?" There's that nagging urge to turn and look behind me, again. Surely, he must be talking to someone else.

"Me?" I point with my hand to my own chest. He laughs, and the sound makes me clench my thighs together. I'm fucking screwed. *At least, I wish I was.*

"Yes, you," he says with a smile on his face.

"Matthias, you don't need to ask me out because you accidentally pushed me in a lake, okay?"

He laughs again. "So technically, we both *fell* into the lake, no pushing involved. And second, nobody calls me Matthias." *Crap.*

"Sorry," I inwardly cringe, "just, um, Georgia talks about you sometimes, and she's always called you Matthias. But it won't happen again, promise." *If there even is an 'again.'*

"No, you misunderstand. Nobody calls me Matthias, but you can. If you want to." His mouth tilts up slightly, revealing a single dimple. He sounds so sincere, but I'm still having a hard time believing this is all really happening. This is all just some fever dream, right?

There's something about his smile though, and if this isn't a joke, there's no way I could refuse him. "Okay, I will then."

"So, does that mean you'll go on a date with me?" *So he's still on that, okay.*

I hesitate but finally answer, "Uh, sure, that sounds great." When he smiles again, damn, it makes me want to jump his bones, but I don't. I head towards my sandals, sliding them on and wait for him to do the same. We walk back towards the pavilion with squeaky shoes, and wet hair and by the time we get back, I'm teasing him about the "snake" again.

"It looked like a snake!" He says, exasperated.

I just laugh and say, "Uh-huh. *Sure.* Well, I'm gonna go find my bag and change."

I head towards the end of the pavilion, but he keeps walking with me and then extends a hand to stop me.

"Wait, can I have your number?" He asks, his hand resting on my upper arm. I think subconsciously, I've been trying to give him an out on this whole "date" thing, but he's not backing down. Matthias really wants to go out *with me?*

"Um, yeah, when we get to my purse, I can write it down for you." He just nods, moving his hand gently to my hip and nudging me to lead the way. We're almost to the table where I left my bag when we have to squeeze between two larger groups of people standing in the way. As we pass, I overhear, *"I haven't seen any cute blondes around, man. Sorry."*

"She was *here! But now I can't find her. I've been looking for an hour now."*

"Hey! Matt!" The first voice calls out. "You seen a cute blonde chick? Liam's looking for her." I stop dead in my tracks. Th-they're not talking about me, though, right? I mean *Liam as in Liam Millar?* Looking for me? I turn to look behind me at Matthias, and he motions to the two guys to look in my direction.

"Is this the cute blonde you're looking for?" The first voice and Mr. Blue Eyes turn and eye me up and down. My cheeks turn bright pink under their gaze. I hardly think 'cute' is how I would describe myself right now in my soaking wet dress with frizzy, air-drying hair. But as soon as Mr. Blue Eyes looks back up at me, there's a jolt of familiarity. Mr. Blue Eyes *is* Liam, William Millar. My mom's other boss. *Isn't that just grand?*

Liam slides a hand behind his neck like he's embarrassed but quickly recovers. "Yup, she's *the one*," he says in a tone that confuses me slightly. Matthias eyes Liam, not understanding, as well.

"Alright, well, Liam, this is Britain, Georgia's daughter. Britain, this is Liam Millar and my little brother Niko." He gestures toward each man respectively.

I extend my hand to Liam first, "It's nice to meet you, Mr. Millar." He pauses before taking it, but when he does, his touch is just as warm and tender as it was earlier in the bathroom.

"Please, call me Liam," he replies, and I give him a gentle smile before turning and offering the same to Niko.

Niko's response is just, "So you're the famous Britain, huh?" My cheeks reheat. Why am I 'the famous Britain?' *Famous to who?* I look back at Liam, half waiting, half staring at him in awe. Liam Millar is Mr. Blue Eyes, *huh.*

"You're really Georgia's daughter?" He finally asks me.

"Yep, that's me," I say with a bashful smile.

"How old *even* are you?" *What?* What does that have to

do with anything? The direct, oddly worded question bothers me.

"I'm 18, *why?*" He just continues to stare at me though, until he finally drops his head shaking it, lightly laughing.

"No reason. I was looking for you to say thank you, for the ice, and the ibuprofen." He gestures towards the red bump on his forehead. *Of course*, that's all he wanted. I just nod.

"You're welcome, and I'm still very sorry about that." He shrugs it off, looking over at Matthias, seeming just now to realize he's soaking wet...and I am too. Liam drops his gaze, giving Niko a pat on the shoulder.

"I'm gonna go grab a beer. I'll see you all around later." As Liam walks away, I get the strangest sensation. It's a bit like déjà vu, but I've never been here before, and I've never felt this way before, but oddly, the feeling is undeniably there — I feel like I don't want him to leave.

NOW

THREE

BRITAIN

12 weeks. Twelve weeks of just the peanut and me. *If it's only been twelve weeks, why do I look 5 months pregnant?!* I pull my camisole down over my belly, stretching it taut. Like if the fabric were tighter, my belly would look smaller. News flash: It doesn't.

I look at my reflection in the full-length mirror. The summer sun has helped put some color back on my pale, life-less body. And thanks to prenatal vitamins, my hair is long, luscious, and golden blonde, passing my shoulder blades for the first time in a decade. Unfortunately none of that is enough to detract from the dark purple bags under my eyes. They're the only visible, outward sign of the pain and turmoil that still haunts me. But luckily, I'm able to play off my lack of sleep on pregnancy woes. *If only that were the truth...*

Cupping my growing belly, I whisper to the peanut, "Just you and me, kiddo. Well, you and me and the girls." I pause, finding the courage to say out loud, "I'm so excited to see you today." Sometimes I think if I say the words out loud, it'll make them more true. *I hope it makes them true.* It's not that I'm lying about my excitement, it's just that there's still so much hurt that it shrouds the excitement, darkening it. Every elation feels less like happiness and more like anxiety. The butterflies feel more like nausea laced with dread than with glee.

I'm trying, but it's hard. It's so fucking hard. To get out of bed every day and pretend like I'm okay when I'm not. I try to put on a brave face for the girls, but most nights I still cry myself to sleep and I pray they won't hear me. Another news flash: I'm normally unsuccessful. Inevitably, one of them will slip into my bed at night. It's comforting having them there, but usually it just magnifies the fact that I'm alone, and there's room for my grown children to try to soothe me to sleep each night. I appreciate them, but I should be nursing them over *their* heartbreak, not the other way around.

I throw on a pair of spandex biker shorts before heading down to the kitchen, well aware the girls are already up. Caroline was texting from bed at 6:00 A.M. before she even left my room. Once she got downstairs and turned on the great room TV, Elodie joined her like a moth to a flame. The girls have always been early risers and light sleepers. *But Peanut, you're going to be my sleeper, though, right? Please?*

I walk out of my primary suite and down the main staircase as the bright morning sun assaults my eyes, streaming through the second-story windows of the great room. I need it, though. I need the sun desperately. Every day feels like a battle not to fall into a deep depression. Sunlight, exercise, and staying busy are my only saving graces right now.

When I get to the bottom of the stairs, I can see into the great room and I smile slightly. Both girls are cuddled in their respective corners of our cloud sectional with throw blankets piled around them, scrolling through their phones while an episode of *Below Deck* echoes throughout the first floor.

"Morning, girls," I call out to them as I make my way over to the sectional to give them each a kiss.

"Hi, Mom." "Morning," they both say, never glancing up from their screens. I drop a kiss quickly on both their heads, then turn toward the kitchen.

"Mom, don't forget, you have your virtual appointment with Carla at 8:00." I feel a stab of shame in my gut at Caroline's reminder. *When did they have to start taking care of me?*

"Thanks for the reminder, baby." I just turn around and give her the warmest smile I can manage, then head straight for the coffee pot. As I make my way into the kitchen, the interior courtyard catches my attention and I make a mental note to do my session with Carla outside.

We're still settling into the new house, and while it wasn't exactly what I was looking for, it's been pretty great so far. I had originally hoped for a large cabin on Spearhead, not this sprawling villa on Robles Lake. But the timing of it all just fell into place, and logistically it just works. I'll always keep an eye out for property on Spearhead, but lakefront lots only come available every few years. Robles seemed like a good compromise in the interim, only about 20 minutes from Georgia's and 25 minutes from Sandy's.

Robles Lake and Spearhead seem worlds apart even though it's a surprisingly short distance in reality. The divergent lakes are about equal in size, but the scenery *here* resembles the valley floor more than the Sierra Nevadas. But

Robles has a certain beauty in its own right, I suppose. It's nestled into the rolling golden hills with sandy beaches and dusty roads, all of it seeming to be perfectly juxtaposed to the turquoise water of the lake. It is, however, a bit ironic that its name means "oaks" when there are so few trees to be found here.

The house itself is beautiful. It's a 5-bed, smooth stucco, Spanish-influenced villa with an interior courtyard and a pool. It blends into the hillside, the color of the house a perfect camouflage with the golden grasses, accentuated with a terracotta tile roof. And while we aren't exactly lake front, we are lake *view*, which is exactly what I have my sights set on...as soon as I get my coffee.

Lately, I've been living for my mornings, almost as much as I dread my nights. The mornings are always the brightest spots of my day. I'm always a bit more hopeful that today will be the day that it starts to hurt a little less, that the tears won't come so easily. Every morning I sit on the patio with my one and only cup of coffee for the day, and I plan. I plan the day and that I will be better. I'll resolve to be stronger, and to be happy, and some of the time it even works. That is, until about 8:00 P.M.

That's when the anxiety and fear set in. It reminds me of when the girls were both newborns, and I was terrified of the nights. I could go through our days with ease, but as soon as the sun went down, I'd turn into an anxious, tearful mess. It was the fear of the unknown that I struggled with. *Would the baby sleep that night? Would I get to sleep that night? What if something happened?*

I did most of the newborn nights alone since Damian was working 40+ hours and going to school for his postgraduate at the same time. Whatever happened during the night, it was my domain to manage. The pressure and the fear ate away at me. So much so, I eventually stopped going to bed, opting to just stay on the couch with the bassinet beside me, crying out of fear until I fell asleep or one of the girls woke up.

It's the same feeling I get now. It's this fear of the unknown. The pressure that it's all on me now, and no matter what happens, it's on me to manage...alone. I thought, *I hoped*, with time, the feeling would ease, but it hasn't happened yet. If anything, it seems to be getting worse. I was doing okay for a little bit, when I was staying at Georgia's with Alex. But once I moved out, every day has been a little bit harder, and I've cried a little bit more.

I can hear Carla now, *"Grief isn't a linear experience, Britain. You are allowed to be okay one day, then not the next."* Carla's right, she always is, and nothing is as true as that statement. Grief hasn't been linear for me. It's been a zig-zagging chart of high highs and low lows.

"Whoa! Mom, you, like, *popped* or something." Elodie sidelines me in the kitchen. I look down at the belly. *She's right*, it wasn't this protruding yesterday. I look up to see Elodie staring at my stomach, too.

I laugh lightly, not whole-heartedly. "Yep, sure did." I pause for a moment, picturing Liam in the kitchen with us. I can see him reaching out for me, obsessed with me and our growing baby. I get chills, and my stomach rolls. I hate that I do this. I imagine the 'might have beens' constantly. The doctors appointments we would go to together. The nights we'd spend lying in bed, my body pressed against his. I imagine the whispered 'I love you's' and the feel of his warm hands on me. *I have to stop doing this.* I have to because not only are these fantasies decidedly not real, neither was our relationship.

"So, I have my appointment with Carla at 8:00, and then a doctor's appointment this afternoon. But other than that, what do you guys want to do today?" I try my best to divert my attention to planning. This is what I do. This is how I survive.

Caroline joins us in the kitchen. "We were actually hoping you'd take us to Gigi's this morning." *Oh.*

"Sure, yeah. I can do that." The girls and Sandy are getting on like a house on fire. I've never really understood that sentiment, but when I see the three of them together, laughing like hooligans, it starts to make more sense. "You want me to take you to the coffee shop or to their house? And then what time do you want me to pick you up? I can come right after the appointment, and we can do Colton's for dinner. All of us together, maybe?"

Elodie and Caroline exchange a look, activating my "mom sense." They're keeping something from me.

Caroline speaks for both of them, "Yeah, that sounds good. We can also just play it by ear depending when you get done. And you can take us to the coffee shop. Grandpa wants our help making the cinnamon rolls for this weekend."

"Mmm hmm, okay," I say with suspicion and a hint of jealousy. I sort of wish I could just ditch my appointment and go make cinnamon rolls, too. Getting lost in the physical activity would be nice. So would hanging out with Sandy, Jim, and the girls. But I should be cherishing this alone time because pretty soon such a thing won't exist.

"I'm gonna go sit on the patio with a cup of coffee.

Anyone want to join me?" Maybe I can get one of them to spill the beans about the look they just shared.

Caroline pipes up before Elodie gets a chance, "We're gonna go eat breakfast, then get ready so as soon as you're done with Carla, we can leave." Elodie just nods along in response. Whenever they're being secretive, Caroline talks for the both of them since Elodie lacks a filter. I was always able to count on Elodie to tattle on Caroline, and herself, when they were littler.

"No problem, sounds good. If you need anything, you know where to find me." I smile and head for the coffee maker that Elodie has already prepped and readied for me, my favorite mug already sitting underneath the drip. The girls make their own breakfast, filling humongous bowls with Cap'n Crunch, while I get out my bowl for my oatmeal filled with hemp, chia, and flax seeds. *Ah, to be young again.*

I'm just getting settled on the patio with my coffee and breakfast when my phone pings. I don't even have to look to know who it is. *Matthias.* It's the same every morning. He's steadfast, still, after all these weeks. My mouth turns up the smallest amount as I read the message.

MATTHIAS

Morning sweetheart. Hope you slept well and you're feeling better.

BRITAIN

Hi. I slept okay, and feel a little bit better. Thanks for checking. 🙂

Lies. I did not sleep okay and my stomach didn't hurt. But I wanted him to leave last night, so I told him I was nauseous and wanted to go to bed. I don't want Matthias to know how bad I'm struggling. So, I hide it from him, which is awful. I know I should tell him, but every time I'm with him, I feel good and I think, *this is all I need, to just be around him, and I'll be fine.* But again, as soon as the sun sets...I get this awful feeling that comes over me, and I push Matthias away.

I don't think he's caught on. At least I hope he hasn't because I don't want him to feel like he's some runner-up or rebound, that I'd rather be somewhere else than with him. I want to be with him, but there's a wall between here and there that I can't seem to scale just yet. I open my phone and add to my 'Things to talk about with Carla list': *Progressing with Matthias, when will I be able to be intimate with him?*

I set my phone down on the patio table and look out over the lake. There's hardly a cloud in the sky, the water smooth as glass due to the early hour, and the memories just as fresh and biting as if it all happened yesterday. The irony that this is where I met *him* is like a slap across the face. I'm sure he barely remembers it, but not me. There was something about him even then that I was inexplicably drawn to and yearned for. Even then, before I knew what it meant, I was *his*.

———

I cuddle into the outdoor sofa with my laptop perched on its arm. I'm still nursing my coffee, stretching it out as long as possible so it feels like my second cup, not my rewarmed first, and I've got my box of Kleenex by my side at the ready. The good news is I don't feel queasy and nervous before today's session like I did last week, which means I'm acclimating into routine therapy again. But I can't fool myself into thinking that I won't feel like utter crap by the time this is over. So with dread, I open the Zoom invite link and wait for Carla to join.

The interior courtyard that sits in the center of the house is still a bit sparsely decorated, but I've got my sofa and side table, my laptop and coffee — the essentials. And the girls made good on their promise to get ready for Sandy's as soon as breakfast was over. They've also made themselves scarce from the main level for my session. I don't ask them to do it, but I'm glad they do. No one wants to watch their mom break down every night, let alone every therapy session, too.

The laptop dings as Carla joins our meeting.

"Wow, Carla. Your hair looks amazing." She's gotten rid of her bob. The severe bob she's had for six years is now a chic pixie cut.

"Thank you, Britain. How are you feeling today?" She never lets me small-talk my way out of discussing my feelings.

"Well, about the same, I guess. I'm still having a hard time at night. Still crying a lot." I shrug.

"Has anything changed over the past week?" She always asks this, it's her underhanded way of inquiring whether I've been in touch with Liam.

"No." She just nods her head, wanting me to elaborate on my answer, but I don't want to. If she asks a yes or no question, she's going to get a yes or no answer. After we're both silent for a moment, she tries again.

"How are things going at the new house? How do the girls feel about their new home?"

"New house is good. Still trying to make it feel like ours, but it's nice. I like that it's sort of secluded, but we're still close enough to town and the doctor's office and hospital. I also like that it doesn't have any old memories like Georgia's house." *Or like Liam's.* "And the girls seem happy. They've bonded with Sandy and Jim this past week. They're actually going to their house today while I'm at the ultrasound. And they're also getting to see Alex more, too, which I think is great. They've never had a ton of family around, besides Damian's dad, so I think they're just soaking up their new connections. If they're unhappy, they haven't said so. But even if they were, I don't think they'd tell me." I laugh ironically, "They're looking out for me now, not the other way around...I feel like a terrible parent." *Ugh.*

Carla nods her head again, "I think it's great that the girls are getting to connect with Sandy and Jim, and that they're going over there today, I think it'll be a good opportunity for you to have some alone time." She doesn't say it explicitly, but the sentiment is clear. *Alone* time. No kids, no family, no Matthias around. They're my crutches. I start to feel anxious just thinking about it. *Alone.*

"Right, alone..."

"Yes, alone." The tears are already starting to cloud my vision. "When was the last time you were alone, Britain?"

"Well..." *Crap,* I don't know. There were those few days in June, after the girls left for Disney, before Sandy and Matthias came out to help me pack. But then Jess was there, so, no. It'd have to be when Liam was in Sonoma for work. *When he picked up my ring. When we were together, and he loved me.* "It was when I was staying at Liam's and he had a work trip."

"Hmm," Carla ponders. "Why do you think that is?" *Isn't it obvious?*

"Because I'm scared to be alone."

"Why?"

"Because then I'm just like Georgia. Because when I'm alone, there's no one to interrupt the thoughts that make me spiral into darkness. Because if I'm alone, I'm scared I won't be able to get out of bed and keep...going." *Ouch.* I know I've subconsciously been thinking all of this, but verbalizing, making it real, feels like a dagger slipping under my ribs. The pain is sharp and tangible. I fold in on myself as the tears consume me and I try my best to hide my face in my hands.

I'm a terrible mother. Pathetic and weak. No wonder he didn't want me.

"Britain, does anyone else know you're feeling this way?"

I sniff out my answer, "No."

"Could you talk to someone around you about it? Maybe Jess? Alex? Or even Sandy?" Definitely not Sandy. I love Sandy, but she's still Liam's mom. I also don't know if she talks to him or not. And not Alex. God, he'd just stick to me like glue, making sure I never leave his sight. *Jess.* She's probably the only person I could tell, but at what point do people get tired of dealing with your lame shit? She must be exhausted by now.

"I could talk to Jess about it."

"Alright," she nods solemnly, "that's part of your homework. Talk to Jess before our next session, which I'm going to move up to next Monday. Okay?"

"Yeah," I sniffle. "Okay."

FOUR

BRITAIN

After my session with Carla, it takes me longer than usual to pull myself together, but eventually I do, like always. The girls are still out of sight, so I hop in the shower to officially finish off my crying and get ready for the day. Then I try to pull myself together a bit better than I've been doing lately. I mean the saying isn't 'look good, feel good' for nothing, is it?

I've just finished putting on some mascara when Elodie and Caroline waltz into my bathroom. Quite literally, waltzing. I laugh.

"What are you girls doing?"

"Just waiting for you, Mother," Elodie says.

"Where did you learn how to dance like that?" I mean really, ballroom dancing, right here in the bathroom.

"School," Caroline spouts off. *Sounds about right.* At my public school, we learned line dancing. Apparently at boarding school you learn ballroom dancing.

I laugh. "Of course. Are you guys all ready?"

"Yep," they say in unison.

"Great. Let me throw something on and we'll leave."

"Ooooh, can I pick it out?" Elodie asks.

I pause, "Within reason, yes." Elodie is fashionable in a way I never was at age fourteen.

"Yessss!" She pumps her arm in the air and darts into my closet. It's not as full as the one at Liam's used to be, but slowly, my new wardrobe is growing. Not that I wear any of it, or will wear any of it now that *I'm* the one growing.

As part of her personal assistant duties, Jess has added styling to her list of responsibilities. She insisted I give her a monthly budget she can use to order me clothes and I caved to her demand. She also forbade me from throwing any of it away, even if I don't want them anymore. I thought she was going to cry when I told her how I let Sandy either burn, trash, or donate my previous wardrobe. *Jess.* I need to call her after I drop off the girls.

"Ta-Da!" Elodie says as she steps out of the closet, dress, bag, and shoes in hand. It's a little dressy for an ultrasound appointment, but if it'll make her happy, I'll wear it.

"That's a lovely choice, Elodie. Thank you, baby."

"No prob, mama." She winks at me. "We'll be waiting for you downstairs."

"Yep, I'll be down in a minute." I take the Zimmermann dress off its hanger and slip it on quickly. I slide on the sandals and grab the purse, but pause. *Should I bring it?* It's 12 weeks today, but maybe it's time I stop doing it. He never responds to me. Ever. He probably doesn't even see my text messages.

I walk into the closet and stop at the built-in charging

station where my old phone sits. I pick it up and check for messages, but *zero unread messages, zero missed calls* stares back at me, just like always. My stomach sinks, which is ridiculous because there's never anything new. Never. But it still hurts each time. I plop the phone back down into its slot. Maybe it's time to just disconnect the line once and for all.

I ended up getting a new phone and number a couple of weeks after Liam dumped me. I wince inwardly at that word, *dumped*. But I suppose it's accurate. He disposed of me easily. My hands get clammy just thinking back on it.

It was necessary to do, though. It was verging on unhealthy how much I obsessed over constantly checking for missed calls or messages from him. Carla actually suggested I change my number to take back some control over the situation, and it helped. I no longer obsess over where my phone is and whether it's charged. But because I'm pitiful, I couldn't get rid of it fully.

So it sits in my closet, and once a week, I send him an update. I try to keep it focused on the peanut, but sometimes my bitterness slips out. Again, those messages probably fall on deaf ears (*or is it blind eyes?*), and I have nothing to worry about.

I do think about Georgia, writing her notebooks to Constantine even after they ended their relationship. She called it a fool's errand. I call my version 'pathetic.' It's the only word that comes to mind when I think about me doing the same thing. What makes my version so pathetic, though, is that no one reads my messages. Constantine always read Georgia's notebooks, but mine probably never even make it to 'read' before he deletes them.

I'm leaving the phone. I nod my head, physically willing

my body to agree with my mind. *Decision made*. If I get home tonight and still want to do it, I can always do it then. I have to at least *try* to stop doing this, this obsessing. *I hate you Liam Millar for ruining me.*

I turn off the closet light and make my way downstairs.

———

"My favorite girls!" Sandy walks out from behind the counter to greet the girls and me.

"Hi, Gigi," both girls say as Sandy embraces them. It's moments like this that I'm reminded why I moved here. *Family, people who care about us.* From the outside, it might seem kind of strange that the girls are already calling her Gigi, but Sandy was insistent that they do. Sandy just folded the girls into her orbit, like she does, so naturally. Like it's never been any other way than it is now. And I get it; she doesn't want the girls to feel singled out when the new baby has a Gigi, but they don't.

It's special because they've never had a grandma like this before. Damian's mom passed away when they were babies, and Georgia was never in the picture, at least physically. Of course, they talked on the phone, but Georgia didn't give them warm grandma hugs and bake them cookies after school. Fortunately, Sandy has zero qualms about filling in for Georgia and playing an active role in her adoptive grand-kids' and her future grandbaby's life.

"Hey, sugar! You're looking great today!" Sandy's radiant smile practically beams at me. The girls don't even give me a goodbye, they just walk straight to the back to find Jim.

I peer around Sandy and call out, "Okay, bye girls, love

you, too!" Then drop my hands to my side in disappointment when they continue ignoring me. So I refocus on Sandy, "Thanks, Sandy. Elodie picked it out." I motion down to the dress.

"I wasn't talking about the outfit, baby." Sandy winks at me. I can't help but smile in return. She's always trying to bolster me and lift me up. Sometimes it works, and for those times, I'm grateful.

"It's the makeup. Without it, I'm basically just a hairless raccoon." I laugh. Sandy doesn't.

"That's not true, Britain. You really are glowing today. I wouldn't say it if it wasn't true." She arches a brow at me, and she's right. I blush over her scolding.

"Okay, then, thank you, Sandy. I probably needed to hear that," I sigh and she smiles at me, but not the bright smile she just gave me a moment ago. This smile is toothless and slight.

"You got a minute to sit down for a cup of joe before you take off?" *Abso-freaking-lutely.* I was mentally creating errands out of thin air so I wouldn't have to go back home before my appointment.

"Of course. That sounds great!" *Oh, shoot.* "Well, a decaf cup of joe. I've already had my allotted caffeine ration for the day." Sandy just chuckles in response.

"I'll be right back." She heads back behind the counter while I snag my favorite table, the one in the window. The town is a lot busier now than it was the first time I sat here. It'll be busier tomorrow and over the weekend, too. But even on a Thursday, the town is bustling and moving. It seems like an endless parade of trucks pulling boats down to the marina. I can practically smell the sunscreen and pine trees, and feel the mist on my face from the wake. *I should ask Alex if he'd*

41

do a boat day with the girls and me sometime soon. I get out my phone and add that to my list of 'Activities to-do before summer ends.'

"Here we go, baby. One cup of decaf and a shortbread cookie." Sandy sets the white mug and plate down on our table before sliding into the seat across from mine. Her presence soothes something inside me, and for a moment I forget. I forget about the last 6 weeks, and the pain, and the crying, and I feel lighter for a moment. *A fleeting moment.*

"Thanks Sandy," I say with a smile, then motion around to the cafe. "You guys are pretty busy for a mid-Thursday morning." Most of the tables are filled with tourists or part-time residents. At least that's what I assume since I don't recognize anyone here.

Sandy looks around, too. "We sure are. You know, if the girls want a little part-time job this summer, I'd love to have their help a couple days a week." *More alone time, great.*

"Oh, you know, you'd have to ask them. But it's okay with me if that's what they decide." Sandy smiles and pats my arm.

"I'll ask em' today!" She's still smiling at me, but it's that closed mouth smile again, and she's not talking. This is very atypical Sandy behavior.

I ask, suspiciously, "Alright, what is it?" She looks away from me for a moment before returning her gaze.

"I've debated even bringing this up...but you seem a bit better today..." *Keyword: seem.* I'm getting better at hiding it.

Sandy drags out her pause, like she's *still* debating it, but I stay silent, letting her come to her own conclusion.

"So...I had a call last week." My stomach falls into my ass, I already know where this is going. "From William."

Whatever glow I was just rocking has undoubtedly left

me. My mouth gets hot and there's too much saliva. When I swallow, it feels like downing a ball covered in sandpaper. My hands start to tremble, so I slide them off the table, clasp them in my lap, and instantly divert my gaze downward, hoping she doesn't notice the pain in my eyes.

"He asked about you..." *Why? Why the fuck would he do that?*

I can't even look back up at Sandy when I respond. "I don't want to hear it," I say quietly.

"He has a new number." *I'm sure he does.* Probably got tired of my incessant text messages. I just nod, though. "I'd be happy to give it to you if you'd like." My gut instinct is to fall to my knees and thank Sandy, to get that number and call him right this minute. But I can't start this all over again. I can't go back to the beginning of calling or texting him and waiting to hear back. The agony I went through, waiting, hoping, praying. I can't do it again. *I know I won't survive it again.*

It takes all my strength not to cry as I respond, "No, that's okay, but thank you, Sandy." When I look back up at her, I can see that our expressions mirror one another. *Heartbroken*, it's written all over both of us. Heartbroken in different ways, but with the same end result, sadness and pain.

"I can't go through it again, Sandy. I'm...I'm barely surviving this go around. I know I seem better, but I'm not." *Do I tell her?* "I'm not sleeping, and then I can't get out of bed unless the girls are there pushing me to get up." I pause to breathe in and out, "And there's a lot of times...I just don't want to keep going because it hurts so bad." Sandy slips a trembling hand over mine. When our eyes meet, hers are pooling with tears. She gets out of her chair and embraces me.

Standing bent over, she hugs me tight. I don't let the sobs out, but I know the tears are still falling. Same as her.

She's still holding me when I whisper to her, *"Please don't tell him."* Sandy releases me, and sits back down in her chair.

Her voice trembles when she says, "If that's what you really want, I won't."

"It's what I need." She nods her head in understanding. I need Liam to think I'm fine. The last thing I'd ever want from him is his pity.

"Are you seeing someone about this?"

"Yeah, I am."

She nods again. "What can I do to help?"

"I don't know if there's anything that can help. I think it's just a matter of time at this point." *Unfortunately.*

"Well, if you think of anything at all, I hope we'll be the first ones you call because there isn't much Jim or I wouldn't do for you and the girls."

"Will do," I reply solemnly. Sandy reaches out and gives my shoulder a warm squeeze.

I try my best to ease the tension, though. "It's just like old times, Sandy. Me crying in the cafe. Except this time, we can't have tequila!" I force out a laugh.

"Speak for yourself, baby!" This time I really do laugh. I start to wipe away my tears and I wonder, *how many more tears will I shed for this man?*

———

I slide into the driver's seat of my new SUV and try to focus on my breathing for just a moment. *Why? WHY would he ask about me?* I don't get it. I wish Sandy wouldn't have told me. I didn't need to know he had a new number and that I've crossed his mind, even if it was only in the politest sense. It changes nothing, but it hurts like hell.

I start the car, but sit in my parking spot at The Grounds for a few more minutes, mostly staring off into space. Without thinking, I start driving. It's like I'm in a trance. I'm *not* thinking, I'm just doing. I wind up the mountain, on the road to Liam's house, mindlessly. As I get closer to the turn for his street, my palms turn damp and I feel like I have to pee, badly, all of a sudden. I'm nervous.

What if he's home? If he is, will I get out? Will I yell at him? Scream at him? Or will I just keep on trucking?

I make the turn onto his street. Even though it's mid morning, the road is still mostly shadowed by the thick pines growing all around, making it feel ominous and dreadful. I begin to slow down as I approach the entrance to his driveway and my heart palpitates.

There's no Range Rover. But there is another car parked right in front of the garage. The jealousy that pulses through me feels like an ice cold I.V. It hurts, and for a moment I feel like I can't catch my breath. I instinctively slam on my brakes. With my arms stretched out in front of me on the steering wheel, I hang my head between them and try desperately to inhale.

That car could be anyone's. It could be the cleaning lady, it could be a tenant. Unfortunately, I can't think that rationally right now, and I refuse to believe it. There probably is someone else by now. Even if there wasn't when he ended things, I'd have to be an idiot to think he isn't moving on, or hasn't moved on by now.

Hell, I actually wish there *was* someone else. Then at least I'd know. I'd get some closure and know how big of an ass Liam really is. And that would make it better, because it's the not knowing that eats away at me and degrades my mental health. Not knowing is like being in quicksand, and the only person that could save me is Liam, but he's just standing there. Ignoring me. Seeing me go down, but never once acknowledging my existence.

I wish he'd just tell me, 'I don't love you. I don't want to be together. I'd rather be with someone else.' *Fuck*, even if he told me he'd rather be alone, *that* would be better than *this*. *Fucking coward.*

The person I was planning my entire life around, the person I would have given anything and everything for is the one person who won't acknowledge that I exist. *Shouldn't that be closure, enough?* I shouldn't need to know *why*, I should just accept that the only truth I will know firmly in this entire situation is that he doesn't love me. He doesn't care about me and my pregnancy means nothing to him. *Fucking accept those facts, Britain.* I seriously need to chin up and move the fuck on.

I ease off the brake and go down to the end of the street where the pavement widens into a dead end. I turn around, and this time, when I drive by, I don't even bother to look. There's something I need to do before I turn out onto the main road, though. I scroll through Carplay, hit Jess' name, then wait while the ringing echoes through the empty cab of my vehicle.

"Hey, babe. I was just thinking about you!" Jess answers the phone cheerfully.

"Hi." My voice falters before I can say anything more, but I don't need to.

"What's wrong? Is everything okay?" Jess knows me. All it takes is a change in the tone of my voice, and she knows.

"Everything is wrong, and nothing is okay." I cry out as soon as the words leave my lips. I cry, hard.

"Oh, Britain. I'm sorry. What's going on?" Jess' tone is subdued and concerned.

"I," I cry out again, "I can't pretend like I'm fine anymore." I keep crying.

"Then don't. Don't pretend to be fine. You shouldn't be fine."

"I...I dropped the girls off at Sandy's this morning and she told me Liam called her. And he asked about me. Why?!" I cry, "Why would he do that?!"

"I have no idea sweetheart. Is that why you're so worked up?"

"It's one of the reasons." I pause to sniffle. "Jess, I...I'm struggling...to get out of bed in the mornings, and to keep going. It just hurts, so bad." The line is dead silent on her end for more than a moment.

"I'll be there tonight, at the latest, tomorrow morning. Okay?" I nod to myself in the car.

"Okay." My voice is quiet and meek. I try to calm myself down enough so I'll be able to see the road and drive back to town.

"Everything's going to be okay. Not right this moment, not even tomorrow, but soon. Everything will be okay, got it?"

"Yep," I sniffle.

"I'm gonna go book a flight and pack. Are you okay to go to your appointment this afternoon? There's nothing wrong with rescheduling it. In fact, I recommend rescheduling it. Go to the store, get some ice cream. Then go home and put on Bridgerton. Before you can even get to Queen Charlotte, I'll be there." Jess is right. Delaying my ultrasound a week won't make a difference. If I'm going to stop pretending to be fine, the first step is taking the time when I need it. I don't need to keep pushing through unnecessarily.

"Y-you're right. I'm going to reschedule," I sigh as my crying fades. Knowing Jess is coming here is already working on soothing me.

"Good, I'm going to let you go, but text me if you need anything. I'll see you soon, okay?"

"Okay, and Jess?"

"Yeah?"

"Thank you."

"Of course. Love you. We're going to be okay, okay?"

"Uh-huh. Love you, too. Bye."

The call ends and I immediately pull up Silas' office number. Hopefully they can get me in next week.

"Dr. Scala's office, how can I help you?"

"Hi, um, this is Britain Scott. I have an ultrasound and check-up appointment with Dr. Scala today, but I need to reschedule."

"Okay, well, there'll be a $50 fee for the late cancellation." The administrative assistant sounds annoyed with me, I don't blame her.

"Right, of course, that's fine."

"Unless you're sick, in which case we can waive it."

"I'm not sick, I just can't make it today."

"Okay, well, let me see about getting you rescheduled. Hold just a moment."

"Sure." The line switches over to elevator music for less than a second when I hear a click.

"Britain?" A familiar male's voice sounds over the line.

"Hi, Silas."

"What's going on? You okay?" *No.*

"I'm fine." *Lie.*

"Okay, do you want to talk about it?" He asks. I sigh.

"I'm just struggling today, Silas. Well, not just today, but today has been a particularly hard day, and I just need to rest and spend the day at home. I'm sorry to cancel on such short notice. I'm happy to pay the fee, or if you even need to bill me for the whole appointment, that's fine, too. I just can't be there today, and pretend to be happy. Like everything's fine when it's not." My voice cracks on my last few words.

"Brit, I'm so sorry. It's completely fine. I'm going to move your appointment to next Thursday, same time. Take the day and rest. Please. Next time, just text me. You don't have to call in, okay?"

"Thanks, Silas." I can't say much more or I'll start crying.

"Do you need a counseling referral?"

"I'm already seeing someone, but thank you."

"Please text me if anything changes or comes up, okay?"

"I will."

"Alright, take care. I'll see you next week."

"Okay, bye."

"Bye." The call ends and I feel the smallest bit of relief flow through me. I haven't just taken a day to grieve since those first few weeks at Georgia's house. Maybe that's why I felt better back then; I was just letting myself feel everything, and maybe that was the healing part.

I open the glove box for a napkin to dry my eyes, but then

remember the car is new and hasn't had its inaugural fast food journey. *No napkins.* I wipe my eyes with the back of my hand and start the drive down the mountain. First stop, In-N-Out, second stop, ice cream, last stop, home. I need this. I need to just let myself be sad, so I can eventually be happy. *It's a plan.*

FIVE

BRITAIN

There's nothing like a dead silent drive down mountain roads to give you a little bit of clarity. So after picking up In-N-Out and my emotional support ice cream, I headed home on a mission. I dropped everything on the kitchen island and bounded straight upstairs to my closet.

Picking up my old phone, I power it off once and for all. I'll officially disconnect the line when I have the bandwidth to deal with the phone company. But this is it; no more weekly texts. No more holding out hope. It's not worth my sanity.

I drop the phone into my underwear drawer — *no need to keep charging it anymore* — and head back downstairs. I grab the ice cream and walk out to the garage to put it in the chest freezer, but I halt when I open the door. My Porsche is parked in here, hidden from my everyday view. I never could bring myself to get rid of it.

I drop the ice cream in the freezer, then move to the car and open the door. It seems like a simple task, but it feels monumental. It's another hurdle to clear on the path to moving past Liam. It's only been driven once in the last month or so, and the last time I drove it myself was on my way to Colton's *that night.*

I slide into the driver's seat, like some sort of exposure therapy I'm forcing myself to endure. Even though it's hot enough to fry an egg on the hood, I close the door. I hate to admit it, but I do it so the smell of Liam's aftershave doesn't fade faster than it already is. I inhale his woodsy scent, thinking about the trip we took to Yosemite right before he left for Sonoma. *Before I spread Georgia's ashes.* Remembering that time feels like a kettlebell sitting on my chest. It probably isn't helping that it's at least 120 degrees in here with the door shut.

I don't want to get rid of this car, but I should probably get an air freshener if I want it to stop smelling like crippling pain. When I open the door and lean on the steering wheel to pull myself out of the low seat, something in the rearview mirror stops me. *His* sweatshirt is draped over the backseat, like a relic from the past. I lean back in to get it, then slam the door shut. I just stand there in the garage, holding the sweatshirt like it's some sort of magical talisman because this is his sweatshirt. Not the one he gave me to wear, but *his.* And it still smells like him.

"Where are we going, babe?" Liam just looks over at me and smiles before extending his arm over to rest his hand on my leg. I love it when he does that. That hand is like an unwritten declaration. Mine. *"You're really not going to tell me?!"*

"If I did, it wouldn't be much of a surprise."

"You're killing meeeee. Please?" I ask, just shy of fully begging.

"Definitely not."

"If I guess it, will you tell me?"

"No."

"If I give you a blow job, will you tell me?"

"No."

"If I give you a blow job right now, in the car, will you tell me?" He doesn't immediately respond this time. I've got him.

"Fuck, Bambi." I smile victoriously. I don't even wait for him to say anything more. I just lean across the center console and start unbuttoning his jeans. He helps me move them down, exposing his cock. Then, holding his dick in my hand, I start by giving him a long lick up the underside of his shaft, pausing at the top to apply pressure to his head.

"Are you going to tell me if I give you this blow job?"

"No shit, Bambi. I'd give you anything right now if you'd just put my dick between your sweet lips."

"Say no more," I whisper before lowering my mouth down around him. He hisses, and the car begins to slow.

"Hold on, baby," Liam says to me as he turns the car off the main highway and onto a heavily wooded dirt road. He puts the car in park and I get back to work. I suck him down, taking him all the way to the back of my throat, before moving my hand onto his base to assist. My mouth sucks, and my hand pulls, and I get wet knowing how much he likes my blow jobs.

"Baby, you're my fucking favorite thing in the world...and this...is my favorite thing you do." He's white knuckling the steering wheel above my head as I continue taking him down my throat until he places one of his large hands on the back of *my head and starts thrusting deeper. He's close, and I let out a little moan, getting so turned on, knowing I get him like this. Whenever he comes in my mouth, he absolutely loses it, bucking his hips and groaning. I suck a little bit harder and pull him a little bit deeper, and he's gone.*

"Bambi, FUCK." He thrusts into me hard as I swallow his cum. "Fucking hell, baby." He sighs out, then gently strokes the back of my neck as he starts to come down. I clean him off with my tongue before sitting back up, and the minute I do, he launches himself at me. Holding both sides of my face between his hands, he slams his mouth over mine not caring that he can probably taste himself on me.

He pulls away just enough to say, "You have no clue what power you have over me when you do that. I'd give you the fucking world, the deed to my house, every penny if you asked." I smile and blush, slightly embarrassed, but loving the praise he showers on me.

"Good to know. But all I'm asking is where you're taking me." He gives me one more peck before sitting back down and refastening his jeans.

"We're going to Yosemite. I booked us a cottage at The Ahwahnee." I'm pretty sure my mouth falls open. How does he just get me? He's moving to put the car into reverse, but I stop him. Reaching over, I grab his face between my hands and I kiss him with everything I have. It's a kiss that says I fucking love you, Liam Millar. *I don't say it out loud, though. It's too soon.*

I release him and he smiles at me, my favorite smile in the world. "Is that alright with you, Bambi?"

"More than alright. It's been on my bucket list. For years. I don't think you understand how excited I am right now."

"Oh, I think I do, baby." He reaches out and runs his thumb over my bottom lip, his gaze set upon my mouth. I blush. He gets just as excited over my blow jobs as I do over a trip to Yosemite. He drops his hand, patting my leg. "Buckle up, buttercup. And no more bjs if you wanna get there before sunset."

"Yes, sir," I say as I sit back in my seat. I've got the stupidest, biggest smile plastered all over my face because of this man. He absolutely blows me away.

———

I drop my head into the sweatshirt and inhale. The memory of us tangled in the sheets that week makes me want to cry all over again. *You suck, Liam Millar.*

I go straight upstairs after leaving the garage. Discarding my dress and panties on my closet floor, I slip his sweatshirt on and walk right over to my bed. Flipping the duvet cover back, I slide in between the cool sheets and lay down. I trail my hands over my breasts, feeling my bare, already-hard nipples chafe against the inside of his sweatshirt. When I get to the part in my legs, I drop my knees open and slip my fingers over my clit and into my hot center.

I'm soaking wet. *Of course I am.* Sex with Liam just did something to me. Apparently it *still* does something to me if I'm dripping wet over a memory. I slip two fingers inside myself and use my other hand to massage my clit, and I think about him. On top of me, sliding over me, thrusting into me. Praising me.

I push my fingers deeper, curling them, and my hips start grinding to get a better angle. I'm already close. I push down on my clit and increase the tempo of my finger thrusts and with closed eyes, my back arches, and I see his face. I see his body towering over mine. I can almost feel the heat radiating off his hard muscles as he tenses because knowing I'm close brings him closer, too. Instinctively, I want to moan his name. It seems like the natural thing to do, but I don't let myself.

I can picture him in my dreams all I want, but his name passing through my mouth gives him credence in this space, and this is a Liam-free zone. So I bite down on my lip, hard, as my muscles tighten and clench around my fingers. My back arches again and I push my hips and feet down into the mattress as my orgasm rocks my frame. *Fuck.* I've forgotten what that's like. It's been...five weeks and...five days since I've had an orgasm. I drop my hands down, onto the bed and sigh.

———

Matthias

I check my watch for what feels like the hundredth time. *She should be here by now.* I scan the parking lot again. *Maybe I missed her?* But no, I still don't see her SUV anywhere. The only thing indicating she might already be here is the BMW loaner car parked right in front of the office door. *Maybe she took her car in for service and she's driving a loaner?* Her appointment is in five minutes, and it's not like Britain to be late.

Fuck. I was really hoping to catch her *before* the appointment, so I could talk to her, but now there's probably not enough time anyways. Her ultrasound's today, and while I've been dying to ask if I can go in with her, I haven't gotten the nerve to bring it up. Or the moment hasn't been right. Or the girls have been around. *Or I've been too scared of the answer.*

She didn't invite me to come, but I knew what time her appointment was today and I wanted to surprise her. Not just with my presence, but also with the rest of the afternoon, too. I'd hoped to catch her as she was walking in, and that's when I'd finally do it. I'd ask her what I've been meaning to for weeks. Because I don't want to be just some guy she's dating, I want to be her boyfriend. Her *serious* boyfriend.

It was always supposed to be me taking care of her and this baby. I can practically hear my Dad's voice echoing in my head about taking care of "his girls." *Yeah, I'm trying, Dad.* And I want to be there for all the baby things, including the ultrasounds. Because if things keep going the way I hope, this baby will be my child, too. I don't want to miss seeing one of their ultrasounds because I was too scared to put myself out there and tell Britain that I see a future with her. A future family, with this baby — *and hopefully a few more.*

But I'm starting to get this weird, gut feeling it's not gonna happen the way I planned. *Fuck it.* I get out of my SUV and head into the office. A quick scan of the waiting room as soon as I walk in reveals what I already knew: She's not here. As I approach the front desk, Silas walks out from the back, talking with a patient, so I wait a moment until he's finished.

"To what do I owe the pleasure, brother?" Silas asks me as he moves to set down a file.

"Hey, is Britain already here?" I don't know why I'm suddenly nervous. *Is she okay?* I haven't talked to her all day in an attempt to hype up the element of surprise.

"You haven't talked to her?" Silas asks. His response puts me slightly on edge.

"No, I was trying to...surprise her." There's that weird feeling again.

"She rescheduled." That's all he says.

"*Why?*" I ask a bit too harshly.

"She just needed to reschedule, man." He's talking to me as Dr. Scala right now, not my brother. *Noted.* I give him my sternest big brother look, but it doesn't work on him anymore. He's not Niko, or even Max, who I can still sway with a look and the knowledge that I sign their paychecks.

I nod my head and scoff lightly, "Alright, then." That's all I can say, not sure if I'm more pissed off at Silas for freezing me out or Britain for not telling me. I turn around to head out the door, but before I can leave, Silas stops me.

"Wanna grab a beer tonight?"

"Ha!" *Silas wants to grab a beer?* Never thought I'd see the day Silas was asking me out for a drink. "Since when do you go out on a school night?" I attempt to rib him, but my tone is pissy, and it comes out mean.

"I don't know, man, since we live in the same city for the first time in years, and you're my brother?" *Suspect.*

"I've got plans, bud." I try to adjust my tone to something less harsh, "Maybe next time." I turn around to leave, but he calls out to me again.

"If your plans change, let me know!" I don't respond, just heading straight out of the office. As I walk to my car, I get that weird feeling again. My gut twists with worry...and anger.

———

By the time I've rung the doorbell a third time, I really start to panic. *Did something happen to her? To the baby?* I'm just getting ready to call her again when she opens the door. The awful feelings coursing through me are alleviated the moment I see her. She must have been taking a shower. Her hair's soaking wet, and all she's wearing is a towel. But just the sight of her like this makes me semi-hard.

"Hi, come in. Sorry, was just in the shower."

"I gathered," I say as Britain ushers me through and over the threshold. As soon as she turns around from closing the door, I grab her around the waist and pull her into me. *I need her so fucking bad.* I drop my mouth to hers and she opens right up.

"Are we home alone?" I ask, releasing her mouth just long enough for me to ask and her to answer "Yes" before I'm all over her again. I've been waiting for this since the moment I saw her at Colton's a month and a half ago, but between the move, and Sandy, and the girls, there hasn't been an opportunity...until now. I pick her up, moving her legs to wrap around me and head straight for the stairs.

I'm almost to the top when Britain laughs out, "Not even a hello? How are you? Just straight to bed?" *Yeah.* I don't think she has any idea how badly I've been needing this. How I need to cement myself in her life. How I need to claim her as mine.

I lay her down on her bed and quickly slip off my shoes. Less than a second later I'm on top of her, nudging her legs open with my knee.

"I missed you, babe," I say as I take her mouth. Slipping my hand behind her head, I stroke her cheek, as our mouths move to the rhythm we've created. The same way we used to.

Never too slow and never too fast, just perfectly in sync with each other. It's always been so easy with her.

I move my hand to her breast and push the top of the towel down, exposing her, allowing me to run my thumb over a nipple. *And fuck,* she looks and feels better than I remember, and when she moans after I increase the pressure, I can't fucking wait. I rip the towel apart exposing all of her, and I freeze.

I lean back on bent knees to admire the sight of her laid out before me. "You're so beautiful, Brit," I whisper and her cheeks turn bright pink. She's beautiful, always has been. But now, she's looking...very pregnant. I go rock hard, surprising myself. I haven't seen her naked since, well, it's been a really long time. *17 years*, I think with regret. And the last couple of weeks she's been wearing baggy sweatshirts and flowy sundresses, hiding *this*. I run my hand over her bump, loving how it feels, how she looks round with the baby.

The sting of jealousy hits me right in the center of my chest. It should have been my baby in there. The feeling only fuels the need I have for her. I haven't felt this kind of lust towards anyone since...her. I glide my hand over her abdomen again, unable to help myself. *Fuck, maybe my kink is fucking pregnant women?*

"Matthias..." Britain says quietly. I'm still staring at her body and rubbing my hands all over her because she has no idea how good she looks, or how unbelievably sexy she is, bump and all. *Especially* with the bump. *God damn.* I grab one of her full breasts in my hand, noticing how much fuller they are than they used to be. Time has been good to her, filling out her breasts and hips.

"So, so beautiful, Brit," I say to her before I drop my

mouth back down to hers. She tastes amazing, leaving me to imagine what she tastes like down there. I push up and away from her mouth and make my way down her body, dropping kisses on her chest, her breasts, and lastly, her belly, before I move to settle in between her legs.

"Matthias, stop." Her tone is firm, the sound abrasive to my ears, leaving me feeling instantly scolded. "I'm sorry, I can't," she says more quietly this time. My cheeks burn with embarrassment. I tense up, feeling the back of my throat sting painfully.

I just nod my head, but I'm finding it hard to meet her eyes. "No. Uh, no, I'm sorry. I don't know what I was thinking." *Not true, I was thinking I want to fuck away all the memories of* him. I move off and away from her, sitting on the edge of the bed to put my shoes back on, feeling the heat of anger spread through me. *It should have been me. It was supposed to be us. That's supposed to be our baby.*

"I'm sorry, Mats." *Mats.* When she says it, it hurts, and I can't help the sarcastic laugh that I let slip out. I used to love it when she'd call me that. Now I'm here feeling chastised and she calls me Mats like it'll somehow soften the blow.

"Why did you reschedule your appointment?" I turn to look at her, and her eyes go wide with surprise. There's a slight bark in my tone that I don't try hard enough to hide.

"Did Silas call you?" She tilts her head slightly in confusion.

"No, I went to his office. I was expecting to see you there for your appointment."

"Oh, you were coming to my appointment?" *Yes, Britain.* I try not to feel hurt by the sound of her surprise.

"I mean I thought I'd kill two birds with one stone. See you, see my brother." The lie comes out easily.

"Right. Let me get dressed really quick and then we can talk, okay?" She rests her hand on my shoulder and I get that awful feeling in my gut again. But I don't let on. I just nod my head and stand.

"Do you want me to get you water or anything? I'm gonna head downstairs." I ask mostly to keep my mind and hands busy, but I know I'm falling right back into the role I was made for — taking care of her.

"Sure, I'll take a water. Thanks."

I walk out of her bedroom feeling burned, and like the biggest fucking idiot. Was I wrong thinking she was ready? I thought we just hadn't gotten the chance to be alone. It never occurred to me she might not want *me*. *I don't fucking get it.*

SIX

BRITAIN

When I get downstairs, Matthias is sitting on the sectional in the great room. His elbows are perched on top of his knees, his hands clasped, and his head hanging low. *Jesus.* He is, without a doubt, the most beautiful man I've ever seen. His dark hair is long enough to rest on the collar of his shirt, and with his head bowed down, several pieces have broken free and fallen onto his forehead. My chest constricts at the thought that I'm hurting him. I desperately want to walk over, push his hair back, wrap my arms around him and apologize until I'm hoarse.

It was evident how disappointed he was when I told him to stop. To be honest, I was a little disappointed in myself. I wanted to go there with him, and be with him like that, but I just couldn't. It felt *wrong.* So far, everything with Matthias has felt good. I wouldn't go as far as saying it's felt "right" because that has a lot of other implications, but it felt good. Knowing we were going to be intimate, *that* felt wrong. Having sex right now would just end up being a disservice to both of us, and Matthias deserves more, way more.

Walking around the arm of the sectional, I move to take a seat near him. But I don't take his face in my hands and push his hair back. And I don't wrap him up in my arms.

"What's the bag for?" I ask, noticing the overnighter I couldn't see before coming around the sectional.

"It was a surprise, but I was planning to take you to the coast for the night." He motions down to the bag. "The girls packed it for you and I picked it up earlier. I was planning to meet you at your appointment." *Oh.* "Don't think we'll be needing it now." He sighs out, sounding downtrodden. *Fuck.*

"I'm sorry Matthias. I was going to talk to you about this, but I...I'm struggling to put into words how I feel." He just turns to look at me, his warm brown eyes penetrating me as a sad expression passes his face. But he just nods, waiting for me to elaborate.

"I've been, um, really struggling lately." I drop my head down in shame and stare at my hands as they fidget with the hem of my shorts. "And I'm not sleeping. And every time I'm alone, I fall into this depressed state that feels impossible to get out of. I'm sad...and I've been pretending that everything is fine because I hoped that if I just put on a happy face for long enough, it would just come true, you know? But it's not fair for me to keep this from you."

"Why would you think you'd need to keep this from me?"

"I don't know!" I say it a little too loudly, exasperated. "Because you shouldn't have to deal with this. It's not your problem, and you deserve to be with someone who is happy and can make you happy."

"I am with someone who makes me happy. I'm just disappointed you don't feel the same way."

"You do make me happy, Mats! That's the problem, though. When I'm with you, I'm happy. You make me happy. But it's a distraction from what I still feel deeply, *painfully*, and it's grief. And I don't let myself deal with it. And I don't talk about it. I just pretend. *That's* the problem."

"So I'm being punished because I make you happy?" *What the fuck?* I finally look back up at him.

"How am I punishing you?" I try to keep my tone even.

"By keeping me at arms length. And not talking to me about the important stuff and the real stuff you're going through. Look, I love spending time with you, and with the girls, but I don't need everything to be rainbows and sunshine. I don't know what gave you that impression." He pauses to shake his head in disbelief. "You still don't get it. I want to be with you. *With you,* Britain. Somehow, though, I've already messed it all up because you won't tell me what's going on. You act like everything's fine, until it's not, but you're not even giving me a chance to show up for you in the first place." *Shit, he's right.* When he speaks again, he averts eye contact and his tone is subdued.

"I showed up at the appointment today," he pauses, like he's debating what he wants to say, "because I wanted to ask if I could go into the ultrasound with you. And I wanted to know if we could put a label, on *this*." He motions with his hand between the two of us. "And then I had this grand idea that I'd sweep you off your feet and take you away for a romantic night." He lets out a sigh. "I wouldn't have planned all that if I had known you're not over Liam. *Not even fucking close to being over Liam,*" he scoffs.

I'm gobsmacked. I don't know what to say, so I sit there saying nothing.

"Do you want to stop seeing each other?" He can't even look at me when he asks. My heart breaks and I know there are tears in my eyes. I respond without thinking. The words are out of my mouth before I can even think twice.

"No." I say it quietly, but it's there, and it's the truth. I don't want to stop seeing him. "I don't want to stop seeing you, Mats, but I don't want to keep pretending like everything's great and I'm happy when I'm not. And I don't think I'm ready for a label. I'm just not ready. Like don't you ever wonder why I don't want to hang out, or go on dates at night?"

"I just assumed you had morning sickness. Well, you know what I mean, the all-day sickness people call morning sickness."

"It's not that. It's because I get so scared and anxious at night that I just end up crying, all night, every night. It's just this bone-chilling fear, and for no apparent reason." Matthias moves over, wrapping me in his strong arms.

"I'm sorry, Brit. I didn't know. You should have said something. I'm sorry I made you feel like you couldn't say anything." He pulls away from me slightly. "What do you need? What can I do?"

"I don't know. That's part of the problem, I don't really know what I need or what anyone *can* do. I probably need to talk about it, but I can't imagine that's something you'd want me to talk about with you." He grimaces for a fraction of a second before he schools his face back into a sympathetic expression.

"If talking about Liam would help, let's do it." He says this with as much enthusiasm as someone getting ready to have a root canal.

"Jess is coming. She'll be here tonight or tomorrow morning. I can talk to her about some of this, too." He looks instantly relieved. "I just want to start by taking today to just be sad. Not try and be happy, but just really be sad. And I want to watch TV, and cry, and then eat some ice cream...and it's probably for the best if I do that alone."

Instantly, his shoulders fall slightly. This feels impossible if I do what I need—at least what I think I need. I'm disappointing Matthias, but if I keep going along like this...I *can't* keep going along like this. It dawns on me that I'm feeling something I used to feel all the time with Damian. It's this internal conflict. I'd feel it when what I wanted, or even who I was, was in direct conflict with Damian and the life we shared. Damian and I only worked when I would bend to him. *Hmm.* I shouldn't waste my time comparing Matthias to Liam, but I don't remember feeling this way with *him. Did you forget, Britain? Liam's not here, though.*

I can't go back to that either. What I need is valid; what I'm asking for is fair. I told Matthias, that day at the hospital, I may not be able to give him the relationship he's looking for. At this point, he can take it or leave it. I'll be sad to see him go, but I won't be sad that I'm standing up for myself.

He sits there for several moments, looking at me. Like he's willing me to buckle, to take it back, to ask him to stay. But I don't. When he realizes it, he finally says, "Alright then. I guess I'll get going." The disappointment seems to roll off him in waves, crashing into me. But I stay strong; I won't cave.

"Okay, sounds good...and we'll talk tonight, yeah?" I walk with him over to the front door.

"Will we, though?" Matthias asks with a sort of chill to his voice. I'm not used to seeing him like this. Matthias has always been a golden retriever, but today was like peeling a layer of an onion back, and I'm not sure I like what's underneath.

"Yes, we will. I'll text you tonight."

He leans down, giving me a gentle kiss on the cheek. "If you say so, Brit." He steps over the threshold and turns, giving me the slightest of smiles. "Take all the time you need, babe. I'm not going anywhere." And just like the flip of a switch, the golden retriever has returned.

———

By two o'clock, I'm wondering about the girls when my phone starts vibrating.

"Hi, I was just thinking about you guys. You ready for me to come pick you up?"

"Uhhh, you're still here?" Caroline asks me cautiously.

"Yeah, I ended up rescheduling my appointment. And baby, I appreciate you and Elodie helping Matthias get stuff ready for the coast...today just wasn't the best day to go. But hey! I have some good news!"

"Oookay, what's that?"

"Aunt Jess is coming today or tomorrow!"

"Yesssss!" Elodie whisper shouts, making me laugh to myself.

"That's great!" Caroline's tone immediately improves, the relief apparent. "I mean, Elodie and I were planning to stay the night at Gigi's, but we can come home if you need us to." The guilt washes over me. They shouldn't have to worry about their mom for one night.

"No, I think you girls should stay if you want to. Jess and I can come pick you both up tomorrow."

"Perfect! Because Grandpa is building a bonfire tonight, and we're making s'mores with Carly's homemade graham crackers! *Homemade* graham crackers, Mom!" Elodie's excitement is nearly infectious.

"Wow! That sounds amazing! Can you girls save me a graham cracker to try, please?"

"We will, and will you call us if you need anything tonight?" *No.* Caroline shouldn't have to take on my burdens anymore. I have to work on getting better, being better so my kids can be kids, not their parent's chaperone.

"Absolutely, I will. You girls have so much fun and let me know what time to pick you up, okay?"

"K! Bye, Mom. Love you!" "Bye, Mom."

"Love you both so much. Bye."

These girls deserve more than I'm giving them right now. I let out a long sigh.

BRITAIN

You're okay with the girls staying over?

SANDY

Are you kidding me? These girls make me feel young again, and they're a joy to be with. They're welcome to stay over anytime.

Okay. Thanks, Sandy. I'm not sure if you were tracking, but I'm not going to the coast tonight, so if they need anything or need me to get them, I can.

Yeah, I was tracking, and that's okay. It just didn't work out today. Get some rest and we'll see you tomorrow, baby!

Okay, thank you.

This is good. I can be alone...for a little bit. Just as I grab the remote to restart *Bridgerton*, the doorbell rings. I'm not expecting anyone and the house is pretty secluded, so I check the Nest cam before answering. It's a young man, with an armload of bags and packages.

I open the door cautiously. "Hi, can I help you?"

"Are you Britain Scott? I have deliveries for you from Jess DiAngelo."

"That's me." I open the door a bit wider and he immediately starts passing over bags and parcels.

"I have more stuff in the truck, I'll be back in just a sec." I nod my head wordlessly and move the bags and packages from the front courtyard into the entryway. After a moment, he's back again with more bags and boxes. Leave it to Jess to find someone who'll deliver anything, same-day, to Robles Lake. We can't even order Chinese food, but here is a man dropping off groceries, a Pack-n-Play, wine, and fresh flowers. *This woman should be president.*

After one more trip out to the truck, the young man pulls out a piece of paper and presents it to me.

"I'm supposed to assemble the Pack-n-Play, install the carseat in your car, and put all the groceries away. Here's a copy of my driver's license and a phone number to call for reference if you want to check with them first."

I should probably be worried, but he seems like a nice kid. And if he wanted to murder me he probably wouldn't have bothered to bring all the groceries in first.

"That's okay. Come on in, but don't worry about the groceries. I'll do those."

"No, ma'am. I've been given strict instructions to not let you lift a finger. It was a stipulation with this job." *Ma'am. Dagger to the chest.* I laugh a bit, though.

"Okay then, have at it. If you need anything, don't hesitate to ask. And I'm Britain, by the way." I hold my hand out to him and he takes it with a firm shake.

"I'm JJ, or James. I'll answer to either."

"Nice to meet you, James." I give him a brief smile before showing him the kitchen and the guest room on the first floor that Jess and Eden can use.

I grab a LeCroix before heading back to the great room, opening my text messages as I do.

BRITAIN

Where do you find people — HOW do you find people to do this stuff for you?

JESS

If I told you, then you wouldn't need me anymore.

Not true, I'll always need you 😉

Fact. FYI ETA 6:30

That's a pretty fast turnaround time. Did you hop on the first flight out?

Don't be mad...

Oh God.

I'm not coming alone...I may have asked Damian if he had any meetings happening on the west coast this week.

Great.

Wonderful.

He just cares about you and wants to check in on you and the girls, that's all. Let him. He let me and Eden stow away on the company jet. K?

Fine, I'll allow it. See you soon.

Jess only responds with a picture of Eden in the arms of a flight attendant aboard a private plane. I can't stay mad at her. Even if hanging out with Damian right now feels a little less than ideal, I know she means well.

I haven't seen much of Damian lately, aside from the prisoner exchange back in Virginia when they got back from Disney World and Summer came with him. *Ugh*, She was wearing the most pitiful smile on her face, like she really took pity on me. Me, the middle-aged woman, pregnant and alone, next to her, a young vibrant woman, just settling down with her new man. That might be my second least favorite memory ever. The first being Liam sliding my engagement ring off my finger in a crowded bar. *I think that'll be a core memory for the rest of my life.* I cringe.

Instead of restarting Bridgerton, I throw my AirPods in and head upstairs. I have to hunt down the new bedding for the baby's room. Damian will have to sleep in the nursery, I guess. It's not decorated yet, but there's at least a twin daybed in there, along with a crib. I'm sure he'll *love* that.

SEVEN

LIAM

I look at the time on the dashboard like my life depends on it. Every minute gone by is another minute lost. *Why isn't she picking up her fucking phone?* Obviously it still works; she just texted me last week. I try calling again (for the hundredth time in the last four hours) but it's the same as every time before — straight to voicemail. Her sweet-sounding voice on her inbox plays back to me, making the pressure in my chest tighter, almost unbearable.

This has been the longest four hours of my entire life. The worst part is, I don't even know where I'm really going. I'm assuming if Silas is her new OB, she's somewhere semi-local to Spearhead or town, and if there's anyone that'll know where she is, it's Sandy. *"She's good, better off without you,"* replays in my mind. *Please don't be too late. Please, please.*

I debated going to the house first, but there's no way she'd be there. That'd be too easy, a fucking dream, honestly. But I do need to know if she read the letter. I have to assume no, since she doesn't know why I left. I explained it all in the letter. And if she didn't get it, is it just sitting on our bed unread? *Our bed.* My bed. God, I've fucking ruined everything.

All I wanted to do was make things right, take myself out of the equation for *them*. But the plan didn't work, and now I've missed out on months with Britain and my child because I had to be some kind of martyr. *My child.* I can't believe I'm going to be a dad, and Britain's going to be their mom. *FUCK, she's my everything.*

In the back of my mind I'm already thinking: *What happens if I can't make this right? What if I am too late and she's moved on?* Maybe her and Matt are happy, and she really is better off without me. I guess I'll cross that bridge when I get there. Or maybe I'll just drown instead. I don't fucking know, but I've gotta get there first, and the first step is to find Sandy.

The steep driveway to their house winds around to the front in a circle. Without wasting a moment, I throw the truck in park right by the front door and practically run into the house, shouting before I can even make it inside.

"Sandy!" I call out through the main level, but nothing echoes me back. So I continue on, walking deeper into the house to the kitchen.

"Hi." *Who is this?*

"Uh, hello…" I respond, pausing to get my bearings. There's something familiar about the teenager standing in Sandy's kitchen. I don't have time to pull the thread, though.

"Is Sandy here?" I ask a bit too brusquely.

"Yeah, she's in the back. May I ask *who* is asking?" The teen questions me, mirroring my less-than-polite tone.

"I'm her son, Liam."

The teen scoffs at me, and if looks could kill, I'd be dead on arrival. "So you're the man who doesn't know how to use a phone? Or a condom?" *The fuck?*

"*Elodie!*" A second teen comes out from the pantry holding chocolate bars. "You can't say stuff like that." The minute I see her, realization hits me. It's like looking at the Britain I met 17 years ago, except this version is a little bit taller and a bit more tan. *Holy shit*, I might cry. Partly from relief that Britain might be here, but also because it feels like getting punched in the gut meeting them like this.

"Why? It's true." The spunky teen with reddish hair just shrugs her shoulders and glares at me, maliciously.

Caroline turns her attention to me. "What are you doing here?" The not-so-warm welcome is almost too much, but I guess I get it.

"Where's your mom? I need to talk to her."

"Oh, you do, do you?" Elodie asks me in what I'm starting to believe is her only tone, moody and accusatory.

"Yes, I do. I've tried calling, but she's not picking up. I need to see her as soon as possible. Please." They both look at each other in a knowing way, having some sort of sibling conversation telepathically. "Is she here?" My heart starts racing. I just need to see her and explain, and tell her about the letter.

"She's not here." Caroline finally answers me. I run my fingers through my hair, pulling on the ends, trying not to break down in front of the girls.

"Can you tell me where to find her then?" The siblings

communicate telepathically again, looking at each other before answering me.

They both reply in unison, "No." They don't even give me a second look, instead going back to their task at hand, which is apparently making a tray for s'mores from the looks of it. It's taking everything in me not to walk over and throw their tray off the counter and yell at them.

"Girls, I don't think you understand. There's been a miscommunication. I have to explain to your mom what happened." I start pacing, the anxiety eating away at me. Caroline keeps ignoring me, but Elodie responds.

"Uh huh, suuurrre. A *mis-comm-uni-cation,* huh? Alright, I'll tell you where she is." *Thank fuck.*

"God, thank you, Elodie–" She cuts me off before I can say anything else.

"When hell freezes over." Caroline shoots her a scolding look, but doesn't reprimand her this time. Instead, we all turn as the door to the back deck opens, and I see my mom at the same time she notices me. We make eye contact before she looks at the girls, then back at me.

"*William,* what are you doing here?" Her tone is unpleasant, not the warm one I'm used to.

"I need to find *her* and talk to her, but I can't get a hold of her." Sandy sort of chuckles before smiling. It's not a happy smile.

"Oh, *you?* You're having trouble getting a hold of her?" Her brow arches. She's pissed. "Girls, why don't y'all head out to the deck and make sure Gramps has all the wood he needs and I'll deal with taking out the trash, kay?" She gives them a wink before guiding them out the back door.

The girls give me the side eye as they leave, but they don't say anything more.

"So am I the trash then?" I ask Sandy once she's back in the kitchen.

"If it looks like a duck and quacks like a duck...you know how it goes, baby." I forget how vicious Sandy can be. The southerner in her comes out, and she's likely to tell me to bless my heart any minute.

"I can explain everything, but I have to find Britain. She deserves to hear it first."

"So you think you can just explain this to her and everything'll be right as rain?" She laughs at me, ironically. "William, I've never been more disappointed in you in your entire life. Britain deserved better. She *deserves* better. So do my grandbabies, and honestly, at this point, they're probably better off without you mucking everything up. *Again*."

"Ouch."

"Somebody's got to be the one to tell ya. Might as well be me."

"You weren't lying when you said you'd disown me, were you?" It's my turn to laugh ironically now.

"Sure wasn't, sugar. I love you, William, but I didn't raise you to be a trash human being. If this is how you want to act and treat people, I'll say goodbye right now. *Now*, unless you have something else to talk about, I'll see you to the door." Sandy moves to usher me out of the kitchen and towards the entryway.

"You don't understand. I did this because Britain is still in love with Matt. I was giving them their chance. I was giving her a choice. Don't you see that?! I didn't tell Matt about Britain being here because I was scared she'd go back to him the second he came around. And then I overheard Britain telling her ex that she'd never gotten over him, and...and I just knew I had to do this for her. And for Matt. And if I didn't, I'd just be this placeholder until she left me for him someday." Sandy gives me a sympathetic smile.

"Then you're stupider than I thought, son. Britain is madly in love with you. Well, she was..." She *was*?

"Was? Past tense?" My stomach sinks, and my heart stops beating.

"Some hurts are so bad they can't be undone, baby." She pats me on the back and keeps pushing me towards the door. I dig in, still unsure whether she's here or not. I look around for any sign that she might be, but I come up empty.

"Is she *here*? *Please*, just tell me that."

"She isn't. You need to go, William. I want to soak up my time with the girls."

"Right..." I can't think, but I can feel. And I feel like if I walk out that door, I'm giving up my chance. I don't know if or when I'll get to see her or talk to her again. "I can't go, Mom. If she's coming to pick up the girls, I can't leave."

"But you can't stay here, bud."

"Fine, but I'm not giving up. I only did this so she had a chance to be happy, even if it meant I was living in hell."

"You think she wasn't already happy? The Britain I saw in your living room, wearing her engagement ring, is the happiest I've ever seen her. And the Britain I saw at the hospital, alone, waiting for you to walk through that door, thinking you didn't want her, is the saddest. So tell me again why you think you needed to do all this for *her* to be *happy*?"

"She was waiting for me at the hospital?" I hardly even recognize my own voice. It's brittle and slight.

"She said she texted and called you to tell you she was pregnant and you just ignored her. You humiliated her, hurt her, and then abandoned both of them." *Both. Fuck me.* I push my hands through my hair, gripping the sides of my head tight, painfully. I close my eyes to try and keep the tears from falling, but it's not possible. *What the fuck have I done?*

"I'll leave, but I'm not going anywhere." *Never again.*

———

Ten minutes later, walking up to my own house, I feel like death warmed over. The only thing propelling me forward at this point is the need to find that letter. I flip on the lights in the mudroom and my breathing halts. Britain's tote is sitting on the bench and her sweater is hung up on one of the hooks.

"Britain!" I yell out, but silence is the only return. I walk briskly through the house, flipping on lights as I go.

"Britain?" Her sandals are on the floor by the sliding doors to the deck, but the lights are all off outside and the door is locked. I take the stairs two at a time to our bedroom. The door is shut, but as I go to open it, I say a silent prayer that she's in there.

"Britain?" I say it more quietly this time when it becomes apparent she's not here. The bed is perfectly made. Not a thing out of place. Nothing's been touched since the last time the cleaning crew was here.

Making my way over to her side of the bed, I see it. Folded neatly and sitting on top of her pillow. She's not here, but this stupid letter is. *FUCK!* I want to fucking scream and the overwhelming urge to destroy something pulses through me. I need a bottle of bourbon and a fucking baseball bat.

One problem: The only person at fault here is me. Am I really going to beat the shit out of myself? *Mentally, yes. With a baseball bat, no.*

I walk over to her closet and turn on the light. It's still mostly full of dresses on hangers I never even got a chance to see her wear. *Fucking hell.* I turn off the light and close the door, heading straight to the bathroom. The need to punish myself is strong, so I turn on the shower as hot as it'll go and start unbuttoning my shirt.

I'm stopped midway by all the shiny glass bottles and cream-colored pots and jars still sitting on top of her counter, neat and organized, fucking taunting me. Everything looks like it did, *perfect*, her life woven into mine. Except it's just an illusion. She's gone. Because of me, she's gone, and might never be mine again.

Fury like I've never felt before comes over me as I slam my fist through the mirror above her sink, shattering it instantly. I swipe all the shit on the counter against the wall with a loud roar as the bottles crack on impact, staining the paint while the smell of Britain's perfume begins to permeate the entire space. *Great, just fucking great.* I'm such an idiot. I'll never be able to get the smell out. I'll have to move into a different fucking bedroom now that this one will smell like *her* for the rest of eternity.

I stumble to the ground, my body trembling with unspent rage as I try to regain my breath. Eventually the adrenaline starts to wear off, and I look down at my hand bleeding all over the bathroom floor. *Hell.* I rip off the rest of my clothes and say screw it. I'll deal with all this shit once I've scalded and scolded myself in the shower.

———

"You look like shit, man." I open the door to nothing less than a verbal assault. *Spectacular*.

"Thanks, Niko. Good to see you, too," I deadpan as Niko walks into my house like he owns the fucking joint, followed shortly after by Silas carrying a duffle. "Good to see you, too, Silas." He looks up at me and just nods before bringing his gaze down to my hand that I haphazardly wrapped with a hand towel. Looks like I'm getting the full welcome wagon tonight.

I shut the door behind them and head for the kitchen where Niko's already pouring himself a glass of bourbon from the bottle I just set out, and Silas has the duffle open on the eat-in table, pulling out supplies.

Niko just stares at me before saying in between sips, "It's been awhile, man."

"Yeah, it's been awhile since I've *seen* you. But you know, it's funny, when I talked to you last week, you never mentioned that Britain was pregnant." He chokes on his sip of bourbon. Once he recovers, he just shrugs. *He just fucking shrugs*. I have to work to try and push the rage back down.

"You didn't ask, and it wasn't my news to share." I nod my head up and down, not trusting myself to say anything back, then look over to Silas.

"HIPPA," is his only response to my query. "I need you to take a seat and let's get that towel removed." I wordlessly do as I'm told. As pissed as I am, Niko and Silas are doing me a solid by coming here to stitch me up.

"So, you had an accident?" Silas takes the seat beside me,

unwrapping my mangled fist. I hiss as the towel gets ripped away from the gaping cuts.

"Yeah, my fist fell into a puddle of broken glass."

"Uh huh. Does *this* have to do with the fact that you just found out Britain is pregnant?" Silas keeps working on my hand while he talks, never making eye contact.

"No." Except now, he looks up at me.

"No?"

"I mean, yeah, I just found out she's pregnant. But this," I motion with my left hand to my right, "is because I fucked everything up and I'm just pissed at myself for not being here for her. I couldn't be happier to hear that she's pregnant." I hang my head, embarrassed. It's the truth, though. Having a family with Britain was all I'd ever wanted, and I ruined it.

"So, she didn't tell you then?" Silas nonchalantly keeps pulling the thread on this.

"No, she did. I just didn't...it's a long story, but she told me when she knew. I just didn't get the news until this morning. She did the right thing. It was just...me. It's all on me."

"Fucking Tori, man." Niko finally pipes up.

"Yep, Tori was the one who told me." As fucking unbelievable as this is going to sound, I'm grateful for Tori for once. Without her, I still wouldn't know. I'd be sitting in my sad apartment in Sonoma, miserable. *Now I can just be miserable here.*

"I need to talk to Britain, but she won't answer my calls. You guys helped her move, though, right?"

Silas doesn't even look up when he says, "HIPPA," and Niko doesn't immediately respond.

"And what's your fucking excuse, Niko?"

He runs his hand down his face in exasperation before

answering me. "Cause Matt's my brother! I don't know, man. I wanted to tell you, but he asked me not to." *What?*

"Wait, he asked you not to tell me about the pregnancy? *Or* where she moved to?" I legitimately might need the baseball bat now.

Niko just drops his head and shakes it, "Both." I clench my left fist so hard, I might bust a vein.

"We're talking about my child, man. *My* kid." I'm seething. *I could fucking kill Matt.*

"Just remember, you won't be able to see said kid if you're in prison," Silas says, reading my mind. I take a deep breath, trying to calm the rage rolling through me. I'll deal with Matt later.

"How is she doing?" I pose the question to both of them.

Niko responds first, "She's good." For a second, I swear it looks like Silas flinched. He stays silent, though.

"Silas?"

It's a moment before he responds, "HIPPA."

"I'm not asking for health information, I'm asking *you* how is she doing as a person? Come on, *please.* Is she happy?" I don't know what I hope the answer is. If she's happy, I'll want to die, but if she's not...I'll still probably want to die.

"Yes." "No." They both answer at the same time. Niko looks at Silas, but Silas remains looking at my hand.

"What-what's going on, Silas?" I ask, legitimately scared of his answer.

"I don't know, man."

"You *won't* or *can't* tell me?"

"*Can't.*"

I just nod in response. God, I hope nothing is wrong with

her. Or the baby. I also selfishly hope this means she hasn't moved on yet. *I hope.*

EIGHT

BRITAIN

"Eden! Come to Auntie Brit!" I reach out for the baby and tears fill my eyes. *Fucking hormones.* She reaches back, and once I have her, she lands a slobber-filled kiss on my chin. I laugh, "Hi, baby. I missed you!"

"Aww, I missed you too, Brit," Damian responds. I just roll my eyes. He bends over slightly, giving me a kiss on the cheek before moving around Jess and me to place suitcases inside. Then he's back out the door.

"How was the flight? With Damian?" I laugh. Jess and Damian always got along fine, but I wouldn't go so far to say they were *tight.* After the whole 'leaving me for Summer' thing, relations haven't exactly improved.

"It was good. He was on the phone the whole time. So honestly, it was perfect." This time Jess laughs, the sound bringing me comfort. I reach over and give her a hug with the arm not wrapped around Eden. Jess being here makes my life infinitely better. She balances me out. She's everything I'm not. She's bold, vivacious, stylish, dark hair and tan skin; she's my better half nowadays, truly.

"I needed this," I whisper to her. "Thank you." She just nods her head and I release her.

"Okay, so show me around. I need to see this place!"

"You're the one who found this house in the first place. You probably know it better than me." I'm not joking. Jess and I spent hours on video calls picking out furniture, walking the layout of the new house.

"But that was just pictures. Also, how did James do?"

"James was great, a perfect gentleman. Very helpful. I did not lift any fingers."

"Damn right," Jess says fiercely. I laugh.

"Alright, ladies. That's all the bags from the car. Where do they go?" *Right.*

"Jess and Eden's stuff goes in the guest room on the main floor." Bouncing Eden on my hip, I guide them both down past the courtyard and my office to the guest suite. Eden giggles when I jostle her in my arms, and I smile down at her. I can't believe I'm going to have another baby. The tears start to form in my eyes and I sniffle, trying to will them away.

"You okay, babe?" Damian places a hand on my back gently as he asks. It's oddly intimate. "*Brit*, sorry. *Not* babe. *Brit*." He drops his hand quickly. Jess looks at me, raising both eyebrows in question, but I just shrug my shoulders in response.

"I'll take her while you show Damian where he's staying," Jess says as she reaches for Eden. I pass the baby back to her mom and proceed to lead Damian upstairs, wondering what the heck that was all about.

"So, sorry this isn't like an ideal sleeping arrangement, but the only other room I have is the nursery." I open the door to the sparse space. The only thing that was done in here was a fresh coat of paint and two pieces of furniture. The crib is sitting on the far wall and the twin daybed is up against the opposite.

I laugh. Damian asks, "What's so funny?"

"The irony is, I don't know how many nights I wished you would've just taken over and slept in the nursery to give me a break every once in a while. And now, here you are, sleeping in the nursery."

Damian rubs his hand across his forehead, sheepishly. "Yeah, uh, I wish I would've done some things differently."

"Yeah." *Me too.* "Of course, you could sleep in one of the girls' bedrooms tonight. They're sleeping over at Sandy's. We can all go get them tomorrow morning."

"I'll just stay in here, it's fine. But, uh, they're staying at Sandy's? What about...you know?" He doesn't want to say his name. *Same.*

"It's not like he's there or around. As far as I know, he's still in Sonoma, and Sandy is good for the girls. Like a grandma they never had, you know?"

"That's great. And hey, I'm really looking forward to seeing Spearhead Lake." He reaches out to gently pat my arm. The awkwardness of the gesture isn't lost on me.

"Sooo, how long are you planning on staying?" I try to ask in my most polite, nonchalant voice.

He laughs, "Ahh, not long, I promise. I just want to see the girls and then I've got a couple meetings in Silicon Valley early next week."

"You're welcome as long as you want, Damian. I wasn't

trying to make it sound otherwise. It does feel a bit weird though, no? I mean staying in the same house but different bedrooms. Me in the primary suite, you in the nursery." Damian is like a security blanket. Part of me wishes he would just wrap me up and cuddle me and make me feel better, but that's not really his role in my life anymore. *I don't really know if he even has a role in my life.* I'm a bit surprised that the thought of it makes me sad.

"I was thinking the same thing. I'd be lying if I said I didn't miss you, Brit. And seeing you pregnant," he motions down to the bump I didn't even attempt to hide, "it's like going back in time. I think, I *wish*, I could do it all over again, you know?"

"Oh, I know. Sixteen years sounds like a long time, but looking back, it all went by in the blink of an eye. And now here I am, doing it all over. On my own." The embarrassment of it forces me to drop eye contact, hoping to avoid the pity in his eyes.

"You don't have to do it on your own. You know that, right? You can come back to Virginia-" I cut him off.

"Come back to Virginia and what? Ask you and Summer to come babysit once a month?" My tone is harsher than I meant. "Sorry, just, I don't think Virginia is the best place for me to be right now."

"No, you're right, of course. I'm also three times busier now than I was when the girls were babies." He pauses to laugh gently. "I just love to find solutions for problems is all." Yes, *I know.*

"Well, I'll let you get settled in. Let me know if you need anything, though I'm sure Jess would be better at helping you find it than me." I turn to leave, but he grabs my hand and pulls me into a big bear hug before I can walk away.

"You're doing great, Brit. You're going to do great, okay? You did all the hard baby parenting *basically* by yourself, for both girls, *at the same time*. One is going to be a walk in the park for you." He runs his hand up and down my back warmly and I just let the tears fall. Damian still understands me. He knows my biggest fear in life is to be alone and he's trying to build me up just like he used to. I nuzzle into his chest, pushing my face into his cashmere polo, but with surprise, I realize he doesn't smell like *my* Damian anymore. He smells like *hers* now. I pat his back for him to release me and he does.

"I'll see you downstairs in a bit," I say as I leave the room without looking back. But instead of heading to the main level, I head to my bedroom for a quick closet cry. Checking my watch in the jewelry case, I realize it's still a bit too early for my nightly anxiety crying. This is just flat-out *sad* crying. My chest physically aches, so I stop trying to hold the tears in and let them out, and then I do what comes naturally. I open my top drawer and pull out my old phone. I hold my finger over the power button, debating.

The temptation is strong. Whenever I feel at my absolute worst, I want to text him. I want to tell him everything I'm thinking and feeling, and I want him to make me better. I want him to want me. I want him *period, still,* and I hate myself for that. *I fucking hate myself.*

Don't do it, the little voice in the back of my mind says. It's my last sliver of self-respect I still have left that says *don't do it.* It tells me *if you do, you'll lose this last shred of dignity, forever*. So I reopen the drawer and chuck the phone back inside.

I should text Matthias, *not* Liam. Pulling myself together as best as possible, I head downstairs.

> What are you up to?

Not much, just back at the office working.

> Getting a bit late, no?

Nowhere else to be, why not?

That stings a bit. He's obviously still salty about earlier.

> Okay, well, Jess and Damian are here now, keeping me company.

There's three little dots that disappear. Then they're back, then they disappear again before they come back.

Damian is there, too?

> Yeah, Jess caught a flight with him. He came to see the girls before some meetings next week.

The three dots appear, before they disappear. Again. I know texting doesn't have a tone, but I feel like his text may as well have said: *What the fuck? Why is your ex-husband staying at your house when you just told me you needed to be alone!?* I'm starting to get that awful feeling like I'm doing something wrong, I'm *guilty* of being wrong, and I don't like it.

> Jess and I are going to watch Pride and Prejudice, eat a pizza, and snuggle with Eden. I just wanted to say goodnight and I'll talk to you tomorrow.

Goodnight.

Definitely still salty.

"So this is the only place that'll deliver to you?" Jess asks as she unstacks pizza boxes on the counter.

"Yep, but it's honestly pretty good." Even though we're closer to town, there's even fewer restaurants at Robles Lake than at Spearhead. Here, we've got one pizza place and a half-decent grocery store.

"I'll be the judge of that," Damian says as he swoops in, snagging a slice out of the box Jess just opened.

"Hey! Ladies first," Jess says, shooting daggers with her eyes in Damian's direction.

"Aren't you a bit too feminist for that sentiment, Jess?"

"Not when it comes to food!"

I roll my eyes at both of them and put two pieces on my plate. I don't know why, but my stomach's already turning and I can tell I'll probably only be able to get one piece down. I instinctively go to put one back, but Jess stops me.

"Uh uh, no. Girl, you need to eat." Resistance is futile, so I slide onto the stool next to Eden who is strapped into her high chair that's mounted to the counter top. She's fumbling for Cheerios, wearing nothing but a bib and diaper. Her dark brown hair is quickly becoming matted with mushed cereal, but even so, she might be the prettiest baby...ever. My girls were adorable, but Eden is gorgeous.

"So, when are you disappearing, Damian, so I can talk to my best friend?" I chuckle at Jess' question.

"Jesus, subtle much? Let me just get another slice and I'll take myself outside. Need to make some phone calls anyway."

"Yeah, don't forget to check in with *Summer*." Jess gives him a pointed look before looking at me. I must look confused because she gives me her signature head nod, the one that says she'll spill the tea once he leaves.

Damian just stares her down, only briefly glancing in my direction before walking out the back door.

"What was that about?" I ask.

"He didn't tell Summer he's staying here. I overheard him on the flight talking to her." *What the hell, Damian?*

"Uhh, not cool."

"Nope. I'm surprised *you're* not more upset about it, though."

I shrug. "Not my circus, not my monkeys — at least not anymore."

"Word."

"Plus, I'm a little preoccupied with my own shit."

"Yeah, so when do I get to meet this *Adonis*?" Jess moves to sit on the other side of Eden.

"Uh, I don't really know. We kind of had a weird day today. I don't know what's going on between us."

"Uh oh."

"It's not bad. It's just I think he wants more than I'm ready to give. Well, actually, I know that's exactly what it is. I'm not ready, but he's feeling ready to be in this serious relationship." I tell Jess about earlier, how he wanted to be intimate and I stopped him. How I told him I'm still dealing with trying to get over Liam, and about the short text messages. I shrug, "It's hard, because I want to be that person, but I don't know that I have it in me right now."

"You shouldn't feel like you need to be anybody else but yourself. If you're feeling otherwise, that's telling you something right there." Jess is right. I should be able to just be me. "Let me ask you this, do you like Matthias?"

"Yeah, I-"

"No, do you like *like* Matthias? Like you want to be around him when he's not near, and you think about him all the time, and you'd be devastated if he stopped coming around." *Not really. Maybe. I don't know.*

"It's not like that with him." My reply is quiet. I hate admitting that I'm not head over heels for Matthias when I should be. "I want to be like that with him."

"Do you really?" If I sit with myself and think really hard, there's the little voice that says no, but then there's the louder voice that says yes. Matthias is showing up where no one else is, and that means something to me.

"I think so. He deserves that."

"Yeah, but it doesn't have to be you that gives that to him." Logically, I know that, but I can't help but feel like it does have to be me. He waited all these years, for me, and me for him, too. Up until 3 months ago, I still pined for Matthias. "Regardless," Jess motions with her hand to figuratively clear the air, "one thing I know for certain is Liam can be blamed for all of this."

I burst out laughing. "Hundred percent, couldn't agree more."

———

I really thought tonight would be the night I'd stop feeling absolutely miserable. With Jess and Damian both here, I was certain of it. But by 8:30 I had to excuse myself to go to bed. I felt sick to my stomach, and if anything, the anxiety seemed amplified tonight. It's not like I have any chance at actually falling asleep, but at least if I'm in bed, my best friend and ex-husband don't have to watch me fall apart.

I pull the oversized pregnancy pillow in firmly to my chest, squeezing it tight. I try to focus all my nervous energy and fear into clenching it as hard as possible, but it does little to ease the pressure in my chest. I release it, flinging my arms back against the mattress in defeat when a gentle knock on the door pulls me out of my misery.

"Come in!" I yell, but I don't even bother to get off the bed.

"How you doing?" Jess asks gently because I'm sure she already knows how I'm doing.

"Ugh, miserable." A small cry breaks free from me at the last moment. "I'm pitiful, I know."

"You're not pitiful, babe."

"I am. Pregnant and alone. Sad and despondent. Tragic. Oh, and weak, too. Is it any wonder why I'm by myself?"

"It *is* a wonder. And you're not pitiful or weak. Someone did this to you, but this isn't who you are." Jess crawls into the bed and lays down next to me, so I roll over to face her.

"Tell me something awful about Tommy so I feel better about being alone, *please*?"

Her response is lightening fast. "He clips his toenails over the bathtub."

I fake a gag. "Yep, that'll do it. All better. I'm cured. I need no man."

Jess just laughs. "Damn straight you don't," making me laugh, too, before she changes her tone. "Can I ask you something?"

"Of course," I reply.

"Do you ever think about what it would be like if Liam came back? Like if he came back here and wanted to be together?"

"I do." The first couple of weeks after he left, there wasn't a day, hour, or minute that went by that I didn't wish he would come back to me. "Well, I *did*. I try not to think about him coming back anymore." It hurts too much.

He still shows up in my dreams on the rare occasion I do sleep, but that's all they'll ever be, *dreams*. It would be a dream, him coming back, wanting to be together. *And* me forgiving him. But that's the most fantastical part of it all, thinking I could forgive him. I honestly don't think I can.

There's no reasonable explanation that would make this all okay. At least not one I can conjure. He made very conscious and permanent decisions that I can't move past. How could I be okay with a man who seemingly aimed to inflict the most amount of pain and humiliation possible and then completely abandoned me? I get the chills when I think about it, but I keep coming back to this same conclusion: *He never actually loved me.*

Was it just an act? I mean, how duplicitous can one person be? I don't even fucking know him. *I never even knew him.*

"Care to share?" Jess pulls me into the present.

"Huh? I don't know, it's all just dark and depressing shit."

"Well, that's sorta the reason I'm here..."

"Right," I sigh. "I just keep coming back to the fact that he probably never loved me. It's the only thing that makes sense. But I can't figure out why he would go through all the trouble of asking me to marry him, and telling me he loved me, when he didn't. What was it about then? Was he just in it for money? Was he just preying on the fact that I'm a lonely, pathetic human, and he knew he could take advantage? What was it, Jess?" I let out another sigh, "What the fuck was it?"

Her mouth tilts up slightly in a comforting way, but not in a smile. "This isn't what you wanna hear, but I do think he loved you. That picture you sent me was worth a thousand, no," she shakes her head, "a *million* words. I don't know why he did what he did, but I do think he loved you. Either that, or he deserves a fucking Oscar for his performance."

"I want to hate him, Jess..." she reaches out for my hand.

"But you don't."

"I don't." She just nods in understanding and it's then I decide to fully come clean. "I haven't told anyone this, but I... I still text him. Once a week, I'll send him updates about the baby, like how they're developing or what new symptoms I have. It's stupid. I'm going to stop, though."

"Does he ever respond?"

"Never." My mouth quivers as I try my hardest not to cry, and Jess threads her fingers with mine, giving them a tight squeeze in support.

"Brit, why don't you just go talk to him? It's not like you don't know where he is."

"We've been over this, an-and my feelings on this haven't changed. I just can't, okay? He made it clear that he did not want me to be part of his life anymore. I don't need to go stand in front of him like a fool just so he can make that distinction clear to me *again*. It just screams desperate."

"It doesn't scream 'desperate,' it screams I deserve a fucking reason why! As the mother of his child, you deserve to be able to tell that child, when they ask why their dad isn't around, *because you know they will*. You'll be able to tell them why. You won't have to say that it's just because their dad is some asshole, even though, I mean, maybe he is. But at least you'll be telling them the truth, *whatever* it is." Jess is right, but she also doesn't know what it's like to grow up with a parent who's supposed to love you unconditionally, instead, cut you from their life. I've been conditioned since infancy that my own father didn't love me enough to stay. I've since learned that was *probably* a good thing, but still. I learned young that when someone shows you they don't want you, just believe them.

Liam showed me what all the men in my life have: I'm not enough to stick around for. I may as well believe him.

NINE

LIAM

After Niko and Silas left last night, I drank one too many glasses of bourbon while sitting in the dark great room. It not only fit the mood, but keeping the lights off kept me from hyperfocusing on all the reminders of her: her favorite throw blanket, my slippers she'd started claiming as her own, the couch that we'd made love on. I still remember the last time like it was fucking yesterday. She drove me into a frenzy that night, the night before I left for Sonoma.

"Where have you been all my life?" I whisper over her head, her body curled against mine as we cuddle on the couch. The way we are together is the stuff of dreams. I'm almost positive she's been asleep for the past 20 minutes, so when I drop a kiss on the top of her head, I do so gently. But after I do, she shifts and starts running her hand up and down my chest. Then she's moving lower, her fingers slipping below my waistband and into my sweats. Fuck me.

It doesn't matter when, or where, I'm ready for her, always. She grips my hard cock running her hand up and down over it as I press my palm into her back, nudging her closer to me before reaching down and grabbing her asscheek. She lets out a little moan and her body grinds towards mine seeking friction and I know exactly how I want her.

"Bambi, get undressed." I nudge her to get up, and she does exactly as she's told, just like the good girl she is. "I want you to suck my cock." Her cheeks stain pink and she moves to kneel down in front of me, but I stop her. "I want you to suck my cock while I eat my girl's sweet pussy." Wordlessly, she moves over me, positioning her face over my dick and her pussy over my face. I grab both of her ass cheeks in my hands and massage them together, revealing how wet she already is. She's glistening. My dick starts to get desperately hard in response.

"Take it out, baby." Britain moves my sweats down over my hips and my cock springs free. She looks back at me for a moment, waiting for permission. "Do you want it, Bambi?" I ask her, and she nods. "Then have it." She immediately drops her head and slides me past her damp lips. A groan slips out of me over the feel of her warm mouth coupled with the sight of her dripping wet pussy. I love the mess she makes when giving me head. Yanking her hips back and down so I can place my mouth on her clit, I suck her in.

This time she moans, and when she does, the vibration makes me want to blow my load in her mouth right this second, but I hold off. I never want her blow jobs to end, so I try my best to focus my attention on her pleasure in hopes it'll somehow stave off my own. I release her clit and bring my tongue down and swirl it inside her, and fuck, she tastes like heaven. When I say I could have her for every meal, I fucking mean it.

Returning my tongue to her clit, I move my fingers that are clenched on her ass closer to her asshole, and slip my thumb in. She clenches down on me hard and releases another deep, vibrating moan.

I stop my assault on her clit long enough to get out, "Come all over my face, baby," then I'm back on it, circling, and pressing her down on my face as she loses it. She releases my cock from her mouth as her back bows and she calls out my name — my favorite fucking sound.

That's right, ride my face, baby, until every last bit of pulsing pleasure subsides. I smack her ass gently when she eases away.

"Waiting for you." She says it so quietly, I'm not sure I heard her right.

"What was that, baby?"

"You asked where I'd been all your life. I've been waiting. For you." Christ. *My fucking heart could burst. She has no idea how long I've been waiting for her. No fucking idea. I'll tell her someday. Without another thought, I grab her by the waist quickly and move her, still on all fours, so that I'm kneeling right behind her. I pull my sweats down a bit more and slam right into her, frantically...and bare. And fucking hell, she feels so incredible I actually get the fucking chills.*

My hands are gripping her hips tightly and when she pushes back against me, I know she wants this, too.

"Make sure to pull out, please," she says while clenching down on me.

"I will, I promise." It'll be painful not to come in her, but of course I won't. I thrust harder and deeper than I ever have

before, obsessed with every second her bare skin touches mine. A thrill goes down my spine when she moves her hands to hold onto the back of the couch for better purchase. Good, because I plan to fuck her hard.

"Do you like the way I feel, Bambi?" I need to fucking hear it.

"So much, Liam. Too much." She turns her head to look back towards me and I can see where she's biting down hard on her lip.

"Come for me again. I want to feel you." I need to feel her.

"Yes, sir," she says.

I release my grip on one of her hips and drop it down to her clit. Less than a minute later she's pushing her ass back and screaming my name. It feels like the longest orgasm because I'm desperately trying to hold back and not come. But as soon as I think she's through with it, I push out of her as quickly as I can and slide my dick roughly between her perky cheeks. I come in an explosion of bliss as my hot spurts paint her back and ass. And I can honestly say, I've never loved the look of her more, covered in me, looking like mine.

———

The irony that she was already pregnant by then isn't lost on me.

The whole house reeks of her and it's driving me insane. I don't know what the fuck I was thinking when I thought I could let her go. *I need her like I need my next breath.*

At 3:30 A.M. I finally moved into the guest room. Between the smell of her perfume and her empty side of the bed, I couldn't take it anymore. Trying to sleep in there without her was torturous. Her absence was louder than a jackhammer on my skull, forcing me up and out of our bedroom in a last ditch attempt at sleep. It worked for two hours, but now it's 5:30 A.M. and I'm already in the shower, my body and mind motivated by a singular task: Finding Britain.

Step one is to get back in Sandy's good graces. Make that Sandy's *and the girls' good graces,* but I've botched it all. Whenever I imagined meeting the girls, I thought maybe they'd be tentative at first, but I'd eventually figure out a way to win them over. I just thought it'd be as simple as getting them tickets to see Taylor Swift. Now I'd probably have to book a fucking private concert just to get them to talk to me. *I make a mental note to check the feasibility of that.*

Thanks to my hand, I move at a sloth's pace while showering and dressing when all I want to do is hit the road as soon as possible. So I don't even bother to make coffee or grab anything for breakfast. They'll have that where I'm going.

———

"You again." *Still pissed.* The sassiness is only part Britain. The rest is completely original, all Elodie. I've decided to take a different approach than yesterday. Yesterday I was desperate and rude. Today I have to be charming, patient, and kind. It's going to be fucking hell.

I plaster on a smile as I approach the counter. "Good morning, Elodie. You're up bright and early."

Without missing a beat and completely straight-faced she says, "Well, when you work at a coffee shop..." *You idiot.* It's unspoken, but the intention is clear. I let her biting tone roll right off my back because that little piece of information has hope swelling in my chest.

If Elodie works at the coffee shop, Britain is absolutely nearby. How many days will I have to come in here before a chance encounter? It doesn't matter, though, because I'll be here. I'm not above stalking right now. She's carrying our child, and I'll do anything and everything to get them back.

"So did you come here for small talk or are you getting coffee?" Miss Sassy Pants asks rudely.

"Both?" I try in a playful tone, but she doesn't budge. "Alright then, I'll take a black coffee and a newspaper, please."

Caroline and Sandy come out from the back carrying boxes of pastries. They both slow down when they see me at the counter. Caroline scrutinizes me, giving me the once over, before her sight lands on my hand.

"What happened to your hand?" *Caroline's asking me a question?*

"I, uh, got locked out of my house and had to break a window to get in." I hold up the hand stupidly.

"Uh huh," Sandy says before moving past Caroline to unload the boxes. "Don't you have those keycode locks?"

"It wasn't working." *Lie.*

Sandy also gives me a once-over before getting down to business, "What are you doing here, William?" I look at both girls to find them staring straight back at me, waiting.

"I'm here for her, okay? You can ask me to leave, and I might, but I'll just be here tomorrow, and everyday after. Even when the girls go back to school, Sandy, I'll be showing up at your house, relentlessly, until you give me something. Anything. Even if I don't get to see her, hopefully you'll at least tell me how she is, how the baby's doing. And I don't want to do this, but I'm not planning to be an absentee parent. So if I have to, I'll petition for my share of custody." God, fighting with Britain over custody will be the hardest thing I'll ever have to do. Every instinct in my body wants to give her what she wants, but if that's full custody, I don't think I can do it.

Elodie turns around without saying anything, filling up a coffee cup and grabbing a newspaper from the stand beside the counter. "That'll be $4.75, mister." Caroline and Sandy continue watching me as I pull out a twenty and hand it over.

"Keep the change." Everyone continues to stay silent, so I move to a table (the one by the window in hopes I don't miss a thing) just as a familiar face pops in.

"Hey, Murph!" I call out to the old guy who just stepped in. He turns in my direction, but his reply is only a low "Hmph" as he walks away. Let me guess, he's pissed, too? How many cold shoulders am I going to have to brush up against? It doesn't matter, though. There's only one person's favor I need or want. The rest of the world can eat shit.

———

Britain

Well, first night sleeping alone in a while and I survived it. It wasn't plentiful or satisfying, but I did eventually fall asleep. And while I almost asked Jess to stay, I decided to woman up. It felt comforting waking up knowing Jess and Damian were here and that I wasn't alone, though, even if Damian...is Damian.

Just like yesterday, I'm a little more hopeful this morning. I feel a little bit lighter and a bit more optimistic. I went past the 12-week mark and I *didn't* text him, I slept alone last night and I've got my best friend here with me today. Oh, and her cute sidekick that I fully intend on cuddling with later, too.

I slip on some silk sleep shorts and a brami before heading downstairs where I find Damian and Jess, already up and about, still operating on Eastern time. Jess is feeding — well, attempting to feed — Eden, and Damian is out back, pacing while he talks on the phone.

"Good morning, sunshine!" Jess sing-songs to me in an overly cheery tone, making me laugh.

"Well, good morning to you, too!" I drop my voice to say hi to Eden, "And good morning to you too, sweetie." She breaks out into a smile and smacks her little hands down on her food tray in enthusiasm. I drop a kiss on top of her head before I make my way over to the coffee maker.

"Did you guys sleep okay? Have everything you need?"

"Are you kidding? We slept great. Without Tommy's snoring, I legit slept eight hours and so did Eden." Glad my heartbreak could be good for something, even if it's just to get Jess eight hours of sleep.

"That's amazing, Jess."

"How about you?"

"Eh, not great, but I did sleep. That counts for something, so I'll take it."

She gives me a half smile before moving on. "So when are we gonna go pick up the girls?"

"I just texted them asking when we should come, but still waiting to hear back. I think Sandy has them working at the cafe with her." Jess' eyes go a bit wide in surprise.

"Really? They want to do *that* on their summer break?"

I shrug my shoulders. "I don't know. Sandy asked me if it was okay first and I told her it was entirely up to them whether they did or not. I think they just like getting out of the house more than anything. We'll see how it goes." I think they could probably use the break from me, too.

As I go to sit down on the other side of Eden, the doorbell rings, startling me. *What the hell?* It's 7:30 A.M. I look at Jess wondering if she ordered something. "Are you expecting someone?" I ask. She shakes her head no. *Alright then.* I head to the front door, checking the peep hole first. *Of course.*

"Hi," I say as I open the door to Matthias standing before me with a huge bouquet of flowers and a very familiar bakery box I just know is full of cinnamon buns.

"Hi," he responds, giving me that dimple-filled smile. *Damnit.* I can't stay frustrated with him when he smiles at me like that.

I open the door further. "Come in. Come in." He steps into the entry in a dark charcoal, three-piece suit and tie, and heavens, it's the sexiest thing I've seen in a long time.

"I have a meeting at 9, but I wanted to come see you. Also, it's Friday," he says, holding up the box of pastries. "And I wanted to say sorry...about yesterday. Yeah, just about yesterday." The sheepish, half smile he gives me makes him instantly forgivable.

"I'm sorry, too. I dumped a lot on you, and really you're great, Mats. Thank you for the flowers and the cinnamon buns." I try my best to give him my warmest smile. The smile must be sufficient because he moves in towards me, giving me a kiss on the cheek.

"You look so beautiful this morning, Brit," he whispers in my ear, making me blush. I turn to face him and just like we always do, we find each other. He moves in, dropping his mouth to mine and I really wish I hadn't turned him away yesterday. *Why did I do that again?* I could have woken up to him in bed this morning. He breaks away from me briefly to set down the box and bouquet, then pulls me into a warm embrace, our mouths reconnecting in a passionate kiss.

The suit, the flowers, the pastries — all of it has me practically panting with need. The spark I've been trying to find with Matthias is reigniting, slowly but surely, and we move against each other, making out like a couple of teenagers in my foyer.

"Ahem," Jess clears her throat and I immediately drop my hands from Matthias' face. Turning to see Damian, Jess, and Eden staring at us from the great room, I drop my head on Matthias' chest for a brief moment before looking back up at him. He just smiles down at me, though, like it's no big deal.

I grab Mats' hand and pull him into the great room. "Jess, I'd like you to meet Matthias. Matthias, this is Jess and her daughter Eden, and then you've met Damian before, right?" Matthias immediately extends his hand to Jess, giving her a firm shake. "Nice to meet you Jess. I've heard so much about you." He then turns to take Damian's hand. "Nice to see you again, Damian." For a moment it seems awkward. I can't figure out what Damian's expression is, but after a beat, it passes and the air clears.

"Matthias brought us some pastries." Turning to him, I

ask, "Do you have time to stay for a coffee?" I find myself hoping he'll say yes.

"I can't, babe. The meeting...but what do you have going on tonight?" *Oh*. I wasn't expecting to feel so disappointed, but I understand.

"Um, no idea yet." I turn to look at Jess and Damian who are just standing there staring at us, so I move Matthias towards the front door and out of earshot.

"Sorry, they're being weirdos," I whisper to him.

"It's okay. They're just looking out for you. I like it. Well, I like when Jess does it..." I laugh and the smile he gives me in return has me getting wet. He's looking at me like he used to, like he could eat me, and I feel my whole body start to heat. "Come outside with me for a minute?" he asks. I give a single nod and we both slip out the front door.

As soon as it's closed behind us, he pushes my back against it and kisses me with an intensity I haven't felt before. It's desperation and yearning, and I feel it, too. *I fucking feel it, too.* The thought alone makes me excited. He moves a hand up into my hair while he sucks on my neck and I close my eyes, relishing the feel of him. I want to feel like this, with him.

"No hickies, babe," I say when he starts to suck harder.

"What about where no one can see them?" *Jesus.* I nod yes, and he pulls my cami up over my belly, holding it just below my breast. Placing his mouth on my rib cage, he begins to suck while groping my breast. I thread my fingers in his hair and for a moment I think about pushing him down to his knees and letting him eat me out on the front porch, but I refrain. After he finishes marking me on the side of my breast, he rejoins my mouth with fervor.

He pushes his long, hard length against me, and I want him. *Why do I want him so bad right now?*

"Brit..." He releases my mouth and pants out.

"I know, I want it, too." I manage to whisper.

"I don't want the first time to be against your front door, though," he laughs. "Well, the first time in..." *17 years,* he leaves it unsaid.

"Same," I laugh, too, and he drops his forehead to mine.

"Tonight?"

"The girls and everyone will be here tonight..." I feel his shoulders deflate slightly. "You're still welcome to come over, I just don't think the opportunity for anything else will be there." He immediately perks back up.

"Then tomorrow night? It's the Greek Festival. Will you come with me?" *The Greek Festival. Our first, first date.*

"Are you asking me out on a date, Mats?" I give him a sly smile.

"I am, Brit. Please say yes."

"Okay then, yes. I'd love to." And when I say it, this time I know I mean it. The thought sends my heart soaring with hope. Hope that I'm finally closing the door on Liam, and opening up to Matthias.

TEN

BRITAIN

Wearing a stupid smile on my face, I walk back inside to find Jess and Damian right where I left them, staring at me from the great room. I blanch.

"What?" I ask them. Damian is just standing there in what seems like shock, while Jess gives me the same stupid smile I was just wearing.

"Girrrrllll. If you don't want him, I do." I burst out laughing, but Damian is still standing there, dead in the water. It's probably pretty jarring to see your spouse making out with someone else for the first time, in...ever.

"Sorry you had to see that, Damian." I say sorry from a place of politeness, but I'm not actually sorry, at all.

"Yeah, I'm sorry, too. Probably could've gone the rest of my life without seeing that." I can tell from his tone alone, he's fucking pissed. Without another word, he walks straight out of the great room, heading out to the back patio. Jess and I just look at each other for a moment.

"Don't even trip about him. He wants to have his cake and eat it, too." Jess is right. He left me. *He* filed for divorce. But somehow he wants me to never move on. I just shake my head and try my best to let it blow over. *Not my circus.*

"Soo," Jess sidles up next to me, "What were you guys doing out there?" I blush hard.

"Nothing. Just talking."

"My ass!" Jess exclaims. I just laugh then head over to grab the pastry box off the entry table. We move back into the kitchen, taking our respective spots around Eden.

"We were kissing." I flip open the box of pastries and pull out a roll for her and me.

"You were kissing, and..."

"That's it, just kissing."

"Girl, I could hear you moan through the door."

"Oh my gawd, that's mortifying. And Damian heard it, too?"

"Uh, yeah, but who cares about that. So, you guys all made up? A quickie against the front door to seal the deal?" Jess waggles her eyebrows up and down in a hopeful expression.

"We did not have sex against the front door, just so you know, but I think we made up. Not that we were really in a fight, but he apologized for yesterday and I did, too. And Jess," I give her a knowing look, "when he kissed me, I felt it again. Like him and I could be something."

"Well, I'd be concerned if you didn't feel anything. I mean, Christ, the man is a walking cologne advertisement. Just hear me out, okay? Look at the child I made with

Tommy. Gorgeous, right? Imagine what *our* children would look like?" I laugh. I know she's joking...I think.

"We'd all look like ogres compared to your family. I know it."

"And you said he has brothers?"

I laugh again. "Yeah, three of em'. Hey, everything alright with you and Tommy?" The question is only partly serious.

"Oh, yeah. We're just in a dry spell right now. Just kind of missing the mark with each other. You know how it goes." *Do I ever.*

"Yeah, I know. But if you want to talk or vent about it, I'm all ears."

"Stop deflecting. When are you getting in bed with Matthias?"

"I don't know, Jess. I want him, and trust, I wanted him to take me on the front porch, but I still think I gotta take it slow. And it's not exactly like we have all the opportunity in the world. Bit of a full house out here. But he did ask me out tomorrow night. There's a Greek festival in town. It happens once a year...it's actually where he took me on our very first-ever date."

"That's sweet. You better have said yes, B."

"I did. I said I'd go."

"Good, I'll pick out your clothes."

"Okay, but nothing too crazy. It's hot at the festival and I just want to be comfy."

"Yeah, I meant while I'm here, period, I'll be picking out your clothes. But don't worry, tomorrow I'll keep it light and breezy." She gets a mischievous look in her eye, and I grow slightly concerned she's going to put me in a wispy, barely-there dress circa Jennifer Lopez at the 2000 Grammys.

———

The drive up to Spearhead was entirely uneventful. Damian didn't say a single word and Jess and Eden both cat napped. As we start to approach the main strip of town, I try to bring them all back to consciousness, gently.

"So this is it, guys. Don't blink or you'll miss it." I slow the car considerably and roll down the windows to let in the scent of the pines.

"On the left is the restaurant, Colton's. We'll have to go there one night. Next to it is Sandy's cafe and Maggio's." Pointing out the other side of the car, "And there's the gas station, grocery store, and diner. And that's it!" I sort of laugh. *Lamest tour ever.*

"Wow," Jess deadpans. *Classic New Yorker.* Damian remains silent. *I thought when you divorce someone, it means you get to stop dealing with their tantrums?* I remind myself, though, *not my circus.*

I park off to the side of The Grounds, behind Sandy's Suburban. Sliding out of the car, I smooth the wrinkles out of my favorite midi dress. Then, standing tall, I inhale the fresh air that seems to roll off the evergreens. My chest rises and falls, slowly releasing any tension I might be holding on to. There's just something about this place that puts me at ease in a way I can't describe. It always smells like better days, happier times. Fresh yet rich.

"Want me to get Eden for you?" I ask Jess. I'm trying to give her as many little breaks as possible while she's here, but it's also good for me to practice for this whole "baby" thing. It's been a lot of years since the last time I've had to do this.

"Sure! She's all yours." Jess moves aside so I can unbuckle

Eden from the carseat. Once she's tucked into my side, I turn around to find Damian waiting right behind me, holding the door. Even when he's grumpy, he's still a gentleman.

"Thanks, Damian." All I get is a wordless nod in response.

"So this is the famous 'Grounds'?" Jess asks.

"This is it," I smile, joining her as we walk to the front door. "Oh, you have to try the pastries. Jim makes everything himself." I pause as we all walk through the door that Damian is holding open. "I'm telling you, his croissants..."

"*Britain?*" *That voice.* Electric chills run down my spine. I turn to look in its direction just in time to see Liam shoot to his feet, sending his chair sliding across the checkered floor. He's as devastatingly handsome as I remember in a plain gray tee and black jeans that look like they were cut to his muscular body. He has a look of surprise painted all over his face and I freeze, my body seemingly turning to stone. *This isn't real. I'm losing my fucking mind because these delusions are getting way too real.*

I turn to look at Jess, but she's looking at me with the same wide-eyed, stricken expression. Okay, so maybe this *is* real. This is happening. My stomach free falls as I try to make sense of him being *here*. He just came back, *I guess*. I mean, I knew it was inevitable, I just didn't think it'd be so soon.

Sensing something isn't right, Eden starts to fidget and whine. With trembling hands, I hand her back to her mom, then turn back to my ex-fiancé. Just hearing the words roll through my brain hurts. *Ex-fiancé. Does it even count if it was for less than 24 hours?* I mentally shake free from that thought. It doesn't matter. I'm nothing to him now. *I suppose that means he's nothing to me either.* I remember my place, and move to excuse myself.

"I-I, forgot something in the car. I'll be right back," I say it more to myself than to anyone else. Ducking back out the door that Damian is still holding partially open, I move with quick strides to the car. *This is good.* I mean, not really, this is fucking awful, but good in that I can do what I'd planned to do if I ever saw him again. I can check another thing off my to-do list, and he can be free of me like he wants.

"Britain, wait!" I hear the front door of the cafe close as he calls out to me, but I don't stop. Unlocking the car, I reach over to my purse and rifle around until I find what I'm looking for. When I turn back, Liam is right in front of me, just like I've dreamed of for weeks. The shock of seeing him is one thing, but his close physical presence is more than I was prepared for. I don't know whether to cry or yell or vomit. All I know is I have to push down the overwhelming urge to throw myself into his arms. So I do. I push that feeling down, deep and far away from my consciousness because he's not holding his arms open for me. That's not who we are anymore. So instead, I hold out the card for him to take.

"What's this?" He asks, taking the card and turning the thick piece of cardstock over in his hand.

"It's my lawyer's card. He has all the paperwork ready for you." He looks at me, completely confused. "So you can officially terminate your parental rights."

———

Liam

. . .

Gut-wrenching. It's the only word I have to describe this feeling. I just shake my head back and forth, trying to grapple with how to respond. All I want to do is wrap her up in my arms, hold her tight, and never let her go. But that's not my reality. The reality is she thinks — *I've made her think* — I don't want her or our child.

"I, uh...I won't be doing that." She tilts her head in confusion before clasping her trembling fingers together. She looks distraught and so fucking tired, and it kills me to see her like this. She's lost weight, too. *Too much*, except for her bump. If you didn't know her, you might not notice, but there's nothing about Britain I wouldn't notice. Even in her loose sundress, I can see where she's swollen and round. My chest feels like it's on fire seeing her...like this.

My eyes fill with tears when I look down at where Britain and our child are growing and more than anything I've ever wanted, I just want to reach out and hold them both. *My whole fucking world standing right in front of me.* I reach for her, gently, testing her comfort level, but she flinches back and away from me. *Yeah, I thought that might happen*, but it doesn't hurt any less. My heart slams into my chest painfully, and I drop my hand back down to my side.

"Britain, I made a mistake. A really awful, terrible mistake. I never meant to hurt you." *Please, baby. Believe me.* She doesn't move. She barely blinks, her expression seeming unmovable. "I wrote you a letter, I left it for you. I thought you would get it when you went home, after you left Colton's that night."

"I never went back to your house after Colton's." *Your*

house. Right, it's not her home anymore. I die a small death at that realization. "You didn't need to write me a letter to tell me you didn't want to be with me. You could have just used your words instead of being a coward. You could have not done it in front of everyone I know here. You could have not left me for dead the second you turned your back on me." *Burn*, I deserve that.

"First, that's not what the letter said, Britain. I never, *not for one minute*, have stopped wanting you."

"Stop lying." Her voice trembles, breaking me. "I don't know what you want from me, or what purpose I served in your life, but you don't have to pretend anymore." She drops her head to hide her tears. *Fuck, no.*

"Britain, stop. The only thing I want, the only thing I'll ever need is you. You just have to let me explain." She doesn't say anything, and now she won't even look me in the eyes. "Baby, please." My words come out choked and painful.

She looks up at me, her eyes pooling with tears. "I've only just started getting used to the fact that what we had or what we were wasn't...real. At least not for you. *Please* don't come back into my life and ruin all the progress I've made. I don't deserve this. I don't know what I did to deserve any of this, but I can't do it again. *Please,* just leave me alone."

My throat starts burning. "I'm not going anywhere, Britain. Not now, *not ever*. What we have *is* real." My voice sounds raspy, my throat strained with pain.

"You know, you really had me believing that," she laughs viciously as tears fall down her cheeks. "You made me promise that *I'd* never leave *you*. But here we are, Liam." Her voice drops, sounding smaller than I've ever heard. "Everyone leaves me...and in the end, you did, too."

Goddamnit, this is breaking my fucking heart.

"You're wrong. I won't ever leave you, or our child. I promise from this day forward, never again. If I had known, I would have never left."

"Well," she scoffs, "I don't want, or need, anyone to stay with me because of a baby. I don't need your pity, Liam, I already get it from almost everyone else. I don't need anything from you. At all." Her voice is so low it's barely perceptible. The odds of me coming out of this with her by my side are starting to dwindle.

"I don't pity you!" It comes out louder than I wanted, so I lower my voice before continuing. "I would have stayed and done anything and everything to make you happy in hopes you'd never leave *me*. Britain, I left to give you a chance with Matthias. That's it. That's the only reason. You need to read the letter I wrote because I'm going to screw this all up, which is the exact reason I wrote it all down in the first place. Not being with you is the hardest thing I've ever done, but I thought I was doing what was best *for you*." She just stares up at me, unmoving and not speaking. I'm just about to speak again when she beats me to it.

"You're a coward, Liam Millar." Her tone is ice cold as she pushes against my chest with both hands before yelling, "YOU'RE A COWARD! I told you I loved you more than anyone else! *Anyone.* I told you that, and you chose not to trust me and then you abandoned me, just like everyone else!" I've never heard Britain shout like this before.

"*Okay,* that's enough." The woman who was with Britain earlier comes around the side of the car. "You need to leave her alone." She looks at me as she says it. I don't know what to do, though. I can't leave it alone — *her* alone — but I'm only making things worse.

Reluctantly, I take a step away from Britain who has gone back to refusing to look at me. Like taking a dagger to the chest, realization is starting to sink in. This is it. *Done*. I've caused irreparable damage. "I'm sorry, Britain." They're the only words I can manage to get out without choking.

"Just leave me alone, Liam." She says it so quietly, I know it's what she really wants, but I can't stop myself from trying one more time.

"Please, Brit–"

"I'm with someone else." She cuts me off and cuts me deep. Just like that, my whole world comes crashing down. There's nothing if she's not in it. *I'm nothing*. I knew this was a possibility, I just always hoped she'd choose me. Britain starts regaining her composure, while mine slowly slips away. My hands start to shake and I feel a tear break free, running down my face and off my chin.

I don't even have to ask, I already know *she's with him*. I take a few more steps away from her, my feet feeling more and more unsteady by the second.

"Okay, I'll leave you alone, and, um, I'll reach out to your lawyer about custody." I hold up the card she gave me with a slight tremble in my voice and in my hand. The woman, who I'm starting to believe is Jess, wraps an arm around Britain and turns her body in the opposite direction as me, like a bodyguard shielding their principal from a threat.

They start to walk away, but I stop them. "Wait," it comes out more like a croak, "your stuff, all of your stuff is at the house. Do you want–"

Britain interrupts me, "You can–" but she's quickly cut off by Jess.

"*I'll* come pick it all up tomorrow." Her tone is authoritative and devoid of warmth, leaving me with no other option than to just nod. I look Britain in the eyes one last time before her friend shields her from me once again. I'll never forget that look for the rest of my fucking life. *She hates me.*

————

Britain

I hoped hurting him would make me feel better, but it didn't. The look on his face when I told him I was with someone else will be burned on my brain for eternity. He's either the best fucking actor, or it really hurt him as much as I'm hurting now.

Jess turns my body away, but I look him in the eyes one last time, and the only thing running through my mind is, *why can't I stop loving you?* But it doesn't matter. I don't trust him. I *can't* trust him, and my heart could never withstand this unbearable kind of pain again.

"Jess," I dig my heels in to stop her pursuit. "I just need a minute. I can't go back in there just yet." She releases me from the firm hold on my shoulders, giving me a stern look.

"Fine. But if you're not back inside in 15 minutes, I'm coming to get you."

"Yeah, I know," I say quietly, shakily. Jess gives my shoulders a squeeze before letting me go and heading back inside.

I'm standing halfway between my car and the entrance, stuck in limbo with Liam behind me and my family in front of me. All I want is to turn around and look at him, to soak him in, even run back to him. But I can't. That's not us anymore. Instead, I'll do what I always do: Break down and feel awful, even if it's just for five minutes. So I walk past the cafe and around to the other side of the building.

Putting my back against the bumpy log wall, I pray it'll hold me up. Then, with shaking hands and legs, I cry. *Why does it have to hurt so much? Why do I still love him? Why am I such a crybaby?!*

Eventually, the gruff sound of a male clearing his throat jolts me back to reality and I open my eyes to see Damian standing in front me.

"Have you come to gloat?" I ask him between sniffles.

"No," is all he says before wrapping me up in his warm arms and comforting me. It's not the kind of embrace you would get from an ex-husband or former lover. No, right now, he's here as my oldest friend, my closest companion, and he soothes me.

"It's okay, darling, let it all out," he says while tucking my head beneath his chin and pulling me into him more snuggly. So I do. I let it all out.

ELEVEN

LIAM

I knew the chances of things going the way I wanted them to were slim, so you'd think I'd be ready for when she told me she was with someone else. *Nope.* The only thing I know for certain is I'll never be ready to hear those words. Not in my fucking lifetime. Her words acted like stray pieces of shrapnel, embedding themselves deeply in my psyche forever.

I can't get my hands to stop shaking as I take the business card she gave me and slip it into the bill fold of my wallet. *She wants me to terminate my parental rights?* Again, not in my fucking lifetime. *Never.*

I know what I need to do, but I can't. Not yet.

Instead, I stand in front of her car for several minutes, unmoving. *Her car,* a new SUV, already with a carseat in the back. Just one decision of many she's probably made in my absence. The realization kills me. She's already dropped me from the roster, removed me from the decision making list, and replaced me with somebody else. Did *he* help her pick out a new car? Do they live together? Is that why she moved? Does he go to all the doctors appointments?

The last thought eviscerates me. My heart's pounding so hard I can feel every vein in my body throb, each beat a painful reminder that it's alone. The one it beats for is lost to me...maybe forever.

As painful as it is, I admit defeat and start the arduous task of moving through life *without* Britain. Putting one unsteady foot in front of the other, one at a time. I step back into the cafe to gather my stuff, but as soon as I open the door, every pair of eyes lands on me with one set standing out above the rest. *Jess.* Her and her vicious glare move towards me in a menacing manner.

"What's your phone number and address?" Britain's guard asks with all the friendliness of a hungry momma bear complete with a baby bear perched on her hip.

"Uh, sure, let me just write it down for you." I head towards the counter for a pen and piece of paper from the receipt printer while my death by a thousand glares continues. The girls don't say a single word to me, and Sandy only gives a sympathetic sigh before shaking her head in disappointment. I quickly jot down the information as the urgent need to leave ramps up. The cafe is starting to feel suffocating. *I have to get the fuck out of here.*

I hurriedly hand over the slip of paper to the dark-haired woman and say, "I'll pack everything up. If you want, I can drop it off and save you a trip up the mountain."

"No," she says as she stares at me harshly. "Britain deserves her privacy. I'll come get it. What time?" Right, they don't want me to know where she lives. That's where we're at.

"Anytime. I'll be home." I can't exactly go into work, and I've got no life. *Where the fuck else would I be?* She just nods curtly at me, and I swear the baby mimics her actions. Even babies fucking hate me. *Unbe-fucking-lievable.* "It's Jess, right?" She just nods once. "Right, I'm sorry to finally meet you like this, but for what it's worth, I never wanted to hurt her, and I'll never stop loving her." I drop my head to hide the tears as I pick up my newspaper and coffee cup, needing to be anywhere but here.

"It's not worth much, but I know," Jess says, then turns around and walks away from me, and I don't know whether I'm glad or sad. She knows I love Britain and I wouldn't want to hurt her, but it means nothing. I've proven to Britain that I'm just like the rest. Like her dad, like Matt, like her ex — I'm just another Walkaway Joe.

———

Britain

Damian's hand moves up and starts stroking my hair softly as he says to me, in his low voice, "I know you don't want to talk about it with me, but I do feel like it's worth saying, I never saw you like this after I left…"

I roll my eyes because talking to my ex husband about the guy I'm still desperately in love with sounds like my idea of hell, but there's the other part of me that knows he's right. I've never felt like this about anyone, and never acted this way either. Not during, and not after. It only hurts this bad *now* because it *was* so good.

I think about Matthias, and what it was like when he dumped me, but I'm coming up empty. I can barely remember how I used to feel before Liam. Like he took up so much of my consciousness, I had no choice but to let go of the old memories, the ones I had no use for anymore. Damian's right that it was never like this when he left me, because I never loved Damian like I love Liam. *Like I love Liam, not past tense.*

Damian keeps going when I don't respond, "And I know it's not my place to say, but I don't think jumping into another relationship is the right thing to do, Brit." I instantly feel ashamed. Of course I shouldn't be throwing myself into another relationship right on the back of this horrendous mess. But at the same time, what do I have to lose? My self-respect? *Practically non-existent.* My reputation? *Also, gone.* I'm an unwed woman who got knocked up after being with her boyfriend for a month. And at this point, what's another broken heart? And why the fuck does Damian think he can give *me* any sort of unsolicited advice? *All this*, coming from the man who literally jumped from our bed to another is bull.

I pull out of his embrace before speaking. "Damian, you have absolutely no right to make that kind of assessment or pass any judgment on me after everything you've done. *You left me.* You don't get to keep making me feel bad about how I live my life anymore."

He reaches out, bracing both hands on my shoulders. "I am not judging you. And you're right that I don't have any right to say this. I'm just letting you know that one of my biggest regrets is going straight to Summer after us." *I don't think he can technically say that since he went to Summer before "us" even ended, but okay...* "I just wish I would've done it differently, that's all. And I just thought I'd give you the advice I wish someone would've given me." I'm a little taken aback.

"I thought you and Summer were doing great, really happy, headed to the altar, no?"

"She's not you, Brit." He gives me a half smile, and his one-sided dimple becomes visible. He shrugs, "But also, I'm not *him*," then nods behind me at the Range Rover that's just pulled out onto the highway. The one day I'm distracted by Eden and fail to scope out the parking lot is the day he comes home. *Of course.* I have the rest of my life to think about that, though. Damian is here with me now.

"Damian...I never wanted you to leave."

"No, but I couldn't stay. We both know that, Brit." He says as he wipes a stray tear off my cheek with his thumb. "We both want something the other can't offer. Doesn't mean I've stopped loving you or wanting you in my life." I nod silently, his words ringing true. I still want Damian in my life, too. But him and I romantically together just don't work.

I laugh softly. "So is this the beginning of a beautiful friendship, Damian?" And he laughs, too.

"Sure is, sweetheart." Using the sleeve of his shirt, he dries my tears then drapes an arm around my shoulder, tugging me to walk with him back into the cafe. "Alright, what's the pregnant woman's equivalent of getting drunk?" I laugh at his question.

"Umm, tacos? Better yet, all-you-can-eat guac! Or..." I rack my brain, "Oh, I know! A second cup of coffee."

"Done, we're getting you a second cup of full-caff coffee

and then I'm finding you the best tacos in the valley for dinner tonight." I pull him to a stop right as we get ready to head back into The Grounds.

"I still love you, too, okay?"

With watery eyes, he nods and says, "Okay," then opens the door to a captive audience.

I chuckle lightly, trying to keep the mood light and not like I just lost my shit in the parking lot on my baby daddy. "No heads up, guys? What the heck?" The girls stay quiet, letting Sandy do the talking.

She makes her way around the counter, coming over to me. "We weren't expecting you till later. Sorry, baby, but it was bound to happen eventually." She squeezes my arm softly before leaning in for a quick hug. She whispers in my ear as she does, "It'll all work out in the end. Don't sweat it, sugar," then moves away to clear a dirty table.

The girls are busy talking to their dad, so Jess moves up beside me. "Are you okay?" She says it quietly.

"Yes. No. I think I'm still in shock. Talking with Damian helped, actually. I just still don't really understand. Liam told me he left to give me a chance to be with Matthias. But...I'm not really sure what to make of that just yet."

"Hmm," is all Jess says in response, then a moment later, "Do you believe him?"

"I don't know," which is 100% the truth. I don't trust him, but it does make things make sense, maybe...sort of. Ultimately, though, does it make things better? *No.* "Does it even matter if I do or not?"

"*Word.*" The way Jess says it gives me pause. There's a knowing in her tone. She knows what this is like.

"Okay, seriously, is everything okay between you and Tommy?" She shrugs, repositioning Eden onto her other hip.

"Yeah, we'll be fine." I eye her suspiciously. *'We'll be,'* not 'we are.'

"Alright, I've got an iced, almond milk, vanilla latte courtesy of the best baristas in Spearhead." Damian announces, handing me over my cup of ambrosia.

"Oh my god, thank you, Damian," I say before calling over his shoulder, "Thank you, girls!" And they smile back at me.

Damian's advice echoes in my mind. Jumping right into things with Matthias might not matter *to me* in the long run, but what kind of example am I setting for the girls? That they always need a man in their life? That they can't stand alone? That's some patriarchal bullshit. *However* I do want the girls to be able to make decisions about who's in their life based on whether that person is good for them, not from some deep-seated trauma their mom pushed on them in their formidable years.

Before I let my mind wander fully into that battle, though, Sandy circles back, joining Damian, Jess, and myself. I assume introductions were made after I ducked out, but just in case, I try my best to do the polite thing. "Sandy, this is Jess, and her daughter, Eden. And then this is Damian, the girls' dad."

Sandy beams at Jess, "Oh yes, we've met already, haven't weee?" She says to Eden in a soothing baby voice. *Born to be a grandma, truly.* "And, Damian." Her tone dries up, "Yes, we've met." *I love Sandy.* A small giggle breaks free from my mouth.

"Well, what time do the girls get off their shift? I can take Damian and Jess down to see the lake if it'll be awhile still."

"Oh no, they're good to go. Girls!" Sandy calls out to them, "You're free! Go pack up and say bye to Grandpa." They just nod and head back behind the curtained walkway.

"Thanks again for having them, Sandy. I really appreciate it."

"They're a delight to have around, baby. And Jess, honey, if you want a sitter so you and Britain can get out, I'm happy to take the babycakes. I gotta practice for the new little one!" She gestures down to my belly.

"I might have to take you up on that, Sandy," Jess says with a smile. The girls come out from the back with backpacks slung over their shoulders. They each give Sandy a kiss on the cheek, then turn toward us to leave.

"We're ready," Elodie says, walking straight into her dad's waiting arms.

As we walk to the car, Caroline finds me at the back of the pack. "Are you okay, Mom?" She asks in the same quiet voice we share. My initial reaction is to say yes, to tell her I'm completely fine, but I'm not. She knows I'm not probably more than anyone. She's seen the tears and the sleepless nights, and while I wish she hadn't, it's okay that she did. Because that's life. Everything doesn't always come up roses. It's hard, but eventually it will get better. That's what I have to show her.

I pull Caroline into my side and say, "Not really, babe, but soon I will be because I've got the best daughters and the best friends in the whole world." She leans slightly into my side as we make our way to the car, and I think I need to start believing that. I just ran into the one person who has the power to bring my whole world crashing down, and I survived it.

———

"Oh my god, Mom, you were so loud," Elodie says to me as we all pile in through the front door.

"No, I was not!" I say indignantly.

"Girl! Yes, you were," Jess inserts herself.

"Mom, I love you, but you sounded like a cat choking on a furball literally the entire car ride home," Caroline interjects with exquisite timing.

I just laugh, "God, that sounds awful. Next time, please wake me up." The last thing I need is to be some viral video the girls post to TikTok. I can see the caption now, "*Old woman sounds like dying cat while she sleeps.*"

Once we've all made it inside, Jess excuses herself to put Eden down for a nap. The girls tromp off to their rooms to drop backpacks and Damian is still outside on a work call, giving me the opportunity I need.

I'm glad I fell asleep on the way home. Otherwise I would have spent the entire time obsessing over what I'm about to do. As I walk up the stairs, my stomach twists and turns with each step. My hands are already sweating and my heartbeat picks up. *There's probably nothing,* I say to myself in preparation for what I assume is the worst.

I walk straight to my closet and open the top drawer. It only takes a second to fish out the phone and power it back on. Once I do, my stomach plummets to the floor as I receive notification after notification. After weeks with not a single one, here they finally are, in the palm of my hand. My fingers tremble as I look to see 10 new voicemails, each one from Liam. I don't hit play, though, I just move on to the text messages. *18 new* text messages and they're mostly from yesterday, before I saw him today...

LIAM

Bambi, pick up the phone.

Please.

I just need to explain.

Baby, I'm sorry. Please call me back as soon as you can.

I'm headed your way, not that I know where that is, but please call me.

Britain?

I didn't see any of your text messages until today. I'll explain it all when I see you.

If I see you.

Please respond, Britain.

And from sometime after midnight this morning:

I understand you're shutting me out, I get it. And I know you might not ever see these, but here's my responses to your messages.

I wish I would have come back that afternoon and talked to you. I wish I would have put my stupid pride aside and told you how much I fucking love you and that without you, I'm nothing. It's only ever been you for me, too.

I don't know what happened and why you're at the hospital, but I wish I was there with you. I could have told you in person how happy I am that you're pregnant. I thought my chest was going to explode when I found out, it was one of the happiest moments of my life, followed by my lowest when I realized I'd fucked it all up.

You didn't do anything wrong and there will never be anyone else. You were it for me. Asking you to marry me was the best decision I've ever made. My biggest mistake was leaving that same day. I'm sorry. You're more than enough, Britain, and I'd gladly spend the rest of my life trying to prove that to you. I'm the fool, not you. Me.

I promise you, the only thing I want is you and our child. I promise. I'm so sorry that I ever made you feel differently. I'm sorry, baby.

This is starting to sound pathetic, isn't it?

When I reread your weekly updates, I feel like dying knowing I've missed out on appointments and taking care of you. You deserve better, Britain. It sounds like maybe you are better off without me.

And from this afternoon:

> I just want you to be happy, Britain. I'm sorry it couldn't have happened with me and I'm sorry for everything I've done to make it that way. Hopefully, though, someday you'll let me be a part of our child's life, and if you feel like letting me, I'll be here. Waiting however long it takes. Again.

> I love you, and our little Bambi, too. Always.

Little Bambi. My chest gets tight and painful, and the tears fall silently. I have been waiting for this moment since the day he left, and now here it is, and I'm paralyzed. I don't know what to do.

TWELVE

BRITAIN

When Damian and the girls head out to pick up tacos, I pull Jess into my room and bring out the phone. I plop Eden down on my bed and play with her while Jess reads the text messages, silently.

"So, what do you want to do about it?" She asks me once she's finished.

"I don't know, Jess," I say solemnly.

"I think after today and all this," she motions down to the phone, "it's pretty clear that he loves you. And it's pretty clear to me that you still love him, too."

"I don't disagree," I reply.

"So?" She holds her hands up like the answer is obvious.

"So...I'm seeing someone else. And it takes more than love to make a relationship work. It takes trust and communication, two things Liam has proven to me to be lacking."

"You do remember yesterday, when I could barely get you to admit you liked Matthias, right?"

"I like Matthias, there's something there."

"Are you trying to convince me, or yourself?" Jess' tone is a little bit bitter.

"Are you mad at me right now?" I ask cautiously.

"I'm not mad at you, but I am frustrated. You love Liam. Liam loves you. From what I can tell, it's the end-all-be-all type of love. The mythical kind of love you read about, but don't experience. And you're just going to mess with some other guy's emotions because you have something to prove to Liam? Yourself? It's wrong. Sit and think on it, and if afterwards you can honestly tell me you are over Liam or don't love him anymore, *then* you should go out with Matthias. But if you can't do that, let him go. Don't make him a pawn in your game because if the roles were reversed, you wouldn't want that either."

I anger instantly, but then her words start to sink in. There isn't one thing she just said that isn't true. I don't know that I can go back to Liam, but I am starting to realize, maybe, I shouldn't be dating Matthias.

"This morning you were pumped about me going out with Matthias, though."

"I think these text messages and Liam coming back make a difference. I know you're smart enough to see that whether you want it to or not, Liam being here changes things. If you feel strongly about Matthias, then wait. Wait till you're sure you can get over Liam. Otherwise you run the risk of doing things you'll regret and hurting people who don't deserve it along the way." She sighs before continuing, "I am grumpy, so I'm sorry this is all coming out in a bitchy tone. I will always be Team Britain, so if you want to date Matthias, I will root you on. I just don't want you to make the same mistake as... someone I know. That's all."

"Someone you know?" I raise an eyebrow in question. Jess has been acting weird ever since this morning, but she doesn't acknowledge my question.

"Want to go swimming?" She sits up abruptly from her spot on the bed.

"What? No, I want my best friend to talk to me about what's going on."

"I'm not ready. Not yet."

"I can respect that. Honestly, I can. But not forever, okay?"

"Okay."

"You know, I'm Team Jess, too, right?" She gives me a look in return that I can't quite make out the meaning of, but she nods anyway. I push a piece of her dark brown hair out of her eyes to make sure she can see how sincere I'm being. After a second, she finally nods in acceptance.

"So then I guess I should make a decision about Matthias, right? Do you think I should cancel our date?" God, I feel awful just thinking about it. I do like him. I do care about him. I don't want to end it, but I don't want to hurt him either.

"I don't know, Brit," Jess says on a sigh. "Maybe go on the date and get your answer that way. Maybe you go, and if it doesn't feel good, you'll know it's not what you want. Or maybe you go, and it's better than you expected, and the feelings deepen, and you realize it's worth it to move forward with Matthias."

"Right...yeah, I think I'm going to go. But after that I have to make a decision one way or the other. Hold me to it, please?"

"I will." Jess stares off after she says it. I wish she would just tell me what the hell is going on, but I'll do my best to give her time. Doesn't mean I won't try to cheer her up, though.

"Wanna start Queen Charlotte before dinner gets here? I'll make you a margaritaaaa..." I use my most enticing voice.

"Duh, yes." She rolls off the bed and Eden and I trail behind her down the stairs. Jess heads for the great room and I branch off towards the kitchen when the doorbell rings.

I stop, calling out to Jess, "Are you expecting something?"

"Nope!" She calls back. I check the peephole before opening the door.

"Hey, what are you doing here?" I ask Alex as he moves right past me and into the house, not even acknowledging me or the baby sitting on my hip.

"Damian called and said he was in town. Said to come for din–" He stops talking and stares down the entrance hall to where Jess is standing, frozen, in the great room, but he quickly resumes, "dinner." Turning towards me so Jess can't hear, he says, "I didn't know *she* was going to be here."

"Mmkay, well, time to grow up. Jess is my best friend and she's doing me a big favor by being here." Damian and Jess look like actual best friends compared to Alex and Jess. They're like oil and water, cats and dogs. Whatever it is, these two just don't mix. He grunts his reply and heads towards the kitchen while Jess stalks him with her eyes until he's out of sight. I drop Eden into her mom's arms before heading into the kitchen to make Jess' marg.

Alex is rooting through the pantry while I stand just outside at the drinks station. "So you'll never guess who I saw today..." Alex turns around holding a bag of almonds. He raises his eyebrows in shock and question, but doesn't say anything.

"Yeah, Liam's back."

"Where?" He sets down the almonds, dusting his hands off.

"At Sandy's cafe in Spearhead. I think he's like back, back." I scrunch my nose at the discomfort I feel even just thinking about him.

"I'm gonna fucking kill him." Alex walks briskly out of the pantry, through the kitchen, and is almost to the front door when I stop him.

"Wait! Wait! Wait! You are not going to kill him. I'm not forgiving him or anything, but I don't think he deserves death."

"Fine, I'll let him live." Alex turns to head back out the door.

"Alex, stop!"

"No, Brit! He wants to show back up here, he can fucking answer to me." Alex is nearly trembling with rage. He needs to do this.

"Okay, but nothing that could get you arrested. No assault, vandalism, burglary..."

He gets a truly devilish grin on his face and says, "No problem," then dips out the door as quickly as he came. I turn around wide-eyed to see Jess with a shit-eating grin on her face.

"Do you think I should call Liam and warn him?"

Jess shakes her head while laughing, "Absolutely not."

––––––––

Liam

Here we go. I pull out her suitcases from the guest room and push them towards my room. I brush the stupid fucking tears I'm crying off my face before laying the suitcases open to fill up. I could leave all this for Jess to do tomorrow, but I'm selfishly motivated right now. There's one thing I can't let her take.

I start in *her* closet, grabbing all the hangers at once and tossing them on the bed. Next I do the drawers in hopes I find it there...and I do. I pull the pink silk nightgown out of the top drawer and it slides over my bandaged hand, slipping to the floor. *Over my dead body is Britain going to wear this thing for him.* I bend over, picking it up, then take it to my closet. Folding it as neatly as I can with one hand, I put it in my bottom drawer beneath my sweats.

As I walk out of the closet, *her* sweatshirt catches my eye. I think about her slipping it on over her naked body after she moved in. I think about cuddling in front of the fire with nothing on underneath. If the pink nightgown is mine, this sweatshirt is hers. I grab it, placing it at the bottom of the suitcase.

Fuck, all it took was putting something in that suitcase and the bottle of bourbon sitting on my nightstand from last night starts calling my name. *Yeah, I'm too fucking sober to complete this task.* I pop the cork off the top and take a long swig, grateful for the low burn shooting down my throat. It's nice to feel something other than heartbreaking pain, and after a few more swigs, hopefully I won't feel anything at all. *Can't fucking wait.*

I go for another long swallow when a pounding fist on my front door stops me. *What the fuck?* I trudge downstairs as the pounding increases in frequency and intensity. Whoever's out there needs to chill the fuck out. I throw open the door and immediately regret it.

"So, you're back." Alexander Palomino stands in my doorway, looking like he's out for blood. *Fucking perfect.*

"Yeah–" Alex's fist interrupts my reply, landing a perfect punch to my left eye.

"Goddamnit, Alex!" I growl out, then bowl over as pain radiates in my skull.

"You're lucky you're already fucking hurt." He basically spits at me, "Do I need to invite myself in, or...?"

I stand up, putting my non-injured hand to my temple. "Excuse me, where the fuck are my manners? Make yourself at home." I turn and head straight for the kitchen, not waiting around or giving a fuck what Alex does. I grab a bag of frozen broccoli out of the freezer, putting it straight on my throbbing head. Peas would have been better, but I fucking hate peas.

Alex heads straight for the wet bar in the butler's pantry, pouring himself a glass of Pappy's that he downs in one large swallow.

"Fuck, man. That bottle's worth more than 5 grand, at least savor it," I yell over to him.

"I know how much it's worth. Why the fuck do you think I'm drinking it?" Alex replies harshly. *To inflict maximum pain,* I fucking get it. I slide into a chair at the breakfast nook and hang my head into the makeshift ice pack as Alex plops down his second very full glass of Pappy's before taking a seat at the other end of the table.

"I don't see you for 35 years, and when I do I find out you got my little sister pregnant. Then you break her fucking heart in front of everyone she knows and leave her hanging out to dry. Who *the fuck* do you think you are to ghost *her?*" He shakes his head in disgust. "She's too fucking good for you." *Yeah, I know.*

"I thought I was doing the right thing. I thought she was still in love with Matt. I've fucked up her life a couple of times now. You think I don't know I'm not good enough for her? Trust me, I fucking know."

"Glad we can agree on that. What the fuck are you doing here then?"

"Are you serious?" I lift my face up off the broccoli to shoot him a dirty look. "The second I found out Britain was pregnant, I came back. I'm not going to abandon her or our child." He just stares back at me, bracing both elbows on the table.

"If you ever hurt her or her children, they will *never* find your body. Do you understand?" I don't know Alex's kill count, but I'm going with high, and I've got no desire to be on that list.

"Yeah, I fucking get it. She has nothing to worry about, though. I'm not even in her life anymore, let alone close enough to hurt her. Who fucking knows if I'll even get to see my child."

"Oh, you will, trust me. Just as long as you understand the second you misstep, I'll be here to fuck your whole world up." I pull my head off the broccoli and pause. *He thinks I'll get to see them?*

"You think Britain is going to let me have joint custody?" His facial expression doesn't falter in the slightest.

"I know she will. Again, because she's too fucking good for you. But in case you've forgotten, *she* didn't have a dad. She'd never keep her child away from the opportunity to know you. Why the fuck do you think she stayed with Damian for so long after he cheated on her the first time? *So the girls could grow up with a dad.* And why the fuck do you think she moved to the middle of fucking nowhere?" Alex gestures with his hands to indicate our area, but I get stuck on something else he said. Cheated on her *the first time?*

"Wait, what? Damian cheated on her before the assistant thing?"

"That's not my story to tell." So that's a yes, and *what a piece of shit.* "Listen, Britain's set the bar pretty fucking low for men in her life, and that includes me. But not anymore. I'm raising the fucking standards. Either meet them or answer to me. Your choice."

"That shouldn't be a problem. I'd do anything to make things better...I just don't know if I can, or will even get the chance to."

"I mean, yeah, she might not let you back into her life, but she'll let you be in your kid's, just don't fuck it up." *Cool, no pressure.* I nod in understanding, though. Alex gets up, walking his half-full glass to the sink before pouring it down the drain.

I roll my eyes. "Fuck, man," I say to him, but he just laughs a "fuck you" laugh.

"There might be hope for you yet, Liam. She wouldn't let me kill you, so next time you see her, a thank you is probably in order." I think he's joking, but maybe not. It doesn't matter because at least Britain thought about me in a non-murderous way today, even if it was just for a minute.

"Yeah, will do." I hang on to the small sliver of hope his words just gave me. *When* I see her, not *if* I see her. Alex sets his glass in the sink and walks in the direction of the door.

He calls out before he leaves, "Vinegar or charcoal!"

"What?" I yell back, dumbstruck.

"It'll absorb the smell of her perfume. Your house fucking reeks, man." My cheeks pinken in embarrassment, but I wonder how the fuck he knows that. I don't get a chance to ask because he slams the front door shut.

That could have gone a lot fucking worse. The front door opens back up a second later, and I call out, "You forget to break my kneecaps?!"

But instead of Alex, Max walks into my kitchen. "You look like hell." *Great.*

"Have you come to shit on me, too?" I ask. He shakes his head, leaning back against the kitchen counter, crossing his arms over his chest.

"Believe it or not, I came to check on you." I pull the bag of broccoli off my face. "Oof, that's gonna be a shiner," Max says.

"Yeah, it certainly feels like it."

"I'm guessing Alex?"

"YUP." He just nods. I drop the broccoli back in the freezer and head for the bottle of Pappy Van Winkles. Now that the seal's broken, why the fuck not? I pour two glasses and slip one to Max on my way back to the chair.

"Is this celebratory?" He holds up the glass in question, "Or end of life and we might as well drink it?" *Fuck.*

"Both?"

Max holds up the glass and says, "Then cheers, brother." He takes a sip before continuing, "Pretty sure I can figure out why it's the end of times, but what are we celebrating?"

"That I'm gonna be a dad and Alex thinks Britain will let me have some kind of custody arrangement, but that's where the good news ends. Oh yeah, and about that," I throw my hand down on the table, "thanks for fucking letting me know."

"You're welcome," is all he says.

"I was being sarcastic, dickhead."

"Oh," he shrugs. "Well who the fuck do you think told Tori to go tell you? So yeah, you're fucking welcome. Matt asked me not to tell you, and being a good brother and all, *I* didn't." *Ahh, okay.*

"Well, then. Thank you, actually." A stray tear escapes, *fuck me.*

"Yup." We stay in the kitchen, awkwardly silent for a few moments before he speaks again. "Listen, I need your help tomorrow night."

"With what?"

"You know what." *Honestly, I don't fucking know.* "The Greek Festival is tomorrow night."

"No." I can't get my answer out fast enough. Absolutely not. Not ready to see the whole Scala clan and my work family.

"First off, you fucking owe me, and second, your answer is yes. Constantine and Julie are both going to be there tomorrow and I need you to referee, run interference, *something*. She hates you the least." What does that say about a person when she hates her sons more than she hates me?

"Ask Silas."

"Can't, her and Silas aren't speaking after she found out Britain's his patient." Christ, this woman's the worst.

"She is aware that I'm in love with Britain, right?"

"Yeah, but you're not with her." He says it nonchalantly, like his words didn't just impale me.

"Fine, but I need you to do me a favor. You know where Britain lives?"

"Yeah, but I'm not going to be the one to tell you where."

"Jesus, I'm not going to fucking stalk her." That's only a half truth, I might. "Her friend is supposed to come pick up all her stuff tomorrow. Can you just take it to her instead so I don't have to wait around?"

"Sure," he says.

"Great," I stand and head for the stairs. "Are you coming? You gotta pack it all up, too, you know, since I'm down a hand."

"Damn, no good deed goes unpunished does it?" Max reluctantly follows behind.

"Sure fucking doesn't, brother." Hanging out with Julie Scala at the Greek Festival sounds about as fun as getting my toenails removed, but for Max, Niko, and Silas, I'll do it. Hopefully this gets me one step closer to restoring *some* of the relationships in my life.

THIRTEEN

BRITAIN

MATTHIAS

Can't wait to see you tonight, babe. I'll be
there in 20.

Reading the text message makes my stomach roll, partly from
guilt, partly from anxiety. I didn't tell Matthias about running
into Liam yesterday...or that I'm using tonight's date as a
litmus test for how we'll move forward. But *I am* looking
forward to seeing him. I guess I'm also just nervous.

When the doorbell rang last night, I actually got excited
thinking it might be him, but it wasn't. It was just Maximus
with all my clothes from Liam's. Jess practically squealed like
a pirate being reunited with their long-lost treasure while I
felt a tad more somber. Seeing my suitcases all packed up, by
him. It had a certain finality to it.

After the shit show that was yesterday, I was mentally

prepared for an anxiety-ridden night of crying and lack of sleep, but 9:00 rolled around and I felt okay. Then 10:00, and all I felt was tired. I hate to admit, but Liam coming back pacified something that was broken inside me. It's always been the unknown that's eaten away at me. And well, now, I know. It's still complete shit, and it still hurts, but just knowing he's *home* comforts me. Knowing he wants this child and will be around helped soothe my subconscious so that I actually slept seven hours last night.

This morning, I let Jess unpack and go through everything from Liam's, not wanting to relive anything, and now we're both in my room getting me ready for the Greek Fest.

"Option one: A linen, square-neck dress by Reformation with Hermes sandals and Jenni Kayne cardigan. OR... Option two: White halter, knit dress from Dissh with Gucci heels." Jess holds up both dresses. Linen would be cool, but wrinkly and non-stretchy. But...the knit dress will leave nothing to the imagination. My pooch will be out for all to see.

"Which one would you choose?" I ask Jess.

"I think it's pretty obvious which one I'd choose," she says. She's right, one looks more coastal grandma and one screams stylish-ass bitch.

"Fine, the knit halter dress," I say with reluctance. Jess does a little happy dance on her way to put option one back in the closet while I slip on the dress and check myself in the full length mirror. *Pregnant.* I look pregnant.

"You look like you're ready for a summer night in Greece, absolutely gorgeous," Jess says, then makes a chef's kiss with her hand and mouth. I'm just going to have to trust her on this one. I can appreciate that this is probably the best I've looked in months and maybe the best I *will* look in months to come.

She's done my hair in beachy waves and my makeup is subtle and glowy with a thinly winged eyeliner, making me feel a bit like Bridget Bardot. The Gucci sandals are still low enough to be comfortable, otherwise I would have nixed them. But right now, I'm just happy for the boost they're giving my bum.

"You look great, Brit." Damian says from the hallway where he's holding Eden on his hip while she sucks on a frozen teething ring.

"Thanks," I say bashfully. I feel like Damian and I have turned a corner since yesterday. We're more relaxed and comfortable, sort of like we always have been, just now there's no sex, matrimony, or sharing of beds. The doorbell rings, so I excuse myself as I pass Damian and head downstairs.

I open the door to Matthias looking like the Greek god he is.

"*Hi.*"

"Hi, darling." He tucks a piece of hair behind my ear, then trails a thumb down my cheek. He gives me a once over, up and down, before his dimpled smile breaks out on his face. "You are so gorgeous, my love." My cheeks heat and my heart skips a beat. He's never called me *that* before.

"Thank you. You," I motion up and down his body, "look amazing, too." His linen shirt is only buttoned halfway up, revealing tan skin and defined pectorals with a dusting of chest hair. "Do you want to come in, or do we need to get going?" I ask.

"We should probably get going."

"Right." I take a step away from the door to call out to the girls. "I'm leaving, family!" Caroline and Elodie come out from the great room for a quick hug, while Damian and Jess hang back and wave from afar, just like I instructed them to.

Matthias slips his hand into mine and I close the door. We walk the short distance to his SUV, but once we get there he pulls me in for a kiss. He threads his hands into my hair, holding the back of my head tenderly, and puts his mouth to mine. He tastes minty and smells like smokey pines. My inner thighs start to burn right as he releases me slowly.

"Do you have any idea how hard it was not to come over last night?" He whispers against my cheekbone. I just bite my lip and look up into his eyes. The dark chocolate eyes I used to drown in, roam all over me, making me buzz with suspense. He removes his hands from my head and opens the door, though. "Princess," he says, then gestures with his hand for me to enter. I just laugh. *That's another new one.*

I buckle up and watch him as he gets up into the driver's seat. He pushes the sleeves of his linen shirt up, showing off his toned and tan forearms. His black hair is slicked back, but long enough it waves and curls slightly at the back of his shirt. He looks fucking edible, I could eat him. *Jesus, am I hormonal?* I went from no sex for months to now desperately craving it. He smiles in my direction, catching me staring at him and I let out a nervous laugh.

We pull out of my drive and head out to the main high-way, and I can't help the feeling of familiarity that pulses through me. Driving through the hills to the Greek Fest, it's literally just like old times. Except now I'm a divorced, mom of two who's pregnant with another guy's baby. *I wonder what he sees in me, honestly.*

"What are you thinking about?" He asks.

"Oh, um...just, did you ever think we'd be doing *this* almost 20 years later?" He extends his hand across the center console to thread his fingers with mine before replying.

"Yes, I did." He squeezes my hand gently and I squeeze back before looking out the window at the golden grasses swaying in the evening breeze and I wonder, *if I'd never left, would we still be doing this?*

"What are you most looking forward to tonight?" He asks.

"Definitely the pilaf and the baklava." My answer is quick and automatic, and of course it's food.

He laughs. "Ouch, I didn't even make the list, babe," he says, making me laugh, too, as warmth fills my chest.

"I am *also* looking forward to spending tonight with you," I try to soothe his ego, but I also realize the words are true. I am looking forward to it.

"That's alright, sweetheart. I know how you feel about food. I'll always be number two in that regard." I laugh again. "But just so you know, you aren't number one on my list."

"Aha! See!" I declare.

"You're the *only* one, babe. It's just you." He turns and gives me his breathtaking smile, and I know no matter what decision I make after tonight, it's going to be hard as hell to do it.

———

The Greek Fest is just getting underway by the time we arrive. Luckily, since the MS Group is one of the largest sponsors, we're able to park in the vendor section saving us a

15-minute walk. Due to the early hour, it's still sweltering out, so that small reprieve feels like a godsend right now.

To be honest, I was surprised when Matthias said we were going at 5:00. The last time we were here, on our first date, we didn't arrive until almost 8:00, just as the dancing and party really started. I think he's taking my tough nights into consideration, which I can absolutely appreciate.

Matthias comes around and opens my door, giving me a hand. As he does he says, "Babycakes," and I can't help but laugh.

"Okay, what's with the nicknames?" I ask him.

I could swear a slight blush creeps up his cheeks, but he says, "Just trying to see what sticks, that's all."

"Uh huh, okay," is all I say. We start walking towards the entrance and he slips an arm around my waist. There's something about the gesture that feels possessive and I can't decide if I like it or not.

At the entry gate is a table with several older Greek women handing out wristbands, and one drop-dead gorgeous woman checking I.D.'s. The gorgeous woman with long black hair, tan skin, and an amazing body nods at Matthias as we approach.

"Hi, cuz," she says to him before looking me over with a discerning glare.

"Gina, this is Britain, my girlfriend. Britain, this is my cousin, Gina." *What the fuck? Girlfriend? That's, uh, yeah, news to me.* My cheeks turn crimson and my facial expression shifts, drawing an arched eyebrow in response from Gina. I work to school it into something more polite, then extend my hand to the woman.

"Hi, Gina. It's nice to meet you." She takes my hand, but

her shake is limp. I can't help but feel her judging me, *harshly*.

"So you're the famous Britain, huh?" Her tone hovers on cold.

I just shrug softly, "I guess. Famous to whom, though, I don't know." I punctuate this with a smile, but Gina just nods with her own smug looking smile, then reaches for my hand to apply a wristband.

"Have my mom or dad come through yet?" Matthias asks her.

"Nope," she says, then reaches out to apply his wristband. "You kids have fun in there." I go to say thank you, but she's already turned her back to help the group behind us.

With one arm still wrapped around my waist, Matthias starts navigating us towards one of the large tented areas.

"Matthias," I say, trying to get his attention, but his eyes are roving all around, clearly on the lookout for something. He doesn't respond, though, caught up in his task.

I try again. "Matthias," I say a little bit louder.

"Yes, babe?" He doesn't stop or look me in the eye.

"Didn't we just have a talk about labels, and how I wasn't ready for one?" This finally stops him, pulling his attention to me.

"We did." *Uh, okay...*

"So then why did you just tell your cousin I'm your girlfriend?"

"Because you are."

"No, we literally just talked about this and I said no." To be fair, I did lie and tell Liam I was with someone when officially I wasn't, but that was more about burning him than me being with Mats.

"Okay," that's all he says. He puts on a half-dimpled smile, then starts tugging me along again. I'm not exactly *mad* at what he just said to Gina, but I *am* starting to get frustrated with how he's dismissing me. I look around and see that a couple people are looking in our direction, most likely because they know Matthias, and I hate that my people-pleasing, good-girl mentality is making me kill this conversation. At least for now.

We arrive at a sectioned-off area in one of the larger tents that has its own separate bar and tables. So far, there's only a couple people milling about in this "VIP" section. Certainly not anyone I know, though that doesn't mean much. I fully anticipate knowing a total of three people here tonight. *Niko, Max, and Matthias.*

Matthias chooses seats for us at the center table, allowing for a decent view of the stage and dance area. "Is this alright?" He gestures towards the seats.

"Sure, it's perfect." I look around, making sure no one is in earshot. "We don't have to finish talking about this right now, but I do want to talk about what just happened." I look him straight in the eye, hopefully conveying how serious it is to me.

He just says, "Sure." *That's it?* I can't help but feel like he's steamrolling me. It's something Damian used to do...and I fucking hate it. I catch sight of Niko making his way over, and decide to stifle my irritation about the situation until later.

"Britain! You look lovely tonight." Niko steps in, placing a kiss on my cheek. I can't help but notice how he looks down at my belly, making me feel severely self conscious suddenly. I should have worn something flowy, not this skin-tight, bare-my-soul-to-the-world dress. My cheeks heat for what feels like the twentieth time of the night.

"Hi, Niko," I say, returning his megawatt smile.

"Matt, you, uh, didn't mention you were bringing a date." Niko says, giving Matthias a look, doing that read-each-other-minds sibling thing.

"Sure didn't." Is all he says in return. Niko just sort of nods pensively.

"Well, this is gonna be a great Greek Fest!" Niko's voice ratchets up an octave. "What are you drinking, bro? Britain, what can I get for you?"

"Just a water for me, man. I've got precious cargo tonight," Matthias says, then reaches over, placing his hand around my upper arm, stroking me with his thumb. Niko just nods solemnly, again.

"Um, I'd love a Sprite or Ginger Ale if they have it. If not, water is perfect," I say. Niko just pats Matthias on the back before heading off towards the bar.

"Are you hungry, bubs?" Matthias asks me. *Hmm, not a fan of bubs.*

"Yeah, I could definitely eat, what about you?" Mats runs his gaze over me seductively.

"Yes, but I'll be eating later." Okay...so that's why we're here at 5:00. Early in, early out. I cast my gaze downward and unconsciously bite down on my lip. When I look back up, I see Niko making his way back to us.

"I think I'd like to go look at the little market, then find something to eat."

"Great, I'll come with you."

I nod, "Okay," then give him a half smile. Niko drops our

drinks into each of our hands and leaves without a word, just staring off at something in the distance.

"Thanks, Niko," I say to his back as he walks off in a rush. *Okay*. Matthias takes the drink from my hand and sets it down on the table next to his.

Slipping my hand in his, he leads us towards the makeshift market set up inside the Greek Orthodox Church. As we walk, I notice the crowd is growing thicker. The line for food is starting to wind down and out of the tent, and the band is starting to prep on the stage. There's little kids running around with balloons, and faces painted with butterflies, kittens, and dogs, and I smile listening to their happy squeals.

Matthias notices me watching and says, "I can't wait till this little one is out there running around," then reaches down to gently press a palm to the side of my belly. The combination of statement and touch feels like an intensely intimate display for *this* public of a place, and I fidget slightly under the pressure I'm suddenly feeling. Matthias doesn't think twice about it and drops his hand a moment later as we continue making our way into the, thankfully, air-conditioned building.

Tables line the perimeter of the space, leaving the middle section open for people to gather. There's a couple tables selling baked goods that instantly catch my eye, but I gravitate towards the brightly colored and hand-painted ceramics, first. Matthias trails behind me, never relinquishing his hold on my hand.

As I peruse the selection, I get a tingling awareness and look up to notice a middle-aged woman with long black hair and matching long black nails staring at me oddly. I give her a polite smile and her expression changes. It darkens, confusing me. I actually take a quick look behind me to make sure her glare was actually intended for me, but there's no one else. She begins moving towards us, so I tug on Mats' hand to pull his attention. He looks up at me, and I motion with my head in the direction of the quickly approaching she-wolf. When he sees her, a look of familiarity takes over his features.

He pulls me in close to him, tightly, lacing his arm around my midsection in the same possessive stance he had earlier, then leans over and whispers into my ear, "Don't worry, bug. I've got you." *Okay, I like 'bug' even less than I like 'bubs.'*

Elvira moves in, standing in front of us, but doesn't speak at first. She's just mad dogging me and pretending like Matthias isn't even here. I'm just about to turn and walk away when she finally says something.

"So it's true then?" She asks, but looks at Matthias for the answer.

"Yes," that's all he says. The woman just nods her head slowly, but retains her cruel expression.

"So you're *Britain*?" She says 'Britain' like it's a dirty word. I'm not liking a single thing about this, but I'm even more perturbed that Matthias is letting this person speak to me like this when he clearly knows her.

"Yes, I'm Britain Palomino-Scott." I extend my hand for a shake, but she doesn't take it. *Rude much?* I drop my hand down, angering more and more with each passing second. If there's only one thing I've learned about being an adult, it's that you don't *actually* have to take people's crap anymore. "Matthias, let's go." I thread my fingers into the hand wrapped around my midsection, turning us to leave when she stops me.

"He doesn't *like* being called *Matthias*." Her scolding sends a chill down my spine. Almost like a reflex, I go to apologize, but Matthias intervenes before I have a chance.

"No, I just don't like it when anyone besides *her* calls me Matthias." *Oh.* Matthias says it firmly while keeping the grip on my hand tender but strong, giving me a gentle squeeze. I get a warmth in my abdomen, appreciative that he is sticking up for me, but also, that I'm the only one who calls him that. That nickname thing is starting to make a bit more sense now. He wants something that's only *his*.

The woman scoffs, "I didn't raise my son to speak to me like that." *Oh. Ohhhh.*

Matthias responds cooly, "And I'd argue you hardly raised me at all." He says it like it's just a matter of fact. There's no bark behind his biting words. *Julie Fucking Scala.*

FOURTEEN

BRITAIN

So this is Julie Scala. All I can think is, *she really is a bitch.* I could understand her disliking Georgia. I mean, after all, Constantine was going to leave Julie for my mom. But her blatant rudeness towards me is a bit uncalled for. What the fuck did I ever do to her?

Julie looks genuinely shocked by Matthias' comment and is silent for more than a couple seconds. I notice her noticing my bump and her expression morphs. In a barely audible voice she gestures down to my protruding stomach and says to Matthias, "Does your father know about *this*?" Her eyes begin to line with tears, but I don't fully understand why.

"Not yet," Matthias says, then gives a tight-lipped smile, "but he will." For some reason, the way it comes out sounds like a threat. Julie just nods, then turns around and walks away like none of this ever happened.

"So, um, that's your mom?" I ask Mats, quietly.

"Yep, that's Julie." I'm looking at him, trying to get a read on where he's at, but his line of sight is still zoned out to where Julie is slowly disappearing through the crowd. Eventually he snaps out of it.

"I'm sorry she was so rude to you."

"Yeah, me too..." is all I say. I guess they can't all be winners like Sandy. Mentally I add Julie to the cons side of my pro/con list for continuing to date Matthias.

"Hey," Matthias turns towards me, using his thumb and finger to direct my face towards his, "I know what will make it all better." I rest a hand on his forearm before replying.

"What's that?" I ask. He leans in, giving me a gentle, but sensual kiss. I can't help how turned on I suddenly become.

He pulls back, lingering close to my lips, "Baklava and ice cream." Not where I thought that was going, but that's probably the more appropriate solution.

"You're absolutely right." I give him a smile. "But first, I want to buy some olive oil and like 15 things of cookies for the girls."

"Whatever you want, buns, it's yours." He drops his mouth to mine once more, and I savor the way his plump lips linger against me. It feels like a promise of more.

When he finally pulls back, I say, "Hmm, I don't know that buns is *the one*, but I like it better than bubs or bug. Bug is *definitely not* the one."

"Noted," he says, then takes my hand and leads me over to the food section of the marketplace. It only takes me a moment because I don't bother to deliberate the choices, I just buy one box of every kind of cookie. The yia-yias all "ooh and ahh" over Matthias and myself while he pays and they package up the goods, and I just stand back watching Matthias as they do. He chats casually with the older women, flashing his dimple-filled smile at them, and then at me and I think to myself, *he's perfect.* The nagging voice at the back of my mind asks, *perfect for me, though?*

Matthias manages to carry all the bags and purchase us both a baklava sundae, all while continuing to hold my hand. *Pro: Does well with juggling full hands.* I can't help but picture him with a baby carrier in one arm, diaper bag slung over his shoulder, and a bottle in hand.

When we get back to our section, what *were* empty tables are now filled with people packed together like sardines. We squeeze through a boisterous group to our spot and Matthias pulls the chair out for me and places the sundaes down.

"Eat this, but I'm going to go get you some real food, okay?" He sets our bags under the table, then gently squeezes my shoulder before walking away. I dive into the baklava sundae eagerly. The warm honey drizzled on top melds with the cool cream perfectly, and when it hits my tongue, I close my eyes to savor it. For once, I'm grateful I don't know anyone here, and am able to eat wholly uninterrupted.

"Britain?" The deep voice echoes to me and I throw my eyes wide open. An older version of the man I once knew stands before me. His hair is still mostly black, but gray now lines his temples. He's still just as tan and ruggedly handsome as always, but with more wrinkles and a certain air of distinct wisdom and warmth about him. Maybe from age, or maybe it's just that I know more about what he meant to my mother now.

"Mr. Scala," I say to him and smile. He opens his arms for me, so I stand and lean into the embrace. It seems to go on and on, but I don't move to break it and neither does he. It feels nice. It reminds me a bit of being with my Aunt Rose. Like connecting with him is like connecting with a piece of Georgia. There's a little bit of her in all of us, I guess. He eventually pats my back and pulls away, revealing teary eyes.

"Really, you ought to call me Connie."

I just smile, "From here on out, I promise I will."

He looks me over once, and says, "You've hardly aged at all, my dear." As I go to reply, Matthias moves in beside me, reaching across to set down a steaming plate piled high with food. I look at the plate with wide eyes, then look at Matthias.

He just shrugs and says, "you should be eating for two, babe," then gently palms the side of my stomach again.

"Matt?" Constantine asks, looking at my belly where his son's hand rests, then turns to look back at his son with the same wide eyed expression I just gave the food.

"Hi, dad." Matthias leans over and the father and son embrace, warmly, but Constantine's eyes never leave mine while they do. Matthias rejoins my side, resuming that possessive stance with one arm wrapped around me.

"Are you two...?" Constantine questions while motioning with his hand between the two of us.

"Yes, dad, we're together." *What the fuck, Matthias?* Literally all he had to change it to was 'we're seeing each other,' and I wouldn't have a problem. I put on a polite smile, though, remembering my manners.

Constantine comes to life before my eyes, before I can even process what Matthias just said. He claps his hands together as his smile beams, reaching from ear to ear. The teary eyes of a minute ago officially let loose a couple droplets, and they travel down his laugh lines landing on his linen shirt.

"I'm going to be a grandfather?" Constantine says lowly, but it's not really a question. I feel a pit in my stomach grow, but I don't have the heart to tell him straight out that Matthias isn't the father. Seeing how he's reacting, it feels cruel to kill the moment.

From across the tent, a group calls out for Constantine, but he puts a hand up to silence them. "Will you come have lunch with me, Britain?"

My natural inclination wants to decline, but I'd love to talk to him about Georgia, quite honestly, so I say, "Yes, I would really love that," instead.

"Great, I'll get your number from Matt, and we'll get it arranged." He smiles at me before bending down to give me a kiss on the cheek. As he pulls away, he says, "My god, how I've missed you." I retain my smile, but the sentiment doesn't make complete sense to me. *Is he drunk? Did he just get me confused with Georgia?*

Once I know he's far enough away that he can't hear me, I say to Matthias, "I literally just talked to you about this."

"Sorry, babe. Can't help it. I just want everyone to know what's mine."

Mine. The word replays in my mind, but I can't quite grasp how I feel about it. I am beginning to feel like no matter my stance on the subject, Matthias is just going to keep declaring that I'm his to anyone who'll listen. There's something possessively sexy about it, but there's something else I just can't place.

"Let's sit down and eat, okay? I can't have the two of you

going hungry." He slides his palm over my abdomen, again, unable to keep his hands off me tonight.

I don't get a chance to respond because it hits me then, like a cool breeze on a stifling hot night, and I feel his gaze instantly. I look around, catching his blue eyes looking at me like I've just stabbed him in the back. My breathing stills as my heart lurches forward in my chest. We stand there with locked eyes for what feels like forever until Gina slides next to Liam, whispering something in his ear, then trailing her hand down his arm, seductively. *Intimately.*

I instantly avert my gaze, feeling the burn of acid rising up my throat. I sit down quickly into my seat, but I just sit there, zoning out, staring into my plate of pilaf and stuffed grape leaves.

"Are you feeling okay, sweetheart?" Matthias asks.

"Um, I'm just not very hungry all of a sudden." I try to keep my voice from trembling, but am unsuccessful.

"Okay, try to eat some of it, though, okay?" I nod silently, and pick up a forkful of rice. Putting it to my lips feels torturous and my fingers fumble to hold the fork steady.

"You know, I actually need to use the restroom. I'll be right back." Without waiting for a response or an offer to accompany me, I drop the fork and move briskly through the tent towards the indoor bathrooms inside the church. There's porta-potties that are a lot closer, but I need a cool, well-ventilated space right now or I might start hyperventilating.

Once I get to the bathroom, I go to the very last stall and shut the door, shakily sliding the lock in place. Attempting to stifle my cries, I cover my mouth and fight against the urge to sob. Unraveling toilet paper, I try my best to catch the tears before they fall in a weak attempt to save my makeup, but I'm failing.

I don't know what feels worse: The look he gave me? Or the look Gina gave him? I thought he was probably already moving on. I knew that. And I am here with Matthias who has gone out of his way to make sure that everyone here knows we're together. I have even kissed Matthias multiple times tonight. I have absolutely no right to feel jealous. *None, you need to stop.*

But I can't help it. My chest is tight, and the smell of the old bathroom, nauseating. I have to get out of here. Pushing out of the bathroom door, I head to the back exit of the church — the opposite direction of the festival. It leads me to a side alley that's dark and quiet, but still close enough I can hear the crowds and music filter over the building. I stand with my back pressed against the cool stone wall of the church and I let the tears fall.

I haven't been out here ten seconds when the back door of the church flies open with such force, the door slams against the stone wall with a loud crack, startling me. I gasp in surprise as Liam steps out into the alley, looking frantic. I quickly inhale sharply, then freeze, like if I don't move, he won't notice me. Which is idiotic; it would be physically impossible unless he was blind. When his eyes land on me, he relaxes slightly.

It only takes two steps before he's right in front of me. "Are you okay?" he asks. I just shake my head, slowly at first, not sure I'll be able to find words without them coming out like a croak.

I swallow in an attempt to coat my bone-dry throat and ask, "Are you?"

"I will be, if you are." Not exactly an answer to the question I asked, but maybe he doesn't want to share that with me. He's doing the thing he does when he's nervous, though, bouncing the palm of his hand against his leg. My stomach sinks the slightest when he speaks again. "I was worried when I saw you take off for the bathroom. I thought...I hoped...nothing had happened...with the baby, you know?" The painful lump in my throat grows. *Right*, that's all this was. Just checking to make sure *the baby* is okay.

"Oh. No, in that regard, everything is fine. Sorry to worry you." I look down in embarrassment. I thought he wanted to know if *I* was okay. *Stupid, Britain. So stupid.* I have to remember that's not what Liam is about. No matter what he *says*, his actions say otherwise. It's *I love you*, but then he leaves. *You're the only one for me*, but then Gina acts as if he's her man. It's confusing, and I'm the fool. Again.

He doesn't make any moves to go, so without looking up, I offer, "Everything's fine. I'll make my way back out in a couple minutes." He still doesn't turn to leave, instead, he takes one step closer. The nearness forces me to look up and into the blue eyes that give new meaning to devastatingly handsome. They absolutely destroy me.

"*Bambi*," he says softly, then moves to wipe the fresh tears off my face, running both thumbs across my cheeks in opposite directions. The touch sends warmth flooding through my body.

"You don't have to do this, Liam. I'm not your problem anymore." My voice comes out in a pitiful tremble.

"Did you read the letter?" I blink a few times, completely confused. "I put it in the black suitcase for you. I understand if you don't want to..."

"I didn't unpack the suitcases." *Why the fuck would Jess keep that from me?* He just nods. His left eye is slightly swollen, but terribly discolored. Without thinking, I reach up and brush my thumb gently over the bruised area. *Shit, I shouldn't have done that.* I've forgotten my place.

"I'm sorry," I say, breaking eye contact.

"Sorry for the black eye? Or for touching me?" I feel him move in closer, his body heat transferring to mine.

"Both," I say, keeping my gaze cast downwards.

"*Baby*, don't be sorry." He lets out a low and ironic laugh, "If it took me getting mauled by your brother for you to touch me again, I'd let him punch me a million more times." My heart starts to beat faster and I look up. He gives me a gentle smile and before I know it, we're reaching for each other at the exact same time. It's instinctual, no thinking required. He pulls my head into his chest under his chin and wraps me up, just like he did my first night in Spearhead.

"I miss you so much, Britain." He says over me softly, stroking my hair before placing a kiss at the top of my head.

I miss you, too. I say it inwardly, unable to reveal my weakness to him.

"Your tears will always be my problem, Britain." His deep voice settles me like nothing else can. I inhale and exhale, relishing the ability to take full, slow breaths. *Where do we go from here, though?*

"Wherever you want, baby," he says as he continues to stroke me gently, his hands passing further down my body to my hips. *Shit,* I didn't mean to say that out loud.

"What about Gina?" *Jesus, Britain, have a little self respect will ya.*

He tenses then leans back and says, "There is nothing

with Gina. The only place I want to be is next to you." My cheeks burn, my pelvis starts to heat, and I have to school myself, harshly, to not go up on my tiptoes to kiss him.

"And what about Matthias? He just told everyone here that we're together." I feel guilt and shame start to burrow their way into my mind.

"Are you not?" Liam asks seriously.

"No!" I say in frustration. "We're not, but he thinks we are, and he's literally told anyone who would listen that we are. I mean, we *have* been seeing each other, but I literally just told him three days ago that I wasn't ready for more, or a label, but he just completely disregarded it, and has been acting like I'm *his*."

Liam grimaces before replying, "So you lied to me when you said you were with someone else?" I drop my chin to my chest, feeling ashamed.

"Yes, I'm sorry. I just wanted to hurt you. It was wrong, but also I have been seeing Matthias romantically, so it wasn't a complete lie." I start to feel sick with guilt. Here I am, in Liam's arms in the alley, while Matthias is probably out there looking for me, without a clue that I'm moments away from falling on my ex's mouth. I push out of the embrace. What is it about Liam that makes me forget so quickly?

"Liam, I can't do this." He visibly deflates. "It's not right, whether I'm actually with Matthias or not. He's been there for me. He's shown up when no one else did. He doesn't deserve *this*," I motion with my hand between the two of us. I'm also not convinced I can ever forgive Liam. *Or trust him either*.

"I need to leave." I'm going to go back to the table and tell Matthias that I'm feeling unwell, and then I'm going home.

"Bambi, please don't leave..." Liam reaches out for me, but I pull back and out of his reach.

"You confuse me, Liam." I shake my head. "Please don't do this to me. *Please.*" I drop my head in shame at the sound of my pleading. Like an old friend, the hurt finds me again, and I remember the knife sliding under my ribs when he walked away from me at Colton's months ago. *Hold on to that, Britain. Don't be fooled by one warm embrace. He is not the person you think he is.*

"Can we just talk, Britain? Just you and me?"

I snap my head up, and face him straight on. "Do you want to talk about how you lied to me? Kept secrets from me? How you left me and just walked away like it was the easiest thing you've ever done? Can we talk about how I don't even know *you*?" I fall silent, realizing I was nearly shouting at him. Liam's gaze darkens and he moves in towards me, crowding me up against the stone church wall. He holds my gaze, leaning over me, trapping me into his hard body.

"*Stop it,*" his tone is low and gravelly. "You're the only person in this entire world that knows the real me. You're the one thing in my life I've never wanted to give up. Fuck Bambi, I couldn't give you up if I tried. I've spent every second of every fucking day missing you. Sick to my stomach, dying every fucking day over leaving you." He takes in a deep breath, then gentles his tone, "I will love you with every breath until my dying day. Baby, always. Do you understand me? *Always.*" He tenderly slides one hand behind my neck and rubs his thumb back and forth across my throat. I feel paralyzed as I grapple with his words. I felt every syllable he just spoke to the marrow of my bones. Each word warmed me, healing something deep within me. But do I believe him? Has too much damage been done?

"Liam..." he moves in closer to me, his body pressed fully against mine now. "Love isn't enough." He doesn't move away from me, though.

"I can't leave you, Britain." His voice is barely above a whisper, but his touch increases in pressure.

Somehow I find the resolve to strengthen my voice. I remember him sliding the ring off my finger. I remember sobbing in the ambulance. I remember Jess peeling me off my bathroom floor because I could hardly take care of myself. I let the memories harden me, strengthening my resolve.

"You can and you will. You've done it before, you'll do it again. Whether that's right now, or years down the road. Whatever we are, whatever we *were*, *love* isn't enough to sustain it. These feelings will fade, and without trust and communication, *we* won't be anything at all, so let's not start this again." I push out and away from underneath him and I don't look back. Not as I walk back into the church, and not as I walk back to the tent. *Don't look back, Britain.*

As soon as I enter the VIP section, I spot Matthias easily, our eyes connecting regardless of the hordes of people. He can see my tear-stained cheeks and starts moving towards me relentlessly, pushing through groups of innocent bystanders. As soon as we're in front of each other, he just cups my face in his hands gently and asks, "Are you okay, sweetheart?" I shake my head, and he nods in understanding.

"Don't move. I'll be back in just a second." He slips away from me, and I take a moment to glance around. I don't see Liam anywhere, but I do notice Gina shooting daggers in my direction. I don't know why. *He's all yours, sweetheart.* My stomach rolls at the thought, but I have to start getting used to it. Liam's not mine. Not anymore.

Matthias comes back and grabs my hand, leading the way out, and says "Let's go." I just nod in response. As we walk to the parking area beside the church, I glimpse those blue eyes watching Matthias and I walking. I raise one corner of my mouth in acknowledgement, but it's not a happy gesture. It's a farewell.

FIFTEEN

MATTHIAS

Damnit. I thought I'd have more time with her before Liam came back. The timing of his return is...less than ideal. I was getting so close. *Finally.*

I saw him chase after her to the bathroom and I thought about following, too, but ultimately I figured Britain didn't need to see me give Liam another black eye. I'm still pissed at him for not telling me Britain was here. For six fucking weeks, she was with *him*. My blood starts to boil every time I think about it, and I think about it a lot. *Britain is mine.*

I'm trying my hardest to calm down before we get to the car because Britain doesn't need me piling on to her problems, but I just hate that he still upsets her like this. In general, I hate that she's upset, period. I wish I could solve all her problems. I wish I could give her a life where she doesn't have to worry about anything. *I know Dad, I'm trying. I'm trying to take care of her.* But Liam messes up my plans, of which I have many...

I look to my right to check on Brit, but she seems lost in a daze. Her tears have dried, leaving little gray lines running down her face from her makeup, and she has that exhausted look about her again. When I picked her up this evening, she looked like the old Brit for the first time, but all it took was one Liam sighting, and we're right back to square one. She has that same dead-tired, barely alive look she had at the hospital. *God, I could fucking kill him.*

The car is already running by the time we get to it, so hopefully it's cooled down enough for her. Wedging between my G-Wagen and the car parked beside us, I open her door.

"Alright, babe," I say as I use my hand to guide her into the car. She doesn't respond, just nods once in acknowledgement and I close her door gently.

Before I make my way over to the driver's side, I stop, leaning back against the trunk door. Not exactly the way I pictured our "first" *real* date going. *Damn.*

Instead of getting in on my side, I walk back to her side, re-opening the door. She looks at me in confusion, but I just keep moving. I slide her heels off her feet, setting them to the side, then recline the seat back for her. I run my hand over her head, feeling her silky hair glide between my fingers, and tell her, "Rest, babe. I'll drive you home, okay?" I turn to shut the car door when she stops me.

She's so quiet sometimes. I smile, remembering, and lean back into the car to hear her say, "I don't want to go home, Mats." She pauses a moment before finishing, "I want to be with you, tonight." Her words are like music to my ears. *Yes, finally.* God, all I've wanted, for years, was to hear those words. My smile goes so wide, it hurts. I'm not entirely sure if she means she just wants to be with me tonight *only*, or together *together*, but I don't give a crap right now. I'll take anything. Her breadcrumbs, her baby steps, *anything*.

"Do you want to go to my house?" She nods, and I smile, leaning over to drop a quick kiss on her cheek. "Mmm, you're a bit salty, babe," I chuckle as I pull away. She blushes, then immediately puts her hands to her cheeks to rub at the tear stains. Crap, I didn't mean to make her feel bad about it.

"I'll run you a bath at the house, if you want?" I rub her thigh gently as I ask. Just picturing her in the tub at my house is already driving me mad with need for her. *I fucking need her.*

"I'd like that," she says, then smiles. She has no damn idea what I'd do to make her smile like that again.

Once I've parked in the driveway, I hustle around to open her door for her. She gives me a sheepish smile and a "Thank you," and when I let go of her hand, the nervousness hits me. I haven't brought her to my house since she's been back. I wonder if she'll like it. My house is nice in that everything is from Restoration Hardware, but it's not 'designer nice' like Liam's. God, I hate that I keep comparing myself to him. I thought about it earlier in the car, too. Like, does she like the G-Wagen more than the Range Rover? Does she wish I was more like him? Fuck, I've got to stop with that stupid shit, though. *I'm Matthias-fucking-Scala.*

We walk through the garage before heading in, but she halts halfway. "You still have it?" She asks as I'm unlocking the door. I'm surprised she can even tell what it is. It's dark and the Camaro is covered.

"Um, yeah. Just never really wanted to get rid of it." I don't know if it's a good thing or a bad thing that I've kept it. Brit probably doesn't have the best memories of it, but the whole reason I kept it was for the memories I had with her in it.

"That's cool," she says. "Does it still run?"

"Yeah, it does. Just got a fresh paint job about a year ago, too." I turn to look at her just staring at the covered body.

"What color is she now?"

I laugh lightly at her question. "Blue," I say.

She turns to look at me and smiles. "I always thought she'd look great in blue."

"I know." I give her a smile back, then slide my hand into hers to guide her into the house. I flip on a few lights before I take her to the primary suite-side of the house, but she tugs on my hand to stop me.

"Matthias, this view is gorgeous." She's staring out at the valley floor that's bathed in orange from the setting sun. My house is one of a small handful on the edge of town that sits on a bluff, providing a view of the river and the land for miles. It's a great lot, but once we build at Broken Ridge, our view will be even better.

"It's not as gorgeous as my view, though." I move behind her, putting my body against her back, my hands falling naturally onto her hips. Fuck me, being here with her is like a fantasy. I don't need anything else but *this*. Her with me. "Let's get you in the bath, sweetheart." She nods her head against my chest, and I can hear how her breath has sped up in response. I don't know if she'll want to be intimate tonight, but when she is ready, *Jesus*. I don't plan to let her out of my bed for a month.

I grab her hand again and pull her down the hall to the primary suite. Once we get to my room, I release her to go turn on my bedside lamp. I unbutton the rest of my shirt as I do, just a force of habit, and turn to see Britain with her eyes trained on my pants. I blush a little because I'm sure she can see how hard I still am for her. I just let the linen shirt fall and head towards the bathroom.

I wish I had some sort of fancy bubble bath for her. *Need to add that to my shopping list*, but at least I have epsom salts. I start the water, checking to make sure it's not too hot, then add the salts and grab a washcloth and towel from the linen closet, setting them and some body wash on the edge of the tub.

"It's ready!" I call out, beckoning Britain from the bedroom. She stands in the doorway, slipping off her heels before padding barefoot across the tile.

"Do you think you could unclasp my dress, please?" She stands in front of me, pulling her hair off her back and over one shoulder exposing the clasp at her neck. I slip the hooks out of their hold, then run a knuckle down her bare spine. It's taking everything in me not to rip her dress off and make love to her in the tub, right now. I just press a soft kiss to her bare shoulder and remind myself I have to move at her pace.

"Do you want something to change into, for after?"

"Do you mind?"

"Of course not. T-shirt? Sweats?" I ask.

"Big tee is perfect." She steps forward letting the dress fall to the floor in a puddle, then steps forward into the tub. I have to take a large gulp to pick my jaw back up to its normal position. *Her pace, Matt, her pace*, I remind myself.

I walk to the closet, hoping to conceal my raging boner and find her a shirt. Kicking off my shoes and clothes, I opt for a pair of sweats instead and scoop up an old soccer league t-shirt for her. Doing my best to give her some privacy, I keep my eyes averted towards the sinks when I set down her shirt.

"It's right here for you, babe. I'll just be in my room if you need anything." I head out, but her sweet, quiet voice makes me stop.

"Mats, thank you...for everything." I just nod my head, staying turned away from her. *No, babe, thank you.*

————

Britain

Did I really just choose? I just told Mats I want to be with him. So yeah, I guess I decided then. *I want to be with Matthias.* I dunk the washcloth to soak up all the soapy water, then scrub at my face in an attempt to remove the tear and makeup stains, but I might have to finish this project in the mirror.

Leaning back against the tub, I close my eyes, peacefully, for just a minute. This feels...right. When I left Liam in the alley, for a second, it felt like I'd made a mistake. I had to fight not to turn back towards him, but by the time I found Matthias, I already knew. I want us to have our chance. I don't want to be 17 years down the road again and wonder what could have been this time. I don't have to live with fear of regret any longer.

I breathe in and out, deeply, happy for the small peace the decision has brought me. But it doesn't last long before my mind drifts to Liam. But just as quickly as he arrives, I push the thought back away. *No.* He doesn't get to just show back up, ruin any progress I've made with myself, or with Matthias. He doesn't get to invade my every waking thought anymore.

Carla's sentiments this past month echo back in my mind, "Take back the control, Britain." And she's right, just like she always is. It feels good to take control over this situation. I can't forgive Liam, and once this lustfulness fades, we'll just be a broken and brittle shell of a relationship. *We're irreparable.*

Okay, enough of that. I want to get back into Matthias' arms. Popping the drain open on his freestanding tub, the water runs off me in streams as I stand. I wrap up in the humongous bath sheet he laid out for me, and take the washcloth to the extra sink. It doesn't look like it's ever been used before. There's not even a hand soap at it and it makes me wonder: Does he ever bring anyone here? I get a little jealous, then ashamed. He's Matthias-fucking-Scala. I'm sure he's bedded many women here before. There's probably so many of them, they don't stick around long enough to even wash their hands.

Stop it, Britain. I can't help but always see us a certain way, though. Him as this gorgeous, intelligent, total catch, and me as the quiet, awkward girl he once fell in a lake with. I use the washcloth to mop up the last bits of mascara, then release the towel to dry off the tips of my hair. I could have really used a claw clip like 20 minutes ago, but oh well now. I throw on the tee he left out for me and examine myself in the mirror. *Damp hair, wasted-away makeup, baggy t-shirt. Oof.*

I hang up the towel on a hook by the rain shower and grab my dress, folding it, then dropping it beside my heels on the floor.

I find Matthias laying on his bed, reading. He's wearing thick, black-framed glasses, a pair of gray sweats, and his chest is bare. He has never looked sexier. *42 looks damn good on him.*

He keeps on reading, but pats the space beside him, silently acknowledging me. I climb on to the king-sized bed, covered in charcoal gray linen, and scoot beside him. He opens his arm to embrace me at his side, and I cuddle right in, so naturally.

"How was your bath?" he asks, then drops a kiss on the top of my head. I bring a hand up, placing it on his bare chest and glide my hand over his pecs. I don't remember him being this hairy. It makes me giggle.

"It was good, thank you."

"What's so funny, giggles?" He finally sets the book down in his lap and turns his attention towards me.

"I just don't remember you being this...hairy," I say, then lightly laugh again.

"Well, I was," he says.

"Really?" I don't remember that at all. In my mind, I picture him with a nearly smooth chest.

"Really. I just don't think we spent much time completely naked when we would...you know." I blush, hard. Yeah, most of our sex was hurried and half-clothed. His brothers always seemed to be around or in the house, or we

179

were at a park...Christ, we probably had more sex outdoors than anywhere else.

"Hmm, I guess you're right, but the glasses are new. You never wore glasses before."

"Yep, I'm old now, babe." I smile at him, because he is not old and he has never looked better.

"You are not. And I love the glasses, very sexy. You have this hot librarian thing going for you right now." I use my hand to gesture up and down his body.

"What do the librarians look like where you live?" He teases me, "Because if they look anything like this, you are no longer allowed to visit there." I laugh and he moves the book to his nightstand, setting his glasses down on top. He pulls me down further on the bed so that my back is flat to the mattress now and as he hovers over me, drinking me in, I grow wet with anticipation.

"What do you want, sweetheart?" he asks, then nudges my nose gently with his. I want him, all of him. I just nod, though. "You're going to have to say it, babe. I don't want to do anything you're not ready for. I've already screwed this up at least once before. I'm just as happy to cuddle, or watch a movie, or go get us ice cream. Just tell me what you want." If I was wearing panties, they'd be soaked by now.

"I want you Mats," I say as I wrap my hand around his arm, stroking him.

"Are you sure, babe?" *Yes*. It doesn't feel wrong anymore. I can honestly say yes.

"Yes." I haven't even finished the word when he slams his mouth over mine, immediately slipping his tongue inside. He moves over me, pushing my legs open with a knee before settling on top of me, his right hand holding the back of my head while his left holds him up, careful to never apply any pressure to my abdomen.

He releases my mouth momentarily to say, "You have no idea how much I want you, Brit." I let loose a small moan when he places his mouth on my neck, kissing and sucking on me with fervor.

"Show me then," I pant out. He stops what he's doing and gives me a deadly serious look.

"There's not enough time, but I guess tonight'll have to be a start." He nods down at my shirt, commanding, "Take it off." I don't hesitate, just slipping the tee over my head. I nod down at his sweats, silently making the same demand, and he does. Moving off the bed, he pushes the large linen duvet back before he drops the sweats revealing his throbbing cock. It bounces in anticipation, and I can't stop staring. *Did it get bigger? What. The. Hell. Maybe it's just been that long*, no pun intended. I laugh to myself.

"Umm, when was the last time you were tested?" I ask, trying to pull my gaze away from his nude form as he crawls back over me.

"When we started dating," he says as he nudges me to expose more of my neck so he can go back to work. "And everything was good. You?"

"Yeah, at the doctor's when I went in for my first prenatal exam. Everything is good."

"Good," he says, then moves back, taking a nipple into his mouth, sucking it softly and causing me to writhe beneath him. Fuck, I want him so bad. I trail my fingers through his thick hair as he sucks and nibbles on my breasts.

"Babe?" I practically moan out.

"Yeah?"

"Can I suck your dick, please?" I feel his cock swell against my thigh in response. He looks at me questioning, almost. I've never sucked his dick before. I was a little shy at 18 and didn't have a clue what the fuck to do, but I want to do it for him now.

"Not before I taste you first." He leans forward, stealing a kiss before he pushes back, trailing kisses across the fading hickeys he left the other day, then moves down, pushing my legs apart. "I've literally dreamed about this, Brit," he says right before he drops his mouth to my clit, laving me with his tongue. I push my hands into his hair to hold him tight against me as I grind, and he moves his tongue over the swollen bud with pressure. He stops his assault just as I'm about to climax to lap up all the juices at my entrance.

"Babe, you taste so fucking good, but I don't want you to come yet. I need to feel it when you do." His words cause me to moan and drop my head back against the bed.

"Then can I suck you now?" I look at him as I ask. His tongue is buried deep inside me, and I clench down, making him moan in turn. He places one last kiss on my clit before sitting up.

"How do you want me?" he asks. I pat the space on the bed beside me.

"Laying down." He nods and moves to the space beside where I just was. Once his back is pressed against the mattress, I crawl over top of him, kissing him gently on the mouth before moving lower. I run my fingernails across his nipples causing goosebumps to form on his arms, and his dick to throb against my inner thigh.

"Do you like that?" I ask, then bite my lip as my inner walls clench around nothing in desire.

"Fuck, yes," he whispers. I don't linger, though. I move further down, placing a soft kiss on his pelvis right above his dick, then gently take his balls in my hand as I run my tongue up his shaft. He starts to leak, so I insert the head into my mouth to suck and swallow what's there.

"Jesus, Brit," he rasps out. I let him go as deep in my throat as possible before releasing him entirely.

"Do you want more, Mats?"

"Fuck, babe, yes." He runs a trembling hand through my hair in appreciation. I nod and suck his dick in again, letting him go a little further this time. I add my hand to help, and I suck and pull, riding his cock with my mouth. I can feel myself starting to drip over how turned on it's making me.

"S-stop, babe. I need you, now." I release him, and his dick slips out of my mouth, making a popping sound. I move over him to drop down on his cock, but he stops me with a shake of his head, rolling me on to my back and pinning me to the mattress.

"No fucking way are you fucking me tonight, sweetheart. I've been fantasizing about this for years." He gazes down at me while he runs the pad of his thumb over my lip, back and forth, then slips it between my wet lips.

"Suck it, darling," he demands, and I do. I run my hands up and down the length of the outstretched arm, watching his dick twitch with desire. "Do you want me, Britain?" he asks. I nod.

"Then take my dick, sweetheart." He presses the wet head against my entrance and starts to ease his way in. Slowly. Too slowly. I want more, I need more. I try to moan out, "More," but his thumb makes it hard to understand.

"I know you want more, babe," he says, removing his

thumb from my mouth, then slamming into me forcefully. *Fuck! Why does it feel a hundred times better than I remember?*

"Matthias!" I call out to him in pleasure.

"I know, babe, your perfect fucking pussy was made for me." He shakes his head, his hair slightly curling with perspiration and falling forward. "No, *we* were made for each other." He thrusts again, pulling out then sliding back in, hard. "It's never been like this with anyone else for me." He thrusts again, grinding down on me as my hips rise to meet him. "I needed this, Brit. I just fucking need you." We thrust and grind again, our old rhythm making its way back to us in a new, yet better way.

"Mats, I'm close," I whisper out. He nods.

"Me too, babe. Don't look away. Don't close your eyes, understand?" It's my turn to nod. I remember now, how intimate sex was with him. It always felt more like making love than fucking, even when he took me hard. Even when he bent me over to seemingly use me, he always brought us back together in the end. Coming together was always his goal, the thought alone brings me to the brink of my orgasm, and when he pushes into me one last time, my climax breaks free.

I scream out his name, and he ruts into me, locking our eyes and our bodies as we both give and take in this intimate exchange. Our bodies are tight against one another, throbbing, when he drops his head beside mine to whisper in my ear, "I've never stopped loving you, Brit."

SIXTEEN

BRITAIN

It wasn't an 'I love you,' per se, but it definitely had the same effect. My cheeks heat and I don't know what to say. Do I love him? I don't know that we're *in* love...yet. I think we could get there. I'm debating how to respond when he interrupts me.

"Don't say anything back. I just wanted you to know that." I *don't* say anything back. I just nod and he pulls back to look me in the eyes, rubbing his thumb across my cheekbone before placing a gentle kiss on my forehead. "God, that was better than I imagined," he laughs slightly, "better than I remembered."

I smile, like he took the words right out of my mouth. "I thought it was better than I remembered, too." He slides out of me, leaving a trail of his cum down my thigh, and the thought of that alone has me wanting him again. Matthias moves back, but doesn't move off me just yet. He drops a kiss to my belly, lets out a chuckle, and rolls off the bed towards the bathroom, so I follow right behind him to pee and clean up.

When I get back to his room, he's pushed the duvet back up and is sitting, waiting for me on the edge of the bed with the tee he lent me hanging from a hand. I stand in front of him, between his legs, and he drops the t-shirt down over my body.

"Can I get you some water? You didn't really eat anything. Do you want me to order something?"

"Are *you* hungry?" I ask, but he tilts his head down at me, giving me 'the look.' "Alright, fine, yes. I'm not super hungry, but I should probably eat." I only got two bites of my baklava sundae and no bites of real food. The last thing I ate was a chicken salad at noon. "What time is it even?"

"It's five after eight," he replies. I laugh.

"Oh, how things have changed. It's 8:00 P.M. on Saturday night and we've already gone out, come home, had sex, and are ready for a midnight snack." He laughs, too.

"I told you I was old now, babe. I think I picked you up *at* 8:00 for our first date. Do you remember that?" He strokes my arms since I'm still standing between his legs and I brace my hands on his thighs as he does.

"I do remember it," I say.

"Did you ever think about me, over the years?"

My cheeks turn hot. Do I tell him the truth? *Yeah, I was basically obsessed with you until...Liam.* No, don't think so, but I also can't lie. My red cheeks are definitely giving me away. He smiles, knowing.

"Yes, I did. Did you? Think about me?"

He nods. "I thought about you a lot. Too much probably."

He reaches up to brush hair out of my face, then continues, "I even went as far as tracking you down...and there may have been Google searches over the years." My cheeks have definitely gone full Flaming Hot Cheeto now. *Matthias Scala Googled me?*

"Well, I can admit I never Googled you. I was always worried I'd see some news article that said you'd married a supermodel or something." I laugh. He doesn't.

"About that..." *wait, what?*

I whisper, "Are you married to a supermodel?" Now he does laugh.

"No, sweetheart. That's not where I was going with that." He pulls me into him, tighter, forcing my arms up and around his neck, then he lifts me to sit on his lap. "I was going to tell you that I actually haven't been with anyone since we broke up. Well, as in a relationship. I haven't been in a relationship with anyone for the last, you know, 17 years." He shrugs, but I'm so astonished I can barely move. I just stare at him.

"Like haven't been with anyone in a serious relationship, like not even sexually?" I don't know if I could believe he hasn't been with anyone, period.

"No, I-I've had sex, I just haven't been in any relationships." He laughs a little, "You're the first woman I've even brought here." He motions with his hand around his room.

"Really?" I ask, with a corny smile on my face. He blushes.

"Yes, really."

I lean forward and kiss him. One of *our kisses*. The kind that could go on for hours, that lives in my head for days, but I pull away before we get too caught up. I have to ask. "Is this why you were so determined to tell everyone we were together?" He looks down, almost ashamed.

"I mean, that's part of it. I just really..." He stops, then regains his composure, "Yes, I want everyone to know you're with me. Yes, it's been awhile since I've done the relationship thing, and I'm still trying to figure it all out. Yes, I am going to get it wrong. Like I did at your house the other day or like when I planned the trip without talking to you. And again, like I did tonight. I'm sorry, Brit. You're the only thing I've ever done right, so if you need there to not be a label, we will not have a label. But to me, we are together. I am committed to you. I probably always have been. I'm happy to wait for you to catch up. I mean, hopefully, you will catch up," he sighs out, then looks at me.

"I think I could be convinced to have a label. Now. I *wasn't* when you started telling people, but I *do* appreciate you explaining where you're coming from. Next time, can you not steamroll me, though? That's something my ex-husband did to me and it drives me crazy, and it hurts my feelings."

"I promise I won't. I care about you so much, Brit. I don't think you have a clue, do you?" He searches my face for the answer, holding my chin in his hand to look at me.

"I'm starting to understand," I say back to him quietly.

"Okay, so does this mean I can call you my girlfriend?" I blush and nod. While I may not be hundred percent ready for this next step, I know Matthias is and I want to give him this chance. He's deserving of this chance. "Great. What can I get my *girlfriend* for dinner? Do you want Chinese, Greek, Kebab?" I go to open my mouth, but he stops me, "Wait, wait, I know. You want Kung Pao chicken with pan-fried noodles from the place on First Street," he pauses. "Did I get it right?"

I can't help but smile. "You got it so right, babe." *How does he still remember that?* He just stands up, holding me in his arms, and starts walking towards the main living area. "I can walk, you can put me down."

He places a kiss on my forehead, and says, "I know, but just let me take care of you, okay? Also, I'm dropping you off on the couch while I go order. You need to pick out what we're watching." He walks us around to the front of his over-sized leather sectional, sets me down in the corner, and hands me an Apple TV remote.

"What are you in the mood for?" I call out to him, but I think he walked into the kitchen.

"Whatever you want, babe!" he yells back. Okay then, Queen Charlotte it is. I open his Netflix, but stop. In his 'Continue Watching,' *When Harry Met Sally* is sitting there, like a movie recommending a person. Like a sign from the Nora Ephron movie gods, I've made the right choice.

————

"Are you sure you can't stay?" Matthias asks me as I put my dress back on. He comes up behind me, refastening the dress, then gently massages my neck. *Oh my god*, how can I say no to this man when he touches me like this?

"It's not fair to ask me when you're massaging me like that."

He chuckles, "Oh, I know."

"I have to go home. The girls are there. So is Jess, and Damian, too." His hand tenses before he stops entirely. I turn to face him, his expression slightly hardened. "Does it bother you that Damian is staying at my house?"

"Yes," he says nonchalantly, just matter of fact. I get it. I guess I'd feel the same.

"Okay, but you do understand that he and I share children? And they're entitled to see their father, and that will never change, right?" I hope my tone doesn't come out as bitchy. I try to say it gently, but firmly.

"I understand why that's important to you, yes."

"Great, because yeah, my own father was a complete waste of human space, but Damian isn't. He's a good dad, and the girls deserve a present parent like him in their life."

Matthias rubs my back in understanding. "I get it, but it doesn't mean I have to like it, okay?" That's fair. If the tables were turned, I'd feel the exact same way.

"Okay," I say, then slip my heels back on. Matthias throws on the t-shirt I was just wearing and a pair of driving mocs. And God, he could wear a garbage bag and still be gorgeous. I can't stop smiling at him when he slides back up to me. He pulls me into an embrace and drops his forehead to mine.

"I wish we could always be like this," his whisper comes out softly. *I wish that, too.* "What are you doing tomorrow?"

"I'm not sure. I might try and take Jess to Colton's for late lunch or dinner. I don't know yet."

"Well, if you can pencil me in, I'd love to see you." My heart falters a moment because I don't know the next time I'll be able to see him, *like this.* The girls will be with me the rest of the summer, and while Jess hasn't given me a definitive departure, once she leaves, I won't feel comfortable leaving the girls at home alone at night. And it's not like him and I can have sex at my place. If the girls could hear me crying, chances are high they'll be able to hear us having sex. I absolutely can't subject them to that. I'm sure I've already scarred them enough with all the excessive sobbing.

Ugh, it doesn't even end there. Then when they go back to school, I go back to Virginia, for at least a month, if not more, while they get settled. Matthias reads me and asks, "What is it?"

"It's just, I don't know when we'll be able to see each other, like this," I gesture to him and me and then to his room, "again." It's certainly not like how it was with Liam. No chance to just hole up and make love for a month straight. Not that that was a good idea. I look down at my pregnant belly. And then what happens when I have the baby? I'll be on parent duty every single day. There'll never be a chance to be like that with Mats. Not for a very long time, if ever. It makes me sad that I won't get that time with him. He's just thrown straight into the lion's den of my life. I sniff and crinkle my nose to try and hold back the tears. *Fucking hormones.*

"We will see each other, babe."

"I know, but we won't just have time to ourselves. Let alone intimate time." I sniffle, then laugh at the ridiculousness of the situation. "I like having sex with you." I give him a mock sad face as real tears fall.

"Okay, babe. Come here." He slips his arms around me, putting my cheek to his chest. "I *love* having sex with you, but that's not all I'm in this for. I want to be with you, and if that means always being around your family, that's what we'll do. And if it means sneaking around to fool around like we used to, that's what we'll do. too."

"Are you sure that's what you want, though? You could be with some-" he cuts me off.

"Stop suggesting that, Brit. I only want to be with you, okay? And if it has to be on less-than-ideal terms, so be it." His hands trail up and down my back seductively and I know I have to have him one last time. Without me saying a word, he reaches up and moves his hands to the dress hooks at my neck, undoing them, causing the straps to fall and exposing my breasts. I let the rest of the dress fall, again, then inch his tee up with my hands.

He sheds the t-shirt, sweats, and his shoes, then lifts me up and sets me on the bed, removing my heels swiftly. He crawls over me, but I shake my head, pushing on his shoulder for him to roll over and he does, falling happily on his back.

"Trust me, babe. I'm going to want this all the time. We'll find a way, I promise," he says, then grips my hips tightly to slide me onto his waiting and ready cock. My hands are placed on his pecs, arms straight as I push down on him and throw my head back in ecstasy. I'm in the habit of no longer accepting promises or making them either, but hopefully, we can try because I want Mats and I to have our chance. I don't want to regret the should have, could have, might haves anymore.

As I slide down, he thrusts upwards and we grind together. His hand comes up to play with my nipples as my nails dig into his chest. The harder I claw at him, the harder he thrusts, and we go back and forth, neither of us wanting this moment to end.

"Stay with me tonight, Brit," Matthias gets out in between thrusts. I can't, though. It's bad enough I'm pregnant with someone else's baby. I have to set a better example than this for the girls, no matter the circumstances. I shake my head no, and he roars when he thrusts into me.

He flips us easily, placing my back against the mattress. "I don't like it when you say no to me," he practically growls. *Fuck yes*, a little role playing is exactly what I want.

"I don't *want* to say no to you..."

"Then don't," he bites back, lifting my left leg to his shoulder and driving into me.

"A compromise?" I wager.

"I'm listening."

"When we're in the bedroom, I won't say no to you here." He drops my leg and braces himself over me, kissing me with his all.

"You've gotta deal, sweetpea." I laugh at the nickname and his fervor both. He rails me like I've never been fucked before. Just as I start to get close, he pulls out and instructs me, "Flip over, babe." I get on all fours in front of him, and he pushes in slowly to start. The change in angle has me clenching my fists in the sheets and he presses down on my back, forcing my ass higher and my chest lower to the bed.

"Brit, not tonight, but soon, your ass is mine, babe." As I'm about to tell him I'm close, he beats me to it, leaning forward to rub my clit. "Come with me, baby," he whispers over me. I nod, and when he dips a hand into my hair, tugging me back, I come hard. I grasp onto the sheets for dear life as my muscles contract and pull his throbbing cock in. He grunts, slamming my ass against him as he fills me for the second time tonight.

We stay like that for several moments until he releases his hold on my hair and moves his cock out of my body, but he doesn't move away. I turn around to look at him, and like the words are written on his forehead in Sharpie, I can see it. He's in love with me.

Matthias opens his mouth to say something, but changes his mind and closes up instead. I turn over to my back and he moves forward, to lay beside me, so I roll to face him. "I'd do anything to make this work, babe. *Anything*," he says.

I just nod my head solemnly and kiss him like it's the last time, with *my* everything. All my hopes and dreams for us, all the years of yearning, but never having. I put it out there. It's not words that say I love you, but it's in my actions. In my touch. There's a part of me that *will* always love Matthias, whether I can verbalize it or not. Whether he's my soul mate or not, there's something between us that's just so right. We come together so...right. When I let his face go and move off the bed to use the toilet, he just says, "Same, babe," to my back as I walk away.

SEVENTEEN

BRITAIN

Matthias squeezes my hand to pull my attention away from the low hills as we drive. "My dad," he clears his throat, "asked for your number. Is it alright if I give it to him?"

"Oh, sure." I go back to looking out the window as we pass a cattle ranch. The moonlight glints off the iron sign at the entrance. I could have sworn it said Scala Ranch for a minute. "Do you know why your dad wants to meet with me?" I turn to look at Matthias.

He doesn't say anything for a moment, just focusing on the road, but finally he says, "I think he just wants to hear what you've been up to. Georgia always kept him pretty well informed about what you were doing, and it's been a couple years since he's had an update." Yeah, not since Georgia passed away. I nod silently.

"What was Constantine like as a dad?" I ask him. I remember being so jealous over the way they were together.

Like Sandy was born to be a mom and grandma, I always sort of pictured Constantine the same way. *The consummate father*, always up for a game of catch, happy to teach you how to change a spare tire, protective and comforting.

"Well, I don't have anything to compare him to, but I think he was a good dad. He taught me how to fish and about business. He showed up to all my soccer games. He always picked out his own birthday gifts for me each year. Which is good because if it was entirely up to Julie, all I would've gotten was socks and underwear." He laughs, but man that woman is...*special*. "I don't know, I mean, I guess I could compare him to Julie, in which case he was a rockstar. Why do you ask?"

"Just curious." I sit and think about how different Alex's life would've been if Constantine would have raised him instead of Ray. What sort of traumas could have been avoided? Of course, I wouldn't even exist in that scenario, though. Or Matthias and I would be half-siblings. *Ick.*

I don't think about Ray much, if ever. Even the sound of his name in my head is foreign. I have absolutely no association with him. It's wild, because I look at Matthias, Max, Niko, and Silas, and to remove Constantine from their lives would be removing what makes them, well, *them*. I can only imagine how different all of our lives would've been if Constantine had just been added to ours. I shouldn't think that because it would've led to the destruction of their family, but I am envious. Probably always will be.

"You're lucky to have him, Mats." He glances over at me and squeezes my hand.

"I know, babe. I hope I can be half the dad he was," he says, then moves a hand over to my belly in a loving gesture.

Dad. Peanut is going to have one hell of a convoluted family dynamic and father-figure scenario. I feel my chest tighten with shame and guilt. Someday will the peanut be wondering why I didn't stay with Liam so they could be raised by both parents in the same home? *Fuck, I've made a mess of my life, my kids' lives.*

I let out an anxious sigh as we start getting closer to my house. It feels a bit like Cinderella coming home at the stroke of midnight. The rose-colored glasses get lifted off, and reality starts to take over. Even with running into Julie and Liam, tonight felt like a dream. Getting to be with Matthias and enjoy each other was something I needed, and didn't even know. But now, all I can think about is Jess, and Liam's letter, and custody agreements (yes, plural,) and bicoastal living schedules. *And it's fucking overwhelming.*

Like a sixth sense, Matthias sees the shift. As we pull into the drive, he relinquishes my hand to maneuver into park. He doesn't immediately kill the engine or move to get out just yet, though.

"I know it's a lot to work out, and a lot to figure out, but I'm here, Brit. I'm not going anywhere, and I'll support you however you need. Whenever you need it." *He's not going to like this request, though.*

"There is something you can support me with..." I say quietly.

"Anything, babe."

"I'm going to ask Liam to come to my ultrasound next week." I pause, trying to gauge his reaction, but it's unreadable so far. "And I just need you to be okay with it." He doesn't say anything, but he turns his head away from me to look out the driver's window. His body language is response enough, and my shoulders drop with disappointment.

We sit there for several minutes, completely silent when I try again, "This baby deserves to have their dad be part of their life, and I can't let my feelings or history get in the way of that." I don't know if Liam will be a good dad or not, but he deserves the chance to at least try. I won't be the one to prevent him.

"Brit, please don't do it," Matthias says, then turns to look at me with tear-lined eyes. I can understand how hard this is, but it's not up for discussion.

"I have to, Matthias. It's non-negotiable. I'm asking for your support, not your permission." I wait, the next move is his. If he doesn't say anything, I'll get out of this car and leave it all behind because I won't fight over this for the next 18 years with a partner. My partner is going to have to accept that I have two exes that have to be part of their kids' lives, or they won't, and they won't be my partner. I'd rather know now, I guess.

"I want to be the one at the ultrasound appointment," Matthias finally speaks up without looking at me.

"I understand, but I don't think having *everybody* at the appointment at the same time is a good idea."

"No, I mean, I want it to just be you and me. Don't invite Liam. He had his chance to be present, and a dad."

"Well, that's not really how parenting works. You don't screw up once and then you're fired. You screw up, and then you get better. That's how it goes."

Matthias turns to look at me, hardly a speck of warmth in his expression. "I know I'm not a parent, Britain, but you don't have to condescend to me." *What the hell?*

"I'm not trying to be condescending. But really, this isn't up for discussion. I just wanted to let you know, and I'd hoped that you could support my decisions like you said you would." It's always, *'I'll be there for you,' but* only as long as it's on my terms and you're doing what I want you to. Maybe he thinks I'm being just as immovable on the subject, but I can't bend on this. I just can't.

I wait, hoping to hear him change his mind, but it doesn't come. He doesn't say anything. At all. But he does move his hands to brace the steering wheel and turn to look straight ahead, giving me the universal sign of 'I'm ready to go.' *Fine.* I unbuckle my seat belt, grab my purse, and get out of the car, but don't shut the door just yet.

"I know it's a lot. I know *I'm* a lot, but don't tell someone you'd do *anything* to make it work or that you're ready to support anyway, anyhow, when it's not true." He doesn't move or turn to me, and he definitely doesn't say anything. So I shut the door and walk up the pathway towards the house, expecting him to stop me. To call out for me and say, "Wait!" But he doesn't. *Wow.* Instead, the only sound I hear is that of his car driving away.

At least I know now. *Damn, Britain, can't you get anything right in your life for once?*

I stop at the front door and hesitate. There's not one part of me that wants to go in. It's only 10:15, and chances are there's at least someone hanging around on the main level making a stealth entrance impossible. *I can't pretend to be okay right now.* So I plop onto the bench in the front courtyard instead. Slipping off my shoes, I pull my knees into my chest so I have a place to rest my forehead, and I cry.

When does this all get easier? Is it when you remove

romantic entanglements? Is that when your life gets simpler? I think back to a couple months ago, when it was just me at the house in Virginia, all alone.

Ha! Things were definitely simpler then. They weren't *better*, but at least I wasn't pregnant, with two baby daddies and a confusing mess of a life. Ironically, if I had just listened to Damian, or even Jess, I wouldn't be here right now. They warned me against moving into things too quickly. And now they're proven right and it's like my 24-hour engagement all over again — embarrassing. Mortifying. Pathetic. *Cringe.*

———

"Britain?" The word echoes in my mind like I'm underwater, or whoever is saying the words is. I just clench my eyes tighter; I'm not ready for consciousness.

"Britain, baby, come on," the voice says, and then I'm floating. I levitate off the bench, weightlessly, into a warm cocoon to travel in. I snuggle in deeper, craving the warmth, trying desperately to get closer to it. *"Christ, you're freezing,"* the voice says, sending a chill running down my spine, yet simultaneously soothing me.

It could have been an hour or thirty seconds, but then I feel like I'm falling, gently. Like a feather falling from the sky, weightlessly drifting into another pile of feathers. I snuggle into the feather bed and practically purr from the comfort and the heat.

"Can I get you something to change into?" The voice wafts over me in waves. It's so deep, it sounds so warm.

"S-ssocks, and a sss-sweatshirt. P-pp-please." I lay back as warm fingers drift over me, moving me, rearranging me. At one point, they even hold me up prone to slip a sweatshirt over my naked body. I'm here, but a million miles away, my head and heart too dreary to join the living world.

"I'm going to leave now, okay?" the voice grows farther away, taking all the warmth with it.

I shiver and chatter back, "P-please d-d-don't l-leave m-me." I feel the presence move closer and I sink deeper when they get nearer. Deeper into my bed, deeper into my slumber, and deeper into blissful warmth.

From the edges of consciousness, I hear the quietest "Never" whispered over me. And then, like a gift from God, peaceful, black, stillness consumes me.

―――――

We're together, in my dream. I can feel him, I can hear him, but he is unreachable. He is all around me, but not connected to me. He is tangible. I just have to wake up and claim him. *Wake up, Britain. Wake up!*

But then the voice is there, soothing me again. Shushing me. The warmth pulls me against their body, and I feel like I'm home. *Wake up!* I can't, though. Not when all I feel is rightness and warmth and happiness right here, right now. I want this feeling to last forever. If I just keep sleeping, maybe it will...

―――――

I wake up to a sharp pain in my neck and an ache in my back. I turn over, slowly, to see the sheets and duvet on the other half of the bed are mussed, like someone else was sleeping there. I try to rub the sleep out of my eyes and make sense of it all, but I can't. *Did Matthias stay over?* The sleep hangover I'm wading through is unlike any I've felt before. My limbs feel heavy and slow, and when I go to sit up, my head slams against my skull painfully and I hiss from the discomfort.

Did someone turn the heat on? It feels like it's 90 degrees. And why am I wearing a sweatshirt? And socks? The last thing I really remember from last night was sitting on the bench outside and then coming to bed. Maybe somebody helped me to bed? But I don't think so.

Ugh, I don't feel good. Dropping back on the mattress, I fumble for my phone on the bedside table. I open my messages and type out a text with one eye closed. The light hurts.

BRITAIN

> What cold medicine can I take while pregnant?

I close both eyes and wait for a response, but it never comes. Instead, Jess enters my room, immediately taking a thermometer to my forehead. She lets out a little huff and then the thermometer beeps loudly letting me know, I'm in the red. I've got a fever.

"I don't want to be sick," I say to Jess, then groan.

"I know, but at least you've got me here to take care of you. Unfortunately, you probably got it from Eden. She had a fever last week. Sorry, babe."

I just nod. "Uh huh. What can I take?"

"What hurts?"

"My head, my neck, my back. But I think the neck and back are from sleeping on the bench outside last night, and–"

"WAIT, why the fuck were you sleeping on the bench last night?!" Jess practically screams at me.

"It's a long story. I'll tell you all about it once sights, sounds, and vibrations stop making me want to puke." I can see Jess simmering with quiet rage.

"Fine, but you will tell me later." She points a menacing, no-bullshit finger in my direction and I nod. Words hurt.

"I'll be back with fluids, medicine, and food. You don't get the medicine until you eat, though."

"Yes, ma'am," I say as Jess marches downstairs. I can hear her yelling at Damian to go to the store for something and both girls making their way up the stairs. Caroline and Elodie stop once they get to my doorway though.

"You have a fever?" Caroline asks.

"I do. I don't want to give it to you, otherwise I'd ask for a hug." I make a sad face.

"Jess is having dad run out for some stuff. Want anything special? I'm gonna go with him." Elodie asks cheerfully.

"I would kill for some rainbow sherbet." I swallow and realize my throat hurts like a mother. *Fuck, I hope it's not strep.*

"Done! Love you, Mom. Feel better!" Elodie chirps out, then bounces away and down the stairs.

"Wh-what can you do to feel better when you're pregnant?" Caroline asks. I can hear the worry in her voice.

"The usual stuff. I'll be fine. Promise. It hurts to talk, though. Wanna come put something on the TV and hang out in here with me?" Caroline just nods and walks over to the loveseat at the foot of the bed and turns on the TV while I shut my eyes and wait for Jess to be back with food and meds. My respite doesn't last long when my phone pings.

"Do you need me to get it for you?" Caroline asks, half out of her seat. I motion for her to sit down, then grab my phone.

MATTHIAS

When you wake up, we need to talk. I'm sorry.

BRITAIN

Okay. I'm sick. Hurts to talk. Head is pounding. Is it okay if we talk later?

Yes, and let me know if you need anything, okay? Feel better.

I drop the phone back on to the nightstand and wait for Florence Nightingale to come force feed me.

———

"Knock, knock. Is it okay if I come in?" It's not even noon when Silas pops his head through my bedroom door. Matthias probably called him.

"Yep," I croak out, then struggle to sit up. "I'm guessing this isn't a social call." I look over to see his medical duffle in hand.

"I mean, if you want it to be, it can," he says jovially.

"I feel like death and talking makes me want to cry, so no."

He laughs at me. "Okay, let me just take some vitals and then I'll check out your throat." Silas takes my temp, my blood pressure and pulse, then asks me to breathe while he listens. I'm a little embarrassed; I'm not even wearing under-wear underneath my sweatshirt, but at the same time, it's

Silas. And he literally watches women take a shit during delivery. I feel like nothing could phase him. He slips the end of the stethoscope up my back, giving me chills.

The feeling triggers a memory from my dream the night before. I had the chills, and someone was comforting me and it felt so nice. I sigh. Not real, though.

"Alright, you clearly have a fever. Otherwise, blood pressure and pulse are good, lungs sound clear. Let's look at your throat. Say ahh." Silas shines a light into the back of my throat as I sit there open-mouthed. "Yikes. It looks angry back there. Good thing I swiped a strep test from the office next door," he says with a devilish grin. Of course, Silas' version of mischief is stealing a strep test. I laugh inwardly. *Such a good boy.*

I go to ask him who called him to come, but my throat burns, and I'm too tired to care. Silas takes the swab and says he'll let me know the results in 15 minutes.

"Don't forget, Brit, lots of fluids, lots of rest, and don't forget to eat." Silas arches his eyebrow at me in his sternest way possible. "We're gonna have words at your next appointment if you've lost weight again." I nod and close my eyes. *I know, I know.*

True to his word, Silas texts 15 minutes later.

SILAS

Strep was positive. I'm going to send the prescription to the Robles Lake Safeway. Do you need me to pick it up for you?

BRITAIN

No, I'll send Damian, but thank you, Silas. I really appreciate it.

> Feel better. I want to see you at my office this Thursday, okay?

> I'll be there with bells on.

Silas taps back a "haha."

BRITAIN

> Can you pick up my antibiotics from the grocery store? Please?

DAMIAN

> Yep, I'll head over now to wait.

> Thank you. Also, did you help me to bed last night?

> Huh? No. I passed out watching Top Gun in bed at like 9.

> Nm. Will you just send Jess or the girls up with the meds once they're here? And thank you, again.

> Will do

It was just a dream. Maybe in my fever-induced stupor, I slept on the opposite side of the bed first, then moved over. I don't know, I don't care. I'm just ready for some meds to kick in and kick my ass.

EIGHTEEN

BRITAIN

"Hey, Brit," Damian nudges me, gently waking me up.

"Mmm..." I groan out and stretch, slowly opening my eyes. "What's up?" He's sitting on the edge of my bed, dressed in a suit, looking handsome and crisp. A stark comparison to my disheveled mess. He pushes the hair out of my face, placing the backs of his fingers flat against my forehead, gauging my temp.

"How are you feeling, darling?"

"So much better. Infinitely better." I swallow and relief floods me when my throat doesn't hurt in the slightest.

"I have to head out. I have those meetings in San Jose, but I was wondering if it'd be alright for me to come back here at the end of the week?" I tilt my head slightly. I'm not really confused, just surprised.

"Of course," I smile at him. "This house is just as much

yours as it is mine." I laugh quietly. I mean, it's basically his money that paid for it.

"It's your house, Brit. Our — and I do mean *our* — hard work has paid for it."

"Okay," I say quietly. Damian's changing. The old Damian wouldn't have flat-out claimed that it was his money paying for everything, but it would have been implied. And yet, now here we are, sitting on my bed, completely comfortable with one another. I feel like we're finally on the same page. We've reached a state of equilibrium, and it feels good. I'm actually going to miss having him around.

"The girls and I would love for you to come back after your meetings conclude." I shoot him a smile, one that he returns.

"If you start feeling worse and need me to come back, just call, okay?" He lets out an ironic laugh, "Honestly, I feel like I'm just a placeholder in these meetings now. I'm just riding this train till we get to my stop, you know?" I do. I know exactly what he means. Life is just pulling you along, but ultimately you have to decide when you're going to get off that ride and start living. I reach out for his hand and he takes it, giving me that one-dimple smile.

"If you ever decide you don't want to do the CEO life anymore, I hope you'll come visit me. My house *is* our house, Damian. We'll always be a part of each other's lives whether we want to or not...but I do want to. I mean, I want you to be part of my life still." I pause, "And I'd love if Summer could join you sometime, too."

Damian's eyes get watery. "You always were too good for me, Brit."

"*But*, if you ever buy a beach house, or an island villa, I hope that 'our house' situation goes both ways." He laughs.

"It will. It *does*. I want you in my life, too, Britain." He squeezes my hand, releasing it, so he can stand up and straighten his tie. He heads towards the door, stopping before he exits. "I'll see you Thursday or Friday, okay? Want me to bring back some clam chowder and sourdough if I make it into San Francisco?"

"Oh my gawd, yes!" He laughs again and turns to leave, but this time I stop him. "Hey!" He turns towards me, "I love you."

"I love you, too. And, B?" His gaze falls to my sweatshirt, "You've been wearing that sweatshirt for two days. You stink." I scoff at him.

"Way to ruin the moment!" He laughs at me before finally leaving. I look down at the sweatshirt and a cold sweat breaks out on my skin. *This is my sweatshirt, the one Liam gave me.* I would never put this on of my own volition. The last time I wore this sweatshirt was the day he proposed to me. I glance over at the other side of the bed where the pillows have been rearranged for sleeping. The decorative euros are stacked neatly on the floor, instead of on the bed like I normally leave them.

Fully aware that I'm losing my mind when I do this, I scooch towards the other side of the bed and smell the pillow. And...it smells like *him. What the fuck?*

"Whatchya doing, weirdo?" Jess asks as she walks into my room. I sit up immediately, like I wasn't just imagining the smell of my ex-fiancé's cologne on my sheets.

"Uh, nothing. I think my sheets smell like a sick bed. Gotta change them today." I shrug it off.

"So does this mean you're feeling better? Because I've been dying to talk to you." I haven't talked to her since she brought me my antibiotics yesterday afternoon. God, that feels like nine years ago, not yesterday.

"Yeah, I feel better. And, *yes*, we need to talk," I say to her, remembering Liam, and the letter, and how she didn't tell me about it. Jess just plops down into the loveseat at the foot of my bed.

"Okay, first things first, why were you sleeping on the bench outside?"

"It was an accident. I wasn't ready to come inside, so I sat down, and *poof!* Asleep. But hey, at the Greek Fest, I ran into Liam again and he said he packed the letter he wrote me in a suitcase." Her face falls. "Why didn't you tell me?"

"I'll get it, hold on," Jess says as she stands up and heads towards my closet. She's back a moment later with a tri-folded letter in hand. "So, when we talked about Matthias and you dating...I was harsh on you. And I felt like I was swaying your opinion or decision, and really how I felt about it was just a reflection of what I'm going through and how crappy I've felt lately. I didn't want to give you the letter combined with my 'don't date him' monologue and have you run back to Liam.

I put it in your closet, so when you got home from your date you'd be able to make an informed decision. I was plan-ning to tell you as soon as you got home. I just thought you'd be able to spend the night with Matthias, then read the letter, and *then* make a decision." She passes me the letter, and I just stare at it. It's a couple pages thick and my name is written in Liam's chicken scratch, scrawled across the front.

"I already made a decision," I say it quietly, my voice still slightly raspy from sickness. Jess' eyes go wide in surprise. "I chose Matthias." Her eyes go even wider, but she doesn't say a word. I look down at the letter in my hands, then back at Jess. "I chose wrong, though." I laugh, lifelessly. "There was never a right choice to make. I'm not going to be with anyone, so none of this matters. Next time, just give me the letter right away, okay?" *Next time.* I laugh in my head. Yeah, the next time you find a long-lost letter from my ex-fiancé, make sure to hand it right over, like it's an everyday occurrence and this is *Days of Our Lives.*

"I'm sorry, Brit." Her tone is solemn.

I just shrug. "It is what it is. I'm just going to focus on trying to be healthier, and the girls, and the baby, and let life be quiet for a while." She nods, the guilt on her face apparent.

"I really am sorry."

"Really, don't be. *I'm sorry* that you're feeling like crap and can't talk to me about it."

"Yeah..." is all she says back.

"Well, when you're ready. I'm here."

"I know."

"Okay, I, uh, desperately need a shower and to change, and then let's have coffee and I'll tell you all about the Greek Fest. Sound good?"

Jess nods. "Yeah, yes. I really want to know what happened."

"Alright, I'll see you down in a minute." Jess just gives a dip of her head and exits, leaving me alone, with *it.* The *full* explanation I've been waiting for. Will it change anything? Do I want it to change anything? *No.* I need to keep a level head.

Damian and I have just gotten to a good place. We're friends who co-parent and care about each other, but without the messy romantic love and intimacy, and now I need that with Liam. I need to uncomplicate our situation. I need to stop hating him *and* stop loving him. I need a co-parent, not a life partner. I already have two of those, Jess and Damian. And it seems like every time I open my heart — *and my legs* — everything goes to shit. I'm closing the door on that part of my life.

Maybe when this baby is in elementary school, and the girls are in college, I can revisit dating, but right now, it doesn't make sense. This mythical person would have to be perfect in every single way. Otherwise, it's just not worth it. Since that's not fair or realistic, and since said perfect person doesn't exist, I just need to let the dream of finding happiness with someone go.

I roll off the bed and walk the letter back to my closet. My old phone, sitting in the charging station, is calling my name and I know what I need to do. There's new messages from Liam, but I don't bother to read them. I just power it off, then place the phone and letter beside each other in the top drawer for another day.

After a quick shower and change of clothes, I check my phone and see new messages from Matthias.

MATTHIAS

Are you going to call me back? We need to talk.

Please, call me.

My stomach turns as I close out those messages and open a new one. My fingers tremble slightly as I type out the text.

BRITAIN

Hi, this is Britain. There is an ultrasound appointment this Thursday at 1:00 P.M. at Silas' office. You're welcome to come, but don't feel like you have to be there. I have a prenatal check first, which usually lasts 30 minutes. If you want to come for just the ultrasound, that's probably around 1:30.

His reply comes through before I can even set the phone back down.

LIAM

I'll be there.

Okay, I'll send you the address.

I don't think I can put the next thing off any longer. I open my contacts, clicking on Matthias' name. It only rings once before he answers.

"Britain! God, I-I-I'm so sorry. Let me explain-"

I cut him off. "You don't have to explain anything to me, Mats. Really. I completely understand where you're coming from and how you feel. If the tables were turned, I would absolutely not want your ex at an ultrasound." I pause, hearing him sigh out in relief. "But I think it's probably for the best that this ends now."

"Don't do this, Brit," he says, his voice low and tense.

"I know you hate hearing this, but you deserve someone less complicated. Someone who can put you first." I don't want to sugarcoat it; the root of some of these problems is that Matthias doesn't come first for me, not even close. There's the girls, the baby, Damian, Jess, and ultimately myself. I would put all of them above Matthias. I love him, but not enough to let the rest of my life fall by the wayside. And I think maybe I'm finally realizing if I'm not taking care of me, I can't be good for anyone else. It didn't work with Damian and it doesn't work with Mats. *Nothing works with Liam, so there's no comparison there.*

"Stop fucking saying that, Brit. I choose you. Wherever I fall in your arbitrary list, I still choose you. Because guess what? There's going to be times in our life where you're not first for me. The company is my life, and I'll have to prioritize that. You will, of course, be the only person romantically, but I get it, okay? I understand, so why can't you just accept that I'm okay with it?"

"Because you're not okay with it! If I prioritize being a successful parent, that means being a good co-parent, and that includes inviting Liam to doctors appointments, and ultimately, to be part of my life. And you really just dropped me off the other night and didn't even say goodbye to me...you wouldn't even look at me because you couldn't support my decision. It's unnecessary stress. I can't be walking around on eggshells about every decision I have to make moving forward. Not that you'll make me ask permission, but I'll be so worried how it'll affect you, it will stress me out."

"You're being really selfish, Britain." *What the fuck?*

"No, Matthias, I'm telling you I can't give you everything you want and need, but that you deserve to find that with someone else. I'm literally doing this for your happiness!"

"Then what happens when you're the only thing that makes me happy? WHAT THEN, BRIT?!" he yells at me.

Lowering my voice, I ask, "Please don't yell at me, okay?" I can hear him clear his throat, maybe not fully aware how loud he just shouted.

"17 years, Britain. I've waited 17 years. I didn't do all that just to fuck you after the Greek Fest and then say goodbye again." The way he says it sounds crass. "Or is that all you wanted from me, huh? Is it?"

"You're out of your mind if you think that's what I wanted. I wanted to be with you. I fucking chose you, and all I needed was for you to support my decisions. But the very first thing I ask of you, you put your feelings, wants, and needs before mine and this baby's. Of which you have every right to do, but that's not the type of partnership that's going to work for me. I can't be with someone who steamrolls me or wants me to ask permission. I'm not that meek girl anymore."

"You were never meek, Britain. You're the strongest woman I know." *That can't be possible.* "Please, give me another chance. I love you so fucking much," he laughs ironically, "so much I hate the thought of sharing you with anyone. And yeah, that includes your kids, but I'm learning, okay? Let me learn how to love you again, the way you need to be loved now, please?" My own words come back to haunt me, *you screw up and you're fired? No, you screw up and you get better.*

"Britain, I know you didn't say it, but I know you love me, too. I know it. I felt it, 17 years, and that never went away. That means something. That doesn't happen for no reason. And yes, we've both changed and our lives are different, but that's going to make it that much sweeter when we figure this out. And we will. Because I was telling the truth when I said I'd do anything to make this work. I'll do anything, including supporting your decision to include Liam in your child's life. I know I'm going to have to give, okay? I know. It's just hard for me...I'm not used to it." I'm not ready to blindly say yes to him, but there's a nagging part of me that knows I'm not ready to fully relinquish this either.

"Can I think about it? I do appreciate you coming around to being okay with Liam being there, but I don't want it to have to be so hard, Mats," I plead with him.

"I know, babe, I'm sorry. I don't want to make any part of your life harder. I promise."

"I'm going to think on it, and maybe let's meet for coffee in a couple days." Hopefully a cool-down period, a session with Carla, and a deep chat with Jess, will help bring some clarity.

"Okay, I'll see you on...Wednesday? Is that okay?" he asks.

I nod silently. "Yeah, Wednesday."

"Okay, and Brit, I'm so sorry. I just hate thinking about you-" he stops himself. "It doesn't matter. I love you. I'm going to keep choosing you and keep showing up. I promise I will get better."

I don't have much to say to that. Talk is cheap. "I'll see you then, and Matthias?"

"Yeah?"

"Thanks for having Silas make that house call. I really appreciate it."

"I don't know what you mean," he responds, sending the hairs on the back of my neck rising.

"You didn't call Silas to come check on me when I was sick?"

"No?" It comes out like a question.

"Oh, weird. Um, maybe Jess or Damian reached out. I just assumed it was you because I had texted you about being sick."

"I should have thought about that. I guess I didn't realize how sick you were, I'm sorry. Just another way I failed, huh?"

"Stop. We're not going down that path." I can hear Jess yelling at me to get my ass downstairs. "Listen, I have to go. I will see you later this week."

He replies, remorsefully, "Okay, I love you. Bye." I can't say it back, though.

"Yep, bye," is all I get out in return. I look down at the sweatshirt I shucked off before showering. *His* sweatshirt. I already know, but I check anyway.

Opening the app on my phone, I check the doorbell camera from Saturday night and there he is. It wasn't my imagination. Liam walks towards my front door carrying my bags of cookies and olive oil, then falls to his knees when he sees me curled up on the bench. *Fuck.* I think about the other night and my deliriousness. About how even in my illness-induced coma, how fucking euphoric it felt, him holding me. *Goddamn it, Liam. Leave me alone.*

I get up from the bed and yell down to Jess, "I'll be down in like ten minutes, okay? Gotta do something." I hear her yell back an affirming sound, so I move on shaky legs to my closet. I hate being so fucking indecisive! *No decision is a decision, though, and inaction is still an action.* I recall Carla walking me through this. I need to know. It's time.

Opening the drawer feels cinematic, like time slows and the paper calls my name. I hold it in the palm of my hand, then slide to the floor, knowing I don't want to be standing for whatever this holds for me. I just want to put this part of my life to rest, and this last piece of the puzzle is it. At least I hope it is.

I flip open the letter. *Dear Britain...*

NINETEEN

LIAM

I've been standing outside Matt's office for nearly ten minutes, fuming, my arms crossed in front of my chest, waiting. I'm itching to say something, but I wait until the call is over to enter. When I do, I don't knock. *Fuck that* and *fuck him*. He sees me enter and it's like a standoff. Who'll make the first move? *Me*.

"Don't you ever raise your voice at the mother of my child. EVER. AGAIN. *Or I will fucking bury you*." He doesn't say anything, just stares at me coldly, making me laugh a sadistic laugh. "And that's if you're lucky and Alex doesn't get to you first." I turn on my heel to leave the office, unsurprised to see Max and Niko standing in the doorway, ready. I nod at each of them and they part to allow me through. Matt doesn't respond until I'm almost in the hall.

"Fuck you, Liam. You don't even deserve to be the father

of her child. You might be in their DNA, but I'm the one they'll be calling *daddy*." *Red*. All I see is red.

It only takes two long strides till I'm in front of him, my fist finding his face easily. The crack is audible throughout the office, followed by gasps from people in their cubicles. But I give zero fucks. I think about the Greek Fest and the way he had his hands all over her the whole time. How he wouldn't stop touching her stomach. *Mine*. He did it because he knew I was there. He wanted to mark his territory. He doesn't even have a clue; she's never been his.

Matt cups his face as his nose spews blood down the front of his shirt while Max and Niko move into the office. They come to stand between him and me, but they don't push me away.

"You're such a fucking bastard, Liam. You might have had her for six weeks, but I've stayed with her for 17 years. And counting." The asshole winks at me as I make a fist with my hand, then release it just to make a fist all over again. Niko gives me a head nod to shoo me out, and I know he's right. I need to leave, at least Matt's office. But I'm done hiding. I'm ready to get back to work.

Matt's not done, though. "If you would've heard the way she was screaming my name this Saturday, you'd know just how insignificant you are to her." I move forward on instinct alone, but I don't get far. Max gets in my space, backing me up, holding me back. I can barely stand the thought of him being with her. *Goddamn, I want to fucking kill him.* I don't have to use my fists to do it, though.

"Oh yeah? This Saturday, when you fucking left her out in the cold on her front porch? You mean this past Saturday, when I put her to bed and she begged me not to leave? Well, guess what? I didn't, and when her body was pressed against mine, she sure as fuck wasn't thinking about you." Matt stands up in response, spitting blood onto the carpet in his office.

"You're lying."

I shake my head, "No, man, I'm not. She might have started with you, but she finished with me." I push Max back gently and walk out of the office. I don't even notice I'm bleeding until Gina stops me halfway back to my own office.

"Boss, fuck! You're getting blood everywhere!" Yeah, must've busted a stitch open. It was worth it. I don't even feel it. Too much adrenaline, too much rage. And *damn*, too much *hurt. She slept with him?* I feel like my insides are caving in on themselves.

"Get a towel, my laptop, and my keys, Gina. We're working from the road." I motion with my non-bloodied hand for her to go ahead of me.

"I'll meet you at your car in five," she says before hurrying off.

Ignoring the stares and whispers as I walk through the office, I don't stop, I just head straight for my SUV in the parking garage. When I get there, I slam my back against the driver's side door and sink to the hot cement floor. It smells like piss in here, but I don't care. *She fucking slept with him?* I pull my phone out to send a quick text, typing slowly with my left hand.

LIAM

> Also bring a bottle of scotch, a good one.
> From Matt's stash.

Gina just taps back a thumbs up.

I don't realize how hard I'm crying until she walks up to me.

"Jesus, Liam. She did a real number on you, didn't she?" No, I did this.

"It's not like that, Gina. It's not like she fucked me over, okay?"

"It sure doesn't seem that way," she says as she slides down to sit next to me on the floor. "What's so fucking special about her anyways? I mean, I guess she's *mediocre* pretty. Is she fucking hilarious? Give a world-class bj? Richer than sin? Help me understand."

"Don't ever fucking talk about her like that again or you're fired." My tone is biting. I love Gina like a sister, but nobody talks shit about Britain in front of me. Nobody.

"You wouldn't get it, Gina," I say, softening my tone. "You'll probably think I'm a fucking sap, but she's my soul-mate. At least I thought she was. Or maybe she'll always be mine, but I don't think I'm hers. I don't know. All I know is it feels like I'm dying." I sniff as more tears fall. Fucking pathetic, just like all those texts I sent her. Just like showing up at her house in the middle of the night.

"Well, fuck her," Gina says.

"GINA, don't fucking say that."

"No, I don't care. My entire life, I've always heard about this *'Britain.' Britain's so good in school. She has straight A's. She's on the varsity volleyball team. She got into Stanford.* And now she inserts herself into all of our lives and fucking ruins the good thing we all had going. Matt was your best friend and now you guys just got in a fist fight in the office over her. It's bullshit." She drops her head to look at her hands, and when she speaks again, her tone is subdued. "I've been trying to get your attention for years, Liam. She wasn't even here for a month and a half, and you have her knocked up and you're dying for her." I look at her, seeing a tear fall. I smile sadly, and swipe the tear off her face. Gina's tears, while they don't make me happy, don't affect me the same way Britain's do.

"Gina, I know it seems like it's only been six weeks, but for me it's been longer." It's been a hell of a lot longer. "I'm not in any state to be good for anyone, probably not even Britain. Not that that's even an option. Just come on." I stand up, offering her my good hand to get up. She takes it, then wipes the dirt off her ass and hands. I wish I was into Gina like that. She's beautiful, but she's not mine. "You're too young and pretty for me, anyways," I tell her, using my shoulder to bump into hers.

"Yeah, and I've got this award-winning personality to go with it." She rolls her eyes. "Can we get out of here now? This place smells like ass." I barely even notice it anymore.

"Yeah, I need to go see Silas." Gina pushes me to get in the passenger side of my SUV while she hops up into the driver's side.

"Okie-fucking-dokie," she says. I can tell she's pissed, but I don't know what the fuck to do about that. She's like family, I don't *want* her to be hurt, but I've never given her any inclination that there could be something between us. Never.

We pull out of the parking garage and the valley sun assaults my eyes. I slam them shut to block it, and when I do, all I see is Britain and Matt. *Fucking*.

"*Goddamnit*," I groan out, putting my palms to my eye sockets, hoping to stop the assault happening in my mind.

When I open my eyes, I see Gina glance over at me, then back to the road with a worried look on her face.

"I'll be fine, Gina. I just need to get these stitches fixed." And then get fucking plastered and forget about the love of my life screaming out some other guy's name.

It doesn't take long before we're at Silas' office. We're immediately taken back and Silas joins us shortly after, ready to re-do the stitches.

"Another glass puddle?" Silas asks. Gina laughs and I glare at both of them.

"Sorry, man, this time it was your brother's face." Silas doesn't even look up, just getting straight to work on cleaning the cut.

"Which brother? What'd he do?" I never realized how much I like Silas. I always thought he hated us. 'Us' being me and his three brothers. He just never wanted to be around us, but I guess if you tell someone you punched their brother and the response is, "What'd they do?" it makes a bit more sense. He knows what they're like.

"Matt. He slept with Britain." That's not all of it, though, "And he fucking yelled at her."

Silas doesn't even change his tone, just says, "What a dick. Is Britain okay?"

"I don't know, man, you tell me. Is she feeling better?" I ask. Other than a confirmation text from Silas that he saw her on Sunday, I haven't heard anything about how she is. It fucking killed me to leave her when she was so sick, but I didn't want the whole house to wake up with me in her bed. And I've been texting her to check in, but I haven't heard anything. Which makes sense, she texted me from a new number this morning. Silas doesn't say anything, he just nods his head and I feel relief.

My stomach twists into knots thinking about how long she could've been out there if I hadn't come along. The valley might be hotter than Hades, but the hills' temp drops low at night, even in the summer. Thank Christ that Niko was feeling guilty about withholding information about Britain's pregnancy. He offered me her address in exchange for dropping off her bags from the Greek Fest on my way home. She could've ended up in the hospital...or worse. *Or worse. Be pissed at yourself, Liam. If you wouldn't have left, you would have been there, taking care of what's yours.*

"So, uh, I'll be seeing you again this Thursday," I say to him.

"Who's gonna piss you off this time? The wall? Your car?" I laugh, then hiss when he touches a particularly sensitive spot.

"Not for this. Britain asked me to come to her appointment this week." Gina scoffs and rolls her eyes and I shoot her a death glare.

Silas looks at me before responding, "I think that's really awesome, Liam. It's a good one to be at." He shoots me a smile. "The baby will actually look like a baby at this ultrasound." *Our baby.*

"Yeah man, I can't wait." At least I couldn't wait, but then I found out she fucked Matt, and there's that hurt and pain again. How the fuck am I supposed to see her and act like that's no big deal?

Silas makes fast work and before I know it, he's done.

"Try not to bust those open again, okay? You don't want permanent scarring."

I just nod. "Hey, Gina, can you give us a minute?" I ask. She doesn't reply, just slides out of one of the extra chairs and heads out. I wait till she's out of ear shot.

"Do you think you could recommend a counselor? For me?" Jesus, I didn't think it'd be this hard to ask. "I'm at a loss for how to deal with all this." I use my non-injured hand to wave around. Silas just looks at me, waiting to hear it all. "I just want to be a good dad, and a good co-parent, and I lack those skills, okay? And obviously this is all the harder because I'm still in love with Britain, but she's not in love with me." Or she is, but she's shutting it down because to her, I'm just some fleeting phase.

Silas pats me on the back. "Liam, you should be really fucking proud of yourself for asking. I've got like four counselors I think could be a really good fit. I also know a good mediator, so when it comes time for custody agreements, you can have that resource, too."

My eyes get a little bit misty. I've been sleeping on Silas Scala. "Thanks, man."

"I'll text them to you in a little, but you gotta go. I need the room." He ushers me up and out.

Gina's standing in the waiting room with her back against the wall, and when she sees me, she pushes off the wall with her heel.

"Where to now, boss?"

"Home. You good to work out of my house today?"

All she says is, "Yup," popping the "p" at the end. *Alright, Liam, time to work and move the fuck on with your life.*

―――――

What the fuck was I thinking? I can't move on. I can't get shit done. I can't fucking do anything. Gina has to keep asking me the same questions over and over because I don't hear her the first time. Then I can't focus on the second, and by the third, I can't seem to come up with an answer.

"I think we should have another scoth-ch," I slur, reaching for the bottle.

"Uh uh," Gina says, moving the bottle out of my reach.

"Plleeasth?" I give her a devilish grin, trying to exploit the fact she has a crush on me. She doesn't hand over the bottle, though, she does something better. She plays back.

"What do I get if I give it to you?" *Yes, let's bargain.*

"A raise," I say, dropping my fist to the desk. It lands hard and sloppy, but luckily I don't wince from pain. The scotch has numbed me right up.

"Hmm," she ponders, moving out of her chair in my office to come closer. She perches on the edge of my desk, a pen in hand still, and taps it to her lips as she thinks. She shakes her head. "Try harder," then gives me a smile. I know what she wants, but I'm not playing *that* game.

"An extra week of v-vacation!" I exclaim. Gina keeps staring at me, though, giving me that fuck-me gaze. She crosses her legs, then uncrosses them, then spreads them wide, scooting to sit all the way on the desk in front of me.

"You know what I want, boss." Gina leans back on the desk, kicking off her heels and scooting over so she's sitting right in front of me.

"Nuh, uh, Gina. Bad idea." I scooch my chair back away from her, but she hooks her legs around the arms and pulls me in closer.

"Let me make you feel better," she croons out, swiping her tongue over her lips.

"Gina, we're not like that."

"But I want us to be. I'm not asking you to put a ring on it." She leans forward to whisper, "Just use me." I feel a bit sick to my stomach at the thought. There's only one person I want to be with. I close my eyes and picture Britain. My chest gets tight, and then I see Matt, railing her. *Fuck both of them.* I know that I left, but I came back! And she still had sex with him. She was with me in that alley earlier that night. *I bet if I tried, she would've fucked me. Is that who she is?*

She slept with him and then curled up next to me, cuddling with me in her bed. She begged me not to go. The more I think about it, the angrier I get. I don't even realize I'm doing it, but I'm squeezing the arm rests of my desk chair so hard my knuckles have gone white, the stitches taut like they might bust again.

Gina sees the tension, but thinks it's for her.

"I know you want this, Liam." She scoots closer to the edge of the desk, sending her flowy skirt falling to the sides. I look and immediately I regret it.

"Where's your fucking underwear, Gina?" She smiles at this small win, knowing I looked.

"They're in your briefcase." I look over to where it's sitting on my desk. But it's what's behind it that triggers me. In a simple silver frame sits a picture of me and Britain from the morning I proposed to her, my hand splayed across her abdomen. *Our first family photo.* She was probably four or five weeks pregnant when we took that picture. I don't know why I did it, but I had it printed and framed, sitting on my desk in Sonoma.

Stupid, really. I still thought I had a chance then. I mean, fuck, maybe I still do?

"Don't leave me hanging, boss." Gina moves one foot off the arm of the desk chair, placing it on my leg, moving it up higher until she's inches from touching my dick. I think she'd be disappointed to find out that I'm not hard, not in the slightest. I grab her foot and push it back over the chair.

"I'm not going to use you, Gina. And I'm not emotionally available, okay?" The intense buzz is starting to fade. My mouth just feels dry and the pain at the back of my throat is back, reminding me the scotch isn't numbing it anymore. Gina sees where my line of sight has landed and reaches over, flipping the frame down.

She drops her head back in frustration. "Ugh, I'm so tired of this bitch ruining everything."

"Don't fucking call her that, Gina." Gina straightens, looking at me — a daring look.

"Oh yeah, you don't like that?" Gina asks, using her legs to pull my chair closer.

"No. I already told you not to talk bad about her. It pisses me off." This just seems to egg Gina on.

"Oh, no," she says sarcastically, "is someone talking bad about daddy's little whore?"

"I swear to God, Gina. One more comment, and I'll..."

"And?" She arches her eyebrows. "And you'll what? Spank me for being a bad girl?" I close my eyes, trying to block out the visual of Gina bent over my desk as I spank her. *No, I don't want that.* She leans down, picking up the bottle of scotch and pours me a tall glass.

"You can fight this, Liam, but it's going to happen." I'm shaking my head in response when she grabs my chin in her hand, her long fingernails digging into my skin, and forces my head up and down in a nod. She finally releases the desk chair with her legs and pushes me back slightly and I sigh out in relief. *Thank fuck, that's over.*

But it's not. She starts unbuttoning her top, and I can't look away. She hands me the glass of scotch and says, "For your viewing pleasure, boss." Then with a wink, she slips the top off and lets it fall to a puddle on the floor. Of course, there's not a bra in sight. She then sinks down to her knees in front of me.

"This is a two way street, boss. You gotta give a little, too." She reaches out and starts unbuckling my belt, and I just watch her in a daze. I don't want this, but also *fuck Britain.* Gina unzips my pants, but that's as far as she gets.

I think I hear a knock at the door, and it pulls me back into reality. *Fuck this.* In my sternest voice, I tell Gina, "Pick your shirt up off the floor and put it back on, *now.*" Gina halts her striptease at the sound of my voice just as there's another knock at the door.

"You want me to get that?" Gina asks.

"No, whoever it is can fuck off. You need to pick up your shit and go." Her eyes seem to cloud slightly, but eventually she drops down to pick up the shirt.

TWENTY

BRITAIN

Dear Britain,

This is the hardest thing I've ever done in my life, but I know I have to do it. If I don't do this now, I know I'll lose the nerve, and never follow through. I'm sorry that this is coming at you with no warning, but it is something I've been thinking about for awhile now.

I should start from the beginning. I've lied to you. I promised I wouldn't lie to you, so I'm going to tell you all the truths now. No matter how ugly they seem, I have to get it out there. Then you can decide how you want to move forward.

First, I was the one who forced Matt to break up with you. I thought you knew this, which is why I haven't said anything about it. I only just found out yesterday, when I called Matt to tell him about us. That's when he told me you didn't know the full story. I had resolved to tell you when I got home, but you were in the bathroom crying. And you'd just found out this awful thing about your family's past, and I didn't want to add to your pain.

I should have told you the moment I knew that you didn't know, and I'm sorry. Truly. The reasons I asked Matt to do it are numerous, and I'll get to them, but in order to do that, I have to go back to the start. Our start.

I lied to you the first time I met you, too. You asked me if I believed in fate, and I said no. When we first met, I couldn't even see you for the first couple of minutes, but I didn't have to. I felt you, and I just had this feeling come over me that you were special. To me. I wanted to get to know you, I wanted to soak up every minute with you in that dingy bathroom. And honestly, I didn't believe in fate, until I met you.

I was standing outside that bathroom when I got what most people would think was terrible news. My girlfriend of five years was dumping me. She'd been cheating on me. I wasn't mad, I wasn't hurt, I was just annoyed, then indifferent. Then you, you hit me in the head with that door, and from the moment I heard your voice, I felt something. You made me feel something in that minute that five years with my ex never even touched.

It only got better when I opened my eyes. You were so beautiful that day. I'll never forget your sun-kissed cheeks and the way you gave me this little half smile. You had the sweetest demeanor and you were so tender about the way you cared for me. You could have asked me for anything right then and I would have given it to you.

I had a moment where I thought, "Is this fate?" Nancy sent me that message just as you opened that door. What are the chances? It felt like one part of my life died and another began in that fraction of a second. Nancy and I had argued the day before and I told her, fairy tales aren't real, fate's not real. This is just life.

I don't know why, but I had to know if you believed in fate. It was a dumb thing to ask, but for some reason I had to know. And guess what you told me? You didn't believe in fate. Believing in fate would mean believing in fairy tales, and you didn't believe in those. I couldn't help but smile. It was like you took the words right out of my mouth. If ever fate existed, it was in that moment, in that bathroom. And I saw you, like the answer to a wish I didn't even know I made.

But then you asked if I believed in fate, and I lied to you. I said no. Ten minutes earlier, and that answer would have been the truth. But after you, I'd always thought it was fate, meeting you that day. I walked out of that bathroom determined. I was going to find you, but when I did, none of it made sense.

You were Georgia's daughter, you were with Matt, and you were 18. I felt like the biggest idiot. I couldn't date you. I was so much older, you were too young. I didn't think you looked 18. You definitely looked younger than me, but not 18. It was like getting punched in the stomach. I resigned myself that whatever I felt for you then was misplaced. Maybe the breakup had been harder on me than I realized and that's all it was.

In the back of my mind, though, I always harbored these feelings for you. I denied them because I wasn't that old guy trying to date someone 14 years younger than me, but they were still there. You've always been there. Which brings me back to why I convinced Matt to break up with you.

The company was under water at the time. We'd made a

couple bad investments, and it was on me to come up with the next thing, so I did. I put all my passion into a project I believed in. It ended up being Broken Ridge, but back when I met you, it was still just an idea. When I was finally able to pull it all together, the entire project hinged on one person, and that was Julie Scala. She had brokered this deal with her father for the land, for us. It was an amazing deal; one I knew I'd never see again in this lifetime.

She had one demand in order to finalize it: She needed me to get Matt to break up with you. I was a bit confused by her demand at first, but, if I'm being honest, I didn't fight her on it. I didn't want you to be with Matt either. You couldn't be mine, but I didn't want you to be his. It seemed like a special kind of torture to have to watch you get married to him someday, have his kids someday, and so I agreed to Julie's stipulation.

When she asked me to do it, she told me it was because you were Constantine's daughter. I don't know that I believed this, but it helped me justify to myself that I was doing the right thing in telling Matt he needed to end it with you. I didn't know Matt would do it the way he did. I thought he would explain it to you, how I had asked him (forced him) to do this. But, he didn't.

A couple months after that, I found out from Georgia that you'd moved away. I thought that was the best outcome for everyone involved, honestly. But I was wrong. Again.

I had no idea that you moved because of Matt, that you never got over him. I thought you moved on, and were probably happy to escape the valley. I didn't know, Britain. I'm so sorry. I really didn't know until I overheard you talking to Damian today.

You've given me the happiest days of my life, Britain. I'm absolutely convinced that if it doesn't work between us, it won't work out for me with anyone. You are it for me. You are everything, my everything.

But what if I'm not it for you? What if I never was?

You spent 17 years never being able to get over Matt. Our six weeks is nothing compared to that. It would be one thing if you never got over him, but Matt was happy and settled in his life. But he's not. He never got over you either. He's still waiting for you.

There's a very large part of me that wants to say, I don't care. I'd rather have you, even if you have one foot out the door, than not have you at all. But what kind of life is that? What example are we setting for the girls by doing that? I want you, Britain, but only if you want me the same way. Without reservation, without caveats, without ghosts from our past looming over our relationship.

You deserve to be so fucking happy, Britain. I can't take that from you. I'd rather be miserable, but know you're happy, truly happy. I won't be the one to take that from you again.

I'm going to give you the space to figure it out. I've let Matt know that you and I are no longer together. Whatever happens next is up to you, and him. I'm removing myself from the equation. I'm turning off my phone and I'm going to go work in Sonoma for the next 4 months. That's all I can give. If you need longer than that, I'll know you can't decide and that's a decision in itself. I can't spend the rest of my life looking over my shoulder, wondering if you wish I was the other guy. And I can't wait longer than 4 months. I want to give you the time you need, but I also need to know how to proceed with my life.

We don't have to have a confrontation about it. You don't need to explain anything to me. If you'd rather be with Matt, just don't be at our house in Spearhead on October 7th. If you're not there, I'll know. I'll pack up the house and move to Sonoma permanently. I will completely disappear from your life.

I still can't believe you showed up at Broken Ridge, that you rented my house. You'll always be a part of me, Britain. Even if you don't choose me, you'll always be the best part of me. I probably won't ever stop loving you, but if you want to be with Matt, cut me loose so I at least have a chance at trying to stop.

If you decide earlier, you know where to find me.

I love you, Britain,

Liam

The tears stream down my face, a drop rolling down my nose and falling onto the paper in front of me. I blot at it, trying to prevent it from making the ink bleed, then set the letter aside and drop my face into my hands. *I love him so much. So fucking much.*

Fuck, Liam. I quickly change out of my leggings and tee, opting for a nap dress and sliding on sandals. A brief look in the full-length mirror doesn't do much for my confidence. I'm not wearing any makeup, and my hair is still wet, but I don't care. I'm moving at full speed right now.

I grab my purse out of the mudroom and run into Jess as I do.

"Whoa, where are you going?" Jess asks.

"There's something I need to do. Can you hang with the girls for a couple hours?"

"Uh, yeah, I guess." I'm already walking away before she

can finish, "Guess you can just tell me about the Greek Fest later then!" Jess calls out after me.

I call back, "Yeah, I will, later. I promise!" I step out into the garage, opening the door while I fumble, searching for my keys. Instead of finding them, my Porsche calls to me. *Fuck yes.* I smile as I duck into the low car, starting it and listening to its purr as the engine turns. I pull out of the driveway and head straight towards Spearhead. I need to see him. I need to tell him I read his letter.

Chances are he's probably home, but just in case, I call. It rings out, then goes to voicemail and I try to tamp down the familiar unease that bubbles up, remembering all my unanswered calls. *Probably working out. Yes, that's it.* It's a little late in the day for him, but not unreasonable. It's only noon. My heart thumps loudly in my chest and I accelerate, my Porsche flying at the same speed as my blood through my veins.

I don't know what I'm going to say. I have no plans other than to tell him I read the letter.

We need to talk, I mean *really* talk, and we haven't done that. We've seen each other in passing mostly, just skimming the surface of it all, but we need to talk. I know it. Subconsciously, I know I just need to see him. *Him.* Liam. My heart flutters as I approach the windy portion of my drive. My hands shake and I slow down considerably to accommodate the steep curves and twists of the mountain road.

Please be home, Liam. Please.

When I get to his house, I say a small *thank you Jesus* when I see his Range Rover parked in the driveway. But then my stomach takes a dive because this means I'm doing this. I snatch my purse up and walk briskly to the door. My hands are bouncing the keys back and forth, nervously, as I wait for someone to answer my knock. But no one does.

Christ, maybe he's in the shower. I knock again and wait, still fidgeting because *shit*, I really need to pee. Maybe it's the nerves or maybe it's my uterus sitting on my bladder, I don't fucking know. I test the door knob and it turns easily. Unlocked. Assuming he hadn't changed it, I could have used the keycode, though.

I step over the threshold, listening for a beat. When I hear nothing, I head straight towards the hall bath, but I'm stopped at the entrance to his office. He's sitting there, full glass of brown in hand, looking a little worse for the wear. If I'm honest, he looks a little like me.

My breathing stops and my cheeks heat while I wait for him to notice my presence. When he finally seems to recognize me, a strange expression passes his face. I lift a hand up and wave silently, giving him a gentle smile, hopeful it's one that says I come in peace. But he doesn't return the gesture.

My mouth is getting hot and I swallow down the excess saliva, realizing I haven't had anything to eat today. Tentatively, I take a step forward and Liam's eyes go wide, giving me pause.

"Hi, I-uh, sorry for just coming in like that," I point back to the front door. "I just really need–" He lifts up his hand to stop me and when he does, I notice...*hair?*

"You know it's rude to break into someone's house?" A woman's voice asks, as a naked Gina rises up from behind the desk. Liam stands up abruptly, his pants unzipped, and his dick hanging out. *Ohmyfuckinggod.* I turn away from the two of them abruptly, averting my gaze then break into an all-out sprint for the hall bathroom, emptying my stomach of bile into the toilet. There's no food there, so as soon as I finish retching, I flush, and book it straight out the front door. I don't know if I'm running or walking, I just know I'm moving — and fast. *Have to get the fuck away from this place.*

I can hear Liam call out to me, but the sound is muffled. My ears are ringing and everything seems a bit spinny. *Huh, is "spinny" even a word?* I lean against my car, fighting for breath as my brain begins what I assume will be a relentless verbal assault. *Mistake, this was a mistake. You're a fucking idiot, Britain. Stupid. Fucking stupid.*

I see Liam walking out his front door towards me, holding up his hand for me to wait, but I just shake my head at him, throwing myself into the car and peeling out of the driveway. Pressing down hard on the accelerator, I almost crash into a tree, but miss it by inches. My car is practically screaming at me with all the sensors going off, but I can't see them, the tears are completely clouding my vision. *Fuck my life. Fuck me. I am so stupid. Britain, why the fuck are you so stupid?*

I throw the car in drive, and the tires screech against the pavement as I floor it past Liam in his front yard. At the stop sign at the end of his street, I just hang my head and cry, but at some point the cry turns to screaming, and I thrash against the steering wheel. I hate this stupid car. I hate that it smells like him. And I hate him, too. I shake my head. *No, I hate myself most.* For believing any of his words, spoken or written. For ever believing a promise he's told me. It means absolutely fucking nothing.

"There is nothing between me and Gina. You're it for me. The only place I want to be is next to you."

Fuck you, Liam Millar. I'm going to find the best goddamn family court attorney that money can buy and I'm going to make sure he only ever sees this baby when I say he can. Fuck splitting custody, fuck co-parenting, and fuck this place.

In the rearview mirror, I can see him start to pull out of his driveway, so I take off at breakneck speed, flying past the main strip and heading straight for Sandy's. It's the opposite direction of town, which is where he probably thinks I'll go. I keep an eye behind me the whole time, but he never shows up in my rearview again. Maybe he wasn't following me. That would imply he cares. Or maybe he's just feeling guilty for getting caught in a lie. I don't know and I don't care.

Damn, I really don't want to go to Sandy's, but I still need to pee like no-other.

Pulling into their drive, I try to collect myself as best as possible before heading in. They might be at the cafe, in which case I'll consider this a great mercy and thank the heavens. I slam the car door shut and pull out my phone to see there's already two missed calls from Liam, but I ignore them. I knock on the front door and try the doorbell, but no luck.

Flipping over the pot on the front porch that's painted with sunflowers, I pull out the hidden key and let myself in, but I call out first, just in case.

"Sandy! Jim! It's Britain! I just need to use your bathroom!" I'm met with silence which is infinitely relieving.

The tears start again, and this time I just let them go. Thankfully, no one is here to see the train wreck I've orchestrated over my own life.

I sit on the toilet to pee and pull out my phone, sending a few messages.

BRITAIN

I need you. Can you please come home?

Then I shoot off another.

BRITIAN

I need the best family court attorney you know. I don't care what it costs.

Fuck, I have to think of something plausible. Why would I just show up at his house? Then I'm reminded of my pillow, my favorite pillow probably still lying on his bed. I wonder if Gina uses it. *Hell.* Then I send another text.

BRITAIN

Hey, so sorry about that. Shouldn't have come by unannounced. I just needed to pick up my pillow. Won't happen again. Have a good day.

The entire thing is a lie, but I can't let him see how much he affects me. He always will, *fucking bastard.* I clean up and wash my hands, then sit on the cool stone floor to let loose a few more tears. Once I feel sufficiently drained, I stand up and open the door.

"Don't you *ever* drive like that again." Liam crowds into my personal space, gripping my upper arms firmly in his hands, stunning me speechless. "I could fucking kill you for driving like that." It's an empty threat, though, as he releases my arms, then pulls me in tight to his chest. He smells like his cologne and scotch. Lots of scotch. My body goes willingly into his arms, even though my mind is screaming in revolt. I let him embrace me, but I don't return it.

"How'd you know I was here?"

"I stopped at The Grounds and asked if anyone had seen which way the Porsche went. They all pointed straight here." *Fucking small towns.*

"Did you see my text?" I try to fortify my voice, "Sorry about that. Hope Gina wasn't too put out that I had to vomit and run." It's hard to keep the emotion out of my voice. The joke sounds neither funny nor crude, just lifeless. A bit like me. I push out of the embrace. "I tried calling, but I promise that won't happen again." I turn to walk past him, but he grabs my arm.

"Stop running from me, Britain."

I glare at him, then down to where his hand is holding my arm. "Stop doing shit that makes me want to run from you."

"That wasn't what it looked like."

"Please don't. You don't need to explain or excuse anything. You are free to do whatever you want with whoever you want." He drops my arm and I start walking towards the front door. I stop and turn before I get there because there is one thing I can't leave unsaid. "I really don't care what the fuck you do, Liam, but don't lie to me. If I can't trust you to be honest, I can't trust you with our child." He takes two steps to slide in front of the door, effectively blocking my exit.

"Is that a threat, Britain?"

"Yeah it is. I know you've never seen the mom version of Britain, but I try really hard to not let my kids be in shitty situations with shitty people. Do whatever you want, but if you want to be a shitty person about it, don't expect me to willingly send my kid to you every other weekend."

"Ouch, every other weekend." He feigns a pain in his chest.

"Right now, you're at supervised visits once a month, at best." His face hardens and transforms.

"This does not have to be like this, Britain." He looks down on me with disdain for the first time...ever.

"No it sure as fuck didn't. Please move so I can leave." I don't know what it is about him that makes me so insanely reactive. *I hate him, I love him, ugh. Why can't I just be indifferent to him?*

"No, not until you talk to me. Not until you let me explain."

"Ahh yes, the epidemic, right?" He looks at me, confused. "Yes, the one where naked women's mouths just fall on your dick. Tragic stuff happening nowadays." I sneer at him and roll my eyes.

"One, she wasn't fully naked. Two, my dick wasn't in her mouth, nor has it ever been in her mouth. And three, you're one to talk! I got to hear all about how much you screamed your boyfriend's name when he fucked you this weekend. Which, gee, he's such a good guy he just left you on your porch so you could get sick. And I don't remember you calling his name out in your sleep. Do you remember that, Bambi?" He asks harshly. "I seem to remember you called out for *me*. You *begged* me to stay."

"He is not my boyfriend and...fuck you, Liam," I say, trying to keep the tears and anger from drowning me.

"Yeah," he laughs cruelly, "I wish you would, Britain! Is there a line I can get in? What's the process for getting in your queue, huh? You know Max, Niko, and Silas are all still single if you want to make your way through them, too." If I wasn't firmly against domestic violence, I would slap him. I try to get the rage under control, but I can't. I try to breathe, but I can't. I try to say something, but I can't. The room starts spinning, and I falter.

"Britain?" The word doesn't come out fully formed, though. Or maybe I don't hear it fully because everything starts to fade and get fuzzy, and the walls close in and I panic before everything fades to black.

TWENTY-ONE

BRITAIN

I wake up on a stretcher in the back of an ambulance with a stricken, white-faced Liam sitting beside me, practically shaking.

"Hi, ma'am. Looks like you've had a fainting spell, okay? We're on our way to the hospital. You're gonna be just fine, but your blood pressure is a little low, okay?" I have no way to answer with the oxygen mask covering my face. I motion towards it, and the middle-aged paramedic removes it.

"What's that, dear?" I can barely form the words, motioning for something, *anything*.

"I-I'm going to be—" Like a light bulb, the paramedic figures it out, and just in the nick of time. A plastic bag with a clampable rim appears in front of my face when I start retching...again. Liam immediately moves closer to me, pushing hair out of my face so it doesn't fall into the vomit. Not that much makes its way up. Just more foul, yellow bile.

"This happen often, dear? The fainting?" I look at Liam, then back to the paramedic.

"Just once before." I drop my gaze, feeling ashamed that somehow this only happens when this man stomps all over my heart. It's not helping that I'm sick, haven't eaten, or taken my antibiotics today. Which makes me feel even more shame. I'm not taking care of my body how I should. Silas was right to scold me yesterday. I need to do better.

"Do you remember what happened last time? What caused it?" Liam moves in closer, placing a supportive hand on my thigh and slipping the other into my free hand. I don't care enough to try and free myself from it right now.

"I passed out, and fell and hit my head. Did I hit my head this time?" I panic, looking from Liam to the paramedic.

Liam finally breaks his silence. "No, you didn't. I was there to catch you." At least there's that small bit of relief. I don't need to destroy what little semblance of calm that's been restored by telling him another head injury could aggravate the existing one, causing miscarriage or other problems.

"Oh, okay, good. Well, um, it was brought on by a combination of things last time. I'm anemic," Liam looks surprised. *Yeah bud, you've missed a lot.* "And I'm pregnant, and under a lot of stress lately..." I trail off, not needing to rehash it.

"I have strep throat. I haven't eaten since Saturday night. I didn't take my antibiotic this morning and It's been a rough start to the day. I'm sure I'm just dehydrated. Do we really think the hospital is necessary?"

"Yes," Liam and the paramedic both say at the same time. I tilt my head back and close my eyes as the nausea starts again. The only perk of being so distraught last time is I was too distracted for motion sickness. *No such luck now, though.*

The hour-long drive down the mountain is relatively uneventful. As long as you consider me dry-heaving every ten minutes uneventful. Liam seemed to improve with each mile as I deteriorated, so by the time we get to hospital, I'm begging for a bag of fluids and some pain meds for my throat that has already started hurting again.

After triage, I get hooked up to an IV as Liam paces back and forth at the foot of the bed in the small, curtained room. The nurse looks at me, then him, and asks, "Sir, what's your relation to the patient?"

"He's just my–" I don't get to finish saying "father of my baby" because Liam cuts me off.

"I'm her husband." My eyes widen in shock and horror, but he gives me a stern look in return, telling me to shut it. Luckily the nurse misses it because they're focused on getting the fluids hooked up.

"Alright, you're all set. The attending physician will be in in a bit to check on you, but just a heads up, we're a bit backed up with all the heat-related illnesses, you know?" I just nod. *Sure, whatever.* Liam softly thanks the nurse, then comes to sit on the bed facing me. I look over at the chair in the corner that he could've taken, but he doesn't catch the hint, so I lean back and close my eyes.

His hand slips into mine, his fingers threading with my cold ones.

"Jesus, Britain, you're freezing."

I shiver slightly. "Yeah, it's cold in here, but also..." I motion up to the bag.

He just nods, then moves to sit *in* the bed beside me, covering me with blankets and pulling me into his warm body. Just like the other night. "Sure you want to get this close? I might get you sick." I don't say it in jest. There's part of me that wants him to move, but also that desperate little girl in the back of my mind that wants him to stay. He threads our fingers together again, cementing his position.

"I don't care." It's quiet for a couple minutes before he starts again, "We need to talk, baby."

I nod, knowing it's true. I can't keep having these explosive events every time I see him. "It hurts to talk right now." Physically *and* emotionally.

"Then just listen. I'll talk," he says. "First, I just want to say I'm sorry. For what I said back at my mom's. I, uh, implied some really shitty stuff, and I didn't mean it. I *don't* mean it. Just hearing you were with him was hard for me. I did not handle it well." *Same.* Yeah, me almost wrecking my car and ending up in a hospital after I saw him with Gina isn't me handling it well either. I just nod to see if he'll keep going. And he does.

"I will never lie to you, Britain. I promised you. I know I haven't been the best, or what you deserve, but I will *never* lie to you." I don't think I can believe him, but I stay quiet to see where this goes. He tells me about the phone conversation and overhearing Matt yell at me. About how he punched Matt and tells him about me screaming his name. I cringe. He tells me about getting the stitches fixed and then drinking half a bottle of scotch on the drive home.

"And I was really wasted, but I am telling you the truth that nothing was going to happen. I had literally just told her to get her shit and get out of my house when you walked in. She was picking up her clothes."

"I'm not as dumb as I look, Liam." I rasp out when he pauses.

He takes my face in his hands. "You are not dumb, you don't look dumb. I'm telling you the truth. I was wasted and acting slow because I was sad and all I could think about was you and Matt having sex." He searches my face, and then his expression changes with realization. "I'm not *him*, baby. I promise." Yeah, the whole fucking your assistant thing hits a little close to home.

I whisper out, "You keep making these promises..."

He nods. "Yep, every single one I intend to follow through on. You want me to fire Gina? Done. You want to go through my phone? No problem. You want access to the Nest cams? Too easy."

"That's not how you build trust." I look up into his eyes — my favorite eyes — and say, "I don't trust you...but I also can't stop loving you." He looks like he might cry. I know I *am* crying.

"How do I regain your trust?"

"Consistent actions over a long period of time." He pulls me in tighter to him and I close my eyes, relaxing into the embrace.

"Okay. Try and get some sleep, okay?" I nod and drift in and out of sleep for what feels like either hours or three minutes. I wake up to Liam stroking my hair and whispering to me. I keep my eyes closed and try to hear him.

"...and I just wish you had read that letter that night...and I wish I would have never written it, because I wish I would have never left..."

"I read the letter, Liam," my voice comes out hoarse and faint, his hand freezing in my hair. "Why do you think I showed up at your house today?" He starts moving his hand, stroking my hair, and I drift off again.

———

I wake up alone, disoriented, and thirsty. So very thirsty. Sitting up in the hospital bed, I look around for my purse, but it's nowhere. Probably laying on the ground somewhere at Sandy's house. Jess and the girls are probably worried sick. *Fuck, and Damian.* He's probably freaking out. I send him a cryptic text and then go MIA. He's going to be losing his mind. *Where is...someone? Anyone?* As I'm about to press the call button, the nurse walks in.

"Well, if it isn't the queen of darkness! Back so soon!" The joke seems in poor taste.

"Yes, I just love the vibes and the food so much," I deadpan.

She laughs. "I hope they admit you, you're fun. Your husband just popped out for some coffee. He told me if you wake up to let you know he'll be back in five and that he's already called the girls." He's completely shameless telling these people he's my husband.

"Oh, okay," I say. *Liam called the girls?* I try to imagine the conversation. Jen — at least I think it's Jen; I don't have a whiteboard in the makeshift curtain room — takes my vitals while someone else comes in to draw blood. A second after they both leave, the attending physician comes in.

"Alright, so let's see here. You fainted." It's not a question, he's just reading my chart. He mumbles over a few lines, then looks up at me and smiles. "I'm Dr. Lopez, we're gonna take a quick look at you, alright?" I just nod. He proceeds to look at my throat, "Oh yeah, we're red back there, aren't we?"

"I had a strep test yesterday, it was positive. I just forgot to take my antibiotics this morning."

"Mmkay, that explains the throat, but what about this fainting? You know, it can be common for hormones to cause you to faint when you're pregnant." Liam walks in with a cup of coffee in-hand and an armful of snacks from the vending machine. He sets everything down at the end of the bed and then turns to the doctor to introduce himself. As my husband. I roll my eyes.

"So, I was just explaining to your wife that fainting can be common during pregnancy due to hormones that affect blood pressure. This is the second time in a couple months." He hems and haws for a moment. "Do you have family or anyone that can be with you during the day? We don't want what happened last time to happen again. I'd say you got lucky this time." *Sure, lucky.*

"My daughters live with me..." I trail off. Well, for the next month they will.

Liam interjects, "And obviously me. I'll be there." He looks at me sincerely, like he really means it and isn't just playing the fake husband role to a T.

"I'm gonna put in a call to Dr. Scala, but I'm not too worried about today. I'm going to hit you with some intra-venous antibiotics to really kick this infection's ass, and then you're good to go. I'll send the blood results to Silas, alright?" I nod and Liam shakes his hand and says thank you as he leaves.

"We've been laying in this bed for six hours, but I knew as soon as I went to get coffee they'd come see you." He shakes his head, looking disappointed.

He says, "I'm sorry," at the same time I say, "Well then, thank you," and he gives me a warm smile.

"You seem a little better after some rest?"

I just nod. "You called the girls?"

"Oh, yeah. I did. Everything's fine. I told them I'd bring you home tonight, probably." He looks at the clock that just hit 7:00 P.M. "You hungry? I tried to just grab a little of everything." I look at the granola bars and bags of chips, none of it very appetizing.

"Hey girl, hey!" Jen pokes her head in through the curtains. "Look what I have for you..." Jen pulls the curtain aside, revealing a tray of assorted ice creams. "I may have stolen these from the break room for you," she says with a wink.

"Wow, thank you so much." This time I actually mean it. I look over to Liam's pile of snacks and Jen does, too.

"Sorry, bud, but ice cream always wins," she says, patting him on the back, then moves over to add a syringe of antibiotics to my drip.

"That's alright, as long as she's happy," he says with a smile. Once Jen slips back out, Liam sits on the edge of the bed to drink his coffee while I spoon through my assortment of ice creams and Italian ices. He sets the coffee aside a moment later, then starts typing furiously on his phone. When he's done, he looks up at me.

"So, Sandy and Jim are driving my car here right now. I had them just throw together an overnight bag for me, but I'll need to go home at some point to get a few more things. Oh, and Sandy made sure to grab your purse for you, too." *Wait, huh?*

"I'm not tracking." I stop eating to stare at him.

"You heard what the doctor said, Britain. I'm not leaving you just to have you faint and get a concussion."

I shake my head. "That's super, super unnecessary, Liam.

251

Jess is there, the girls are there. I can always call Alex. Damian's probably already on his way back. He's been staying with us, and...and there's not even enough beds." Who knew I'd ever be in a scenario to need three guest bedrooms. Unbelievable.

"Well, then everyone could move to Spearhead. With the garage apartment, and the basement, I have enough rooms." He says it so nonchalantly.

"No, you don't. You have the garage apartment, and three guest bedrooms. Do you know how to count? Caroline, Elodie, Jess, me, Damian," I use my fingers to demonstrate, "You're one short." He gets a smile on his face.

"No," I say, shaking my head vehemently.

"How am I going to keep an eye on you at night if we're not staying in the same room?"

"Liam, be realistic." He just chuckles, then takes a sip of his coffee.

"I am being serious." He sets down the coffee, scooting closer to me and taking my hand in his. "Last time this happened, I wasn't here to take care of you. Just let me do this. I need the both of you to be healthy, okay?" I stare at him a little while longer.

"What about Matthias?" I ask him, gauging his reaction. He flinches. It's barely perceptible, but I see it. He leans back a little.

"Would you rather Matt move in with you?" *No. Not even a little bit.* I just shake my head, unable to verbally say it aloud. He nods in response. "Then it's all worked out. I'll stay with you at your house tonight, and then we'll all move up to Spearhead tomorrow." *Uh, no.*

"No, I thought you were going to come stay at my house."

"Well, doesn't it make more sense for you to come up, what with the girls working for Sandy and everything? And it's summer, it's the best time to be at the lake. And Damian can have his own apartment. Or Jess can. Plus, I can have Carly come cook all your favorites, and the girls can go over to Sandy and Jim's whenever they want." He's making some very valid points. The most compelling one being Carly.

"And is Alex welcome over to your house?" I ask warily.

"Yep, he is my brother-in-law after all." Liam shoots me a wink and I roll my eyes. I feel like somehow, Liam has just tricked me back into his arms...and his bed. But I meant what I said about trust: *Consistent actions over a prolonged period.* We'll see how he does.

"Fine, on one condition..." He nods, pushing me on. "You have to convince all of them to move to your house." I shoot him a smirk. Fat fucking chance that's going to happen.

All he says is, "Done." And flashes me back a smile. I get the feeling I've just been played. As in "it's done," the decision has already been made — before he even asked me, he asked them.

———

It's 8:30 P.M. when Liam pulls his Range Rover into the roundabout in front of the hospital while I wait in a wheelchair on the sidewalk. It feels weird. Definitely like déjà vu. I try to push the uneasy feeling away, though, as Liam walks around to the passenger side of his car. He opens the door for me then waits with an outstretched arm like a valet.

When the nurse who wheeled me down passes me off to him, she says, "She's all yours, now."

Liam smiles and says, "Yep, she's all mine." I roll my eyes. We still have so much to talk about and figure out. As soon as he gets in and buckles up, I plan to make things crystal clear for him.

"None of this means we're getting back together. We are *not* together, you know that, right?" He looks at me, just giving a sort of sad smile.

"I know."

"Okay, good. And we still have a lot of stuff to talk about and figure out, least of which is our relationship." He just nods. "I don't even want it to be a discussion, Liam. I have so much going on right now." I start to feel the stress. Jesus, how weirded out are the girls going to be if we move to Spearhead...with Liam. I know logistically it makes sense, and makes some things easier in regards to doctors appointments and having Liam around to help. But there's no way they're going to want to do that. I'm pretty sure they hate him. Jess, too.

Liam slides a hand over to my leg while he drives and... damn him. I hate how good it feels. I hate that I don't make him move it. I just settle back in the seat and watch the hills flash by as we drive to my house.

When we pull up, it's dark out, but I can see a couple figures outside, like they're waiting for us. Elodie is practically bouncing up and down with excitement and I turn to look at Liam, who just gives me a sly smile.

"What'd you have to do?" I ask seriously. I swear, if he bought them cars, I'm going to lose my mind. Liam puts the car in park and I move to open my door, but he stops me.

"Bambi, really?" He gives me the side eye and I concede, sitting back while I wait for him to come open my door.

"Hi, girls!" I call out to them, and Elodie immediately rushes over to me.

"Mom! Are you okay? How are you feeling?" I laugh lightly at her over-eager questions.

"I'm alright, feeling so much better." *Just deathly exhausted*, but I can barely finish because she's talking again.

"Liam got us Taylor Swift tickets!!!" she squeals with barely contained delight. Caroline joins her sister. She's smiling, but not quite as ecstatically.

Once Liam has his bag, he comes to stand next to me, putting his hand at the small of my back, rubbing the area gently. I try to hide how much the gesture makes me want to melt into a puddle, right here. I'm surprised when Caroline speaks next, directing it towards Liam.

"I just want to say thank you, Liam, for being there for my mom. And also for the tickets, and the hotel...and the Disneyland passes." *Ohh, he went all out.* I look at him, looking bashful.

He leans down to whisper in my ear, "I'm not above bribery." I laugh, and then he guides me into the house with the girls leading the way.

TWENTY-TWO

LIAM

Britain's house isn't what I expected. The first time I was here, it was dark, and I headed straight for her bedroom. But walking in with all the lights on, I can see how nice it is. But it's not our home and I need to have her home.

Jess greets Britain in the oversized chef's kitchen with a big hug.

"Girl, I could kill you! I nearly had a damn heart attack," she chides Britain. *Same, though.* When she fainted, it was like seeing everything I've ever wanted slip through my fingers. It was a fucking wake-up call. There's absolutely no way I'm letting her get away. Screw Matt, screw the business — none of it matters if she's not with me.

Jess glares at me, finally acknowledging my presence. I thought getting her to agree to relocate to my house was mission impossible, but she folded surprisingly easily. Her text said, *Fuck it up, and I'll help Alex bury you.* Message received. I have absolutely no intention of fucking it up. Even though this morning — or was it afternoon? — was pretty fucking close.

That reminds me, I need to email Henry about reassigning Gina to someone else. Then I'm going to do what I thought I never would: I'm going to sell my part of the business. My father's probably rolling in his grave that I'm even thinking about it, but I can't be partners with Matt. Sitting in the back of the ambulance with Britain, the decision came easy. I want to be able to go where she and the baby are, and it's not fair to the business for me to just shirk off for months of the year.

So when the girls go back to Virginia, and Britain does, too, so will I. I know the baby won't be born by then, but who the fuck is going to look after Britain when she's there? *Me. Simple.* Easiest decision I could ever make. Her and our little Bambi mean more to me than everything.

As much as I hated today, I can't help but feel...*happy*. So fucking happy. And that probably makes me a sick bastard, but this is my opening, my chance. I have a lot to prove and I intend to do it. I'll show Britain how much I love her every day for the rest of our lives. I don't want another day to go by when she doesn't feel cherished, respected, and most of all, safe. She's so used to people leaving and betraying her, but that won't ever be me. *Never.*

"I think I'm just going to get some water and head to bed," Britain says quietly to Jess and the girls. They all agree and head to their own respective bedrooms, but first Caroline gives Britain an extra long hug. She tries to hide it, but I notice the tears she wipes away quickly. I wait for Britain to get her water...and then continue to wait. I think she's actually forgotten I'm here, and I'm proven right when she turns around to see me standing there in the kitchen, alone with her, and she startles.

"Jesus, Liam. I'm not used to you, I guess, being here." *Get used to it, baby.* I just let her comment go, though.

"Are you ready to head upstairs?" She just nods her head in response and I turn to let her lead the way. My heart starts beating faster in anticipation. Not because we're going to be intimate, but because I'll finally get to be alone with her. Even if it's while she's sleeping, just being with her is all I want. I can almost pretend that we're back together, and that she's sleeping in our bed. Fuck, I just wish it was tomorrow already.

Britain opens the double doors to the primary suite, revealing a neutral, modern space. It's not decorated fully yet, but there's something about it that doesn't feel like she belongs here. *Because she doesn't. She belongs at our house in Spearhead.*

When I close the doors behind us, my pulse ratchets up and my hands get clammy. Fuck me, I'm nervous.

She sneaks a peek at me over her shoulder, double checking I'm still with her, then points to the bathroom and says, "Feel free to get cleaned up. I'm just gonna go change in the closet real quick." She doesn't wait for a reply, just heading into her walk-in closet and shutting the door behind her. In the bathroom, there's dual sinks. Hers is covered in products, all lined up neatly, while the other sink is barren, only a soap pump. Good, it looks like Matt wasn't a regular overnight guest then. I slip out of my dress pants and shirt that still smell like scotch, and opt for a quick shower before bed. I'd hate to nauseate Britain with my alcohol stench.

She has towels stacked neatly on a shelf by her tub, so I grab one, then hop in the shower. It's almost pitiful how fast my cock gets hard, because all I'm thinking about is how close I am to her. I'm thinking about when I'd fuck her in the shower at home, and how I wish she was in here with me now. I'm thinking about crawling into bed with her, her naked body pressed against mine, but I stop. That's not what tonight is about. It's about me being here for her. Making sure she's okay. Making sure she has anything and everything she needs. That's all.

When I turn off the water, I reach for my towel and see that Britain is standing stock still in front of the shower, staring at me. My dick doesn't get the memo that it's not play time and stands at full attention, throbbing for her. Her cheeks blush and she turns around fast, and I hate that that's how it is now. Hopefully in time we'll get back to the way we were. When my naked body was her favorite thing, and hers was mine. I mean, it still is for me — clearly — I'm just not that for her.

I do a quick dry off, wrapping the towel around my waist and tucking it in. We brush our teeth in tandem, she washes her face while I put on moisturizer, leaving us finished with the bathroom at the same time. I wait for her to walk back to the bedroom before I hit the light, ditching my towel before following behind her.

"Whoa, whoa, I'm gonna stop you right there," Britain throws a hand over her eyes so she's not looking at my naked form. "There are teenage girls in the house; you can't sleep in here naked." Right, *fuck*. I turn around, grabbing a pair of boxer briefs and slide them on. When I come back, she drops her hand and rolls her eyes. "That's only moderately better, but for tonight, it's fine." I notice she's not sleeping naked either. She has on a baggy t-shirt, but I can't tell if there's anything underneath. Definitely not a bra, though, I can see her hard nipples popping against the fabric and my dick swells with excitement. This might be more problematic than I planned.

She doesn't say goodnight, or anything else for that matter. She just takes a drink of water, turns off the bedside lamp, and sinks into the bed, fluffing the duvet until she's comfy. Should I say goodnight? Do I just let her sleep? I reach towards her to rub her back, but pull back before I can. I don't want to scare her, or make her think I'm wanting more, but I do want to help her relax and rest. She needs it. She looks so tired and underweight, I get pissed off thinking about how she needs to be taken better care of.

She would've been if I'd never left, so that's on me, and that's what pisses me off the most. I lay on my side, staring at her back for longer than I should when I finally decide to say goodnight to her. I lean up and over to kiss the top of her head goodnight, but at the same time she rolls over, her elbow colliding with my face.

"Fuck," I whisper-shout, holding my nose as my body falls back flat on the mattress.

"Oh, fuck, Liam. I'm sorry. I didn't know you were right there!" She whisper-shouts back at me.

"It's okay, baby. I'm sorry. I...I was just going to say goodnight." She sits up, placing one hand on my bare chest as she leans forward, trying to see my face.

"Are you okay? Do you have a bloody nose?" I can see her frantically trying to search me for injury.

"No, no. Lay back down. Go to sleep, okay?" I whisper

back to her. She doesn't say anything back, just laying down on her side, facing me this time. I roll over to face her, too, and wait for her to fall asleep. But thirty minutes later, she's still laying there with her eyes open, not looking at me.

I ask quietly, "Do you want to talk about anything?"

"Oh, um. Yes...no. I want to talk about everything, but then I remember I'm mad at you, and then I don't." She shrugs, then resettles into bed, slightly closer to me this time.

"I'm sorry, Britain."

"I know. I'm sorry, too."

"For what? You have nothing to be sorry for." I close the distance between us, scooting a little bit closer so I can stroke her hair. She relaxes into my touch easily.

"I slept with Matthias. I was with him. I don't know." I grimace, fighting down how angry I feel every time I think about them together. She wasn't doing anything wrong, though. She wasn't.

"It's not like we're together, though." I laugh quietly, "you have made that very clear to me."

"So you don't think I'm a whore for being with him?"

My hand freezes. "No, not at all. I shouldn't have implied such a thing earlier." She nods silently. "I'm sorry, baby. Really fucking sorry. About all of it."

"Stop saying sorry," she whispers at me.

"I will when you forgive me." I wait for her to say something. I'm not so lucky to think she'll tell me she already has, but if she says she never will...well, that's going to be hard to come back from.

"I'll let you know when that happens then," she says quietly, then finally closes her eyes. My heart could practically burst. She said, *"When that happens."* I keep stroking her hair until I'm absolutely certain she's asleep, and then I watch her for hours. Maybe I'll fall asleep eventually, but right now, I just want to soak this up. Her proximity, the way she smells, the sound of her breathing right beside me. Her presence alone makes me smile, and every time I think I can't possibly love her any more, she always seems to find a way to prove me wrong.

Britain

I wake up to the smell of pines and fresh coffee. My throat no longer hurts, and I'm feeling rested and warm, so I snuggle in deeper, keeping my eyes closed against the still-dark room. I want to stay just like this all day.

I move my hand, stroking idly against his hard chest. The constant *thump, thump, thump* of his heartbeat lulling me back into slumber as his warm fingers play gently against the small of my back.

When I drop my hand down past his chest to adjust the hem of my shirt, I brush against his rock-hard cock. It bumps against me, causing heat to pulse between my legs. *Fuck.* I open my eyes. *FUCK.* I push away from Liam.

"Baby, what's wrong?" He sits up and asks as I scoot away from him.

"We're not supposed to be cuddling."

He looks sad for a moment before recovering. "Okay, I'm sorry, but you know, to be fair, you made the first move."

"I did not!" I say fervently.

"Yes, baby, you did," he says with a sly smirk on his face. *Ugh.*

"Then I'm sorry, I shouldn't have." I get up out of bed and head straight to the ensuite to pee and change. One perk of sleeping in the same bed as Liam, I'll be getting up early from now on just so we spend less time together.

I slip off my oversized tee and rifle through my drawer for something slightly more conservative than my normal clothes. *No baby tees and sleep shorts today.*

Something about being in the same bed as him has me hot and bothered. The heat between my legs pulses and my muscles clench together desperately. I have to stop what I'm doing to catch my breath. When I do, I look up and notice I've left the closet door open and Liam is staring right at me, the heat in his eyes apparent. I can tell he's staring at my midsection more than anything, my bump. I turn my back to him and reach for another nap dress off a hanger.

"C-can I see?" He scares the shit out of me. I turn to find him in the closet with me. Instinctively, I hold the dress over my bare body.

"I'm sorry, what?" I ask.

"I just want to see your bump, Britain. The baby?" *Oh.*

"Um, sure, I guess." I move the dress to the side, but continue holding it against my breasts, trying to keep covered while still revealing my stomach. He drops to his knees right there, never taking his eyes off me.

"Can I touch you there, please?" I have to bite down hard on my lip to prevent me from reading too deep into his request. He wants to touch my belly because that's where the baby is. That's all.

I reply quietly, "If you want to."

He brings his hands up, then gently presses them against my abdomen, taking his time. Savoring this. I'm just staring down, watching him, when he looks back at me with tears in his eyes. "You're so fucking beautiful like this, baby." My heart flutters, my cheeks heat, and my inner muscles clench, begging. Begging for something, *anything. Let me go, Liam.* He doesn't release me, though. He just moves his hand over the area, feeling me and when he speaks again, it's not to me.

"Hi, baby. I'm your dad, and I can't wait to meet you." He leans forward and presses the gentlest of kisses on my womb. I close my eyes and tip my head back, savoring the heat he sends spiraling through my core. Then he does it again, placing a gentle kiss on the other side, and then one on the other. I want him so bad. *I hate that I want him.*

His hands start to move away from my belly now. They slide down over my thighs, then he grips them tightly before releasing and gliding his hands up to my back side. He brushes so gently over my ass, the sensation causes me to release a small moan.

"You are the most beautiful fucking woman, Britain..." His breathing hitches when he settles his hands at my hips. "Do you want me to stop?" *Fuck, no.* I shake my head, and he repeats the movement, running his strong hands down my legs, then back up to land on my ass. This time, he doesn't drop his hands back down, but skims one hand around to the front of me, slipping underneath my underwear.

I swallow and try to even my breathing, but I have no control when it comes to Liam. I never have. He pulls my panties lower and places a kiss on the bare skin, the contact making me reach out to put a hand in his hair. He pulls them lower still, placing another kiss, and this time I drop the dress I'm holding to place my other hand in his hair.

He looks up at me, a question in his eyes. *Are we doing this? Yes. Fuck me, Liam. Yes.* I give the smallest of nods, but he sees it. He stands up in front of me, pulling me against his hard chest. He drops his forehead to mine, both of us breathing raggedly.

"Do you want to go back to bed?" he whispers.

I shake my head. "No, right here, right now." With those words, Liam drops his mouth to mine. His kiss is like molten lava. He pours himself into my mouth, and I feel it everywhere. The heat sinks down to my pelvis causing me to swell and dampen. My toes curl and tingle, and my palms get hot and wet.

He breaks the kiss to bend down and take off my panties, sliding them to the ground, but he doesn't move to stand back up. He takes one of my hands in his for balance, then places one of my legs over his shoulder so he can put his mouth on my clit. *And fuck me.* He knows exactly what to do. He remembers exactly what will get me there and each time he does it our hands squeeze tighter together, both of us knowing.

"Liam, s-stop," and he does, immediately, setting my one leg back down on the floor. I want him in me, but I don't think I can say it out loud.

"Say it, Bambi." Liam uses his stern voice that makes me start to leak in anticipation, but I shake my head. I can't say it. I can't tell him I want him. It's like revealing all your cards in poker. You're relinquishing control.

"This doesn't change anything, okay?" I can't say what I want to, that I want him, desperately. I can't give in like that.

He doesn't say anything back, just nods his head, then tugs on my hand to pull me down to the floor. He slides off his boxer briefs, then lays me out beneath him. He puts my back against the plush carpet, then spreads my legs with a knee to settle between me.

There's no backing away from him now. He's staring at me so intensely, it's like he's boring his way back into my soul. His gaze drifts down my body, like he's committing it to memory all over again. And I need him with a desperation that feels so vast, I'll never be fulfilled.

He drops his lips to mine, leaving a searing kiss on my lips just as he starts to enter me, and I have to bite my lip hard to not scream in ecstasy. I close my eyes and embrace him into me. All of me.

I've just lied. This changes things. He changes me each time he touches me. Each time he loves me, each time he's inside me, I change. I fall. I let him in.

He thrusts into me gently, rocking against me, our eyes connecting. I don't want to look at anything else. I want to see him. I want to see what I do to him because I hope it's at least a fraction of what he does to me.

We move against each other on the closet floor like we've done this a hundred times, but it's still the first time. Our bodies synchronized in this dance we both love. Neither one of us talks the entire time, because we don't need words here. We don't need to role play or talk dirty. Even though we both love that, right now, we love coming together more. And we are, I can feel it. He's burrowing his way back into my life.

He doesn't have to burrow back into my heart, he's never left. He's in my bones, he's in my DNA. He's who I want and

I never want this feeling to end. I want him like this every day. Every morning. Always.

"I'm going to fill you up, baby." Like he isn't already, but the words set me on fire. No one has ever fulfilled me like him. My muscles convulse and pull and strain, and Liam drops his hand to my mouth so my family doesn't hear me cry out his name. And I do. I let his name leave my lips in this space for the first time. The second he hears his name, he loses it, pressing himself tight to me as his thick cock throbs and spills against my walls. He leans down, biting my shoulder gently to keep from yelling himself. Our orgasms seem to last forever, each of us riding out every second like it's a lifeline and as soon as we let go, we're dead. *I don't want to let go.*

When our pulsing subsides, Liam makes no move to release me. Instead, he places soft kisses across my collar bone and then my chest.

"I love the way you smell, Bambi," he whispers softly.

"And what do I smell like?" I ask, quietly.

"Mine," he says, then looks at me. I nod. I get it. I really fucking do. Because every time I smell him, I think he smells like home. And safety. And it's the only thing I want, and he's the only place I want to be.

TWENTY-THREE

BRITAIN

When I come out of the water closet, Liam is standing in front of my sink. He has on dark gray jeans and a gray t-shirt that hugs his broad shoulders. Damnit, *I love him.* He holds out the dress that I dropped in the closet and helps me slip it on over my head. He doesn't back away though once I'm dressed. He gets closer.

"Do you still mean what you said back there?" I give him a look of confusion, so he clarifies, "You said it wouldn't change anything." *Oh.* Of course it changed something.

"It can't right now. There's just a lot of other stuff we need to take care of first."

"That's not really an answer to my question, though, Bambi." He's impossibly close, so he moves his arms around me so I don't lose my balance when he presses in again.

"Of course it changes things, Liam," I say quietly, admitting it. I look up at him and ask, "Did you mean what you wrote in the letter, the part about wanting me that first day we met?" He nods his head.

"I wanted to make you mine the moment I laid eyes on you, and that feeling hasn't stopped since then." My cheeks heat and I feel like I could cry. All this time, it could have been us. I lean in and he meets me, our mouths colliding in pain, and ecstasy, and want. He strengthens his grip around me, as I thread my hands into his hair and we get lost in each other once again.

"Oh my god, Mom!" Caroline exclaims, then covers her eyes with her hand. *Shit.* I push out of the embrace, taking a step back and away from Liam. It could've been worse; she could've walked in 15 minutes ago to see me getting fucked on my closet floor.

"Caroline, open your eyes, but maybe next time, let's knock and wait *before* walking in?" She drops the hand and looks between Liam and myself, her cheeks a bright shade of pink.

"Okay, sorry about that. I'll knock and wait next time. Um, I just came to see when we're leaving because Sandy wants Elodie and me to come over this afternoon." I smile because if I'm honest with myself, I want to leave as soon as possible. I can't wait to be close to the lake again, and to go see Sandy every morning at The Grounds. And I want to smell the pine trees and sit on the deck with a book. I look to Liam for his thoughts on timing, though. He double checks his watch before answering.

"There's a cleaning crew there right now, so I think let's plan to leave in a couple hours, give them time to do their thing?" I nod in agreement.

"Does that work?" I ask Caroline.

"Totally. I'll go tell Elodie to start packing, and then you're cool if we go to Sandy's?"

"Absolutely," I tell her.

She turns around to leave, but shouts over her shoulder, "You guys could also lock your door, too!" My cheeks turn bright pink now because there's a part of me that *does* want to lock the door right now. I look over at Liam, and he's wearing a shit-eating grin.

"I swear, it feels like you plan this. I was just about to tell you I don't want my family to know about *this*," I motion between the two of us, "but that's out the window now." He reaches out to pull me back into his embrace.

"Baby, we're adults. Sleeping in the same room. With one bed. They would've figured it out."

"I know. But can we not do obsessive PDA in front of them? The girls have only ever seen me romantically with their dad, and now we're all just moving into your house, and I feel like I'm really fucking up their lives." He brushes my hair out of my face with both hands.

"You're not fucking them up, okay? I talked with the girls about how much I love and care about you, and how I just want to take care of all of you, including them and the baby. I also told them I wouldn't rush anything, but that I needed you guys close so I can do that." He gives a small laugh, "They're so fucking smart, just like you. They understand."

"When did you talk to them?"

"In the hospital, while I was getting coffee."

"So before the doctor even recommended having someone with me during the day?"

"Yes." He's shameless, but I laugh. "Also, you should be proud, they drove a hard bargain."

"Oh, that's all Damian's doing. Not mine."

"Speaking of, he's the only one I haven't talked to."

"Yeah, he texted me he couldn't make it back until Wednesday at the earliest, so I'm not really worried about his situation." Liam breaks out into a big smile. "*What?*"

"So you're telling me you had an extra bed last night, and you didn't tell me? Were you hoping to seduce me, Britain?" His tone is teasing, but I blanch. *Fuck.* Why didn't I think of that last night? My subconscious knows why, though. It's because I wanted him in my bed. Plain and simple.

———

Jess and all the girls are in my SUV, driving behind Liam and me up to his house. It's the strangest thing to be able to fall right back into this level of ease and comfort in his presence, but somehow, I do. He has that effect on me. He absolutely makes my blood boil with lust, but when it's just the two of us, I feel at peace and relaxed. I look down at where his hand hasn't left my leg the entire drive, making me smile.

"Why do you have stitches?" He doesn't move his hand away, just answers me.

"About that...your mirror, at the house...I ordered you a new one, but until it gets here, you can use my sink, okay?"

"You punched a mirror?!" What the hell?

"I'd just found out that you were pregnant, and that I'd missed everything that happened at Colton's, and I was furious with myself over leaving. I'm sorry." I nod.

"Um, so how did you find out that I was pregnant? You just decided to check your messages or something?" He squeezes my leg.

"You aren't going to believe this, but it was actually Tori." A cold shiver snakes up my spine at the mention of her name, but I don't say anything, waiting for him to explain. "She came to tell me that you and Matt were together, to rub it in my face. And also," he takes a deep breath, "she's the reason why you're pregnant." *THE FUCK?*

"EXCUSE ME?"

"When she broke into the apartment, she went through and poked holes in all our condoms."

"Uh, *that* is the most *insane* shit I have ever heard. That's not real, right? Like she just made that up to screw with you?"

"No, I checked the ones we still had, and they all had holes in them." I feel sick to my stomach.

"I got pregnant because a psychopath wanted revenge for losing her job?"

"Baby, I'm so sorry." He sounds so sincere, but still, I start to breathe a little bit faster. I get angrier, too.

"Are you sorry? You wanted this, even when I didn't." *Oh my god*, could he have planned this? "Please be honest, did you have anything to do with that?" I wince, like I'm bracing for the worst, clutching the door handle till my knuckles turn white.

"Britain, no, of course not. I respected your wishes. I'm not a fucking monster. Baby, look at me." I take a deep inhale, then turn to face him. "Of course I didn't. If you would have decided you didn't want to have this baby, I would have supported that decision, too! I'd even accepted we'd never have our own, okay? I promise." I tilt my head back in frustration.

"The promises, Liam! You keep making promises. Can we find another word, please?" That word is grating on me.

"What's wrong with a promise if I mean it?"

"I'm feeling a little bit scarred by that word. Maybe it has to do with you making me promise not to leave you, and then you left. Or how you promised not to lie to me, and then you did. Are any of those instances ringing a bell for you?"

"You're right, I'm sorry. Consistent actions, not empty promises. I'm working on it, Britain. I am." I breathe in and out deeply, slowly calming down, but a bit enraged at Tori.

"Do you think there's some legal action that can be taken against her?" I ask, then look to him.

"If it's important to you, I'll hire a lawyer to figure it out. Do you want me to?" *Ugh.*

"I don't know that I want to add one more thing to deal with. What's done is done, I guess." Liam squeezes my leg.

"Hey," he says gently, "do you *want* to have this baby?" *Yes.* I turn to look at him again.

"I do, but thank you for asking and considering that this might not be what I want. Granted, some of the conditions haven't been ideal...but we are very lucky, and I know this baby was conceived in love." *Unlike me.*

He moves his hand off my leg to reach up and push the hair off my shoulder and away from my face. With his hand clamped around and gently massaging my neck, his thumb strokes my cheek. "Our baby was absolutely conceived in love, Britain."

Our baby. Hearing him say those words makes me feel something. It's happiness and excitement, and it's the first time I'm feeling it for this child. Maybe that makes me a horrible mother, but I needed Liam to make this all right. I just hope to God he does.

"*Wait*, how did Tori know I was pregnant? Like do I need a restraining order?" *Is she stalking me?*

"Well, Max was actually the one who told her. He did it on purpose because he wanted her to come tell me. Matt told his brothers not to tell me you were pregnant and–"

I cut Liam off. "Are you being SERIOUS right now?" I don't know that I've ever felt this kind of anger in my life. I'm seething. *Matthias prevented Liam from finding out about his child?*

Liam eyes me cautiously before he speaks again. "Yeah, Matt told them not to tell me, and Max was trying to be a good brother, but thought I deserved to know. So he did it in a roundabout way. I'm guessing you didn't know that?"

"NO! Oh my god, Liam. I thought you knew I was pregnant and just wanted nothing to do with me. I was devastated. I even asked Matthias about you, and he said you'd called to let him know about Sonoma, so I assumed you'd checked everything. And that you'd seen my calls and texts and were just done with me. I couldn't even get out of bed some days it hurt so bad." My hands are shaking.

"Britain, baby. It's okay, I'm here now and I'm so sorry there was a time when I wasn't. It's not an excuse, but if I'd known about the baby, the hospital, any of it, I would have been back in the blink of an eye, okay? I really thought I was doing the right thing by letting you go."

"This is a lot, Liam. Can we just not talk the rest of the way home? I need to think." He breaks out into a huge smile, though. "*What*, Liam?"

"You called it *home*, baby." His smile stays plastered on

his face the rest of the way, and we don't talk again. I just sit with my thoughts. They're all over the place as I hop from one thought to the next. *Tori is insane. Matthias is deceitful. How did she poke a hole in the condoms? Matthias said he'd do anything to make this work — except being supportive and honest. How could he? He had to have known how hard I was taking it all. He fucking saw me at the hospital.*

A gentle leg squeeze pulls me out of my mental typhoon.

"We're almost there. Do you want to stop for coffee? Or head straight home?"

Home. That's exactly how it feels and that's exactly where I want to be. I give him a little smile. "Home is good." This time he threads our fingers together for the last mile.

When we pull up to the house, a car I recognize is parked in the driveway. *Carly.* I wait for Liam to come open my door, and when I step outside, I inhale. The smell of pines and damp earth grounds me, and I release the tension from our conversation. Liam rubs my back in understanding, and I give him a small smile. I never thought I'd be happy to be back here, but here we are. He takes my purse and his overnight bag to set inside while I wait for the rest of our group.

The girls and Jess pile out of my SUV, but before we can even start unloading, a familiar face greets us, reaching for the bags first.

"Hi, Mrs. Scott. It's good to see you again." The young man grabs two huge suitcases at the same time, like they're filled with air.

"Hi, James! What are you doing here?"

"I came to help out my sister for the day, and she said Mr. Millar could use an extra hand with luggage. So here I am, happy to help. I'll be back for the rest, so please don't lift anything." As he hauls away the suitcases, I notice Jess, Elodie, and Caroline all staring at his backside.

"That's *the* James who delivered all my stuff to your house?!" Jess basically shouts. I laugh.

"Yeah, why?"

"He's hot! Duh!" Jess exclaims. I laugh again.

Elodie and Jess work to get Eden out of her car seat, but I notice Caroline still staring at the door James just walked through. Liam walks back out and he looks so happy. I just smile.

"Alright, girls," he calls out to us. "James and I will get all the bags. Carly's serving lunch, come on in." As if on cue, my stomach rumbles. So I abandon the cars and head for the door.

"Hey, Liam, this is a cool house!" Elodie is staring up at the large modern cabin before her.

"Thanks, Elodie," Liam says bashfully.

"Just wait till you see the inside, girls, his fireplace is carved from a boulder and there's a rope swing on the dock outside." I don't want to oversell it, but I hope they like this house as much as I do.

"Oh my god, no way!" Elodie exclaims, nearly sprinting into the house. Caroline plays it cooler, though. She just nods her head, but I see her cheeks turn to cherries when James walks through the door just as she's going in. Jess glances back at me and we exchange knowing looks. I walk past Liam, but he snags my arm, halting me. He pulls me into him, and I know my cheeks probably look just like Caroline's.

"Bambi," he starts.

"Yes?"

"I'm going to make you happy, I'm going to take care of

you, and I'm going to love you every day." I wait for the *"I promise,"* but it doesn't come. And *that* makes me smile.

"We're still not together, though. Just so you know..."

He laughs at me. "I get it, gotta keep your options open." He releases me with a pat on my ass, and I blush all over again.

When I walk into his house, it's strange. Everything is new and old, all at the same time. There's fresh hydrangeas in all the vases and a Trudon candle burning in the foyer. And while it's just as beautiful as I remember, now there's the added comfort of home this time. It's a belonging.

I purposefully avoid looking towards his office as I walk through the great room to find my family in the kitchen with Carly, everyone's favorite place to be.

"Britain!" Carly exclaims when she sees me. She sets down her whisk to come around the counter for a big hug. "Oh! It's so good to see you!"

"Hi, Carly! I'm happy to see you, too." She releases me, giving me her luminous smile, her chestnut eyes shining bright. "Oh, and hey, I met your little brother. He's such a gentleman!"

She turns bashful. "Aww, thanks. He is, isn't he?"

Jess interjects, "Yes, quite the gentleman. How old is he?" I nudge her with my shoulder and laugh.

"Oh, yeah, he's 17. Sorry, Jess." Glad to hear they've already made introductions. "Everybody, go sit down, eat! Lunch is on the table!" The girls bound over to the eat-in, but I hang back a moment longer to chat with Carly.

"Liam said you'd be cooking. I didn't realize we'd get to see you today, but I'm so glad we did."

"You're just saying that because you can smell the cake

baking..." Carly gives me the side eye with a smile while she keeps whipping cream.

"Maybe..." I reply, returning the smile.

"Well, you're going to be seeing a lot more of me! Liam hired me full-time for the rest of the summer. So five days a week, I'll be here to do breakfast, lunch, and dinner!"

"That's amazing, Carly. We're so lucky to have you. Honestly, I've missed you so much." She looks at me, probably noting how much weight I've lost without her cooking.

"I've missed you guys, too. Glad to be back...Now go eat!" I laugh, then sit next to Elodie on the bench.

There's a family-style spread laid out before us. A greek salad, summer pasta, grilled salmon, and focaccia. And for once I actually want to eat. Jess sits with Eden in her lap, feeding her pieces of bowtie pasta.

"Jess, give me Eden so you can eat." I hold out my arms to prompt her.

"Nuh uh, girl. You gotta eat first." I roll my eyes at her, but make myself a plate instead. "James is putting together her high chair right now, anyways. So we're good. But hey, this is like a really nice *cabin*." She uses her one free hand to make air quotes. "As in, I didn't know cabins could be this nice."

I laugh at her. "Yeah, Liam designed it himself. It used to be just a basic log cabin, but he re-built the entire thing a couple years ago."

"Wow, that's really cool." Caroline chimes in, surprising me. "Can we go down to the dock after lunch?"

"Definitely, you absolutely can." God, please let them fall in love with Spearhead, too.

"I'm really starting to see the appeal," Jess says to me, making me smile.

"Oh yeah?"

"Yeah, gorgeous house, private chef, on the lake, and, bonus, he has a nice ass."

"Thanks, Jess." Liam says as he comes to take the seat beside me, dropping a kiss on the side of my head. "Carly! You and James should come eat with us!" he calls out into the kitchen.

After Carly finishes whipping her cream and James brings in Eden's high chair, we all share an enjoyable family meal. There's laughter, and teasing, and the food is insanely good. For the first time in months, my cup is starting to feel full. I look at Liam and then at the rest of my family, and I'm in awe. I didn't know it could be like this, but *fuck*, I'm so happy it is. Even if it's just for this moment, I'm going to savor it.

TWENTY-FOUR

LIAM

"You're spoiling us," Britain says, like it's a bad thing. She's sitting in our bed, against a wall of pillows, with her Kindle in her lap. *I'm never going to get tired of that view.* I drop the towel from my shower over the tub and make my way back into our room, and this time, I make sure to lock the door.

I crawl into the bed next to her and say, "Yeah, so what if I am? You all deserve it. I'm here to take care of you and I'm not going to let you forget it." I place a kiss on her forehead before settling back with the TV remote. I'd rather be crawling all over her, but I'm trying not to smother her. She's also made it very clear: We. Are. Not. Together. *But we will be.*

"Do you want to watch something? Or if you want the sound off, I can just read, too." I stop flipping through Netflix and look over to her. She's smiling at me. *Damn*, I want her smiling at me, for me, forever. "What is it, baby?"

"I was happy today." She gets teary eyed a second later.

"Hey," I reach over and pull her into my side. "That's great, baby."

"*You* made me happy."

I chuckle. "Again, you're saying it like it's a bad thing."

"Well, I just...there's just this part of me that wants to stay mad at you, but you're making it hard." I start running my fingers through her hair. I get it. It's hard to let the go of the anger sometimes.

"I know, baby. I'm sorry." We just cuddle for a little while until the TV auto turns off and the room gets thrown into darkness.

"You ready to go to sleep?" I whisper over her in case she already is. She doesn't respond, so I start to move gently out from underneath her when she stops me.

She whispers back, "No," then sits up, pulling off her oversized t-shirt and sliding her underwear away. That's all it takes for me to get rock hard. I don't make a move, though. Maybe she just wants to sleep naked. I'm fully prepared for this morning to be a one-off. I have no expectation that we'll fall back into our twice-a-day routine, as unbelievably amazing as it was.

But then she surprises me when she gets on top of me, straddling me. She leans down to kiss me and I reach for her, slipping my hands into her hair. I want her so bad. My dick, my body, my *being* aches for her. I crave it. I *need* to be inside her. She breaks the kiss and starts to make her way down my chest, kissing me.

"I love you so much, Britain," I whisper to her. She looks back up at me, but doesn't say anything in return. That's okay, I don't need her to. At least not yet.

My fingers trail through her hair in her descent. "Baby, you don't have to. I'm the one who should be taking care of you."

She silences me with a finger to my lips. "I want to, Liam. I miss doing this for you...I love doing this." *Fucking hell.* I won't last 30 seconds. When she finally makes her way down and slips her lips around my cock, I have to fight not to bust in her mouth. *How does she do this to me?* It doesn't seem fair that I've met the person who is so right for me in every way. Her body, her mind, her voice, her laugh. Everything about her life blends into mine seamlessly. She swirls her tongue around my head and heat floods my groin. I'm burning for her.

"Baby, I don't want to come in your mouth tonight." She nods in understanding, releasing me, then crawls back over to straddle me again.

"Do you want me to ride you, daddy?" *Fuck. Daddy.* Sparks fly in my head at the sound of her voice calling me daddy. My head and my heart feel like they'll explode if I don't get inside her.

"Yes. Be my good little girl and ride it." She slides down on me, her tight pussy pulsing already. She wants this, too. *Thank fuck she wants this, too.* "Britain, I fucking love you." I place my hands on her hips and help her grind as I thrust. She lets out the sexiest little moan when I hit her in the right spot. So we keep at it, but not for long. She slams down onto me, her pussy pulling me in tight as she tilts her head back and moans my name. Loudly. *Fuck.*

"Baby, shhh..." Sex with kids in the house is going to be a struggle with this one. She bites her lip to prevent any more sounds from coming out as she rides out her orgasm. As soon as she's passed it, I flip her on to her back and slam back into her.

"I'm going to have to get you a gag, Bambi." She laughs at me, then lifts her hips to meet me as I thrust. Every thrust brings me closer, but I keep holding back. I want her to come again. I want us to come together. I want to feel my girl take what's hers. My thrusts, my cum, my love. It's all hers. So I slow the pace and grind with her.

Running a hand along her breast, then pulling a nipple into my mouth, I can feel her tense before she even knows it's coming. Instead of leaving it to chance, I slam my mouth over hers and swallow her pleasure. Her pussy tightening around me brings me home, and I let go. Nothing could ever compare to this feeling of completeness, with my entire world here in my arms, in our bed. *I'm home with her.* My body releases, and releases, the spasms fucking pure bliss as she claws at my back and we grind out another orgasm for her. My body is satisfied, but already craving more.

"I'm never going to get enough of you, baby." I drop my mouth back down to hers, slipping in my tongue, not leaving her body a second before I have to. She pushes hair out my face, gently, and my heart slams into my chest. I pull her hand over my heart, holding it there.

"*That*, beats for you. I couldn't get out of bed some days either. And if you wouldn't have let me back in your life, well...I don't know where I'd be. Because truly, this is for you, Bambi. All of it. Everything I am, I have — it's all yours, Britain. I've *always* been all yours. From the moment I saw you, I was yours." She doesn't say anything, but she pulls my mouth back down to hers in a kiss that could end all kisses, and I grow hard again, never having left her body.

She starts to move against me when she feels my hardness, and I move, too. It's frantic this time, and punishing. She pushes me, asking for me to go harder. And I do. Like the deeper I bury myself in her, the harder it'll be for her to ever get rid of me. And she's not *ever* getting rid of me, ever again.

She comes before me this time, but I follow right behind her. My muscles contract and release in burning ecstasy, and I love every fucking second, wishing it would last forever. I make a promise to myself: *I'll be this person for her, forever.* When our breathing finally returns to normal, I slide out of her, pressing a kiss to her bump, before heading to the ensuite. And just like we used to, I feel our routine start to come back. She uses the toilet while I wash up, and then we come back together in bed.

She doesn't put her clothes back on, just sliding in next to me and I curl behind her, pulling her in tight to my chest. I stroke her hair for a couple minutes and then I can't help myself, and I move my hand down to cradle our growing child. I realize with stunning clarity, *this* is the happiest I've ever been in my life. With her and our family under one roof, us loving each other. I don't think I can go back to living without her. Not now that I know what this is like.

You made me happy, too, Bambi.

———

When I roll over in the middle of the night and reach for her, my hand comes up empty. *She's not in bed.* I flip over my phone to check the time, 4:06, then get up and head towards the bathroom, but I don't find her there either. My pulse picks up instantly with panic. *Did she leave?* I throw on a pair of sweats and head downstairs in search of her.

"Britain?" I whisper her name when I get to the bottom of the stairs. Nothing answers my query, but I do hear the faintest sound coming from my office. When I get to the entrance, I see her huddled in my office chair, her knees pulled into her chest, and she's resting her head down, crying.

"Baby? Is everything okay?" She looks up at me, surprised I'm there, but just shakes her head in response.

"What's wrong? Talk to me. Please." Her tear-rimmed eyes cause me anguish, and I have to fight the urge to pick her up and place her in my lap. I don't do it, though. I just move closer, leaning against the edge of the desk.

"I just — I feel awful. I feel like a terrible person." She stops to cry for a second before launching back in, "I slept with your *best friend*. Like three days ago! And now I'm here, living in your house, sleeping with you, and I feel like I'm making all the same mistakes all over again."

"Do you want me to move to the garage apartment?" *Fuck*, I really don't want that, but if she needs space and to slow down, I will.

"That's the part that makes me awful, I *don't* want that. I'm happy being here and I'm happy being with you. But I'm supposed to be mad at you. And I'm supposed to stay single because you're not supposed to relationship hop, and I'm sure there's some etiquette rule about waiting a certain number of days between fucking best friends. And then all of that makes me a terrible mother, right? What am I teaching the girls?" I lean forward to wipe a tear off her face.

"You're teaching them that your, *their*, happiness is important. You're showing them that life's too short to waste time being with the wrong person. You're teaching them that a family can grow in ways you'd never expect, but that we're all the better for it.

We're going to show them what it means to care for one another, and what *they* should expect from a partner. They're going to learn to never accept second best because this," I motion between the two of us, "exists, and it's worth going through hell and fighting for. And if you're worried about what other people might think about what's going on here, I'm going to stop you right there. I don't give a fuck what they think. The important people only care that you're happy and healthy, and that's all that matters. And I think you should sit down and talk to the girls about what's going on. Because I think I'm right, that their opinion matters the most to you, yes?" She nods solemnly.

"You're making it so hard to hate you, Liam." She sniffles. "Don't you hate me, though, for being with him?" *No.*

"Not even a little bit, baby. Did it suck when I found out? *Absolutely.* It fucking annihilated me, but I don't hate you for it and I don't think you're a terrible person. I do need to know, though, are things over between Matt and you?"

"I ended things with him on Sunday morning, but then he asked me to reconsider..."

"And?" My heart rate runs rampant with fear. *Please don't rip out my heart right now.*

"And I'm going to tell him today that it's officially over." *Thank fuck.* I kneel down in front of her, falling to my knees, then placing my hands on her legs. "What are you doing?" she asks with a look of confusion.

"Begging for forgiveness, Bambi." I pull each leg down so

that she's no longer hugging them into her chest, and I move forward between her legs.

"I won't make you any promises, Britain. I'm just going to tell you what I'm going to do. And then hopefully, someday, I'll have earned back your trust, and your love, and the privilege of being your partner." I take her left hand in mine, rubbing at the spot on her finger where my ring used to sit. "First and foremost, I'm going to choose you every day, Britain. I'm going to take care of you, and the girls, and our baby. I'm going to respect and support you, and I'll move heaven and Earth just to make you smile. The only thing I need from you is a chance. To earn your forgiveness, and your love, and the place next to you. Please, Britain, can you give me that chance?" She nods, tears filling her eyes, and my heart soars. It's not forgiveness...*yet*. She hasn't said I love you...*yet*. But it's a step in the right direction. She's closing the chapter on Matt, and giving me a shot.

"This doesn't mean we're back together, though," she says as she leans forward.

"I know, baby. You're gonna make me work for it, aren't you?" She nods, then licks her lips before she drops her mouth to mine. It's a gentle kiss, but I don't push for more. Not right now.

"Do you think you can forgive *me*?" she asks. *I already have.*

"There's nothing to forgive, Bambi." Seeing her faint, then in the ambulance — it was so clear to me that none of that matters. I don't care if she slept with Matt. I literally left her to give her that opportunity. It's the going forward part that matters. That's it. And I know I have a shit ton to prove to her. I slide my hand up around her neck and stroke her cheek. "Can we go back to bed now, Bambi? You need to get some rest."

She nods, and we both stand. "Put your arms around my neck," I whisper to her. She does, and I lift her body, moving her legs to wrap around me. I sink a kiss onto her lips, then carry her upstairs to our bed. My dick throbs the whole way, but I don't make any moves to do something about it. I need to show her I can take care of her in ways that don't involve sex.

She basically said as much in the alley, that these feelings of lust will fade and without trust and communication we won't have anything left. Well, I'm going to build that for us. I'm going to give her my consistency, my trust, and my voice, and hopefully someday she'll do the same.

I close the door behind us in our room, making sure it's locked. When I get to her side of the bed, I set her feet on the floor gently. She's wearing her oversized t-shirt again and I motion to it. "Do you want to sleep with this on or off?" Before, she always slept naked, but that's when it was just us...and we were together.

"Off," she says quietly. I nod, and lift the shirt off her slowly, the fabric gliding over her breasts, revealing hard nipples. My dick throbs again. I let her shirt fall to the floor and take her in. It's dark, but I can still see her curves and her pebbled nipples. I see her lacy underwear, and how it dips to accommodate her growing abdomen. I swear her bump grows every day, and I fucking love the way she looks, swollen with my child.

I can't wait to knock her up again, but I hesitate to tell her. I'm trying really hard not to scare her off. I slide a finger under her panties at her hip and ask, "Do you want these on or off?" My voice comes out raspy with need.

"Off, please." I nod, then use both hands to slip her underwear down her legs. My dick swells fuller when I can see all of her, but I still don't make any moves. I'll let her initiate for a little bit. We're on her timeline now. I'm hers whenever she wants me, but I won't push it. I pull back the duvet and usher her to climb in. Once she's covered, I drop my sweats and get in on my side of the bed. When I lean over to press a kiss on her shoulder, and whisper "Goodnight," I can tell she's already asleep. *Good.* She fucking needs it.

The odds of me falling back asleep now are slim, so instead, I lay there wide awake, plotting. I plot how I'm going to win her back. How I'm going to show her how much she means to me. I think about how I'll do that, and what's important to her. And what's important to her are the girls, Jess, and Damian. *Damian.* I don't know why he's staying with them, or what the deal is there, but I do know I'm not worried about it because I trust Britain. I want to talk to her more about it, but it can wait.

When the clock finally hits 5:45, I crawl out of bed quietly. I scrawl a note for Britain and set it on her bedside before heading downstairs. *I've got someone to see and work to do.*

———

The door chimes when I walk into The Grounds. There's no one else in here, which is typical of 6:00 A.M. on a Wednesday morning.

Sandy walks out from behind the curtained back, but

stops short when she sees me. "William," she says with surprise. Her words don't pack the same bite they did last week, though.

"Hi, Mom." She moves to stand behind the register, but she doesn't come around the counter to greet me like she normally would. "I could use a coffee, but I was hoping you could talk, too." She nods, filling a travel cup with black coffee, then brings it around to a table for us to sit.

"Is it true? The girls said Britain and them were staying at your house now."

I smile. "Yeah, it's true."

Sandy chuckles, but eventually breaks out into a smile, too. "How much is that costing you?" She arches an eyebrow when she asks.

"Ha!" I laugh. "Yeah, um, quite a bit, actually. But it's worth it."

"Damn right they are." *I know, Mom.* "So, what brings you here then?"

"Well, as part of making things right with Britain, I need to make things right with you, too. I've missed you, and I'm going to need your help with the baby coming, and I don't want things to be weird between us. You're going to be the best grandma and I just don't want you staying away because I fucked up."

She gives me an endearing look, sliding her hand over mine. "Honey, you couldn't keep me away from my grand-baby even if you tried." I laugh and roll my eyes. *Of course.* "And, as long as you're making things right with Britain, we'll be alright..."

I nod. *I will make things right.* "And I don't mean to say that you need to get back together for things to be alright, but

I need you to be respecting her and treating her like the goddamn queen she is, you understand?"

"Understood," I nod. "Does this mean I can come off the shit list?"

"You're on probation, bud. But Liam?"

"Yeah?"

"I'm real proud of you, son. Just don't fuck it up this time." *Oh, I won't.*

"Thanks, Mom. I should probably get going. Full house and all..." I reach for my wallet, but she stops me.

"This one's on the house, sugar." I laugh, leaning over to give her a kiss on the cheek.

"Love you, Mom."

"I love you, too, William."

TWENTY-FIVE

BRITAIN

As I come to consciousness this morning and stretch, I realize I'm smiling. Because I'm happy. Talking with Liam last night helped subdue my anxiety and cemented that I'm making the right decision.

How I feel when I'm with him is undeniable. He's my safe place, and my home, but he also makes me burn with hunger and want. I roll over, out of instinct, to his side, but find it empty, surprising me. *Did I sleep in?*

I roll back over to check my phone, and see a note in his horrendous chicken scratch.

> *I hope you get some more sleep, Bambi. I'll be downstairs waiting for you when you get up, but I just wanted to let you know I love you, and I'm here to support you today.*
> *Always, Liam*

It takes me a moment to realize what he means. *Support me*, in talking with Matthias. *Right*. I have to do that today. I flip the phone over to see it's 7:45 and I have no new messages. After I talked to Matthias on Monday, I thought for sure I'd hear from him between then and now, but it's been nothing but radio silence. If I'm being honest, I'm glad he hasn't reached out. It's been a crazy couple of days, but even though I've been here with Liam, I've still thought about him.

I finally had my session with Carla yesterday where I dropped everything on her — the good, the bad, the ugly. She walked me through a couple exercises to help calm my mind in hopes the answer would reveal itself to me. But what really did it was when I asked her if she believed in fate.

"Do you believe in fate, Carla?" She shows little to no reaction to my question, at least not one I can perceive through my laptop screen. I fully expect her to say no. Carla seems like the type of person with an "everything in its box, Excel spreadsheet, pro/con list with a statistical chance of success" view of love.

"Yes." Seriously?

"Wow, um, really? I just mean I took you for someone with a very pragmatic and calculated outlook on love."

"I'd like to think of it as a more holistic approach. I look at all the factors of love and relationships together, but I understand that how someone makes you feel is one of the most important elements. And sometimes, there's no explanation for why. In my line of work, I've seen it all, Britain. And I see how against all odds, people come together under the most adverse of circumstances. For you, Britain, you need to figure out who it is that brings you happiness and peace."

———

I close my eyes and I let the past fade away, and I think about who makes me happy. Who am I able to be completely myself with? Who feels like home? Who feels like safety and warmth and peace? And it's easy, I see *his* face. He's waiting for me downstairs.

My excitement propels me up and out of bed. I quickly throw on a Skims boyfriend tee and boxers and head down to see my family.

I find Jess and Eden in the great room, watching *Bluey*. "Do you need coffee?" I ask before I walk into the kitchen. She just shakes her head, no, then gives me a smile.

In the kitchen, I find Carly and the girls. "Morning," I say to them. The girls are sitting at the island stools, perusing their phones while Carly carves up a pineapple.

"Good morning!" "Hi, Mom." "Morning, Mom!" They all return. Someone's missing, though. Caroline notices me looking around.

"He's working out, Mom." *Shit. Obvious much, Britain?*

"Okay." I smile at her, then pour myself a cup of coffee.

"So, this morning I have a frittata, fresh fruit, and blueberry waffles for everyone," Carly announces.

My mouth salivates. "Did I mention how lucky we are to have you?" I move to stand next to Carly, leaning back against the kitchen counter.

"You did." She smiles, continuing her precision butchering of the pineapple. "It'll be on the table in 5 minutes."

While she keeps working away, I decide to chat her up. "I didn't know you had a little brother." Caroline perks up at the mention of James. "Does your whole family live around here, too?"

A slight blush creeps up Carly's cheeks. "Oh, no. It's just the two of us, him and me!" I'm a little surprised, but at the same time, if there's anything I understand, it's weird family dynamics.

I wait to see if she wants to expand, but she doesn't. Understood. "Well, it's awesome that you guys have each other. He seems just as amazing as you are. You know, he's welcome to come over here any time. I'm sure the girls would love hanging out with someone their own age. Or maybe he can show them around, if he's free." Caroline is fully invested in my conversation now.

"Next time he's free, I'll have him tag along. Thank you." She smiles at me and I smile back. I ask her if she's still working for Sandy and Jim, which she replies in the affirmative, and I don't know how she does it. Working full time for us, doing all the prepared meals for them, caring for her younger sibling full time — she blows me away.

I hear the door to the mudroom open and the butterflies in my stomach activate in his nearby presence. Caroline still hasn't gone back to looking at her phone and I find her just staring at me, so I try to school my face into not smiling like an idiot, but it's hard when you're this happy.

"Hey, girls, I'd love it if we could go for a walk this morning. I can show you my route. It's got an awesome view of the lake?" I ask Caroline and Elodie.

"Sure, Mom. Sounds fun!" Elodie replies, but Caroline just nods her head, silently.

When Liam finally rounds the corner, toweling off his sweaty face, he says, "Oh, damn. I was hoping to finish before you were up. Sorry, baby." I smile at him with the knowledge that I'd keep on choosing him, *every day*.

"It's okay. Thanks for leaving the note."

He nods, "Of course," then makes his way over to give me a kiss on the forehead.

Caroline hasn't stopped staring at me the entire time, but Elodie with her face still turned down to her phone says, "Eww, gross! Get a room!" I laugh.

Carly finishes plating the last of the pineapple and lets us know it's time to eat. When I instruct the girls to each take a plate to the table to help, I feel his hand wrap around my arm and pull me gently back to the mudroom.

"I just want to say good morning, properly," he says before he drops his mouth to mine in a kiss that makes my panties wet. I don't want him to stop, but he does. I lick my lips when he's done, tasting his salty sweat.

"Mmm, you taste salty," I tell him, and his broad smile comes out.

"I love having you back home, baby." That's not what I was expecting. I can practically hear my heartbeat in my ears, and feel it in my pelvis when he says this.

I go up on my tiptoes to whisper in his ear, "And I missed having you in bed this morning."

"Christ, baby," Liam says, pulling me in tight to him. I can feel his hard length come alive against me.

"The baby needs to eat, babe," I tell him when he doesn't immediately let me go.

"Okay," his voice comes out strained. "I'll be out there in a minute." He releases me and motions down to the raging hard on. I just laugh at him, then join the rest of my family for breakfast.

"Can you join us?" I ask Carly before sitting down.

"Yep, will do! Just let me get out the syrup and butter."

When Jess and Eden make their way over to the eat-in, she eyes the spread, then looks up at me, "Girrllll, don't fuck this up." We both laugh.

While I help her get Eden strapped into the high chair, I ask, "I'm taking the girls for a walk after breakfast to talk about everything. Do you want to come? Moral support?"

She looks at me with a smile. "No, I don't think so. But...I think you and I are overdue for a girl chat this afternoon. During Eden's nap?"

I nod, we are more than overdue. "So about that...I'm supposed to go get coffee with Matthias sometime today. I was wondering if you'd take me. Just be there, in case things are..." I trail off, looking over to the girls, then say, "weird."

Liam chimes in, making his way to the space beside me and says, "I'm going to take you."

"I don't know if that's such a good idea based on what happened last time." I look at the stitches on his fist.

"I don't want him yelling at you, again," he says it low, just for me to hear, but that doesn't matter.

"Matt yelled at you?" Caroline asks, looking a bit stricken. I eye Liam, then turn my attention back to Caroline.

"Unfortunately, yes. He was upset, I don't think he even realized he did it. I asked him not to, and he didn't do it again." She looks distressed, though. Jess sees it, too.

"Can he come meet you at The Grounds? I can bring Eden with me and we'll hang out with Sandy while you talk, but then I'm still there for support if you need it. We also won't be too far to put Liam at ease, as well." It sounds like the perfect suggestion to me.

I look to Liam for confirmation. "If that's what you want to do, then I'll support you," he says. "But if you change your mind, I'll be right there." He drops a hand to the small of my back, rubbing the area gently.

"That's what I want," I say and he nods in affirmation.

"That's settled then. Let's get everyone fed. We've got a big day!" Liam says while guiding me to my seat on the bench.

"A big day?" I ask.

"Yep, after your walk, I could use the girls' help, actually." Caroline and Elodie look over to him. "I need some help picking up the paddleboards I ordered from the marina. James is coming over at some point with the truck, but I thought it'd go faster with a few more hands."

Elodie is talking as soon as he finishes asking. "Oh my god, yes! Can we use them? I mean, like are we allowed to use them?"

Liam chuckles. "Yeah, I mean, I bought them for you girls to use."

Elodie pumps her fist up in the air in a loud "Yes!"

Caroline just says, "I could help...if you need." She's trying so hard to play it cool, but I don't miss how quickly she scarfs down her breakfast to go get ready.

When I've finished eating, I glance over to Liam. He's sipping his coffee and reading the news on his phone. His silver hair is mussed from working out and his shirt still slightly damp with perspiration, but I've never wanted him more. He looks in my direction, noticing me, and we exchange smiles. I love him so much. *Ugh*, I *want* him so bad.

We all help pick up from breakfast and then I excuse myself to go get ready for the walk. I'm hoping he'll follow me, so when I turn back on the stairwell to see him several feet below but gaining on me, my muscles start clenching with anticipation. He's looking at me like I'm his next meal, and I can't fucking wait.

I turn on the shower in our ensuite, strip, then wait for him. As soon as he walks into the bathroom, I'm on him. I run my hands up his shirt, then help pull it over his head. Next, I work his shorts down, his thick cock greeting me once it's free. Then taking his hand, I guide him into the heated shower.

"You messed up our routine," I say to him. It looks like he blushes.

"I don't want you to think that's all we're about, Britain." That's my fault. I told him once the lust fades, there'd be nothing left of us. I already know that's not true.

"I know it's not all we're about," I say, going on my tiptoes and pulling him down to my mouth. He wraps his arms around me, lifting me up with both hands on my ass cheeks, and I wrap my legs around him. He moves us, pinning me against the shower wall and I'm already soaking wet. So when I feel him near my entrance, I adjust slightly and he glides right into me.

"Fuck, Bambi," he groans out as he thrusts against me and I run my hands up his neck, and into his hair.

"I wanted this the second I woke up this morning," I whisper into his ear as he thrusts then grinds against me.

"Baby, there's never a time I don't want you," he says, dropping his mouth to mine. We work together, pushing and pulling in our give and take. He pulls out slowly before slamming back into me, pinning his hips against mine, then whispers in a gravelly voice, "I want your pussy full and dripping my cum the rest of the day, so that when you're sitting with *him*, *I'm* the one inside you." His words set me on fire.

"Fuck, daddy. Yes, please. Pleaseeee..." I beg and moan, and I'm so fucking close.

"I want the whole world to know you're mine, Britain. I want my ring back on your finger, yesterday. I want you having my babies, and I want everyone calling you Mrs. William Millar." *Jesus.* I tilt my head back and moan out his name. "Do you want that, too, Mrs. Millar?" *Of course I do.*

I pant out in a moan, "Yes, daddy. I want that, too." And with that, we both lose it. He roars, and I try not to scream when his name comes out of my mouth as all my muscles contract around him, over and over. His heat fills me, fueling me as I grind down against him, driving me into another orgasm right on the back of the last.

When the tension starts to leave his body, and our breathing slows, he rests his forehead against mine. "I meant what I said, Britain, but I can wait till you're ready, okay?" I nod and he drops his mouth to mine. Gliding his tongue into my mouth sensually, my pussy clenches down on his still throbbing cock. *I'll be ready soon.* I don't say it out loud, though. He could stand to keep groveling.

He slides me slowly off his dick, setting me down in the shower. I duck out quickly to pee, but then come straight back to join him. While he's scrubbing his body, I move under the massive showerhead and let the water soak me. When I step out and reach for the shampoo, he stops me. He puts a large amount in his own hand, working the suds up, then motions for me to turn around.

His fingers working the shampoo into my scalp feel fucking orgasmic. I think I even moan when his pressure increases. When he finishes my scalp massage, he places a gentle kiss on my shoulder, then says, "I'm going to take such good care of you, baby." And I feel it in my bones. He's going to take care of me and our family, and it's like it's all I've ever wanted — the way his words fill me up and soothe me. I want so badly to tell him I love him, but I'm going to wait. When the time is right, I'll let him know.

He helps me rinse my hair, then apply conditioner, and when it's time to scrub my body, he does all the work for me. Scrubbing an area clean, then covering it with kisses and love. He spends extra time on my abdomen, running a large hand over the area, then looking up at me from where he is on his knees.

"I just can't believe our child is in there, Britain." The look and smile he gives me after he says that makes me feel like a powerful goddess. That I am amazing and divine for carrying our child. He makes me feel like I'm magic. I look down at him, and push a stray lock of hair out of his eyes, and smile back. He's magic, too. My magic.

"This is the second time today you've gotten down on your knees for me, Liam." I laugh slightly at that fact. *I bring Liam Millar to his knees.*

"If that's what it takes, I'll fall to my knees for you every day. You're my queen, Britain." He pulls my hand to his mouth, placing a soft-yet-sensual kiss there.

"We should probably finish up, our family's waiting." I give him a hand to help pull him back up, and he looks down at me with a radiant smile. I'm about to ask him what he's smiling about, when he beats me to it.

"I like the way that sounds, baby. *Our family.*" *Me too, Liam Millar.*

TWENTY-SIX

BRITAIN

I feel nervous and shaky when I send the text message.

BRITAIN

Can you meet for coffee at noon?

His reply is almost immediate. I wasn't expecting that after not hearing from him for days.

MATTHIAS

Yes, at La Boulangerie?

Actually, I was wondering if we could meet at The Grounds in Spearhead?

This time the reply isn't immediate. There's three little dots that come and go multiple times before I finally receive a reply.

Why Spearhead?

I'm staying here right now.

I don't want to lie to him, and if he asks, I'll tell him the truth. But I don't want to hurt him unnecessarily either.

WHERE are you staying in Spearhead?

Fuck, in all caps, too.

I'm staying at Liam's house. I ended up in the ER on Monday, and he's been looking after me since then.

I hope that isn't too much of a white lie. The flat-out truth would be because I love him, and I'm happy here, and he's taking care of me. I wait for the reply, but then fumble my phone when it starts ringing in my palm. *Shit,* Matthias is calling. I'm in the primary suite upstairs with Liam, but I'm supposed to meet the girls in ten minutes for our walk. I hit decline, feeling like absolute shit when I do it.

I can't talk right now. I'm going for a walk with the girls. I can call you afterwards, or we can meet for coffee.

The girls are staying at Liam's house, too? What the fuck, Britain? Pick up the goddamn phone!

He immediately calls after sending the text. Liam hears the ring this time and walks out of the ensuite to check on me.

"Everything okay?" I'm sure he can see the look on my face that it's not. I shake my head, and he comes over to where I'm sitting in an overstuffed armchair in front of the fireplace.

"What's going on?" he asks, and I tell him about texting Matthias, and that I didn't lie to him and now he's calling me over and over. And just like on cue, my phone rings again with another incoming call.

"I'm supposed to meet the girls downstairs in five minutes for our walk. Do you think I should just take the call? I mean, I feel like he's not going to stop." I can feel the anxiety creeping in.

"If you want some privacy, I can tell the girls the paddle-boards are ready now, and then you guys can walk when they're back home?" he asks.

"Do you mind? I think it's probably better if I just take care of this now."

"Whatever you need. I can stay, too, and just have James take the girls if you need some support."

I do want him to stay. I know if he's here with me, I'll be safe. But also, it'll be good for him to get time with the girls. "Just go, it'll be okay."

He looks slightly uneasy, but then concedes, giving me a kiss on the forehead. Before he leaves, though, he tells me, "I love you, Britain. No matter what, okay?"

I nod my head and say, "Okay," and then he's out the door. My phone rings again, and with a tremble in my finger, I slide to answer. "Hello?"

"Britatin, WHAT THE FUCK?" he yells at me. *That escalated quickly.* I immediately regret sending Liam away now.

"Please don't yell at me, Matthias."

He just ignores my request, though. "You have got to be FUCKING kidding me! Wait, are you fucking *him?*"

I'd be lying if I said his tone didn't scare me. Do I say yes? This is the ugly side of it all; I feel like complete shit and the guilt is overwhelming.

"I am," I say quietly. I know this is going to hurt, but it's the truth. I brace myself for his response, knowing it's going to suck.

"Wow, Britain," he scoffs. "You're quite the little *whore* aren't you?" My stomach sinks into my ass, my cheeks burn with shame, and the urge to curl into a ball and die is strong. "I didn't believe Liam when he said he was with you the night of the Greek Fest, but that was true, wasn't it? You told me you wanted to be with me, but then you turn around and fuck us both in the same night. Fucking unbelievable, Brit."

"I did not have sex with Liam after the Greek Festival. I was sick and he carried me to bed. That's it." I try really hard to keep my tone even and strong...I'm probably failing.

"Like I'd believe you." His tone is pure poison. It's hateful.

"You don't have to believe me. I ended things with you on Sunday, and I was not with him before then." I think it's telling he doesn't give a fuck what happened to me that I ended up in the ER. He only cares about someone else putting their dick in what he thinks is his.

"Do you want my brothers' numbers? Huh? So you can go FUCK THEM, TOO?" he yells again. I'm not sure if it's him raising his voice at me or that he's saying the same thing Liam did, but it stings. Harshly.

"If you yell at me again, I'm hanging up and blocking your number."

He laughs a mean laugh at me. "No you won't because you're just a desperate little slut who's daddy didn't love her enough," his voice rasps out, maliciously. "Speaking of, just wait till Constantine hears about this."

Why the fuck would I care what Constantine thinks? It throws me off, until I remember what a huge dick he's being. I can't believe I ever had second thoughts about this. "I don't even know who you are, Matthias. All I wanted was to tell you that I don't want to reconsider being with you. Whatever we had is fully in the past, but I do want to thank you for putting any doubts I was having about my decision to rest. Please don't call me *ever* again." I end the call, set the phone down with shaking hands, then move to the bed where I curl into the fetal position and cry.

What in the actual fuck just happened? It's like he flipped a switch and morphed into Mr. Hyde. I know realistically I'm not a whore, or a desperate little slut with daddy issues, but on some level, the words sting — and maybe he's not wrong? I cry a little harder, but I'm thankful when the phone doesn't ring again.

I lay there for two hours, crying on and off again, wondering what the hell just happened? Is this who he is, or did I just hurt him that bad and this is my fault? Maybe he's justified? Maybe I was a whore. I mean, I did sleep with best friends, days apart. Maybe that does make me desperate. And yeah, I know I have daddy issues.

I'm so lost in my own thoughts, I don't hear the bedroom door open. Liam climbs into bed, pulling me into his arms to cradle me. He tries to soothe me, brushing the hair out of my face, then rubbing my back, until finally he breaks the silence.

"I'm sorry, Britain. I know that was a really hard thing to do."

I laugh, then sniffle. "No, it was actually exceedingly easy to do. I'm just crying because he was a total prick."

Liam tenses behind me. "What did he say?"

"Oh, you know, the usual. Called me a whore, a desperate little slut with daddy issues, yelled at me, asked if I wanted his brothers' numbers so I could go fuck them, too."

"I'm going to fucking kill him," Liam whispers behind me.

"It's not worth it. As long as he stays away from me, I don't care anymore. I just can't believe I was doubting myself. I was so worried I was making the wrong decision, but um yeah, that definitely solidified it for me."

"Well, you're not a whore, or desperate, and who doesn't have daddy issues? Even I have daddy issues, for fuck's sake!" I laugh at his comment, then roll over to face him. I don't want to talk about this anymore.

"Distract me. How did picking up paddleboards go?"

"Ahh, I think it went alright," he says while gently stroking a thumb across my throat. "I took them all for a quick lap around the lake in Lucille. Elodie loved it. Caroline looked like she was holding on for dear life. Well, when she wasn't looking at James, she was." I laugh, and he continues, "She's got it bad, sweetheart." *She's not the only one.*

"Thanks for doing that. Did you already get them unloaded?"

He reaches over, pushing my hair away from my face. "We did. They're already out there with them if you feel like sitting on the deck or dock to watch. We can do lunch out

there, too. I think Carly said it's only like 45 minutes out."
Christ, it's already almost lunch.

"Yeah, I think I'd like that."

"Any chance I can convince you to put on a swimsuit and
go for a swim?" He gives me that same 'I could eat you' gaze.

"You really want to see all this in a swimsuit?" I motion
down to the belly that, thanks to overeating at breakfast,
seems bigger and harder than it was earlier.

"Fuck yes, Bambi. You're so damn sexy. If the kids
weren't here, I'd get you in the lake naked and fuck you right
on the shore."

"Really? Even with the sand?" He laughs at me.

"Fine in the dock storage closet. Fuck, even just on the
dock. I want to fuck you in every room in this house, baby." I
just nod my head and smile.

"I'm surprised we haven't already." I mean, we really got
around the first time.

"Yeah, about that, we're starting from scratch, so we'll
really have to commit to working on that if we want to get it
done before *this* baby comes out."

"*This* baby?" He said it like there'll be others.

"I'm just being hopeful. If you're done after this, we'll be
done. I'll go get a vasectomy as soon as you're done giving
birth. But as of right now, yeah, I want another one." He gets
a little more serious, his voice a bit quieter. "I want to be there
when you take the pregnancy test and when we hear the
heartbeat for the first time. I want to be at the ultrasounds,
and I mean, I fucking love the idea of getting to knock you up
again." My cheeks heat. *Fuck me.*

"Hmm, I really want you to fuck me right now." I lean
over to give him a kiss. "But I think I'm going to put on a

swimsuit instead." I sit up and head to my closet. He trails behind me to watch me undress, so I make sure to take my time, giving him a show, touching my breasts and pulling on my nipples before I tie my top. When I look over to him, he palms his rock-hard cock, watching me, sending a gush of warmth between my thighs.

I step both feet into my bottoms, then turn around, bending over slowly to bring them up to my hips. When I'm finally fully standing, he's right at my back, running a hand down into the front of my swimsuit bottoms.

"We don't have to fuck to make you feel good, baby." He slips a finger between my already slick folds, running it up and down, and my head falls back against his shoulder in response.

"I know, but I think I'd rather just wait. I want you begging for it."

"I'll get on my knees and beg for it right now, baby."

I shake my head, though. "No, I want you desperate." I spin around, standing right in front of him and palm his thick cock over his jeans.

"I'm pretty fucking desperate now," Liam says a bit breathlessly.

"How desperate?"

"I might die if I don't taste your sweet pussy." I pretend to ponder his level of desperation.

"Hmmm. Maybe you can watch but no touching?"

"No," his tone is firm, unrelenting. "I need to touch you, Bambi. I need to taste you and I need to be inside you."

I'm curious. "When we were apart, did you ever touch yourself and think of me?"

"Every. Fucking. Day," he replies.

"Show me." He doesn't say anything back, he just unbuttons his jeans and drops his fly, revealing his bare cock. He wraps a large palm around the thick shaft, making a tight fist, but his eyes never leave me. He stares at my body like it's the hottest thing he's ever fucking seen, making my chest swell because that's absolutely the way I see him.

He starts stroking, up and down. And I start salivating over the muscles and veins in his forearm that pop and throb as his tight hold grips his length. "What would you think about?" I ask quietly.

"I'd think about the first time I came inside you. I'd think about bending you over our kitchen island, or taking you up against the wall. I thought a lot about the time we did 69 on the sofa and I painted your ass with cum." I'm going to have to change swimsuit bottoms; it's starting to feel like I sat in a puddle.

I can't take it any longer. I move my hand down, sliding it into my bikini bottoms and he moans at the sight. I push the bottoms to the side, and let him watch as I insert a finger, then two. I use my other hand to push my swim top over and pinch a nipple. The heat of his gaze is overwhelming me, and I press my palm to my clit.

"Don't you dare fucking come, Bambi," he says, eyeing where my fingers are entering my body so I ease up on the pressure. "Fuck it. Get on your hands and knees." His voice is commanding and *fuck yes*, I love when he tells me what to do. He drops his jeans to the floor and rips off his shirt, turning to close and lock the closet door. I watch him from my hands and knees, my pussy tight and vibrating with anticipation.

"Crawl to me, Bambi," he says, getting down on his knees. "You're going to suck my cock, before I rail that ass." My cheeks flame and I nod before I start crawling to him. Maybe it's demeaning, maybe it's sick, but I don't give a fuck. Because if Liam Millar tells me to do it, I will...and I'll fucking love it.

When I get to the point where his dick is inches from my face, he instructs me. "Be a good girl and open wide." I do, and he thrusts his cock into me. I moan, and feel him tremble from the vibration. Wrapping my lips around his shaft, I suck, and work up and down, moving my tongue around his head. The tip is already dripping, and I savor the bit of cum already there.

"Are you ready, baby?"

I nod and moan out, "Yes," and he grunts, but has to pull back to keep from blowing in my mouth.

"Turn around, Bambi." Of course, I do as I'm told, releasing his dick, then turning around to give him my ass. He quickly unties my bikini bottoms at the sides, then discards the fabric to the closet floor.

I can hear, then *feel*, as he spits on my ass. The sound is so dirty, so fucking erotic my clit actually vibrates. *Fuck me, that's hot.*

He rubs the lubricant between my cheeks and around my hole. The sensation feels fucking euphoric, causing my fingers to dig into the plush carpet. His dick throbs between my thighs, but he doesn't enter me. Instead he warms me up, slipping in one finger, then slowly adding another to my asshole. *Fuck, Liam, please.* The thrill of anticipation heightens the feeling of the cool air hitting my nipples and clit, and like nothing I've ever wanted before, I want him in me. Touching me. Claiming me.

"More, daddy. I want more," I tell him.

"Of course you do, Bambi," he chuckles, "because you're fucking perfect." He removes his fingers, and my body aches from the emptiness. He spits on my ass again, and my pussy leaks down my inner thighs. "You're so fucking beautiful, Bambi. Your ass, this pussy, and that filthy fucking mouth. Tell me what you want."

"I want your thick cock to fuck my ass hole and some day soon, I want you to fuck me with both holes filled."

He grabs my chin, turning me to look at him. "You want a butt plug, Bambi? Because I'm sure as fuck not sharing you." *God, I love this man.*

I laugh, "Yes, daddy, that's what I meant." He spits on my ass once more, then slides his cock past the tight ring of muscle. *Fuuuccckkk.* I cry out from the mix of pain and pleasure. I can hear him moaning behind me, but I focus on my breathing to get the discomfort to subside.

"I don't know if I can keep from moving much longer, baby. I'm fucking dying over how tight you are." I push back against him, letting him know I'm ready and turn my head so he can see my smile.

"Fuck me, *daddy*."

A truly devilish look comes over his face in response to my words. "Oh I will, baby. I've been dying to fuck this pretty little hole for awhile now." He laughs maniacally, "But if you want to come..." *Damnit*, I should have seen this coming. He thrusts in and out of me slowly making my clit throb, begging for attention, and when he slides out, my pussy aches and clenches for him. "You're fucking mine."

"I've always been yours, Liam."

"I want everyone else to know it, too." *Shit*, I was hoping to hold it over his head a while longer.

"Something else." I try to prolong the inevitable. He thrusts again, and I cry out with desire.

"*No.* Fucking keep this up, and you'll find yourself engaged before you get to come." The need to come is so intense, my body feels like it's on fire.

"Fine! *Fuck.* We're together!" I'm the desperate one now. I need him touching my clit. I need him grabbing my full breasts, hard. I need him to quench the burning from the sting of him stretching my tight hole. He reaches around placing a damp finger to my clit and I toss my head back, intoxicated by this man. "Yes, fuck me...fuck, baby. I don't know if I can keep from screaming." I don't want to keep from screaming, I want to scream his name at the top of my lungs. I want everyone to know that this man claimed *me.* Wants *me.* Loves *me.*

"Try, Bambi. I'm close, though," he says when we both hear it at the same time, a door opening, and we freeze.

I turn back to look at him with horror on my face, and he slams a hand over my mouth. It's too late, though, I'm already coming. I rock back against him, and bite one of his fingers, and then I feel him erupt inside me. As if this wasn't already the best orgasm of my entire fucking life, my tight asshole can feel each time his spurts of cum release, extending my orgasm even further. We stay as quiet as possible, dying together, when we hear the door finally closes again.

"Fuck, that was close," I whisper out.

He nods in agreement. "But goddamn, it was so fucking hot. *This* is going to be a core memory, Bambi."

He slides out of me slowly, trailing kisses down my spine and then with a quick pat to my ass, we both get up and head to the bathroom to wash off. When I come out of the water closet, I'm laughing to myself. I turn on the shower, but Liam stops me first.

"What's so funny?"

I laugh out loud again. "When our grandkids ask us, 'How'd you and Grandma get together?' are you going to tell them it was over anal on the floor of my closet?"

He laughs, then walks towards me, placing a kiss on my lips. "This fucking filthy mouth." He kisses me again. "I love it."

TWENTY-SEVEN

BRITAIN

I change into another bikini and throw a sleeveless knit dress over, while Liam walks out of his closet in just a pair of swim trunks. I bite my lip and smile when I see him. *He's fucking mine.* He joins me as we open the door, giving me a quick kiss and running a hand over my bump. Then we turn to make our way downstairs when the sound of the front door slamming shut startles me. Liam immediately bypasses me on the stairs, putting his body in front of mine.

He walks straight to the front door to open it, and when he does, I hear yelling. *Matthias.* I blanch and freeze, fear taking hold. Liam looks back at me and says, "*Stay*," in his sternest voice, then closes the door behind himself.

Carly, hearing the commotion, comes out from the kitchen with a concerned look on her face. But after seeing me, her concern turns to fear. "What's wrong, Brit? Are you okay?"

I just nod. "Are the kids still down at the lake?" I ask.

"Yeah, do you want me to go check on them?" I nod vehemently.

"Yes, please. Make sure they stay there for right now." She turns and heads straight to the back deck.

On shaking legs, I walk towards the front door and when I get to the foyer I can make out loud voices, but the words are imperceptible. I press down on the latch to release the lock, and immediately the yelling fills my ears.

It's not what I hear, but what I see that surprises me most. Alex stands between Liam and Matthias, trying to prevent them from coming to blows. *Alex is here?* I stand frozen on the front porch as I watch the scene unfold.

"All of you, and that fucking whore, are nothing but scum of the Earth white trash. I mean, who could blame her, though? It's not like Georgia could keep her legs closed. Is it any wonder Britain can't either?" The pain I feel from Matthias' words is searing. *He told me he loved Georgia.*

Liam gets a murderous look on his face and is just about to speak when Alex beats him to it. "The only reason you're not already unconscious is because you're too fucking weak to take a swing," Alex says viciously. "Your ass would be fucking toasted and you know it. But if you really wanna talk about scum of the Earth, it's you, bud. I should've fucking ended you 17 years ago. You've grown to be such a big man, talking about women like this." Alex scoffs, "Pathetic. You are your mother's son, Matt."

At that, Matthias loses all control and takes a swing at Alex. And surprisingly, it lands. Alex only takes a step back for a moment, then slams him back with a deafening blow. Matthias falls down, and stays down, clearly knocked out cold. When I gasp, Alex and Liam immediately turn to look at me.

"Baby, I told you to stay!" Liam yells as he runs over to me. "I need to make sure Matthias stays down. Alex already called the sheriff. They'll be here any minute."

I ignore Liam trying to usher me back into the house and walk over to Alex. "I'm so sorry, Alex. Are you okay?" I look up to see the red mark where Matthias caught his jaw.

"I'm alright, Brit. I had to let him hit me so I could lay his ass out," he punctuates the statement with a charming grin. It's almost enough to make me smile, too, but then I look down at Matthias. *Who are you? Did I really hurt him so badly?* I want to feel guilty, and maybe I do a little bit, but the things he just said...he was unhinged. And mean. *So mean.*

"When did you get here, Alex?" I ask.

Alex looks to Liam, then back to me. "Ahh, a couple hours ago. Liam asked me to come hang out for a little while he took the girls out."

"I didn't want to leave you alone, in case something like *this* happened," Liam rubs my back supportively.

"Um, th-thank you then." I direct my thanks to Alex.

"Britain, can you please go back inside? I don't want you to have to deal with this when Matt comes to and the sheriff gets here." I nod absentmindedly and head back through the front door. I walk, in a daze, to the back deck, and wave for Carly to come back in.

When she gets to the top level of the deck, I let her know that it's taken care of and the sheriff will be here soon.

"Maybe we should take lunch down at the dock, if that's okay?"

"Absolutely, I'll bring it out as soon as it's done," she says.

"Sorry, to make it difficult, Carly. I appreciate it."

"Brit, please don't worry about it. I'm happy to help." She lowers her voice, "Do you think I should send James out there?"

I shake my head. "No, not at all. Alex could take the whole town of Spearhead single-handedly. They'll be fine."

Carly laughs. "Oh, okay..." but trails off to head back into the kitchen.

I make my way down the steps to the dock to find Jess sitting in an Adirondack chair with Eden in a Pack-n-Play napping beside her. Caroline, Elodie, and James are all out in the cove paddle boarding. *Thank god.*

Jess sees me and immediately knows something is up. "What happened?" she asks, sitting up abruptly and sliding her sunglasses to the top of her head.

"Umm, Matthias is probably getting arrested on the front lawn right now."

"Shut the fuck up!" Jess says, little to no real concern in her voice. "I thought it was weird Alex was just hanging around this morning. Girl, what is going on?" She gets up, pulling another Adirondack chair closer to hers, then guiding me to sit.

"So much, Jess. So, so much. I don't even know where to start."

"Well, start at the Greek Fest because I've been dying to know what's going on since then."

I inhale deeply, and I back it up and tell her. All about the Greek Fest, meeting Julie, running into Liam, deciding between him and Matthias. *Ha, that's fucking laughable now.* I tell her about sleeping with Matthias, and how he left things on Saturday night. I tell her about Liam finding me on the porch, and staying the night. Then me reading the letter and coming here. I conveniently leave out the part about Gina. I'd like Liam to stay in her good graces.

But I tell her about the argument and how that led to me fainting, the hospital, and Liam staying with us, just to have us now staying with him. I tell her about us fucking in the closet that morning, and how since then we can't seem to stop. She finally interjects on that note.

"Yeah, I mean, I could deduce the fucking. I would highly recommend not giving one of the girls the room I'm staying in because I can hear you guys, FYI." *Fuck. Good intel, though.* I tell her about Liam begging for my forgiveness, and how I'm still so fucking madly in love with him.

"And so you knew I was supposed to meet with Matthias today. I was going to tell him that it's officially over, but when I texted him, he got pissed and called me. He was yelling at me, calling me a whore and a desperate little slut with daddy issues. And yeah, it was a lot, but I thought that was the end of it. I felt like crap about it, so I stayed upstairs just fucking crying until Liam and the girls got back. And then we, um, had a thing in the closet, and we're back together now. But when we came downstairs, we heard a door slam, and Liam went out, and there's Matthias yelling at Alex."

"Whoa, he was fucking closet crazy?!"

"I guess. It doesn't fully make sense to me, though."

"You fucking ripped his heart out," Jess says.

"But that's the thing, I don't think I did. He's pissed, but like he was fighting more with Alex than Liam. That's weird, right?"

Jess shrugs. "I don't know, girl, but apparently that's one powerful pussy you have right there. You've got one man falling to his knees and another losing his mind."

I burst out laughing. "Okay! Shut the hell up! But, hopefully, that's the end of all that craziness because I really just want to hang out with you and enjoy the lake."

"And get some good dick," Jess laughs out.

"Are you talking about me or you?" I turn to look at her, but she's sort of staring off now. "Jessssss," I shake her arm, "talk to me, please. I just told you Liam forced me back into a relationship over anal. Come onnnnn."

Jess looks at me and says, "Okay, yeah. I need to hear how the fuck that happened because you left out a few crucial words when you just told me a minute ago." I laugh at her.

"Not until you talk to me first." I'll take a page out of Liam's book.

"It's just really hard." When she turns to look at me, she has tears in her eyes. I don't think I've ever seen Jess cry. Scratch that, *I know* I've never seen Jess cry before.

"Babe..." I reach out for her hand, and she lets me take it.

"Tommy wants to open up our relationship." *Oh fuck.*

"Oh, okay. How do you feel about that?" Open relationships aren't bad, just as long as both people want it.

"Like I don't want to have an open fucking relationship with my husband."

"Yep. Understandable." I nod my head up and down.

"And you won't fucking believe this, but–"

Jess is interrupted by the sound of Carly coming down the deck stairs. "Lunch is ready!" Carly's timing, always impeccable.

I squeeze Jess' hand. "I want to hear the rest of this,

okay?" She just nods, but then seems to glass over, dropping her sunglasses back down. Damn, I hope she'll tell me soon.

I stand up to call the kids back in, then move chairs to get the outdoor table on the dock set up for lunch. Once the kids are close enough to the dock that they can hear me, I ask them to head upstairs and help Carly with the rest of lunch. James is the first to respond.

"I'll help her, Mrs. Scott." *Mrs. Scott.* It doesn't even sound like my name anymore. *Mrs. Millar sounds better.*

"James, you have to start calling me Brit or Britain, okay?"

"Okay, yes ma'am," he says as he helps pull the girls' boards out of the water, racking them up. *Ugh, ma'am.* I mentally roll my eyes, even though I *do* appreciate his manners.

When I turn around, Liam and Alex are walking down the stairs, arms filled with plates, napkins, and serving platters. Liam and I exchange a knowing glance and he nods in affirmation. *It's all taken care of.*

He sets down his load and comes to me, pulling me in tight, then whispering into my ear, "I'm sorry, baby. That won't happen again."

I run my hand up and down his back, appreciating how warm and safe he makes me feel. I won't worry about it because I know he'd never let anything happen to me or the girls. Not even Jess or Eden. My heart swells for this man.

He releases me when the girls make their way over to the table. "James, go tell your sister to come down and eat, yeah?"

"Yes, sir. I'll be right back," James replies, then jogs up the stairs, taking them two at a time.

I watch everyone get settled in, but I focus on Liam. His calm demeanor, the smile he gives the girls. The way I feel towards him seems impossible. I didn't think I could love him anymore, but seeing him interact with our family, it's like he was made for this. He's the missing puzzle piece of my life. He was meant for me.

———

As soon as we're done eating lunch, I know what I need to do. I really need to talk to the girls and make sure that they're okay with being here. If they don't like it, even a little bit, we'll move back to the Robles Lake house. It would suck for me, but if they need that, we can.

"Hey girls, do you think you're ready for that walk now?"

The girls both look at each other and Elodie shrugs, so Caroline says, "Yeah, let's go."

Liam gives me a look of slight concern, though. "Can you take your phone and not go too far, please?" he asks. I nod and make my way up the deck stairs to wait for the girls.

When I go to pick up my phone, my hands get clammy. I'm scared of what I'll see. I'm imagining 20 missed calls, and a slew of nasty text messages, but luckily, there's only one.

> **UNKNOWN**
>
> Hi Britain, it's Constantine Scala. I just want to apologize on behalf of Matt about today. It will not happen again. I also wanted to see if you would come have lunch with me this Friday? (This invitation is unrelated to anything that happened today.) I would love to catch up and chat. Let me know.

I know he said it's unrelated, but I can't help but feel like he's going to sit me down and preach to me all the virtues of his son. Or maybe he just really wants to talk about Georgia. *Georgia.* I've been so busy the last week, I've hardly thought about her at all. A pit in the bottom of my stomach grows when I realize I've left her box at the Robles house. *Shit.* I need that here. It's become something of a security blanket the last few months; I don't like being away from it. More than anything, I'm terrified that something could happen to it, and all of Georgia's memories would be gone forever, just like her.

BRITAIN

Would Matthias be at this lunch?

CONSTANTINE

No.

Okay, then yes, lunch would be nice. Let me know where and what time.

Does noon at my house work?

His house? I've never been to the Scala family house before. Matthias drove me past it a few times when we were dating the first time, but he never took me there. Him and his brothers shared a house closer to the college, which is where we were most of the time.

Yes, I will see you then.

Wonderful! I can't wait!

His response makes me laugh a little bit. *Constantine is not Matthias, I remind myself.* He's a good man, he treated

Georgia with love and respect — at least I thought he did. I hope he did.

"Mom! We're ready," Elodie yells up to me. Right, our walk. As I walk down the stairs, I realize I'm nervous. I want so badly for this to all work out.

I find Caroline and Elodie waiting for me in the foyer. Elodie is bounding on her toes, ready to go, but Caroline seems to be carrying herself in a somber manner. Crap. Hopefully we can talk through it. I'm sure she knows what's coming.

We step out into the afternoon sun and head north, down the main road. I let us fall into an easy gait as I formulate how to approach this all. The girls remain quiet, clearly wanting me to lead this.

"So girls, I, um, really wanted to talk to you about everything that's been going on lately." I pause, waiting to see if they have any feedback, but neither of them says a thing. *Okay.* "I know this has probably been really confusing, and I'm very sorry that you've both been caught up in it. I never wanted either of you to have to deal with any of this–"

Caroline cuts me off. "Mom, just out with it, you're speaking in euphemisms." She surprises me.

"Oh, okay. Well. I really love Liam, and I want to be with him, and I want to make sure that that is okay with the both of you. And if it makes you uncomfortable at all, just tell me and we'll move back to the house at Robles."

"I like staying with Liam at Spearhead," Elodie says. Well, there's at least one.

"I mean, aren't you worried he's going to hurt you again?" Caroline asks, her tone a bit colder than I anticipated.

"No. I mean, the realist in me knows it's a possibility, but that could happen with anyone. Liam makes me happy." I shrug, I don't want to deep dive on my feelings with the girls because Liam makes me feel a lot more than just happy. He makes me feel everything.

"I know, Mom. It *has* been nice to see you smile lately." When Caroline says this, I think about Georgia, and how foreign it was for me to see her smile. I want the girls seeing me smile all the time.

"I really love being here, but it's important to me that the both of you can also be happy here. We are a unit, okay? We *all* deserve to be happy, so I'm asking you both: Do you want to stay? And are you okay if I get back together with Liam?"

"Does this mean we'd have to go to school here?" Elodie asks. I laugh lightly.

"No, not at all. I'd still go back to Virginia with you when school starts."

Elodie nods. "Okay, then yeah, I want to stay. And it's okay with me if you get back with Liam."

We both turn to look at Caroline. "I mean, I don't hate it here...and I know Liam makes you happy..." she trails off in thought. "I *guess* it's okay with me."

Her tone and her words don't match. She's saying yes, but everything else says no. "Caroline, just be honest. I want to know how you really feel." She doesn't say anything for several moments, just kicking a pebble down the road every couple of steps.

"I mean, don't you think he needs to work a little harder to win you back? He, like, really messed up your life, Mom. And I just think it's too soon. And I don't like him."

I know she's probably right about the first part, but I have to know. "Is there a reason why you don't like him? Did he do something?"

"I just don't think he deserves you mom. I don't like him for you."

My shoulders droop in disappointment at Caroline's words. I knew it was probably too good to think both girls would be on board with this.

TWENTY-EIGHT

BRITAIN

"Okay, then," I let loose a long sigh, "let's work on packing up when we get back to the house. Your Dad will be here this afternoon and he can drive us down, okay?"

"What, Mom? No! I want to stay!" Elodie exclaims, getting worked up.

"I understand, Elodie, but if I'm not getting back together with Liam, I can't stay here. It's too hard and confusing, okay?"

We keep walking in silence and I crinkle my nose as I fight the urge to cry. We come to a break in the trees, revealing a small trail, and I lead them to the end. The trees part the closer we get to the water, eventually revealing a massive boulder with a view of the entire lake. I sit atop the boulder and pat the spaces beside me, and they both join me, one on either side. I stare out at the water, watching boats zoom by and birds fly overhead. I breathe in the smell of the pines, and I mentally say a small farewell to the lake and to the spirit of Georgia whose ashes have blended with the wind and the water here.

It takes Elodie wiping a tear off my face to realize I'm crying. "Don't cry, Mom."

I sniffle, and try my best to hold it in. I can't talk about this anymore. "So, have you decided who you're taking to Taylor Swift?" I overheard Liam mention he got them six tickets, so they could each take a friend.

"Do you think Liam will still give us the tickets?" Elodie asks, disappointment apparent in her tone.

"Oh, um, I can always buy them off of him..." I say, trying to repress the tears. "Hey, wh-what if you guys ask Summer if she'd want to go?" They'll have more fun with her anyways.

Elodie just shrugs, "I guess," and Caroline doesn't say anything at all.

My phone pings and I look down to see a text from Damian.

DAMIAN

I'll be there within the hour!

"Well, we should probably head back, okay? Your dad said he'll be here within the hour." I stand up, dusting the pine needles and debris off my butt. We all stay silent on the walk back, but as we near the house, I ask them to do a few things.

"Please pack up. Pick up the room you were staying in, and I'd like you to write a thank you note to Liam for letting us stay here for a couple days, okay?" They both nod. When we get back to the house, Liam is waiting on the front porch.

He gives me a smile, and when I don't return it, he knows. His smile slides right off his face.

Caroline doesn't miss it. She looks at me, then looks at him, and as soon as we're at the front porch, she walks quickly inside, avoiding eye contact with Liam. I push for Elodie to follow her sister.

"I'll be up in a couple minutes, okay? Can you go tell Jess to get ready, please?" Elodie nods and shoots Liam a tight half smile. Once they're out of ear shot, Liam launches in.

"Doesn't look like it went the way you hoped." I shake my head.

"No...it didn't. Um, we're going to move back to the Robles house today." His face falls. "Thank you for letting us stay here while I recovered." I have to stop talking to keep the sob from coming out. Liam just stands there not saying anything at all.

"I-I should probably go get packing, but, um, I'll still see you at the ultrasound tomorrow, okay?"

When it becomes clear, he isn't going to say anything back, I drop my head and walk into the house, heading upstairs and straight to my closet floor. I let the tears fall silently as I fold clothes and put them in my suitcase. A gentle knock on the door frame makes me wipe the tears away, and I turn to see Elodie and Caroline staring down at me.

"Oh, wow, you guys are fast," I laugh out, between a cry. "Come help me then."

"Mom," Caroline says, "can you stop packing? I don't want to go."

I pause my folding. "Caroline, don't feel sorry or change your mind just because you see me cry, okay?"

"It's not that, Mom. I just, what I said on the walk, I didn't mean it. I guess...I just wanted to feel like I had some control and then you mentioned Summer, and I realized I'm not being fair. You gave us a vote, but dad never did. And that makes me mad, and I'm taking that out on you. I'm sorry." *Oh, baby*.

"Honey, *I'm* sorry. I wish we would've never put you in this situation in the first place."

"It's not your fault, Mom, it's Dad's–"

I cut her off. "It is *both* of our faults, okay?" I set down the clothes and stand up to face them. "I want you to be honest with me, even if it hurts, okay? I can take it, and I know you both can, too, which is why I wanted you to have a say. So just be honest with me, Caroline."

"I want to stay and I think it's okay if you get back with Liam..." she trails off, then looks down at the floor.

"Are you sure?" I ask.

"I am." She seems to gain some resolve. Looking back up at me, "I want you to be happy, Mom. Really." I nod my head, and then bring them both in for a hug.

"Should we go let Jess know to stop packing?" I release them, reluctantly, from my embrace.

Elodie pipes up first, "I never told her we were leaving." Then flashes me a radiant smile and I laugh.

"Okay, alright then. Um, maybe I should go talk to Liam then?" They both nod and head towards the bedroom door. As they walk out, Liam walks in. He just gives the girls a sad smile, leaving extra room for them to walk past.

"Do you need any help?" he asks calmly.

I shake my head and whisper, "No." He moves in, taking me in his arms.

"It's my fault, Britain. I'm sor–"

I cut him off, though.

"No, we changed our minds. We're staying." He pulls me back and stares into my eyes. His look just like mine, tear-filled.

"Thank Christ," he says, then pulls me back in, tightly. I giggle, then squeeze a hand between us to wipe away my tears. "Bambi, I don't want to be apart from you, ever." He kisses the top of my head, giving me a tight squeeze.

"I don't want to be away from you either...but, speaking of, don't you need to go into work?"

"Nah, I'm not too worried about that right now. I have more important things going on." He looks down at me, smiling, his beautiful blue eyes looking luminous. He tugs my hand and leads me over to the armchair by the fireplace, settling me into his lap. We sit there silently, him stroking my hair, and me just holding on tight for a while.

"So, which one was it that voted me off the island?" he finally asks.

I laugh. "Does it matter?"

"I just need to know who I'm buying a puppy for."

I laugh even harder. "I will murder you if you get us a dog."

He gives me a side eye. "It's inevitable, Britain, but I think it's cute you think we have a choice."

I lean back. "So you're going to get up with the dog at 4:00 A.M. to take it out to tinkle? And who watches the dog when we travel to Virginia, and stay there for extended periods?" I'm making a lot of assumptions here, based on the last time we were together. "I mean, that's if you come to Virginia."

"Well, that's easy. Yes, I'll get up with the dog, and then we fly private and the dog comes with us. And obviously I'll be coming to Virginia with you." He sets a palm on my bump. "Where you and the baby are is where I'll be." I nod my head up and down, so grateful for him, so madly in love with him.

I know now is the right time. "I love you, Liam Millar," I whisper to him.

He nudges his nose against mine and whispers back, "I love you more."

————

"Are you excited?" I look over to Liam as he drives us down the mountain for our appointment with Silas. He nods, looks over at me, then back at the road.

"And nervous," he says a bit quietly.

"Don't be nervous. If anyone should be nervous, it's me! Silas is going to be pissed if I've lost any weight." I laugh, trying to lighten the mood. He just moves his hand over, placing it on my thigh, and we both relax into the touch. The rest of the drive is spent talking about Damian and Summer, our newest house guests.

"It really doesn't bother you to see them together?" Liam asks.

"No, not even a little. I think it probably would've at some point, but not now that I have you."

"Huh, alright," is all he says.

"Damian is the girls' dad. He's a really good dad at that, and he's still one of my closest friends and I'm trying to make an effort with Summer, too. The girls deserve a family where everyone gets along and we can enjoy being around each other. Listen, I'm a bit of a package deal, Liam. I come with a lot of side characters. If it's too much, you just have to be honest and upfront with me now."

"What?" he asks. "No, god, I don't care that you want Damian to be an active part of the kids' lives. Not at all. I'm glad that you can have them staying with us and it's not a big deal. I was just curious because Alex mentioned to me once that this wasn't the first time Damian had done something like this. And, well, I wondered if it was hard for you to — I don't know — see it or relive it."

The first time. I think about it, but the sting is brief, barely palpable. So much has changed since then. "Not anymore," I say, then give him a soft smile.

———

After a quick prenatal check, which revealed I did not lose any weight (thank heavens), Silas walks us to the room for the ultrasound.

"I'm glad to see you're doing well, Brit," Silas says, helping me to lay back on the slightly reclined exam table.

"Thanks, Silas."

"And I'm sorry my brother was a total ass to you. Really, super sorry." I laugh awkwardly.

"Um, it's okay. Water under the bridge."

Silas just looks at me dead serious and says, "It was not okay." I just nod, at a loss for how to respond. "The tech will be with you in just a second, okay? Just don't forget to let them know if you want to find out the sex or not."

Liam chimes in, "There's a chance we could find out if

the baby's a girl or boy today?" He looks to Silas for the answer.

"Sometimes it can happen this early, but if not, 20-week ultrasound for sure. That's why, just in case, let them know, alright?"

"We will," I say to Silas as he moves to walk out. Liam stands up, giving him a handshake and a pat on the back before he says goodbye.

"So..." I look at Liam, "do you want to know or do you want to be surprised?" I ask.

"I mean, of course I want to know," he looks a bit bashful, "but if you don't, we won't."

"No, let's find out. Just be prepared, we probably won't know today. It's still early. But, um, what do you hope it is?"

Liam shrugs. "I don't know. I kinda like being a girl dad." My heart beats harder. *Fuck I love him.* "But I'll be happy either way."

"Same," I say, giving him a smile.

The ultrasound technician joins us a couple minutes later. She spreads the warm jelly across my abdomen and soon the rhythmic sound of the heartbeat can be heard. Liam slips his hand into mine, holding it tight. He's completely fixated on the screen, but I can't help but fixate on him. His eyes are watery and he's wearing the brightest smile. It's enough to make me want another baby.

"So..." the ultrasound tech starts, "did we want to know the sex today?" I look at Liam with a bit of surprise, but I nod my head, and he does, too. I let Liam answer for us.

"We do, if it's possible. Um, if it's not, you know, no big deal." I smile at his awkward answer.

"Well, you're in luck," she says.

Liam squeezes my hand tighter, and I can feel that his pulse is as quick as mine. "Your little guy is in just the right spot. We can see his genitals right...there." She clicks on the screen, taking a photo. "Congrats, Mom and Dad, it's a boy!"

It's a boy. All I see is the picture of Liam in Sandy's house, the one where he's on a tricycle. Bright blue eyes, blonde hair, and the biggest smile, and I can't wait.

Liam squeezes my hand tight, looking between the screen and me, then finally he lets the tears fall. He leans down, kissing my forehead, and says, "I love you so much, Britain."

I just nod, too scared I'll end up ugly crying if I try to speak.

———

There's no holding the news in. As soon as we're home, Liam announces to the household, "It"s a boy!" He pulls out the good bourbon for Damian and himself, and Carly starts on a cake to celebrate.

Jess walks over, giving me a massive hug, nodding down to Eden and says, "Arranged marriage?"

I just laugh. "Like any daughter of yours could ever be forced to marry someone not of her own choosing."

Jess nods, "True, true."

The girls' reactions surprise me the most, though. "I'm so glad it's a boy," Caroline says.

"I wanted a little sister," Elodie seems deflated.

"That's because you've never had one," Caroline rolls her eyes. "Trust me, we're better off with a brother." We all laugh, and the girls hug me tight. Summer even makes her way over hesitantly for a quick hug and a word of congratulations.

Then, as if she has a sixth sense about these types of things, Sandy walks in on the celebration. "Okay y'all, what's going on? I need to know!"

"It's a boy, Sandy," I tell her.

Her eyes instantly fill with tears, but then she clasps her hands together and lets out an excited shriek. "Carly! I need your help making a margarita, baby!" she yells out, and then heads straight towards the kitchen.

I look around for Liam, and find him staring straight back at me. He mouths to me "Thank you," and I smile because, really, I should be thanking him. For making all my dreams of what our family could be come true. It's just a shame Georgia isn't here to see it.

TWENTY-NINE

BRITAIN

It's something of a gothic mansion in the heart of town. Surrounded by fig groves and perfectly manicured shrubs, the Scala house screams *old money*. My point is only drilled home when I pull up to a gate with security at the entrance. *Seems unnecessary.* After I show my ID, the guard instructs me to park in the roundabout and that someone will greet me at the front door.

The house is domineering and cold looking, and I already regret not letting Liam bring me. I drive up to the roundabout, complete with a fountain in the middle, and put my car in park. The front entrance features an arched double door with dark, wood paneling and iron bars over the window. It's *a vibe,* but the cherry on top is the face that greets me. And by "greet" I mean looks at me like I'm a pile of dog shit she's been forced to clean up. *Gina.* My internal instincts are all telling me to turn, run, do not pass go, do not collect 200 dollars.

But just like curiosity killed the cat, here I am. I'm thankful I at least let Jess choose my dress for my lunch with Constantine. It's another flowy Zimmermann midi, and even though it's stunning, I look like I'm wearing a potato sack next to Gina in her high heels, wide-legged trousers that cinch at her petite waist, and a silk shirt. *Why does she have to be so pretty?*

I leave the comfort of my car and walk slowly up to Gina. Her expression doesn't wane in the slightest when she greets me. All I receive is a, "He's waiting for you," and a swish of her hair in my face as she turns to lead me to what I'm beginning to assume is my death. *Okay.*

Even though the exterior of the home is dark, cold stone, the interior opens to a bright and light space. The walls are painted cream and the furniture is modern and overstuffed, everything done in perfectly worn leather or mohair. *Nice.*

Gina takes me down a long back hall that's filled with old black and white photos. *Family maybe?* But not anyone in this family. The photos all look like they're from another generation, probably even a couple back.

We stop outside an open door where Gina knocks gently and Constantine calls her in. We walk into the room that looks more like a library than an office, but nevertheless it is. A glossy, oversized mahogany desk sits in the middle of the room, with Constantine sitting behind it. He stands when he sees us, and breaks out into a wide smile.

"Britain!" he practically shouts, coming around the desk to greet me with a big hug and pat on the back. I return the embrace, but can't help but notice that Gina is still standing there giving me a death glare. When Constantine releases me, he motions and says, "Gina, have you met Britain before? She's Georgie's daughter. Our girl!" *Our girl?*

"Yes, I may have run into her once before," Gina says dryly.

"It's nice to see you again, Gina," I offer up politely. She doesn't respond, though, just turns and walks away. Right before she gets to the door, she calls back, "Lunch will be served in 30 minutes, Uncle!" And then she's gone. *Good riddance.*

Constantine is still standing at my side and I look to him, hoping he'll lead since I'm still at a loss for why I'm here. He places a hand over the top of my shoulder and says, "Come, let's sit down. We have so much to talk about." *We do?* He sits me down on a chesterfield sofa by the window, taking a seat across from me on a mirroring sofa.

"Hi, darling," he starts. It's an oddly intimate endearment, but I just smile. "You must have so many questions." His eyes turn watery.

"Um, yes, I suppose I do." Not that I could think of a single one right now. "Maybe you could just start with why you asked me to lunch today. I'll be honest, after everything that happened with Matthias, I didn't think I'd hear from you...and I know this is uncomfortable, which is why I didn't want to bring it up at the Greek Fest. But he's *not* the father of my baby."

"Oh, I know. Liam's the father." *He knows?*

"Oh, okay," I say, then wait for him to answer the rest of my question.

"Britain," he pauses to scoot forward on the sofa so he's

closer, "I'm assuming you've gone through Georgia's personal effects?"

"The notebooks, you mean?"

"The notebooks were only part of it." I wait for him to elaborate. It was basically just a box of notebooks, and then some old photos and birthday cards. "Did you look at any of the photos or read the birthday cards?" *No.*

"Um, no, just the notebooks."

"Ahh, okay, then we have a little explaining to do, don't we?" He gives me a warm smile, standing to go get a box off his desk. He walks back over to me, setting it beside me on the sofa and then sits himself on the other side of the box. I turn towards him as he opens it.

If what Georgia left me was her life and memories in a box, what Constantine has here is my adolescence in a box. My old teddy bear and baby blankets are immediately recognizable. There's a box with an old rattle and baby bootie. There's my artwork from the second grade. And the book on sea otters I wrote in the sixth. I place my hand to my mouth in astonishment, and when I look up at Connie, he has tears in his eyes.

"Now, I don't have as many photos as Georgie does, but I have some." He opens a manilla folder and I can't hold back the tears. The photo on top is of Georgia in the hospital, a little me swaddled in her arms, and Constantine right beside us with a massive smile on his face.

"You were there when I was born?" I set the photo down to wipe the tears away from my eyes and he reaches a hand over mine in a soothing gesture.

"Of course I was," he says softly. He continues on, showing me photos of my first Christmas. There's a photo of a 10-month-old me pushing a baby carriage and Constantine right behind me, spotting me in case I fell. There's photos of my first birthday. I'm in a high chair with cake all over, and Georgia and Constantine are standing on either side of me, also covered in cake. I laugh because in the photo Georgia is laughing. She's happy. *She was happy.* I laugh again, and then choke on a cry.

"I never knew. You came around?" I shuffle through a few more photos, spotting a dark-haired boy carrying me in his arms. *Matthias?* I stop and pick up the photo.

"I came around as much as I could. All the big days and a lot of the not-so-big days, too." Constantine pauses when he sees the photo I'm holding. "Matt would come with me sometimes. It was very sweet. He'd dote on you, very protective..." he trails off. I set the photo back down, still torn between the different versions of the man that little boy grew up to be.

It's not hard to notice there aren't any photos of me with Connie past the toddler stage. He has photos of me with Georgia. And some of my sporting events, and school graduations. But there's no photos of him and me beyond the early years.

"Why did you stop?" I ask quietly. I know the answer, but I want to hear it.

He sighs before speaking. "Well, Georgie asked me to stop. I came over after work one night, and you ran into my arms and called me Dad, and after that, I wasn't allowed to come over." *Oh*, that's not what I was expecting. I thought he'd tell me how he was busy, he had his own family to tend to, not *that*.

All I manage to get out is, "Oh." When he doesn't say

anything, we just sit there in silence as I finish shuffling through the photos, and the contents of the box.

He chuckles, finally breaking the quiet and says, "I used to have this little pocket notebook where I'd write down tidbits or things Georgia would tell me about you. It had everything: favorite movies, favorite food, funny things you once said. I hate to admit that I lost it somewhere along the way, though."

I look up at him, and I wonder, "Did you love her? I mean really, truly, because I know she loved you."

"That's like asking if the sky is blue, Britain." He laughs softly. "I love her...still." On his last word he chokes, then lets a few tears fall. This time I reach out my hand to comfort him, and he takes it.

"I'm very sorry that you two couldn't be together then. It was a tragedy." He nods in agreement.

"I'll be honest, my biggest regret in life is not being with her when I had the chance."

"When *you* had the chance?"

"When I finally decided the kids were grown enough and I didn't need to worry about Julie interfering with custody, Georgie wouldn't have me." He chokes slightly. "I understood. I'd made the rest of my life a priority for years. It wasn't fair of me to expect her to just jump."

I laugh. "She was stubborn, huh?" He laughs, too.

"Oh yes, was she ever." We sit there in amiable silence for several minutes, when there's a knock at the door. I instinctively drop Connie's hand when Gina walks in, carrying a tray from the kitchen. I couldn't eat right now if my life depended on it, but Constantine gets up, takes the tray and thanks her before shooing her back out again. I don't miss her glare before she leaves, though. Jesus, she hates me.

"Did Julie know about this?" I motion down to the box, and he nods his head.

"I wasn't a very good husband to Julie, maybe ever, but after everything that happened to Georgie, I was even worse. I never tried to hide any of it. In fact, at one point, your school pictures were hung on the fridge right next to the boys. I'd talk to them about you, too. It um, was probably hard for her, but we'd always had our issues." No wonder Julie thought I was his.

I just nod. He motions over to the food, "Hungry?" I give him a half smile, and shake my head no. "Yeah, me neither, kiddo," he says, coming back to sit down across from me this time.

"So, in Georgia's box then..." I'd like him to fill in the blanks there.

"Right, so every year, I'd send you a birthday card. You should find those in there. There's probably even a couple from Matt, too." I feel guilty when he says his name.

"How is Matthias doing? I'm really sorry that things didn't work out."

"I'm really sorry about how that turned out too, dear. I'd be lying if I said I didn't have high hopes for the two of you. Always did. I thought..." he laughs. "I always hoped it'd work out between you two. I'd selfishly thought, what could be more perfect? I'm afraid I have to accept some of the blame there. I probably pushed him a little too hard." Constantine pats his legs nervously.

"I never meant to hurt him," I say quietly.

"No, no, and I'm sure he never meant to hurt you. Sometimes the apples don't fall too far from the tree, though." He chuckles. Yeah, I'm starting to see just how toxic Matthias' family life probably was.

"I was a little surprised when we never heard from you after Georgie's death, though."

"I'm sorry, I just wasn't emotionally ready to come back here."

"I understand, sweetheart. But I am glad you're back now. I've been waiting for this moment for a couple years now. Really ever since I retired." I give him a smile.

"It was really nice getting to talk to you, too, Connie."

He gives me a silly look before launching back in. "As you know, Georgia's estate passed over to Alexander, but we did it that way because when I pass, my portion of the business will be split between Matthias and you both, equally."

I freeze, unsure what to make of that. "Oh, Connie, that's a lot, and also really unnecessary."

"Of course it's not. Georgie and I wanted it this way."

"I could never accept that, Connie. It's your family's business."

"And you're my family, Britain."

"What about Max and Niko and Silas? Your sons? Aren't you worried what they'll think?" He smiles at me gently.

"You asked if I loved Georgia, Britain, really truly." He pauses. I nod and then he continues, "The answer is yes. If I wasn't with Georgia, I wasn't with anyone." I sit with his words for a moment and let them sink in. My eyes must go wide in realization.

"Matthias is my son by blood. You're my daughter by love. And Max, Niko, and Silas are my sons by choice. I love them, I raised them, but they are not mine."

I'm almost too stunned to speak. "Do they know that?"

"Matthias, Max, and Niko know."

"Well, I think Silas will figure it out when you leave half your share of the company to me."

"Maybe, maybe not. He never had an interest in the business, and he'll still get his inheritance. I don't expect him to be too upset about it."

"I don't think I can accept, Mr. Scala."

"Please, call me Connie, darling."

"Does anyone else know you're planning to do this? I just, I can't accept."

"It's been in my will for years, Britain. Matthias is the executor, so he knows. Other than that, I'm not sure, and it doesn't matter because it's what I want. I didn't get to be there, raising you, day in and day out like I should've. You didn't even let me pay for your college tuition, which, by the way, I'm still salty you didn't go to Stanford." He gives me a fake angry glare. "My other kids have had me and my financial support for decades, it's the least I can do for you." My cheeks turn pink. The sentiment of it all is overwhelming. *Is this what it's like to have a father?*

"If you're not interested in the day-to-day running of the business, we'll keep everything as it is now. Matthias will manage and earn a salary, but my profit share will split between the two of you. And, of course, you'll have voting rights."

I shake my head. "But that's not until you pass away. That could be 30, 40 years from now."

He gives me a sad smile. "I don't have that much time left, darling." I look at him, and while he's lost some muscle mass, he still looks like a vibrant, healthy man.

"I still think you should reconsider, Connie. I don't deserve this. I know nothing about the business. I'm just a stay-at-home mom now."

"Don't say that, Britain.You're talented. I know what kind of work you did for Scott Technologies. I feel that I'm leaving part of the business in very competent hands. And again, you don't have to dive in, but maybe you save it for the girls some day? Caroline and Elodie, maybe they take an interest?" It's funny to hear him say their names.

"I'm not going to stop trying to talk you out of this, you know that, right?" I point a finger at him.

"Stubborn, just like your mama," he says, making me smile. *Just like my mama*, words I would have hated hearing previously start to take on new meaning. This wonderful man loved her. Maybe being a bit like her isn't so bad after all.

We spend the next hour or so mostly talking about Georgia. I ask if I can have some of the photos and he lets me choose. We talk more about me and my childhood, and then eventually about the girls. "I'd love for you to meet them sometime," I say to him, and he nods silently, unable to speak without choking up. "I'm glad I got to talk to you today, Connie, and I hope we'll see you at Sunday dinner sometime soon?"

"You got it, peanut." I laugh and cry at the same time.

"Did you used to call me peanut?" He nods yes. "I call this one peanut." I place a hand on my abdomen and we both look at each other and smile.

It seems like a nice moment to end things on, so I smile and stand and he does, too. We walk over to his desk where he presses a buzzer for Gina. I look at the collection of mismatched frames scattered over the surface, and sure enough, there I am, and so is Georgia. There's even one of Alex in his dress blues. I smile.

While we wait for Gina, I glance around at his office. His bookshelves are filled with awards and more family photos, and I do wish he could have been my father. *I wish.*

The ceramic urn above the fireplace catches my eye, though.

I point to it and ask, "Is that Georgia?" He looks slightly bashful.

"Alex gave it to me. He said you wouldn't mind if I had a piece of her, too." I don't mind at all.

"I think you've always had the best of her, Connie."

He gives me a smile and we embrace tightly until Gina clears her throat and breaks the moment.

"Alright, darling. Let's chat soon, okay?" he asks and I nod.

"Goodbye, Connie." My voice nearly breaks, but I hold it together for a few more moments.

THIRTY

BRITAIN

I sniffle and wipe my eyes as Gina escorts me back to the front door. We're steps from the exit when she turns around.

"Did you think they actually liked you, let alone *loved* you?" She laughs in my face harshly. My mind gets whiplash over the comment.

"I'm sorry, wh–"

Gina cuts me off.

"Did you *actually* think Liam and Matt would be interested in *you*? You're just a barely B-cup, average white girl who's lucky enough to afford Botox and veneers. You are nothing special, and everyone can see it, even Liam and Matt." *What the fuck is her problem?*

I move to walk around her towards the front door, but she slides in my way. "They only want your share of the business, sweetie." *Oh.* "Yeah, lightbulb. You're a real genius, huh?"

My stomach roils and I get hot, and suddenly it feels like

the walls are closing in. I practically run back to Constantine's office. *I need to know.*

I can see he's surprised when I ask, "How long have I been in your will?"

"Since you turned 18, why?" I don't respond, I just walk back down the hall, around Gina, and out the front door.

I drive aimlessly for the next two hours. Mostly around town, past my old schools, down Aubrey's street and eventually I find myself parked in front of Georgia's, well, Alex's *now*. My phone rings again, but I just hit decline like I have the last 15 times. I've passed the point of any hysterical crying, and now I'm just feeling flat-out exhausted. It's like I'm in a dream where nothing is actually happening. I'm just going through the motions.

With the girls at Sandy's until sometime after dinner, I'm still left with a couple hours before I have to figure out what I'll do. I just know, right now, that doesn't include going home to him. *Home.* Ugh.

I grab my purse out of the car and walk to the front door. I still have my key from when I stayed here last, so I don't bother to knock. I just let myself right in. Alex is sitting at the kitchen table when I do, slamming his laptop shut when he sees me.

"Brit, is everything okay?"

I shake my head. "I just need sleep."

I don't say anything else. I just walk down to Georgia's room, pull on her old robe, curl up on top of her grandmother's quilt, and I sleep. I hate being awake sometimes.

———

Liam

Where the fuck is she? It doesn't take 4 hours to eat lunch. I knew I should have gone with her, I fucking knew it.

I'm pacing in my office when my phone pings with a new text. My hands tremble as I look down, but disappointment floods me when I see who it's from.

GINA

> Finally figured it out. I knew you didn't actually love her. Let me know if you ever want to be with someone who's a little more your league, xoxo.

What the fuck? I have no idea what she's talking about. Maybe she sent it to the wrong number. I don't bother with a response, just hitting Britain's name in my call log instead, and waiting. This time it doesn't go straight to voicemail and my chest hitches in anticipation that she'll pick up, but she doesn't. It rings, then eventually hits voicemail.

Did Matt show up? Did she get in a car accident? My brain goes into overdrive thinking of all the bad things that could've happened. I walk out to the kitchen to find Jess and Carly chatting.

"Have either of you heard from Britain?" I ask, not caring that I just interrupted them.

"No, I haven't," Carly says.

Jess pulls out her phone and pulls up their text thread. An hour or so ago, Jess asked how the lunch was, and all

Britain responded with was: "Lunch was good and bad and Gina's a bitch. I'm going to Alex's for a bit."

"You didn't think this was something worth telling me about?" I ask Jess, my frustration misdirected at her.

"She's at Alex's, she'll be fine."

I run my hands through my hair, but make the decision quickly to grab my keys and head to Alex's house. Except for one problem. "I don't know where Alex lives."

Jess looks at me like I'm stupid and says, "He lives in Georgia's old house." That doesn't help.

"I don't know where that is."

"She never took you to Georgia's house?" No, and I never asked to go. *Fuck me.*

"No, she didn't."

Jess rolls her eyes at me. "I'm sure I have an address in my email or something. Give me a minute."

I can't wait, though. "Text it to me, please?" I don't wait for a response, just heading straight out the door and into my car. I call Alex as soon as the bluetooth connects.

"What did you do?" Alex answers the phone in a biting tone.

"I don't know! Is she there?"

"Yeah, she is. She's sleeping right now."

"Is she okay?"

"No, she's not okay. She walked in here looking fucking catatonic like someone just blew up her world. What. Did. You. DO?"

"Nothing! She was supposed to have lunch with Constantine today, and then she wouldn't respond to my messages, and then my calls, and I don't know what the fuck is going on, but I'm coming to see her."

"Whoa, whoa. Pump the brakes. Let her sleep. Maybe she's just upset about Georgia. She sure as fuck shouldn't be out driving, though." My stomach rolls with anxiety, and fear.

"I guess just let me know when she wakes up and if there's anything I can do." My tone is completely defeated.

"If she wakes up and I find out you fucked her, you're gonna want to to run for the hills."

"I didn't do anything. I don't fucking get it!"

"I'll let you know," Alex says, then hangs up the phone. Jess texts me a minute later with the address. I won't go there, yet, but I'm not going back to Spearhead either.

———

When I get out of my SUV at Max's house, I slam the car door shut and a rooster crows at me when I do, walking past me in a hurry. *Fucking excuse me.* Max is sitting on his front porch waiting for me and he laughs at my reaction to the poultry.

"Trouble in paradise so soon?" Max asks.

"Fuck you, man," I reply.

"So that's a yes." *Yeah, it is.* "What'd you do?"

"Seriously, nothing. She went to have lunch with your dad, and then I don't know, but she won't answer my calls or texts." I shrug.

"Come on, man." Max ushers me inside where his house-keeper, Anna, greets me.

"Liam! Are you hungry? Come, come, let's get you boys some dinner!"

I don't have the heart to tell her no, so we follow her to the kitchen where she starts pulling trays out of the fridge to reheat. Max gestures to the wet bar, motioning towards the bottles lined up, with a question.

"Small glass, really small, I want to be able to go pick her up," I say as he pours himself a healthy glass of Eagle Rare and drops a splash in one for me. I think he does it as a joke, but it's fine. I want to stay sober so I can go get my girl if needed.

In an attempt to keep the conversation off me, I ask Max, "So have you told your family yet?"

He shakes his head no. "Nah, I'm going to let Matt sweat for a bit. Let him wonder."

"Can't say I blame you," I laugh.

"I can't believe you really did it, man. We're going to miss you."

"I mean this in the nicest possible way, but I'm not going to miss *any* of you." We both laugh. "But hey, thanks for buying me out." I hold up my glass to his, in a toast.

"Thanks for thinking of me first," he says, then slams back his full bourbon.

Anna pushes plates in front of us, and we both reluctantly eat. I'm pretty sure Max inherited Anna when his father died and left him this ranch. She only knows how to cook for ranch hands, so while it's hearty food, it's doused in gravy with extra butter and extra lard in everything. Perfect for a hangover. Not so perfect when you're sick with worry and can barely hold it down.

Max and I talk a little bit about the next steps and paperwork for him buying me out. Then Anna asks me about my new girlfriend. And damn, I hate hearing Britain referred to as my girlfriend. I want people calling her my wife.

She cries happy tears when I tell her I'm going to be a dad, then eventually excuses herself to her cottage for the night. Max is sitting there looking at me like I'm foreign, though.

"What?" I ask.

"I just never thought it'd be you, man. To settle down, wife up, three and a half kids. It's like that movie *Instant Family* or some shit. And you're giving up the business for it, too?" He shakes his head in disbelief. "Fucking wild, man."

"Just wait till it's you," I tell him.

"Ha!" he laughs, but doesn't say anymore, which is good because no matter what he would've said, my response would have been, 'That's what they always say.'

It's 9:00 PM, when I look down at my phone for the thousandth time. Still nothing from Alex, and nothing from Britain. That's when I decide I'm done waiting. I throw Alex's address into Google Maps and get up to leave. When I go to say bye to Max, his phone rings. He answers, so I wait till he's done. He gets a weird look on his face, though, and drops the phone away from his ear to put it on speaker.

I can tell it's Gina. "And can you believe Constantine would do that?" My heart rate picks up. If Constantine did something to Britain...

"And now it all makes sense. Matt and Liam were just fighting over who would have more shares of the business. They didn't actually like her." *The fuck?* I look over at Max who looks just as confused as me.

"You said he's leaving Britain with half of his part of the business?" Max asks for clarification.

"Yeah, 50% to Matt, 50% to Britain. She didn't even understand until I laid it out for her that they were only inter-ested in her because they want her portion of the business."

Damnit, Gina *is* a bitch. I don't say anything, though. I just nod at Max and take off, feeling the smallest pang of relief that I actually did the right thing this time. Now I just have to convince Britain of it.

————

Britain

"Baby," he says, gently rocking my shoulder to wake me. "Let's go home."

I keep my eyes closed and try to push away the pain that's coursing through me, but it hurts so fucking bad, all over again. If what Gina said is true, I don't think I can bear to look him in the eyes ever again.

"Go away, Liam," I say, turning, trying to burrow my way deeper into the pillow, and away from the world.

"I'm not going away, Britain. Never," he says calm and cool, with all the confidence of a man who knows he's dating someone well below his league. Like I should just be so grateful he's given me the time of day.

"You can have it. I don't even want it. Just leave me alone, okay?"

"I don't want it either, Britain." His words give me pause, but I keep my eyes shut, my body can't stop leaning into the pain all over again.

"You don't have to keep up the charade anymore. I don't care about it, have it. You can stop pretending, okay?" He laughs at me and I crack an eye open. He looks so handsome, and I hate him. I hate him even more for making me look like an idiot.

"Why would I want 25% ownership in a company I just sold 51% of yesterday?"

My other eye pops open and I slowly turn to look at him.

He nods his head. "I don't care what you do with your 25%, if and when you ever get it. Well, I sort of hope you don't give it to Matt, but otherwise, I don't care."

I pull myself up to sit. "You sold your part of the business?" I ask in disbelief. That business was his life. His family's legacy. The MS Group was *his* life's work.

"I did. Max and I agreed on a purchase price yesterday. I wanted to surprise you with the news once I knew it was a sure thing."

"Seriously?"

"Seriously."

He can barely finish getting the word out before I throw my arms around his neck and hug him tight. He just wraps his arms around me and nuzzles into my neck, pulling me onto his lap. "I've spent enough of my life devoted to work, and now I want to devote the next half to you, and the girls, and this baby, and any others...and the dog."

I stop him from continuing. "We're not getting a dog."

"We're definitely getting a dog," he says and I laugh because I know, *we're getting a dog*. "Baby, I'm a little hurt you thought that's what *this* was about." He brings my hand to his heart, then places his hand over mine. "What do I need to do to prove to you that it only beats for you?" He nuzzles deeper into my neck until he can kiss me.

"I don't know, Liam. I just—it all just sort of made sense. I've never felt like I'm good enough for you, and it was like duh, because I'm not." He pulls back, grabbing my chin in his hand.

"I don't ever want to hear those words come out of your mouth again. You're too good for me, Britain. Everybody knows it, alright?"

"Try telling Gina that..." I whisper out.

"Screw, Gina," he says.

"Please don't," I whisper, and he gives me a look. "I know, I'm being insecure, okay? It just really hurt, and I felt like I couldn't go through all of this again."

"You never will, baby. I'll never let you go through that again. Listen, I've loved you since before I even knew who you were. You were the most beautiful woman I'd ever seen in that little black dress, nursing me, smiling for me. I loved you then." I nod and he drops his forehead to mine, then kisses me gently.

"Why didn't you just come home, Bambi? I could have saved you a couple hours of doom crying." He says it light-heartedly, and he's right.

I shrug. "Just my trauma response, I guess. To be here." I look around. "As close to *her* as possible." He gives me a sad look, but it comes with understanding.

"Alright. Let's try and retrain ourselves to come to me, okay?" I nod. "Okay, can we go home now? Please?" I nod again, and he lifts me straight off the bed and heads for the door.

"Wait!" I try to stop him. "I'm wearing Georgia's robe. I need to take it off." He sets me down, and I slip the robe off, hanging it back over the closet door just like she left it. "Okay, I'm ready," I grab my purse off the dresser and Liam lifts me off my feet.

"I can walk!" I yell at him.

"Yeah, but I don't want to take the risk of you walking away from me." I smile and shake my head. Slim chance of that happening.

Alex watches us from the living room. And I call out to him. "Thanks for letting me nap here. Come to dinner on Sunday, okay? Love you!" I say as Liam walks us through the front door, putting me straight into the passenger seat of his car.

"Wait, I can drive home. What are we going to do about my car?" He closes the door on me, then hops into the driver's side before answering.

"Again, can't take any chances of you escaping. And I've been meaning to ask, did Matt help you pick out that car?" *Yes.*

"Yeah," I say quietly.

"Thought so. We'll get you a new car tomorrow. Tonight, I just want you in our bed, at home, everyone under the same roof." My cheeks turn pink. "And you better believe, we are going to have words over you not answering my calls or texts today. I was losing my mind, baby, sick to my stomach with worry that something bad happened."

"Well, now you know how it feels," I rib him.

"I think somebody needs a spanking," he deadpans back.

"Oh no, anything but that!" I joke, and he turns, giving me a devilish look. *Fuck.* "I'm not going to be able to sit down, am I?" He shakes his head.

"Nope, your ass is gonna be as pink as your cheeks, Bambi." *Can't wait.*

Liam is in bed waiting for me when I come out of the ensuite. I untuck, then throw my towel over the tub, and he watches me walk to the bed, stalking me with his eyes like I'm a tasty snack. I crawl over, straddling him, and he reaches around, grabbing my ass cheeks. He releases them, pulling both hands back, then brings them down in a hard slap.

"Ahh!" I cry out, then look down at his sick smile.

"That's not even a glimpse, Bambi."

"I know," I say, then drop my mouth to his. I slide my tongue along his lips, and he opens for me. As we kiss, I grow damp and wet for this man, and without even thinking, he's inside me. It's so natural to be with him like this.

"I was planning to go straight to sleep tonight, I swear!" I say.

"Same. I thought you needed the rest, but here we are, baby. We can't fucking help it." Nope, we can't. We're like magnets, inexplicably drawn to one another.

"I love you, Liam Millar," I say, then drop another kiss to his mouth.

"And I love you, Britain Millar." *Fuck me.*

THIRTY-ONE

BRITAIN

I wake up early, and roll over to watch Liam sleep. I'm tempted to burrow into him, but I don't. I just want to enjoy this moment. His muscular arms are wrapped around the pillow, and even just seeing his bare back makes me appreciate how beautiful he is. And he is the most beautiful man, inside and out. I sneak out of bed quietly, pulling on his sweatshirt and some biker shorts, then head downstairs.

Jess and Eden are already up, playing on the living room floor.

"Hi," I say, coming to sit down next to my best friend. She seems worn out today. Maybe she's just tired?

"Hey babe, everything okay?" Jess asks. "Kinda worried about you yesterday."

"Everything is just fine. It's a long story, but it's all okay." I bounce my shoulder off of hers. Eden squeals when she realizes I'm there, too, reaching up for me to take her, so I do, setting her on my knees.

"I would be soo happy if we never had to talk about my dramatic life *ever* again. I would much rather talk about you. I'm sorry I haven't been a good friend these last couple months."

She shakes her head at me. "No, you've been a great friend. Your dramatic life has been the perfect distraction. And then I flew on a private jet to this fancy-ass cabin, where a private chef cooks for me, there's a crew of people to clean, and I have Caroline and Elodie for on-demand babysitting. Honestly, my life is a fucking dream because of you."

I laugh. "Well, that sounds like a start, but maybe I could be the listening kind of friend now?" She looks down at her hands where she's pulling her wedding ring up and down, on and off, over and over.

"I don't know, Brit. I thought Tommy was *my* Liam. I thought he was *it*, but apparently he thinks someone at his office is *it*, too."

"Wait, what? I thought you said he wants to open your marriage up. Did he already..."

"He's been having an emotional affair, I would call it, for...awhile now. *A long while.*"

"Wow, I'm so sorry, Jess." I know firsthand how damaging an emotional affair can be, and I don't mean Damian, I mean me. I was in love with someone else most of my entire marriage, even if it was just the idea of that person.

"The only reason it probably hasn't been more is because *they* work at the firm's office in Taiwan." Ahhh, okay.

"I see. But he's not there right now, is he?" I haven't even asked about Tommy, I've been such an asshole. She looks at me and I know. "He left the day you were being salty with me?" She nods her head up and down and I pull her in tight, wrapping my arms around her.

"Should I send Alex his coordinates?"

Jess laughs at my question. Even though she's crying, she genuinely laughs. "No, I don't know that we're at that stage yet. I just know I'm in NO hurry to go home. Do you mind?"

"Not even a little bit. Like move here. Stay here. Whatever you need. I can make your salary full-time and start paying you to a different bank account, if you know what I mean?" She laughs at me again.

"Not necessary, but I will take a roof over my head, though, and some good company."

I release my hold on her. "I can do that. We're team Jess, okay? You don't need him. I know he felt like the one, and maybe he's not, but either way it doesn't matter, because we've got you."

"Thanks, babe."

"Love you, JJ," I say.

"Love you, too, but I fucking hate that nickname," she says back when I notice a bare-chested and disheveled Liam standing at the top of the stairs, like he ran out of our bedroom looking for me. I smile at him, and he gives a wary smile back.

"I promise I'm not a flight risk," I call up to him and he laughs. As I watch him come down the stairs, I literally salivate and lick my lips.

"Maybe we *aren't* getting you a new car today," he jokes, coming over and picking Eden up off my lap. He tosses her into the air and she coos and squeals with delight before settling her on his hip. *Me next?*

"What happened to your car?" Jess asks frantically. "Did you get in an accident?"

"No," I stand up, laughing, "not at all. Let's just say, we are very anti-Matthias at the moment." Jess looks between me and Liam. "Come on, I'll tell you all about it over coffee."

―――――

"So you think Matt was just like trying to be with you this whole time because of the business share?" I shrug my shoulders.

"I mean, why else would he have wanted to date me?" Liam and Jess both give me a death glare when I say this, but I just sip my coffee. It's the truth. Why else would he have pursued me? I mean, it all makes sense. Even at the picnic, he didn't want to take no for an answer. He knew who I was and what that meant, and that's why he asked me out. I'm sure of it. I'm not bothered by it because I met the man of my dreams that same day. He didn't know me and I didn't know him, but the connection was there, instantaneously.

"Shut up," Jess says. "He might be stupid hot, but if he's that big of a dick, it's not surprising he's been single all these years."

"I don't know," I say, then think about Matthias and I together. There was something there. I mean, I don't think anyone could fake all of it. Every word, every touch. I can see how some of it was a show. Maybe he hoped Constantine would just leave everything to him if we ended up together. Or maybe he was banking on the fact that I was just this meek, desperate woman and he'd end up with control of my shares. I don't know, and I'm starting to feel like I don't care if I ever know.

I have everything I've ever needed or wanted right here, at home. Which reminds me, we're missing a few people.

"Hey, isn't Carly coming today?" I ask Liam and he looks at the oven clock.

"Yeah, she's not normally late. "His mouth slides to the side in contemplation.

"I thought she had the weekends off?" Jess says, confused.

"Monday and Tuesday are her days off. If she's not here in an hour, I'll give her a call, but in the meantime, who wants scrambled eggs?" Liam sets down his coffee and moves to the fridge. He still hasn't put on a shirt, and Jess and I both ogle him, watching him work.

"How old is he again?" Jess whispers to me.

"He'll be 50 in October."

"And no brothers?" I laugh at her question.

"Sorry, babe, no brothers."

"Damn, alright. I know we hate Matthias now, but do we hate his brothers, too?"

"Nope. Love Silas, still my doctor. Max just bought Liam out, so love him. And Niko, well he's impossible to hate. Want me to set you up?" I ask excitedly. She looks excited, too, for a second before shaking her head.

"Nah, but it's fun to dream." I nod in agreement. I get it.

The sound of the sliding door opening pulls our attention. We all turn to see Caroline walk in through the door that leads to the back deck, freezing when she finds us all watching her.

"I, uh, couldn't sleep. Just went and sat down by the lake this morning," she says.

While mildly believable, the lie is obvious. I mean, I was a teenager once, too. I nod, but motion for her to come sit next to me, and when she does, I just lean over and give her a big hug.

"I love you, Caro," I whisper in her ear. "You don't have to tell me the truth now, but I'd love to hear it some day." I pull away to see her cheeks turn bright pink then lean back, giving her a loving pat on her leg.

"I was wondering if we could have a big Sunday dinner here tomorrow night?" I look at Liam for his thoughts.

"Whatever you want, baby," he says, turning back to the eggs in the skillet. "Caroline, what can I make you? Toast, scramble, fried egg?"

"Uh, scramble, please," she asks hesitantly, at first. "You do the eggs, I've got the toast." She slides off her stool to grab the loaf of sourdough on the counter and when I look at Liam, he shoots me a wink. He knows it was Caroline. We'll probably have a dog by the end of the week. *Damn.* I laugh to myself.

"I'll invite Alex, Sandy, and Jim, obviously, but I was wondering if I could invite Constantine, too? Maybe Max, Niko, and Silas?"

Liam doesn't hesitate in answering. "Definitely," he says, then walks around to slide eggs onto the plates Caroline's laid out.

The mudroom door opens and Carly comes bursting into the kitchen, looking horrified when she sees us getting ready to eat.

"Oh my gosh, I'm so sorry. Liam, give me the skillet."

He laughs at her, and rebuffs her advances. "Carly, it's fine. It's just some scrambled eggs. We got up a little early today is all. Get some coffee. *We're fine*," he says again, when Carly just keeps standing there.

"My car wouldn't start this morning," she says in a rush, then looks to Caroline and then back to the floor. "And then I had to wait for James to give me a ride." *Ahhh*. Time to have another "safe sex" talk with Caroline. She's going to *love* that.

"We were just talking about getting rid of Britain's SUV. You're welcome to use it, if you need?" Liam offers it to her, and I don't care at all. He doesn't even need to get me a new car, I don't want to go anywhere for the rest of the summer. I just want to sit by the lake and watch the girls enjoy the water, talk shit with my best friend, and love my man. And maybe have a couple Sunday dinners every now and again.

"Oh, um, that's too kind, but I can't really afford a BMW." I don't know Carly's situation, but I know Liam is probably paying her out the nose for her to be here full time. I can tell Liam is thinking the same thing.

"I never said you needed to buy it, just use it. You know, until you get your old car fixed, or a new one. Or just as long as you need, okay?"

I know it's going to take a lot for her to accept, but reluctantly she does. "Fine, but put down the cooking utensils and let me finish breakfast. Jiminy Crickets, Liam, you're giving me a heart attack." She throws her long brown hair up into a claw clip, then heads over to the sink to wash her hands. Liam sets down plates in front of our stools, and Caroline slides a piece of toast on each of them.

"Thank you, Liam," Caroline steals the words right out of my mouth, but I'll gladly take the progress. I smile at Liam and he comes around the island to give me a kiss on the top of my head.

"You don't mind about the car, do you?" He whispers and I shake my head no. He steals an extra piece of toast, then excuses himself to the office to go do "car research." Before I start eating, I can feel Jess' gaze on me so I look over to her. She slips Eden a piece of toast to chew on, but keeps looking at me.

"What?" I ask her.

"I'm just wildly jealous, that's all," she says, then corrects, "Not of Liam. Fuck, you know what I mean."

I do. Because I remember sitting at lunch over margs, feeling jealous of Jess, and Tommy, and Eden, and now look where we are. Things can change in the blink of an eye, I just hope for my sake, things stay the same, at least for a little bit.

On Sunday afternoon, I slip on my favorite Dôen midi dress. Looking at myself in the full length mirror, I can see just how happy I am. There's color on my cheeks from spending all day on the lake yesterday. My breasts seem to be getting fuller by the day, and thanks to Carly's cooking, my belly does, too. I'm hitting my peak pregnancy body and I make a mental note to try and savor it because I'm sure in just a few short months, I'll be hating life and uncomfortable 24/7.

I know I look happy, but I *feel* happy too. Somehow "happy" doesn't even begin to describe it, though. *Happy* isn't encompassing enough to define how I feel. I'm with the man of my literal dreams and my kids have fallen in love with Spearhead, my favorite place in the world. I have family in my life for the first time in decades and I'm finally building the life I've always wanted, with a family I've chosen and chooses me in return.

Alex was kind enough to drop off Georgia's box this morning, and since then, I've been holed up in my room for hours going through the photos and cards that were stashed away beside her notebooks. I read all 18 birthday cards Constantine had written to me, and they were beautiful. Filled with his hopes and dreams for me, his regrets, his sadness. But most of all, his love.

Liam's footsteps draw my attention as he walks into my closet, coming behind me and embracing me, letting his hands rest on my bump. "I love you, Bambi." I smile at him through our reflection in the mirror.

"I love you too, Liam." We stand entwined for a couple minutes, but eventually he releases me.

"We should probably go downstairs..." The way he trails off gives me pause.

"I just finished doing my hair and makeup," I remind him, "and it's only been like 5 hours since you last had me."

"So? I always want you."

I laugh at him. "Not right now. Sandy'll be here any minute."

He mockingly rolls his eyes at me, "Fine." He turns around to walk out of my closet, but stops, turning back. "Is it too soon for you to start wearing your engagement ring again?" I'd almost forgotten about it.

"Well, seeing as how you haven't proposed...yes."

"Ahh, you're going to make me do that again?" I look at him, dumbfounded.

"Yes," I say completely straight faced.

"Right, no, you're right," he says, then walks out of my closet, opening our bedroom door for me.

The house seems eerily quiet. *Huh.* I thought there'd be more hustle and bustle and prep happening for dinner. When we get to the foot of the stairs, I turn to head towards the kitchen, but Liam stops me, taking my hand to head out to the deck.

"I want to show you something," he says, squeezing my hand a bit firmer.

"Sure," I say in return. It doesn't take long for me to realize something is afoot. When we step outside, the whole back deck is covered in flower petals and the stairs leading down to the dock are lined with large arrangements of white and blue flowers. On the dock itself, I can make out what looks like...a string quartet?

"Wh-what's all this?" I ask Liam with a trembling voice.

"Just dance with me, Bambi, nothing crazy." He leads me down the stone stairs, all the way to the dock, and when we're almost there, the quartet starts to play. I recognize the song, instantly. It's "The Chair" by George Strait.

There's a small open area on the large floating dock, and he pulls me into his arms and we dance. It feels just like the first time, except infinitely better. Because I know him, and I love him now.

When the song ends, I lean back and say, "That was nice," and he just smiles back at me, cupping my face in his hand, and stroking my cheek gently. The quartet starts the next song, and my tears start falling without my permission. It's "I Will Always Love You" by Dolly Parton and Liam's eyes turn watery, too.

He gets down on one knee, and pulls out a familiar ring

box. "Britain, I won't make you any promises. We never even have to exchange vows if you don't want to. But I want you to know, I will always love you. That is a fact. It's who I am. I am the best version of me, for you, because of you. You changed my life before I even knew you, Britain. I was always yours, and you were always mine.

You're my home, and my favorite person, and I don't want to spend another day where you're not mine forever." He pauses to swallow, then says, "I'm already the luckiest bastard alive because you're here. Can you make me the happiest one, too, and marry me?" *Yes*. It's a no-brainer. I fall to my knees beside him, and kiss him like it's the end of times. But it's not, it's just the beginning of our beautiful life.

I release his mouth and whisper out, "Yes," as tears fall down my face. He kisses me again, then opens the ring box to slide his ring *back* on my finger, where it belongs.

Liam looks down at my hand, then back up at me, and I can see how much he loves me reflected in his eyes. When the song ends, the group of musicians set down their instruments to clap and cheer, but it's the high-pitched yapping sound that pulls my attention away from my fiancé.

I look at Liam with wide eyes and he nods. "You didn't," I say.

"I didn't, but *we* did." A golden retriever puppy comes bounding down the deck stairs, a large bow tied around its neck. The girls follow closely behind and when the puppy gets to the bottom, it bolts straight for us, jumping on my chest to give me kisses. I laugh because, damnit, I knew we'd have a dog before the end of the week.

"Hi, puppy!" I laugh at the way his tongue tickles my chin. The girls join us, dropping to their knees, too, as we all huddle around the newest family member. Eventually Caroline and Elodie offer us congratulations, giving me, then Liam, each a hug.

"So, what's the pupper's name, huh?" I look around to the girls and Liam.

"Well, we're a bit undecided at the moment," Liam says. "I like Harry."

"And I like Fang," Elodie adds.

"But I think Draco is fitting," Caroline says. I can't help but agree, the puppy has really light, almost white, fur.

"Wow, we're really leaning hard into the *Harry Potter* theme then. So, it's a boy?" They all look at each other then shake their heads no. "No? Well, isn't it obvious then? Her name should be Luna."

"You're so right, Mom!" Elodie exclaims. "Luna Lovegood Scott-Millar is our new puppy!" I smile and look at Liam, and he smiles back at me. Caroline picks up the puppy, nuzzling its soft fur, and Elodie claps her hands with excitement. This time it's my turn. I turn and mouth a "Thank you" to Liam.

Eventually there's clapping and cheering coming from the top deck, and reluctantly we make our way back up to the house. I thank the string quartet before we leave, and then Liam's right behind me, a gentle hand on the small of my back supporting me the whole way up.

I double check the ring on my finger, and just like everything with Liam is and has ever been, it fits so naturally, perfectly. It's just right.

THIRTY-TWO

BRITAIN

When I go to crawl into bed at night, I find my pink negligee laid out on top of the duvet. *I wonder where he's been hiding this?* But I smile, slipping it on over my naked body, then wait for him. He comes in through our bedroom door, making sure to lock it behind him, then starts undressing.

From my spot on the bed, I watch him strip for me, savoring how handsome he is. Admiring how his abs look cut from a slab of marble. How his hair falls slightly forward, the silver strands catching in the low light. My core turns to liquid heat, pulsing with need when he drops his pants exposing his long, thick cock. I bite down on my lip, not even bothering to avert my gaze from my favorite part of his body.

He crawls onto the bed with me, but he doesn't make any moves to be intimate. He just pulls me tight to him, my back flat to his chest and my ass up against his engorged cock. He moves one hand over my belly and the other bends down, resting softly on my breast. When he touches me, I can't help but push my ass back against him. The heat gushing between my inner thighs has me clenching and needy for my fiancé's touch.

"I used to dream about this, baby. You, in our bed, pregnant with our baby, my ring on your finger," he says softly in my ear, making my skin flush. I'd be lying if I said I didn't have those same dreams.

"Yeah, were we doing anything in this dream?" I egg him on.

"Sometimes," he says, leaning over to run his tongue along the edge of my ear before he bites down softly. "I just want to eat you, baby. I can't fucking get enough." He grinds his dick between my ass cheeks at the same time I push back, and we both moan. "I just feel like the luckiest bastard alive... I don't deserve you, baby."

"We deserve each other, Liam," I say, sliding a hand over his, where it sits on my belly. He moves his hand down, though, reaching to the hem of the negligee and sliding it up over my hip. He checks me first, slipping a finger between my folds. It comes as no surprise I'm already slick with desire.

He removes the finger, then slides it in his mouth, sucking it clean. My breath starts coming in short bursts, and I beg. "Liam, please. I need you inside me."

He lifts my leg and adjusts slightly, then slides deep inside. I arch my back into the feeling of my man inside me, where he belongs. Bringing my leg back down, the tight pressure causes me to clench down hard and grind my ass back.

"I'll only be good for 2 minutes, if you keep that up," Liam says, a hand coming down on my ass hard, spanking me.

I cry out, but he shushes me. "I'm going to have to start punishing you every time you scream, baby."

"I can't help it."

He thrusts into me hard, and brings his hand over, between my legs to rub my swollen clit. "You better start learning to try, Bambi, or you're going to find yourself bent over and I won't let you come." *Fuck me.* I reach up and pull my breasts out of my negligee, to roll and play with nipples. Liam licks his lips in response, his eyes plastered on watching me play.

"You're just going to use me, daddy?" I ask, eliciting a moan from him.

"You'd like that wouldn't you?" I nod my head up and down against his back as he continues thrusting.

"You can have me, use me, anytime you want. I'm yours, William." His grip on me tightens, loving the words coming out of my mouth.

"You're *my* little slut aren't you? You want me to fuck you anytime, anywhere, is that right?" *YES!* I fucking love when he talks to me like this. I want to scream, but I try to hold it in, the pressure building to its crescendo.

"Yes, daddy."

"That's right, baby," he laughs a low, seductive laugh at the use of my name for him. His finger increases the pressure on my clit in approval, but it's his words that send me flying. "Who does this pussy belong to, Bambi? Your asshole. Whose is that? Those sweet lips around your filthy mouth. Who owns them?"

"You!" I whisper-shout as my back arches.

"*Mine,*" he says gruffly, slamming into me as we ride out our orgasms together. I make smaller pants and noises as we experience the last of our release, and Liam laughs at me lightly.

"It's impossible for you to be quiet during sex, isn't it?" I nod in response as the last of his throbbing subsides and he starts showering me with kisses across my shoulders and neck.

When we crawl back into bed after cleaning up, he pulls me in tight again and moves his hand instinctively to its new favorite spot, my belly, and holds us close. I find myself smiling uncontrollably. *Home. Mine. His. Ours.* He's the only person who's ever felt like home to me. He's the only place I want to be, and the only one I'll ever want. I feel like I've never truly belonged anywhere because all along, I'd belonged with him.

I might have had something with Damian, even something with Matthias. But with Liam, it's everything. He's *always* been my everything.

EPILOGUE

LIAM

"We aren't having any more kids after this, Britain." I slide my hands through my hair to try and release the tension. "I can't take it." When I look up to where she's sitting in the hospital bed, she laughs at me. Fucking laughs at me!

"I didn't know you wouldn't be able to hang today," she says with a smirk on her face.

"I just watched them insert a needle into your back that was the length of my forearm!"

"And look how much better I feel already? Relax, come here." She gestures for me to join her on the hospital bed. I sit down beside her, almost scared to touch her with all the wires, and monitors, and drips she's hooked up to. "Do you want to watch a movie? We probably have a couple hours," she says while she gently rubs my back. *My wife is too good for me.*

"Fine, sure." She laughs at me again, then tells me to pull

a chair over so we can watch TV while we wait. "How bad is the pain now?"

"I can't feel a thing, and I won't. Silas will have to come tell me when to push because I won't know it's time." I nod silently. She's a fucking warrior. When we walked into labor and delivery, I could hear the screaming and I knew I wouldn't be able to take it if Britain started screaming in pain. But, of course, all my girls are fucking champs, and Britain just bared the pain quietly, clenching her eyes, squeezing my hand, and then releasing a deep breath when the pain subsided. I don't know how she does it.

Luckily, the epidural kicked right in, and she's even fallen asleep.

I check my phone, seeing texts from our girls, Sandy, Alex, Constantine, Max, and even Jess, but I'm waiting. I'll let them know when it happens and not a minute before. I just want to be in it with her.

Silas knocks on the door before entering.

"Hey, man," I greet him. He's only checked on Britain once since we got here. I think he said she was at six centimeters then.

"Hey, Liam, you ready?" He greets back, and I nod. "Alright, Britain," he says gently, patting her leg. "Let's see where we're at." Britain wakes easily, nodding along, and giving me a reassuring smile. Silas lifts the sheets and does a quick check.

I move to hold her hand, and then Silas looks at us and smiles. "You ready to push, Brit?" he asks. She nods ecstatically. Thank god she's a seasoned pro at this. I'd be dying if she showed even the smallest amount of worry, but I'm happy she's excited.

Silas calls in a slew of additional people and it quickly becomes overwhelming, if not a bit frightening. They turn on lamps over the baby bed, and start getting out all kinds of supplies. It's a flurry of movement.

But Britain is just sitting there, smiling, chatting with Silas like this isn't the most important moment of my entire life. Silas repositions the bed to get her ready to push, and I zone out at the monumental shift I can feel happening right beneath my feet. I'm going to have to share Britain with this other human. What if this changes things? *What if I'm not good at it, and she resents me?*

"Liam, Liam?" They have to say my name twice. Britain laughs at me again, taking my hand in hers, like she's supporting me now. She never ceases to amaze me.

She tells me, "We're just waiting for the next contraction and then I'll push."

"Okay, how long will you push for?"

"I dunno," she scrunches her nose. "I spent 3 hours pushing with Caroline and 10 minutes with Elodie." *Oh my god, I can't take three more hours of this.* She just shrugs, though.

"Alright, here we go, Brit, you know what to do," Silas says and with that, Britain bears down while a nurse counts beside her. Then Silas is telling her to stop. And they do that 3 more times, when I hear *the wail.* Britain sits back looking instantly relieved, like she just finished a light jog, not bringing a human into the world.

I lean forward to look at my son, and yeah, my whole fucking world just changed. Like I'm the fucking Grinch who's heart just grew three sizes. I turn back to Britain, gripping her face in my hands and I kiss her hard, my affection and adoration for this woman at an all-time high. "You are a fucking rockstar, baby. I love you so much, Britain Millar." She nods, holding onto my arms.

"How is he?" she asks me and Silas both.

"Perfect," Silas says, bringing the babe up to her bare chest, laying him down. Silas elbows me as he moves to sit back down at the foot of the bed, and says "Congrats, Dad." All I can muster out is a nod because it's taking a lot of strength to not break down and cry right now. I want to cry from relief, but mostly because I'm so in love. With Britain, with our son, with our family. *How did I get so fucking lucky?*

While Silas works on Britain, he asks, "Do you two have a name picked out?" *We sure do.* I look to Britain and see she's crying as she coddles our son.

"I think we're going to let his namesake be the first to know, though," I answer for the both of us. And Silas just nods.

"So, no William Millar the third?"

"Not this time." *Yeah, now that the birthing part is over, we are absolutely doing this again.*

———

Britain

When the peanut falls asleep, I give him a gentle kiss on the forehead and breathe in his baby shampoo and newborn smell. My heart warms a few degrees and I smile. *Our baby is perfect.*

I reluctantly pass him off to Liam so I can stuff my face

with the box of food Carly delivered to the hospital. There's a small quiche, and cinnamon rolls, and chocolate chip cookies — all my favorite things.

I look up to see Liam watching me, so I cover my mouth to talk, "Giving birth made me ravenous. Don't judge."

He laughs. "No judgment, baby. I hold you in the highest esteem, always. You are a fucking goddess." He stands there swaying with our newborn and I dust the crumbs from the quiche off my baby blue striped pjs Jess gifted me for the occasion. I know people will be here any minute, but this is the best they'll get from me.

"How much longer till they're here?" I ask him.

"Any minute, darling." I nod. "Are you nervous to tell them?" I nod again. "You're more nervous about this than you were about giving birth!" That's only partly true. Liam looked moments away from having a panic attack the whole time, so I put on a brave face in hopes he might eventually enjoy it. I think it worked.

There's a gentle knock at the door, and Alex enters. He has a huge bouquet of flowers, a gift basket, and a teddy bear. He heads straight for me, giving me a kiss on the cheek.

"The teddy bear's from me," he says and I laugh.

"Your wife did the rest?" He nods sheepishly and I smile at him.

"Knock knock," a deep voice calls from the doorway, and Liam calls for him to come in.

Connie walks over, heading straight for the baby, looking at him with awe. He holds up a 4-foot stuffed giraffe and whispers, "This is for you, bud," and I smile. The only thing missing right now is Georgia.

I sit up in bed a bit more and start. "I'm so glad you guys

could both make it, because I wanted to introduce you to your nephew," I motion to Alex, "and your grandson," I motion to Connie. "Constantine Alexander Millar, we'll call him CT for short." Alex's eyes mist. He comes over, giving me a hug and a kiss on the cheek, but doesn't say a word as he takes his namesake from my husband.

Connie makes his way over next, giving me a kiss on the forehead then leaning back with tears in his eyes he says, "Thank you, peanut. Your mom and I are so proud of you."

I can't hold back the tears and neither does he, so we embrace and cry lightly against each other. We don't mourn, we celebrate. The love that was, the love we found, and all the love we still have left to give.

BONUS EPILOGUE

MATT

I open the glove box, and pull the small notebook out, telling myself it's the last time even though I know, it's probably not. *Fuck*. I had every chance, every opportunity, every advantage (like this little notebook) and I still couldn't close on Britain Palomino.

I guess the fact that I still refer to her like a business deal is partly the reason why.

I didn't expect to ever have feelings for her. I thought it was all business. I was doing what was right for my family, keeping the business in Scala hands. I thought I was doing what my dad had always wanted of me by taking care of her. I thought, if I could do this one thing, he'd be proud.

The jokes on me though. Britain was beyond what I'd bargained for. She was more. So much more. She was pretty, even though I'd had prettier, but she was also smart, and kind.

Humble and empathetic. She loved me more than anyone had ever loved me before. And I loved *that*.

I think above all else, I loved her loving me.

The door opening to the hospital draws my attention away from the notebook in the palm of my hand to see my dad walking across the parking lot...beside Alex Palomino. I try not to let it get to me, but it does. He loves Britain and Alex like they're his own. I'm his own. I'm his only *own*, yet he never ceases to split himself amongst my brothers and Georgia's kids like they belong to each other.

I watch as Alex and Constantine embrace, my dad giving him a firm pat on the back and then moving closer to our parking spot. I don't miss the way Alex glares at me as he walks by. But he doesn't stop, doesn't say anything, he just heads straight past us as Constantine opens the door, pulling himself up into the car a bit more slowly than I'm used to.

That's another thing. Everyone else gets to see the strong, happy, healthy Constantine while I get the other version. He lets his guard down with me. He moves slower. He lets me see the illness eating away at his insides.

"Why do you have *that*, Matt?" My dad asks without an ounce of warmth or kindness to his voice. I'd been so busy watching Alex, I forgot to put it back away. We both look down at the small notebook in hand and I'm too stunned to say anything for a moment.

"I'll take that back now," Constanine says, extending a hand towards me, waiting for me to place it in his palm.

Like a nail in my coffin, I relinquish the last scrap of Britain I had left and place the notebook in my dad's waiting hand. It's probably for the best.

"How long?" I knew he'd ask. He's always been keenly perceptive.

"Since the first time I met her." I don't bother to lie. My dad knows who I am. He knows what I am. More than anything, he knows I'm not like him. I'm like *her. Julie.*

He shakes his head in disapproval. The sight is like needles to my eyes. Just another way I'll disappoint him.

"Dad,-" I start, but he quickly ends it.

"Don't. There's no point in it now. I'm just glad to have it back." He looks straight ahead, waiting for me.

"How long until your treatment?"

"We've got about an hour, let's get something to eat, alright?" I nod, starting the car, and heading towards the exit. When we get to the stop sign, I just sit there and wonder. How many more days will we spend at the hospital? How many more times will I bring him here? How many more lunches will we get to share together?

"Dad," I say, looking at him. "I'm sorry."

He turns, giving me his full attention. "You're saying sorry to the wrong person." Tears rim my eyes. "I don't need you to be sorry, to me. I need you to be better. Understand?" I nod, but don't verbally respond.

He leans forward placing a hand around my neck, pulling me into him and I meet him halfway. He presses his forehead against mine and says, "Listen, son. There is nothing you could do that would make me stop loving you. Nothing. I'll always be proud to call you mine." *Fuck.*

Maybe someday, I'll be a fraction of the man he is. Until then, I'll take one step at a time. Making amends where I can, and hopefully in time, I can make him proud once and for all.

ACKNOWLEDGMENTS

Thank you to my amazing friends. I know I've dedicated this book to you, but I can't go without acknowledging and thanking you all again. I sincerely don't know that I would have continued without your rallying, cheering, and all the hyping you've done. From all the grass roots, and whisper campaigns you've started to spread the word about my books, to the events, and just general support you've shown me, I feel entirely undeserving of it all.

Thank you to my beta readers, Laura, Alix, Kristie, and Ellyn. Your feedback has been so important and hugely helpful in molding this book into the best version I can make it.

Thank you to my copy editor, Sara, who carves time out of her beautiful and busy life to help me, and help shape these books into something readable.

Thank you to all the readers who gave Georgia a chance. Special thank you to those who then found me on Instagram and slid into my DMs. You'll never know how much those messages have meant to me.

And of course, thank you to my husband, D. For continuing to support this endeavor with me.

ABOUT THE AUTHOR

E.L. Stevens is a book loving, low-key sneaker-head with a mild obsession for baked goods and Dr. Pepper.

Her love affair with reading and romance novels started in the seventh grade with Jane Austen's Pride and Prejudice and hasn't stopped since.

An overactive imagination and obsession with the genre led her to want to write her own books, incorporating life experiences, love of her hometown, and *of course*, baked goods.

When she's not writing, she's voraciously reading, walking her labradoodle, Maggie, chauffeuring tweens between sports and extracurriculars, shopping for sneakers, or baking in the D.C. exurbs.

 instagram.com/e.l.stevens

ALSO BY E.L. STEVENS

GEORGIA

SPEARHEAD LAKE BOOK 1, BRITAIN'S STORY PART I

CONSTANTINE

SPEARHEAD LAKE BOOK 2, BRITAIN'S STORY PART II

JUNE

SPEARHEAD LAKE BOOK 3, ALEX'S STORY

COMING JUNE 2024

SAY SOMETHING

NEW STANDALONE ROMANCE

COMING 2024